FIGHTER
PILOTS

A NOVEL BY

KELLY ROLLINS

FIGHTER
PILOTS

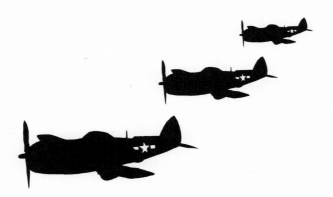

LITTLE, BROWN AND COMPANY   BOSTON · TORONTO

FIRST EDITION

LIBRARY OF CONGRESS CATALOGING IN PUBLICATION DATA
Rollins, Kelly.
Fighter pilots.
1. World War, 1939–1945—Fiction. 2. Vietnamese
Conflict, 1961–1975—Fiction. I. Title.
PS3568.O542F5   813'.54   81–5978
ISBN 0–316–75453–6   AACR2

MV

Designed by Janis Capone

Published simultaneously in Canada
by Little, Brown & Company (Canada) Limited

PRINTED IN THE UNITED STATES OF AMERICA

FOR JAMES SALTER

PART
ONE

1

ENGLAND

IT WOULD BE interesting to know where we are. Probably east of the Rhine, somewhere near Frankfurt. Ahead, it's dark and spooky, but the undercast looks thinner. Maybe there will be a few holes. I guess the colonel knows where we are. Certainly the *Luftwaffe* radar controllers do.

Back during the Great War, when ten thousand feet was high, this business was a lot more glamorous. Our pilots wore tunics with wings on their chests, Sam Browne belts, riding breeches and boots. Sharp. When someone lost a buddy, he'd drink to him, throw his glass into the fireplace, then have his doting mechanics wheel his Nieuport or Spad out of the hangar. Dusk patrol, but this time alone and with a chivalrous challenge wrapped around a wrench.

"Contact!" his chief mechanic would echo, and bravely spin the wooden propeller. If he wasn't run over by the brakeless airplane, he might even manage to return the pilot's calm salute as he ducked under the wing into castor oil fumes.

In contrast, here I sit, looking like some sheep turned inside out—leather outside, fleece inside—wearing a G-suit that inflates at random times, long handles, winter flying coveralls and sloppy, fleece-lined boots that insulate my feet from the warm air coming in by the rubber pedals. Outside it's fifty below, inside only minus forty. I have to keep stamping and clapping like Cheetah. My oxygen mask valves have frozen closed so that when I exhale, the mask makes this farting sound and lifts off my face. But I must be getting oxygen, or I'd be unconscious or something—hypoxia, like in the altitude chamber. The inside of my canopy is so covered with frost that I have to scratch peepholes to see Ken. Ken's my element leader; he's a first lieutenant and he's almost as old as the colonel—twenty-four, he says. But I've begun to realize that he lies a lot. He told me to drink more, and the alcohol fumes would thaw out everything. Over the weekend when fog moved in from the Channel, I did, but I just got sick. Watching me drink scotch and ginger ale, this Limey got sick, too.

Actually, I bitch too much, Ken says. I could be in the infantry, slopping around in the mud and waiting for the big day. All over England you see them marching or sitting around in these tent cities. But, as one of them reminded me, "Every day here is one less day there." And, too, that mud on the Continent is probably even worse. But, Jesus, those bunkers and pillboxes are all along the coast. I've seen them from the air. I couldn't take all those dead bodies. And shooting people. . . . And getting shot without anyone noticing.

So I'm lucky to be flying the Mustang. It's a great bird. It will even outperform the Krauts' FW-190, they say, now that it has this Rolls-Royce engine. We have the "D" model with six caliber-50s, instead of four, and this opaque bubble canopy. They say that some genius at North American named Edgar Schmued designed the P-51 on the back of an envelope. It takes a Kraut to beat a Kraut, I guess. And *pretty!* It makes you feel good just to look at her, unless you're in the *Luftwaffe,* or you fly P-47s. The Jug pilots are envious, so they say, "Yeah, she looks okay, but she can't take it." The Jug, the P-47, is a tank. And it climbs like a tank. We always tell Jug pilots that they should have just enlisted in armor, if that's what they admire in a machine. And sometimes this leads to fistfights because they're so immature and defensive.

Two hours ago I took off as Blue Four, but then Ken's gunsight went out, so we swapped positions. An element leader has to have a good sight. All a wingman has to have is good eyeballs, a radio and the ability to stay with his leader even when the idiot is flying backward. I should know because I've flown wing during seventeen combat missions. Several times I've been "in on the kill," as they say, which means a kind word or two from Ken, but nothing else. He's the one who has all those swastikas painted under his canopy, I notice, and he's the one that gets the medals, even that time when I got half my tail shot off.

"Hey, Johnny, *nice!*" he says to me later. "You fly nice wing, kid. I couldn't have done it without you."

But I don't have anything except the big blue-and-white insignia painted on my fuselage. And a few Air Medals, which come regular as clockwork, one for every five missions. They're like coupons. When you get so many, they give you a DFC, and you can go home. Still, my dad—I've got this snapshot of him wearing a gas mask—tells me I'll never forget my days with the AEF, and he keeps asking how many

Boche I've shot down. But I just keep describing old cathedrals and thank them for the brownies. Dad doesn't seem to understand that a wingman is simply the eyes of his leader. That's what our group commander keeps saying. Yeah, the eyes, and sometimes the ass, I say to myself. Anyhow, if our leaders' tail warning radar worked, we wingmen could stay home. Naw, we couldn't; we'd be sent to the infantry or somewhere, I guess. To *bombers*. Jesus. That's the thing about the Army: if you screw up, they've always got somewhere even worse to send you.

Well, back at five-thirty, the sun is setting. It's all apricot colored but getting paler and pinker every minute. Up ahead it's gray. I haven't seen a single puff of flak. My eight-day clock says it's 1630, but it's always said that. Why is it that no one can design a clock that will work in a car or an airplane? They drop them off buildings and hit them with hammers to test them, but mount one on an instrument panel and it quits ticking. My GI wristwatch says that we're supposed to rendezvous with these bombers in seven minutes, if there are any bombers left. The poor bastards have been to Nürnburg, which is as far as Munich. We don't have enough of these 108-gallon drop tanks to go that far yet. The bombers had to go the last hundred miles without friendly escort—God knows they didn't lack *German* escort. Two hundred miles of absolute hell. I suspect that a few of those guys might settle for a transfer to the infantry about now. "The Greatest Fighting Team on Earth," the recruiting ads say, and there's this picture of a B-17 or a B-24 with all its guns spurting flame while the German fighters fall burning. The truth is that being in a bomber is like being in a tank or a submarine where every minute or so someone lifts a hatch cover, throws a grenade down at you, and closes the cover. They can have it.

I'm finally leading an element, and the first shot I fire will be in total darkness. Typical. In high school, my coach, who used to have a heart attack every game, wouldn't even send me in until the score was 60 to o—either way. He said I wasn't aggressive enough, that I had to be competitive and step all over them. Otherwise, I might as well go out for tennis like some girl.

Boy, a target over five hundred miles away is bad news when the *Luftwaffe* is up, and they usually are. It's like this movie I saw one time, a James Fitzpatrick travelogue or something—not Tarzan, or I'd remember—where these cattle were fording a stream in Brazil (or Florida, maybe) and these little fish attacked them. There was this pink froth and the cattle were bawling and thrashing around. The *look* in their eyes just before they'd go under. Instant skeletons. And that's the way it is up ahead, you can bet, except that they usually become black metallic clouds first. I don't like to get too near our bombers for two reasons: first, they blow up if you look at them, especially while they're still full of bombs and gas, and, second, their gunners don't know a P-51 from a dirigible. They get trigger-happy after a while, especially when there are ME-109s around. I guess we do look alike from certain angles.

5

Last fall, before I got over here, the B-17s went to Schweinfurt, and they lost sixty of them. *Six hundred men.* That almost put a stop to daylight precision bombing. I guess the RAF guys had a hard time keeping their gentlemanly mouths shut.

"Yellowstone, go Channel Dog," the colonel calls. So I punch "D" Channel, which is our rendezvous frequency, and, when my VHF rechannelizes, it gives me goose bumps just to listen. Sounds like the end of the world, that Orson Welles thing, or Gettysburg after Pickett's charge. Men are screaming things no one could understand, and this one guy keeps calling for Little Friends—us. The colonel couldn't get in a word if he tried. I can't see them because of cirrus and my canopy.

My windshield defroster is working better. I can see from about ten-thirty to one-thirty, and, if I lean way forward, I can look down through the quarter panes. But we're still above cirrus, so all I can see are flashes through it. It's as though this deck of cirrus is hiding a thunderhead.

"Little Friends . . . ," the voice keeps calling mechanically. He sounds like he's just given up, like those cows in the travelogue.

"Jupiter, Yellowstone," the colonel replies calmly.

"YELLOWSTONE! *Oh, thank God!* Where are you, boy?" He must feel like Marconi.

"We're at your two o'clock, above the cirrus deck, Jupiter. Now, *listen:* we'll be coming in from five to seven o'clock in about one minute. Notify your gunners. Acknowledge."

"Roger, roger. Wilco, buddy. Just get these bastards off our backs."

"Drop 'em, Yellowstone," the colonel calls to us. I reach down for the drop-tank jettison handles, jerk, and feel her jump. Jesus, you can actually see the airspeed needle leap. It really gives you confidence.

The colonel is flipping up on one wingtip and then the other to check our six o'clock. He doesn't trust anyone. I guess he learned the hard way when he was in Eagle Squadron. Only the cautious guys are still around.

And, still leaning forward, I see the shelf of clouds end—Holy Sweet Jesus, *there they are.* It's not even a formation anymore. There are almost as many stragglers as there are birds in formation. And fighters really love stragglers, birds with feathered props, blowing oil smoke out of missing cylinders, half the gunners lying dead or wounded on the spent brass in the waists, or in their shattered turrets.

It's quite a sight: Custer's Last Stand updated. The B-24s are all trailing some color of smoke, the healthy ones white condensation vapor in endless, merging parallel streams, the sick ones gray, or even black. Shuttling in and out in high glinting trajectories, specks near our horizon, are the enemy fighters. Focke Wulfs, I think. Bad news.

I'm not exactly scared, just excited. And if we didn't have full fuselage tanks, I wouldn't even be worried. But with our center of gravity so far aft, these birds behave a lot like loaded pickup trucks. You can't just jerk back on the stick or you'll swap ends, or snap-roll if you're feeding in too much rudder.

"Red and White, take the left flank," the colonel says, "Blue and Green, the right." So cool. We could be back in the States bouncing Jugs, to hear his voice.

Like Saint Michael the Archangel, he plummets, a slim hawk against the dark ground, dwindling and merging, his flight following. Then White. I watch Blue Leader and his wingman. They are playing the turn longer, curving back toward the right flank. Nobody says anything. The colonel doesn't like unnecessary transmissions. Blue Leader has a target now, so I take Ken farther to the right and pick an element just reversing from left to right bank in their pursuit curve. My controls are so rigid at this speed that I'm having to use my trim tabs just to fly this thing. Even so, I'm standing on the left rudder pedal. Yeah, they're Focke Wulf 190s. All engine and cannon and armor-plated bellies. When they fire at a bomber, they roll onto their backs and throw that armored belly up for the gunners to shoot at. But our belly is where our coolant is. If that's hit, you'd better crawl over the side while you can.

I can just imagine all the excited German calls now that they know we're around. Surely they've seen us by now. I keep waiting for these clowns I'm after to do some tricks, but either they're maniacs or blind. . . . The '190 is supposed to be fast as hell, but even though I've got my power way back, I'm about to run all over this Kraut. If he sees me, he must think I'm trying to ram him or something.

My gunsight reticle keeps flopping around, but I'm so close, who needs a gunsight? I squeeze the trigger, and miss. *I* need a gunsight. He's firing, too, at the bomber. *Whoomp!* That was the bomber's wash we just went through, and now he's rolling over, still firing. I squeeze again, but I'm afraid of hitting the B-24 so I can't raise my tracers up to him. Instead, I just let the FW fall into them.

And, suddenly, *everything seems to stop.* For a second, everything is quiet. I'll never forget it, if I live to be ninety.

It's unreal, like slow motion. He just sits there motionless in my bright circle of diamonds, trembling and sparkling, with little flecks of debris hurtling at me. It's as though I'm pinning a big mottled butterfly, still alive, to a display board. Then smoke rushes back and, for a second, I can't see anything. When I see him again, he's sideways to me, and his prop has stopped. All this in a thousandth of a second, as I whip by him. There wasn't time for any evasive action. He's gone, the bomber is gone, and, for all I know, Ken's gone. No, there he is. For an element leader, he flies pretty good wing.

For some reason, I'm upside down, and we're out ahead of the bomber box. The speed has defrosted my canopy and, looking down, I see three flamers. It's like a dream, all this brilliant orange against the darkness, and all the skywriters.

"Break right!" this voice calls. No call sign. So every P-51 over Germany flips up onto her right wingtip and skitters away. Me, too. Then, sheepishly, not seeing anyone back there, I roll out again. Boy, I can just hear old Ken when we get home. He's so old, anyhow, and here I am flinging him around after a hard three days down in London. We'd dated these two WAAF girls—not officers, just enlisted women but classier than us—and my date kept looking at my mustache and laughing.

"*How* old are you?" she kept asking; and Ken, the bastard, would fall down. You can barely see it because I'm blond and I've only been growing it two months. After a few beers I told him to shut his bloody mouth, and then he really did fall down laughing, especially when my date explained why I shouldn't say "bloody."

Where'd everybody go? Our frequency is so crowded with calls that we must be bumper to bumper. Oh, yeah . . . the FWs have pulled out to get organized and the '51s are over to our left, about ten of them. Gee, look at those FWs *climb*. They are already way up there. We begin essing to stay with the bombers, essing and climbing.

"Twelve o'clock, Blue Three," says Ken. Holy mackerel, it looks like those cavalry movies where the scout would point, and the whole ridge would be feathers. A whole fresh squadron, it looks like.

Hey, guys, I think, let's get organized. Where's the colonel? Where's Blue Leader, for that matter?

Instinctively, we, too, form in line-abreast. Here they come, and at one o'clock the initial bunch is curling around like a big, black whip to form a second wave. This is so bad, it's funny. I bend to my sight, recheck my gun switch. It's like that time I was in for the kickoff, and we were running down the field in a wave, yelling. We need a bugler and a guidon like the cavalry.

Come on, engine. I'm bending the throttle. Two engines in five days, six during the past month. Flash, flash, flash—that's his cannon. One more second. *Now.* I squeeze and feel the bird vibrate. Six smoky lines and a shower of pink tracer converge near him. *Whoomph!* We pass— lucky we didn't both pull up—he ducked at the last second. He wasn't more than twenty feet below me. Oh, mean-looking with that villainous paint job and big wicked cowling. Blunt nose, prop spinner, short wings, no tail to speak of. Black-and-white crosses on the wings.

And here comes the next wave. This time I feel a few nibbles from his machine guns. He fires, and I fire. A few sparkles on him, and then their whole line just splits up without firing much, some climbing, most diving. We flat-chandelle back over the bombers and complete the circle to parallel them. I can't have much ammo left, but I doubt that anyone does, which probably explains why they broke off the attack.

For some reason, everyone is forming on me. No, just three of them. The other four are forming a second flight. Oh, I get it: my bird has "Jenny" painted on the nose and, from a distance, it looks like "Jeannie," which is on the colonel's bird. But they'd know better if they looked at the big letter behind my star. Now they see it's just me, but what the hell. Jesus, imagine, a second lieutenant leading a flight.

Ken tells me I've got a little battle damage under my fuselage near the coolant radiator. Guiltily, I look at my engine instruments for the first time in half an hour, but everything's still in the green. We check each other over as we ess, one flight on each side of the bombers. I don't see any FWs anywhere, but it's pretty dark now. They're probably on the ground drinking beer. We're already west of the Rhine, I think.

I can still see that picture in my mind: the FW sideways just before it blew up. When I think of finally getting a plane, I feel pretty good, but when I think of the pilot, I don't feel so good. Of course, the Germans aren't like us; they're warriors. I remember in freshman lit about Sigurd and Siegfried, and those who migrated to England. They'd fight *anything,* old Tristan weakening this giant—Urgan?—you know, severing parts, following the bloodstained track, and everything. Maybe that guy I shot down felt like old Tristan every morning when he'd take off. Anyhow, he's gone now.

From the tail numbers, I'd say that we're a blend of the original four flights. Crazy. Ken is still with me, but the rest of Blue Flight is missing. If I know Blue Leader, he's coming home on the deck. He loves strafing. I hear distant voices, and a few sound familiar. Yeah, I guess they're down there raising hell with trains and trucks. It's not like the colonel to leave the bombers though, and I feel about escort as he does. It's important, even now at dusk. You can't tell about the Germans: some of them may not be drinking beer. And one or two of these bombers can't keep up much longer. I'd hate to see *their* engine instruments. Every needle has probably gone around twice, especially the cylinder-head temperatures. It's amazing how they can keep going, even without enemy action.

I see water. The undercast is broken here. Probably the Zuider Zee. They say it's full of ditched airplanes. We're still essing, the other flight swinging away until they're specks, then curving back like our mirror image. Hey, there's the Channel. It's black, with whitecaps. I think we'd better break off now, or we're going to be hurting for fuel. I start angling down and away from the bombers. We waggle our wings.

"Thanks, Yellowstone. Thanks, guys," their leader calls. "You saved our asses."

I give him two clicks of the mike button—that's how the colonel acknowledges everything—and lift my hand. Then I look back at Ken, but he shakes his head. He's content flying wing sometimes. Says it beats thinking, the bastard.

I ease the throttle back a few inches of manifold pressure and trim her in a hands-off descent. I like to fly smoothly. Ken does everything spastically. When he brushes his teeth, you'd better move farther away or you'll get hurt. And he wants to become a *surgeon?* Jesus, I can just see

9

him with a scalpel. Appendicitis? Okay, rip! He'd open you up from neck to crotch like a fish. All the nurses would faint.

There's Colchester, all blacked out. Even these little villages look dead and empty until you notice the wisps of smoke from the chimneys. There go the '24s; they're angling up toward Norwich. We went up there one time to see the cathedral, but ended up at this big dance hall, the Sampson and Delilah, with two NAAFI girls. Jesus, with all these planes around, we'd better show some lights. There are so many airfields that the traffic patterns overlap. Everything is losing color down there, but along the horizon flow red and green navigation lights.

"B-17s at eleven, Yellowstone Leader," Ken calls. I nod. I've been watching them for five minutes. Oh . . . now I get it: Yellowstone *Leader*. Yeah, I see now. The other flight is still with us. I'm a big deal. I nod and mark one up on the canopy for him. I can barely see his face framed by the leather helmet and his dangling mask until he draws on his cigarette and smiles. Bastard's gonna blow us both up some day smoking around oxygen.

We ease by the B-17s. First Division birds. I waggle my wings at their leader. He's doing something, waggling in slow motion maybe. Gee, that must be like flying a house around.

Okay, from here a 360-degree spiral should be perfect. We'll be right on initial approach for Boxstead. I have to look twice to see our runway, but I don't dare to keep my eyes on it, not with all these colored lights skimming along. To the south I catch a last glint of the Thames. Everybody is hurrying home. The ground crews are watching from all the flight lines, and around the bases are emplacements of antiaircraft guns. ATS girls serve as their crews. One girl says she is really going to shoot Ken down if she gets a chance.

I flap the stick sharply to the right and back. Obediently, the element settles and slides under us into Echelon Right. It's a nice feeling to be leading. Tomorrow, though, I'll be back there at the end of the whip again, looking up the staircase instead of down it. We burr along in the evening over the farms and cottages of Essex. British engines come home again, these Merlins, still sweet and strong after a hard day. We are curving down in a gentle left spiral, clearing ourselves as we descend. To my right are aligned wingtips and, as we roll out on initial approach, the canopies blend in perspective. I can picture us, slim and graceful as arrows humming across the dark fields, strings of lights along our silhouettes. The second flight is taking interval.

Ahead is the channel of dim lights. It seems to rush at us out of the dusk. We are doing 350 as we level at two hundred feet. Just short of the overrun, I come right back on the stick and blend in left aileron and rudder, honking her up and hard around so they can fan out into landing interval. Base leg. Gear and flaps. My throttle is full back, the exhaust stacks are popping blue fire. Three green lights, full flaps. Trimming as I go, I let the runway tilt up at me, blip the throttle to clear the plugs, and then have to slip her in. Landing lights foolishly on, then off because of the usual fog and that blindingly bright disc of the prop. The slim nose rises and blocks out the runway, but, peripherally, I see white lights flashing by. I'm okay, I've got it made. I'm looking out the quarter panes, fluttering with exhaust. A hair more back-stick. Kiss. Grease job.

I know when I see the flashlights who is who. My crew chief doesn't flash his on the tail numbers. He shines it right into my eyes, and then he waves it around like he's wringing a chicken's neck. I don't know what that means except that that's where he is. Nobody else likes him. I don't either, but I'm stuck with him, and I've got to admit that he turns out a bird that's clean and ready to go. It's just that he lacks any conception of what our mission is. To hear him talk, you'd think it was still 1938 at Selfridge Field, and we are after some flying-time record. If he tells me one more time how Colonel Johns flew for six months without an engine change, I'll . . . well, I'll just stand there and take it as I always do.

Finally, he lifts his two flashlights to form an X. I press the brake pedals all the way down and move the mixture knob to idle-cutoff. Above the dying flutter of the prop, I hear him down there clopping the wooden chocks on the ramp. Here he comes, struggling from the left tire up onto the wing. He shines a flashlight right into my eyes. Maybe he thinks I'm a Kraut. His breath smells of beer, but what the hell, all old sergeants drink. Using his light, I recheck the panels one last time, then switch off the battery. I hand him my leather helmet and mask, some maps I never use, and throw back the shoulder straps.

"Okay?" he asks. Not me, the airplane.

When I mention the damage, he scowls. Colonel Johns *never* brought back a damaged plane. When I admit that I had to use his engine pretty hard, he closes his eyes. We crawl beneath the wing to inspect the damage. There's a ragged hole on the lip of the scoop and another lower. Two more inches and I'd have lost my coolant. I could be telling some Kraut my name, rank and serial number. I ask the chief about the colonel and the others, but he's too mad to hear anything more from me. He kicks his tool box. Last week he was really pissed off: I came back with seventeen holes in the empennage.

"Well, Lieutenant, I'll get hold of the sheet-metal guys. There ain't any more engines, so you better go easy on this one." Blindly, he almost walks into a parked gasoline truck.

Using the wing for a desk, I fill out the form. Two holes in the radiator scoop. Three hundred and fifty hours on the airplane. That's about what my own logbook will say. That's an impressive total, especially with my eighteen combat missions. I'm getting to be an old head. When Ken finishes his tour, I'll probably become an element leader.

The other engines are quiet now. All I can hear are the cooling ticks of my bird and the little whir of the dying gyros. I'm tired, by God, suddenly. It's all fading, and I'm hungry and crippled from my frozen feet. I wish I had the guts to write up that heating system, but the chief doesn't like write-ups.

"Just tell me, and I'll fix it," he warns. "It looks bad to have a bunch of discrepancies in my form." Okay, I've told him seventeen times, so I'm gonna write it up. And, if that truck doesn't get here pretty soon, I'm going to have to step over there into the weeds. The chief grumbles every time I use his relief tube. They ought to retire anyone who's thirty-eight years old, I think.

In the truck, I hear that the colonel went down. Everyone quits talking. He was twenty-six. I think about it for a minute, then shrug. We rock along, our cigarettes glowing under the canvas, our chutes lying in the aisle between the side benches. I'm at the rear, so occasionally I lift the canvas flap, hoping to see more lights on initial approach. At debriefing, we hear that two recovered at Manston. There's no word on the other six, and we are beginning to realize that there isn't going to be.

Frankly, it wouldn't make me mad if the Continent is socked in tomorrow. But I guess the Krauts feel the same way.

2

WILLIAMS

JANUARY, 1947. The Army Air Force has been dismantled. It's just a bunch of ghost bases now, of pictures in deserted headquarters buildings. Everyone has gone home to have babies, to get educated in one way or another. We who remain try to go through the old military motions, but everything is coming apart or disappearing under dust. Grass is taking over the ramps—ironically, pavement cracks are the only place in west Texas where I've seen grass grow naturally—and these old green-lumber tarpaper barracks are still noisily changing shapes. Leave a door open and sagebrush blows in. Close it and sagebrush still blows in.

Pilots have to help maintain the few birds not grounded. I helped change three engines. We had to cannibalize the hangar queens. No spare parts, and no money to buy them. Well, the chief was right: changing engines is work. Now I never use full throttle unless some Navy clown wants to mix it up, they or the Guard. Besides, we are getting tagged with so many additional duties that there isn't time to fly. Somebody had to refuel the birds and stand fireguard during starts. This week I'm a supply officer. Training? Hell, read the manuals. Yesterday we counted four thousand blankets. I was shy twenty-three hundred. This sergeant looked incredulously at me, grabbed the form, and changed it. Sergeants instinctively understand Supply.

We lock up whole blocks of two-story barracks. Pinups are still on the walls, Rita Hayworth's bare shoulders going to waste as she kneels there, her sexy eyes still waiting. Finally, we switch off the water and power, swing the base gates shut, and join another unit. I usually fly a bird. In time, I guess, as the cadres consolidate, we'll have enough people and machines to form a squadron.

I'll tell you, it's a little eerie sitting out here in the panhandle when the wind is blowing cows around and you've got all the birds lashed down. Last winter we ran out of coal and had to burn old chocks in our stove to keep warm. Once, still only a first lieutenant, I was charged with responsibility for a whose base. My dad told everyone I was now a base commander, and my three sergeants thought that was pretty funny. I guess I shouldn't have showed them the letter, because familiarity breeds contempt. Anyhow, it was a relief to get rid of that base. A bunch of civilian sharpies came in with ridiculously low bids, and the government had to accept them. Everything went—blankets, mess kits, the works. They bought the whole base for about one hundred dollars.

Last year, out at Kingman, Arizona, there were thousands of birds aligned in the desert, some brand-new. Papers were signed, and these guys with torches came in and cut them up. The engines, some of the instruments and radios, they saved. The rest went, dust to dust, back to being pots and pans. It made me sick, because I had delivered a few brand new '51s and Jugs there. I saw B-24s with paper still spiraled around their cosmolined guns. They still *smelled* new, some of those birds. But, Jesus, some of those sweet Mustangs—it was like taking prize shepherds to the pound. Maybe it's just as well that I didn't see my old bird out there, or I might have done something foolish. I couldn't afford to buy it and a car though—these new cars are almost the same price—and even if I'd just stolen it, flown it back to Indiana and hidden it in a barn, I couldn't ever afford gas for it. Sixty gallons per hour at cruise, and that the expensive, high-octane stuff. No first lieutenant can afford *that*. It would be cheaper to keep a movie star as a mistress and, if it came down to it, I guess I'd rather have Rita Hayworth. Ken wrote me to get out and become a doctor on the GI Bill, but I didn't like dissecting frogs in high school. He's dissecting people, the bastard.

Instead, I applied for a regular commission, which is supposed to be such a big deal. And I guess it is. I've already taken all these tests and met this screening board where this old, bleary-eyed colonel kept asking me why I wanted to become a regular officer. Why? Well, I say to myself, why not? I mean, what's better than to fly fighters in peacetime and belong to a sort of gentlemen's flying club? There won't be any more wars because we have the A-Bomb, and no one else does. But I told him how I'd always aspired to the military ideals of Duty, Honor and Country. And, finally, he'd nodded and asked the other officers if they had any questions.

So now it's just me and the West Pointers. They look for my ring and make casual inquiries, but as soon as I open my mouth they know I'm no Academy man. A few act like General Pershing, but most of them are okay, I guess. It's just that they think I'm pretty naive, especially when, after a few drinks, I tell them that all I'd had was a couple of years of ROTC in high school and one in college. Coast Artillery, I'd explain seriously and watch their faces.

"*Really?*" one asked. "Coast Artillery?" I could tell he was stringing me along.

But I'd never have gone on for ROTC Advanced with all those buttons on my epaulets and that silly saber. Well, I'm lying, I realize. The truth is that I'm piss-poor at math, and the Advanced cadets had to compute powder temperatures and trajectories. They all looked alike, those Advanced guys—glasses and slide rules and no sense of humor. And the dumb guns would just sit there in their batteries in these quarrylike forts. They couldn't do anything but shoot. About every ten years, the cadets would shoot a projectile as tall as a man, and that thrill had to last them. That wasn't for me.

No, I knew what I wanted the first time I saw those P-26s at that air show at Chanute Field. They had come down from Selfridge Field in Michigan, *nonstop,* to perform at the big fair. It was the most impressive thing I'd ever seen. They'd dive right at us, line-abreast, streaming colored smoke, and then pull up into loops or Immelmanns, their engines cutting out, while all the girls went crazy, pointing and shading their eyes. That evening, riding my bike home, I decided that, by God, *I* could do that. Heights didn't scare me. I had this big tree house thirty feet up in a maple, and I'd even sit up there during storms with the tree swaying and my scared sister indoors frantically playing the piano.

"Johnny!" my mother would call up at me, "come down before you get electrocuted." But I never did.

Anyhow, when I mention that airshow, these West Pointers grin and look at each other. Not many of them seem to know what a P-26 looked like. I guess they'd decided to make it a career for more mature reasons.

"Yeah?" they say, and nudge each other.

One guy who doesn't think he's Pershing said that he'd grown up on Army posts, that's all. Another, who walked home from the movie with me last night, said that he was in the Air Force because his dad had been an infantry officer, and all he knew was that he didn't want *that.*

I get to know some of them fairly well when we go out to Williams Field, Arizona, for jet upgrading. Williams has become a sort of citadel for fighter jocks, Williams and Nellis, up near Las Vegas. Everything else seems to belong to SAC, and these bomber guys are so swollen up with their mission that they don't waggle wings much now. Well, I don't know. It's true we'd be in one helluva fix without them and the Bomb. Churchill has been saying that the Russians are bad news instead of allies. There's always some country you can't turn your back on.

Anyhow, Williams handles the jets and P-51s, Nellis just the P-51s. I'll never forget seeing these underpowered old P-80s trying to clear the irrigation dikes around the base on a hot day. This is upgrading? Then we see them whistling down like kids' jacks through that big hot sky, little silver crosses a mile ahead of their sound, and we change our minds. Some of the instructors have formed an acrobatic team, a tight little cross of crosses; and when, at 1700, you expect to hear the Retreat cannon —*whoomp!*—there they are, arching up from behind the hangars into a rustling, then almost silent, loop, still welded together, wings almost humorously overlapped, pausing at the top, then slowly revolving into the first half of a Cuban-Eight. Little wisps of fuel stream while they twist down again. *Whoosh!* Over us they go again, and when they are close and head-on, you can see them working, bouncing in the thermals. Up, up they go, rising through the red sun, posing unforgettably. I guess that's what finally interested me, that fuel-streaming cross of aluminum flat against the sky.

"You gotta watch your throttle movements," our instructor says, looking up through his sunglasses at us four leaning into his cockpit. "Now watch the tailpipe temperature when I nudge it too fast. You can melt the fucking tail right off."

They are delicate, these jets. We hear the words "flame out" a lot. Too fast a throttle movement, or negative Gs, and you are suddenly flying a glider, a *fast* one.

My first ride. Everything's so smooth and quiet. We sit in tandem beneath this double-length Plexiglas canopy. It reminds me a little of my uncle's Cadillac. He let me open her up one time. The speedometer registered 105, and I couldn't believe it until I looked out at the blurred shoulders. That's what this jet is like: not much acceleration but fast and smooth once you're moving. A little jiggling of the shock-mounted instrument panel on takeoff but, once airborne, just silk. Nothing like that street rod my oldest friend, Jimmy, and I built in high school. She had a bored-out Ford V-8 block, full-race cam, two big Carters, headers and a chromed Dago front axle. The cops didn't like it, not even after we had the valve covers chromed. The '51 is a hot rod that will burn rubber but won't match top speeds with these P-80s; with these jets, you could just run away from a fight. The '51 does two things better: first, she doesn't need half of Arizona to get airborne, and, second, she will climb and turn like a dream. Rate of roll, top speed and zoom are something else.

Every bird has its Achilles' heel, and the P-80's is that if someone leaves the fuselage fuel tank cap loose, you become a Roman candle. Fuel siphons into the plenum chamber intake. That's what got Dick Bong, they say. Another killer is the nose compartment doors. If they flap open, you go careening away like a drunken seagull. So we wear out our screwdrivers checking caps and latches. Wear out the caps and latches, too.

The acrobatic team has a slot man who shot down a lot of enemy fighters over Germany, and he said that he's going to shoot down a few friendly fighters over Arizona if we don't shape up. He's a big, gray-haired guy with mean eyes. Even the other instructors seem a little afraid of him. Flying is his whole life, and he doesn't want anyone flying jet fighters who feels differently. When he taxied in yesterday afternoon with his vertical stabilizer black with soot from riding so close to the leader, he crawled out and, while he was hunching to unsnap his chute straps and G-suit, he gave us hell about our sloppy traffic patterns. Why don't we go fly bombers if we like big patterns? Some day one of us is gonna flame out and crash, and he doesn't want whichever one of us it is to say he wasn't warned.

One morning, abruptly, he asked the whole class who Ernst Udet was. No one knew for sure. He was German, I said, and I'll never forget the look on his face.

"Who was Douhet?" he growled at someone else. "Billy Mitchell?"

"He was court-martialed."

"Yeah? Why?"

There was always another question. "And?" he'd ask, strutting over to the window. "*And?*"

Sometimes at beer call on Friday evenings, we approach him, expecting a more sociable person. But he's always the same. One day, the day I soloed, he was up on a test hop and he flamed out. Gliding home, he set up a spiral. Mobile Control ordered everyone else out of the pattern.

"Negative, negative," he interrupted impatiently, "this is Dutch. Let 'em land. I'll squeeze in. No sweat."

Once I had a check ride with him in the two-place P-80, the T-Bird, and he treated me as if I were a Primary cadet. I hadn't even started the engine before he began. Once airborne, he got me so rattled that I didn't know my name. He'd pop the stick, or take the bird and black me out while he explained what he was doing. I never *saw* anything, of course. Then I got mad and jerked her up into a string of vertical rolls. At the top she even spun one turn before I could catch her. I pretended it was deliberate.

For a while, he was silent, and then he seemed to become my old trigonometry professor who, without realizing that he was an artist, would take my chalk and quickly draw a perfect circle. For me, that was the end of the lesson. I'd just stand there looking at the circle and not hear another word. Dutch's demonstration was like that. You could have dropped a plumb bob down through *his* vertical rolls. I had been using too much back pressure, he said quietly.

Later my instructor showed me my grade folder. "Good spirit," Dutch had written.

3

HAMILTON

AT THE VERY TIME when the Air Force became independent, I got married. Her name is Jenny, and she's this crazy girl I named my P-51 after. She had a recipe for sugarless tollhouse cookies, and all the time I was in England, half of each convoy was tollhouse cookies. Ken tried one and said it was *very* good, but he never tried another one "because of his teeth," whatever that means. Well, there was more to it than cookies. I mean, we weren't Romeo and Juliet, or Tristan and What's-her-name, but we did meet in the fifth grade. While Mrs. Moore was posing intriguing math problems, we were both busy sketching her. Jenny's sketches were so good that I'd just nod and crumple mine. But I was better at drawing airplanes, because I'd built all these models and knew quite a bit about them. What was funny was that when art period came along, and the teacher (who looked exactly like Zazu Pitts) would ask us to draw a box, we'd draw a tree or something, and she'd give us poor marks. I realize now that she was just acting military. One morning when she insisted that we draw a box, Jenny drew this tricky perspective which made the teacher look slit-eyed at her.

When I went home on leave in 1943, I called up all the girls I used to date in high school, but half of them were married or seriously engaged, and the others were so eager I backed off. A few were away at college but, of these, by coincidence—an aunt's death or something—my old fellow-sketcher, Skinny Jenny, was home. When she answered the door, I couldn't say a word. We just stood there looking each other up and down. I'd finally outgrown her, and she had nice boobs and great legs. And she always did have the heaviest hair in class. It's blond and so coarse and straight that she breaks combs. Her mother was both the 1918 County-Fair Queen and the Victory Bond Girl, I learned later, and is, in fact, still beautiful, but noisy. She cans a lot. Jenny attended Bennington, which is a big deal in Vermont, I guess, but unknown back home. I mean, it's *not* Purdue, is it? And I went to Purdue for a year. Anyhow, she was, and is, the same fool except for her build, and I'm beginning to realize that I was really lucky.

After my tour at Williams, I had a few pangs because my old friend, Jimmy sent me a graduation announcement. He has an M.S. now, from Cal Tech, and he's living in a wind tunnel or something. Jimmy was always great with math, but he can't write a simple declarative sentence. His letters look like some monkey in an altitude chamber wrote them, or a doctor.

Well, the Air Force sent us up to Hamilton Field, sixteen miles north of the Golden Gate, and Jenny and I just took our time getting there, using all four days of my authorized travel time. That was our honeymoon, that trip, and we drove up the coastal highway. Everyone said it's scenic and everything, but there was fog nearly all the way. What my folks should have given us for a wedding present, instead of all those silver goblets and tureen spoons, are Marchal fog lights.

It's crazy, I know, considering that I'd been to Piccadilly Circus, but for two of those four nights of our honeymoon, we were both virgins. And then, later, even when I'd think about something peaceful, like fishing or cross-country flying, I put on a ridiculous performance. She should have married Clark Gable or someone.

"No," she says, "you're fine, Sheik."

After we bought this new Ford convertible—boy, is she *pretty* driving it with the top down and her hair blowing—there wasn't any bank account. All we have is in our wallets, which explains why we stayed two nights at Pismo Beach and only one at Carmel. When people ask us where we honeymooned, I say Carmel, but she gives me this amused look, so I have to add Pismo. It's a good thing Jenny has a sense of humor because the fog at Pismo was so thick we nearly walked off a cliff, and our little cabin was so cold no one except newlyweds would have undressed.

Hamilton! Although I have warned her that most Air Force bases are in swamps or deserts, she took one look around, threw her arms wide, and hugged me.

"Jenny," I kept saying, "Jenny, this is the country club of the Air Force, this and March and Langley."

Even the enlisted barracks are permanent buildings here. The PX is Spanish, stucco and tile. All the hangars are camouflaged, concrete things. Sprawling up the hill are the officers' quarters. We drive up a winding road past the club to see them. A poor man's Beverly Hills; Spanish architecture, impressive landscaping. Slowly, we move past the low houses and she reads off the ranks of the occupants. There aren't any first lieutenants' shingles on the lawn; they're all senior officers. I expected that, of course, but it's sad to watch her eyes.

On the crest is the general's mansion, around it the colonels'. At the foot of the hill are little signs saying Major So-and-so. In other words, you can tell a guy's rank by the altitude of his quarters. As a first lieutenant, I don't qualify for anything on base. In fact, we don't even rate sea level. We rent this basement apartment in a sleepy little town sixteen miles to the south. The house itself is right out of a Charles Addams cartoon, Victorian Spooky. But no bats, and it's clean and, best of all, it overlooks the marina. There's only one grocery in town, no restaurants, one movie theater. Sausalito, the sign says. Gulls wake us up whenever the foghorns at the bridge don't. We try to make the early movie; everyone in town does, and we stand in the short line, arm in arm, wearing sweaters even in July. Tickets have gone up to fifty cents.

Although our apartment isn't too enchanting, it does have a view and wainscoting. Jenny is painting a couple of oils to hang: an impressionistic scene of the marina with Angel Island in the background, and a still-life of morning light on our dining table.

"Draw a box," I tell her.

When we taxi out in the cool mornings, I look across the wet grass and the ramp to the camouflaged hangars. Right after Pearl Harbor, they say, an army of painters had attempted to camouflage the whole base, even the ramp and the runway. From ten thousand feet it was supposed to look like a golf course or something. Now they're trying to get the paint off. Mount Tamalpias, the hill patterns fringing San Pablo Bay, and all the peninsulas were a dead giveaway. No Japanese would have been fooled.

On takeoff we skim this low dike which keeps San Pablo Bay from turning our runway into a seaplane lane and, within seconds, we are over dreamy peninsulas and white regattas. With justification the sailors and captain of the Richmond Ferry view us with alarm—sometimes at eye level—and we really work the Navy over. Flying under the Golden Gate is no challenge, but looping a span—I haven't tried that yet—might be.

I should be using the past tense because last week we got in a new squadron commander who considers buzzing childish and buzzing rich yacht owners stupid.

"What does it prove?" he asked quietly that first day. "Listen, if you want to see this base closed and be shipped back to Texas or somewhere godawful, why just keep it up."

Smart. He couldn't have picked a better way to get to us. If someone ordered any one of us to start deleting bases, Hamilton would be the last to go.

"You're supposed to be *defending* these people," he continued, "not harassing them. They are our employers, gentlemen. Now, can we start acting like adults?"

Well, we settled right down, and community relations improved overnight. I like this CO, even if he did fly Jugs. A smart farm boy, he had been studying to become a veterinarian when the war came along. He's thirty but, with his salt-and-pepper hair, he looks thirty-five or forty. When we are flying around the Bay Area, or on a cross-country somewhere, he is as professional as an airline pilot, but when we're out in the acrobatic area north of Point Reyes, you realize that he's no old lady. He will follow you up through any kind of maneuver and still be on your tail when you run out of airspeed and ideas. Then he rocks his wings, assumes command, and leads us sloping down toward the shore and the clean, white city, spiraling with serious regard for the blanketing airways and formally requests landing instructions before he enters Hamilton's control area. He even says "Thank you, sir," to the sergeants in the tower.

And his traffic patterns are right by the book: he pitches out exactly from one thousand feet and curves gently around as though he were driving an egg truck. Following him, we almost go to sleep and forget where we're landing, but we have quit losing guys in the traffic pattern. Let the other squadrons laugh, I finally decide.

"*Professionalism*," he repeats during postflight critiques over coffee, and his Saint Bernard eyes rest on each of us for a few seconds. "Whatever is appropriate for a given situation, neither more nor less. Tangling with the Alameda guys in the tactics area is one thing, jumping a sailboat is something else. Even an F-84 can beat a sailboat—*every time.* So what's the point?"

Until he came along, our squadron wasn't very mobile. If CONAD had ordered us to redeploy, it would have looked like a Three Stooges comedy. I guess we'd have tried to take these beautiful, well-stocked hangars with us. These roots worried him from the first day, so he had the sheet-metal shop construct some aluminum bins, so many for the tool crib, so many for the maintenance manuals and essential spare parts. Even the orderly room had one for the typewriters and records. Then he had them stenciled and packed. Once they were loaded and everybody had muttered about new brooms sweeping clean, he had the hangar doors closed and locked.

"Okay, you're at an abandoned base in North Dakota," he told us, "and you'll be here until further notice."

Our line chief's eyes narrowed, and it's the first time I ever saw his jaw muscles still. Then, with enviable expertise, he spit tobacco juice six feet into a trash can and tugged his herringbone twill cap around by its bill. By God, he had put in twenty-eight years in this man's Air Force, and this was the most *pointless* and *foolish* operation he ever saw. Henry—we company-graders don't call him that, of course: not more than once—is from Petaluma, right off the end of the runway. For eighteen years, including all of World War II, he's been stationed right here at Hamilton and going home every night.

But no one listens much to Henry anymore. When the major gathers his staff around him every evening to see how it's coming along, he invites his line chief and his four flight chiefs, NCOs almost as senior. Only Henry, it seems, can find it in himself to object to a military unit being somewhat mobile.

"If we leave," Henry shouts, "who defends San Francisco? The Presidio?"

"Now," continued the major, as though Henry were just another engine to speak above. "Is there any reason we couldn't deploy within twenty-four hours?" (Jenny, my mind answers.)

Henry jumps up, muttering, and turns away to spit downwind.

"Within twelve hours?" the major asks. I wince, thinking of my tool crib, and we hear Henry choking on his tobacco juice, but no one even looks at him.

What I like best is that the major isn't doing this to impress the colonel. All that impresses the colonel is flying time. Which of our three squadrons will be the first to log a thousand hours in one month? It's never been done with jets, he reminds his squadron commanders pointedly. Training is important, sure; but right now, gentlemen, *time* . . .

We have the F-84, the "D" model. "D" for dog, I guess. The engines are heavy and don't develop much thrust. What's incredible is that we have been designated a fighter-interceptor group. By the time we could get up to thirty thousand, the war would be over. SAC likes to rub it in. When they send bombers in from the north, we don't get the word until they're within two hundred miles, *and* we run for our birds, *and* we taxi like the base was about to sink; but they're always down over San Jose before we can catch them. I forget how many times San Francisco and Oakland have been atomized.

"Okay," the major decides, "if we really thought they were Russian, we'd be waiting at the end of the runway, wouldn't we? We'd gain five to seven minutes right there." No, we won't have everyone on cockpit alert, just one flight. The rest can sit here in Ops reading *Esquire,* but we can attach a trailer to our jeep so that when the klaxon goes, they will have a fast ride out to the most distant birds.

In practice, this theory becomes less attractive. If we are on cockpit alert, the klaxon automatically seems to go right after some buddy has handed you a brimming-full chocolate shake. And there's no way to get a crew chief's attention once a klaxon blows. The APU exhausts stutter up the scale, and the mechanics start running around like we are crash-diving on a submarine. So you gulp a big swallow and take off with the shake slopping over your G-suit.

And if you're in Ops when the call comes in, either the jeep won't start, or Lucky Teeter—that's what we call our hell-driving sergeant—nearly slews us off the jeep trailer. Once, too, the trailer hitch came loose and, like some parade float hurrying to catch up, we went seesawing independently right down between the long rows of birds. Whatever happened, our crew chiefs would always have our engines idling and, having discarded the metal ladders as time-wasters, would be crouched with laced hands to hurl us up into (or *over*, in the case of little Clayton) our cockpits.

When SAC began sending B-36s against the Bay Area, usually at thirty-five thousand feet, even the major's spirit wavered. Every pursuit curve was a series of stalls, every strip of gun camera film a source of embarrassment.

Our group commander, a crazy Irishman—Jenny always says there's redundancy in the term "crazy Irishman"—told us not to worry. It was the same in 1939 when he had flown P-35s against the new B-17s. One year fighter pilots are mushing around looking up at the bombers, the next a new fighter rolls out and the bombers become cows again. Reminiscently, he laughs, rubs his broken nose, and crosses his old flying boots. I thought they must have belonged to Rickenbacker at one time, but the colonel told Sergeant Gonzales, our Operations specialist, that he'd gotten them off a dead Mexican.

"Yeah, Christ," the colonel says and looks out the window. Everyone waits respectfully. With the colonel, you never know whether he's through or not. This time he's not through. He clears his throat.

"In 1942, they were still saying that the B-17s didn't need fighter escort." He gazes around at us with his bleary-eyed grin. "And then the next year they went after the ball-bearing plants at Schweinfurt. *Ha!*" He closes his eyes, and his head lolls back. I wonder if he's been drinking again but, no, when his head rolls sideways and I think he's gone to sleep, his eyes open and he's looking right at Mac.

"Quit nodding, you bastard. You were still in high school."

"Colonel! I was in the ETO flying B-26s . . ." Mac raises his hand to his mouth. He's been tricked again.

"Ha!" the colonel nods. "Bomber pilot! A Polack *bomber* pilot."

"Polack? Sir, I'm a Scot."

"Scot, Polack—what's the difference?" The colonel grins and shrugs.

"Sir, may I be insubordinate?"

"It's a free country. Of course, I may ship you back to Poland."

"Hee, hee, hee," laughs Sergeant Gonzales.

"Why are *you* laughing, you Spic? I'm gonna ship your ass back to Juarez."

"Good," Sergeant Gonzales says, "I'll be a brigadier general in the Mexican Air Force. Big *hacienda,* no bullshit from gringo colonels who pad their flying time . . ."

"Haw!" yells Whispering Mac.

"What's this?" askes the colonel, scowling. "What's this about padding time, Private?"

Sergeant Gonzales ducks behind the Operations counter, then his wide, beautiful grin reappears. "You flew maybe twenty minutes last night and logged two hours, gringo-Colonel. Pancho Villa come and fix you."

"What? *What?*" the colonel can't quit laughing long enough to look outraged.

"How many thousand hours you say you fly, sir?" Sergeant Gonzales's chin rises speculatively as he hefts the colonel's Form 5. "Maybe you fly . . . oh, say, five hundred . . ." He bursts out laughing and ducks the colonel's hurled cup.

Tears streaming, the colonel seats himself again. "Ahh," he sighs weakly. "Major, I want *that* one, and this fat bomber pilot here, shipped to Poland this afternoon."

"Yes, sir. TDY or PCS?"

"Forever." The Colonel nods. "Now where was I?"

"I can tell you where your head was, Colonel," Mac volunteers, his lips pursed. "Gringo-Colonel."

"Poland!" The colonel points eastward. "Hey, you want to see a bomber guy turn red? Just say, 'YB-17.'" He says it to Mac, who simply looks puzzled. "See?" the colonel continues. "He *was* still in high school. The YB-17 was a B-17 Q-ship, with guns sticking out everywhere. No bombs, just guns and ammo."

"Sounds like a good idea," Mac says, and rolls his eyes away from the colonel's withering expression.

"It didn't work?" Will asks.

The colonel smiles beatifically. "Sure, it worked—for about ten minutes. Then the *Luftwaffe* had them for dessert." Contentedly, he clasps his hands in his lap. "Lots of crow feathers sticking out of doctrinal mouths then, gentlemen. Yes, sir. Then they began to wish they hadn't hogged all the development money. But . . ." He opens his hands, his smile broadens. "We didn't have a decent fighter with long-enough legs."

We absorb this, the old struggles in the War Department, at the Tactical School at Maxwell. An ancient feud stretching back through the Depression, back through Arnold and Spaatz, Royce and Andrews, Harold George and Chennault, to Mitchell and the foreign airpower theorists—Trenchard, Douhet. The colonel had flown P-26s with Chennault at Fort Knox in 1933. Despite Chennault's primitive telephone and radio warning network, established temporarily for the maneuvers, the P-26s had intercepted the blue-and-yellow B-9s and B-10s.

It's going to rain hard. Excusing himself, the major leaves to check that all the canopies are closed. The roof of the hangar is beginning to drum. Gulls swing up to stall on the Rescue boathouse and retract their wings. Calmly, the colonel reaches over and two-fingers a cigarette out of Mac's shirt pocket. Mac's eyes follow the theft.

"Button that pocket, Captain," the colonel says, exhaling in Mac's face. The latter looks around at us. "Jesus," he breathes.

"Yeah, we had no money, no rank, no birds," the colonel continues. "Nothing."

"No cigarettes," Mac adds.

"You know what won World War Two, gentlemen?"

"Sure," Sergeant Gonzales volunteers. "The A-Bomb. The A-Bomb and the six-by-six."

"No," the colonel says. He looks around at us. "The *drop tank*. That's right, the old drop tank. We had nothing with legs that could fight, and vice versa. So we experimented with pressed-paper tanks. Hooked them on bomb shackles, Rube Goldberged the plumbing. The Jugs and the P-38s moved deeper into Germany and then we got the Mustang. And that was it. Oh, sure. The infantry won the war—they always do, the last bit—but not without air superiority. And we didn't have that until the bombers could go anywhere, and that meant fighter escort. Escort, gentlemen, meant drop tanks."

Leaning dangerously far back in his chair, the Colonel says, "Yes, sir. The drop tank—and the Merlin engine."

With that addition, he is careful not to look at Mac, who still swears by Pratt and Whitneys. Almost imperceptibly, Mac's foot eases toward the colonel's chair legs. Just as he hooks his toe behind a rung, the colonel casually rocks forward, runs his fingers through his wavy gray hair, rises, kicks Mac's chair off balance, and strolls out.

In 1949, the First Fighter Group down at March Field trades in its F-80s on the first F-86s to roll off the line. Promptly the colonel goes down to check out. He returns, nodding, and says, "That's it, gentlemen. The first real fighter since the P-51."

But when the First flies up to party with us two months later, the colonel tells their colonel that he's glad that we aren't getting such an *ugly* bird, Hamilton being such a scenic base and everything.

"It looks like a cross between a tadpole and a parrot."

Inhaling, the other colonel rises. "Okay," he says, "outside."

"Remember, Jack, I boxed Golden Gloves."

"Big deal. Outside. I'm gonna flatten that ugly nose until you look even more like a frog."

Outside we go, to watch. But they're so drunk, neither can land a punch. Each swing ends with one of them rolling down the hill. Finally, both of them are laughing and hanging on to each other.

Like a rival gang we had met them when they entered our territory, and the fight had swarmed all the way northward from San Jose to Hamilton. I did everything but crash trying to shake this lunatic in his parrot-beaked, swept-wing machine. At one point we were in a daisy chain whistling down Market Street. Some of the windows were above us. God, it was *fun*. When we landed, the general grabbed the two colonels, and they disappeared in the staff car. I heard there were public apologies to the mayor of San Francisco, and that the chief of staff is furious. And our club officer, surveying the acrobatic pyramids of pilots, of beer cans, of broken glass, isn't exactly happy. Nor is Jenny, I imagine. But we are.

The First is having trouble with their birds, they admit. We are sprawled in a BOQ room, barely visible below the smoke. There is always some new problem to ground them, they say. Warmed by their frankness, we confess that it's not all roses with us either.

"Yeah? A reliable old bird like that?"

Out along our right wings through the aluminum skin ahead of the landing gear well, mysterious cracks have appeared. Day by day, despite drill-holes, despite fewer Gs, the cracks lengthen. Today's fight hadn't helped.

Two days later, after we'd waved good-bye and watched those sweet '86s accelerate away like scared fish, old Will loses a wing and goes flipping down into the Vallejo marshes. When they locate the bird, they find helmet paint all over the canopy. We are shaken, of course, but we have to keep flying the birds; there is no one else to defend San Francisco. We tell our wives that the problem has been corrected, but Jenny says I'm lying. Her eyes are red.

"Why didn't he eject?" we jocks angrily ask each other.

If his shoulder harness had been locked, we reason, maybe his head wouldn't have been thrown around so wildly. We begin locking ours, in case that might help.

Will had been leading the element, and the flight had been all stretched out in desperate trail, everyone practicing keeping his gun-sight pipper on the bird ahead, glinting up into the white sun, streaming fuel from vent drains, compression shedding swaths of vapor from the whole span of their wings at times. I can see it in my dreams: curving joyfully up into the blue void with the Gs melting me, relaxing inverted under the lighter G-loads on top, then falling, plunging down the back side of the loop or cloverleaf or whatever we're doing. Will, meticulous, Academy grad, had come along too late for the war and, lacking such a basic credential, he had to work hard to prove tiger status. Tigers maintain precise interval at all times. Will had simply tried to close a gap; his professional pride was at stake. But machines don't know about gaps or pride. They know about transonic compressibility and a few other things which maybe someone down at Cal Tech could explain to me. All I know is that every airfoil has some critical limit, and ours goes crazy at Mach 0.82. Exceed the red-line at low altitude, and the bird tries to do a half gainer, pulling (or trying to pull) about fourteen Gs. At twelve, the wings start folding. In a way, then, Will's accident is more the result of a failure in judgment than a failure of metal.

For a while, as we digest this wisdom, the flight leaders take it easy. And then we get into a hassle with those Navy clowns from Alameda and quit thinking about the wings. It is a matter of professional pride.

"No, it isn't," the major says while Mac and I writhe at attention. "It is a matter of stupidity. Now I have tried to explain the concept of professionalism to you. You are both grounded until further notice."

Gradually the cracks exceed all expectations. One morning we come to work and find all the birds on the red cross.

"Grounded?" Mac howls.

"What's it to you?" Sergeant Gonzales asks him. "Sir?"

Only in an actual emergency can we take off. But, naturally, the major insists that we maintain our usual alert posture—four on five-minute, four on ten-minute—relaxing it only for a couple of hours this particular morning so everyone can attend the big briefing over at the base theater. Several civilian experts from the factory have tried to assess the situation. They begin by showing us some charts about this phenomenon known as compressibility, and then the structural engineer who had designed the wing goes up on the stage. He must have overheard our remarks about tinfoil wings because, quickly, he flashes his credentials: he had designed the Jug's wing. There is a spattering of applause from all the ex-Jugheads, of course; and he smiles appreciatively and says, "Well, this one is even stronger, gentlemen."

What's wrong, he tells us, is the aerodynamics. It's an old airfoil, and the leading edge of the wing isn't swept back. The F-84 was designed during the war, before American designers knew much about sweepback. We learned a lot from captured German prototypes. Later models of the F-84 will have swept wings. Meanwhile, the wing will be patched, beefed up a little, and we will simply have to remember the red-line on the airspeed indicator. I wonder why he'd flown all the way from Long Island to tell us this.

Next, the company's chief test pilot. We had heard of him, and I decide that he is the slim, handsome civilian sitting in the front row. But when the famous name is mentioned, the wrong guy stands up. Slim is simply an engineer. The test pilot is the dumpy one who looks like a Jewish salesman. His suit is rumpled, and his slacks hang down over his shoes. He laughs a lot and asks which one of us is Snake. Snake holds up his hand.

"*Eleven* telephone poles?" the test pilot asks admiringly.

"Right."

"By God, that's a new record. You landed in the rain and saw these headlights coming? So, then what did you do? I heard this story at the bar last night and I said, Jesus, that sounds like my luck. . . ." This for our benefit.

We are familiar with the story. Lost over Pennsylvania in a rainstorm, Snake and his wingman had tried to land on a rural highway. When headlights appeared, Snake had applied full power, hopped over the car, but had stalled and lost control. The car didn't even stop. Dazed, Snake had looked at the scythed poles and limped to a farmhouse where the farmer—rocking on his porch, if we can believe Snake—told him it wouldn't do any good to come in because all his telephone wires had been knocked down. Strong wings, as the structural engineer had said.

"Jesus. *You* get up here; your stories are better than mine, but what the hell. . . . Okay, it's gonna get pretty deep in here—say, Jim, why the hell *did* I come out here? . . . Really? . . . Oh, *noo-o* . . . I've got a wife and kids, man. Get Snake to fly it. . . . Where was I? Oh, yeah, well, I'm testing the first, the very first P-84, see? It's 1930 or something, when I looked like Clark Gable, and I am flying this silly bomb around over Long Island, and it's a beautiful morning, and I'm writing on my kneeboard how perfectly everything is going when I hear this little puff. Puff!" He crouches and tiptoes around the stage. "Well, I decide it's nothing so I keep writing, and then I realize that the airplane is *gone*. Gentlemen, I quit writing because, well . . ."—he taps his head slyly—"I realized, being a test pilot and all, that I should *do* something." (Giggle)

"I mean, who wants to be buried on Long Island? So, I unstrapped, kicked the seat away, and pulled the ripcord."

He nearly falls off the stage laughing. We laugh a little, too, and recross our legs.

"You see," he continues, "the point I wanted to make—uh, would any of you like that exact sequence repeated? no one is taking notes?—is, ah, Jim, which bird do I have to fly? . . . oh, *no-o-o,* Old One-Wing?"

Actually, the previous day, a Sunday, he had flown it. Donning a flying suit, he had prowled our ramp, found the bird with the worst crack, and taken off. At twenty-five thousand, he had eased her into a dive. He finally tells us this matter-of-factly. From shore, the crash boats were putting out. Another company pilot was chasing him in a T-Bird.

"And I was sitting up there, draped with rosaries, and I told them, 'Release the buzzards.' Okay, I'm at eight-one now, and I put both of these steel hands on the stick, my elbows resting against these bands of muscle." (Big grin, whipping his microphone cord straight and pacing the stage like a comedian) "And I wait, see, for the white needle to cross the red one . . . or is it the red needle crossing the . . . well, Jesus, no wonder!"

He pauses. His eyes quit smiling and, for a second, we see who he is. It becomes very quiet. Gradually, his full grin returns, then the comic grimaces and winces, but it's not the same. He is no longer a Jewish comedian. We had seen *him.*

"Well, eight-three and I'm beginning to think you guys made all this up about pitching-up, when clunk!—this big piston hits me on the top of my head, this godlike head, and compresses me to, well, this height. Two days ago I was six feet two, gentlemen. So I don't know what the hell happened. I blacked out, and said a lot of things about engineers that I now regret, but . . . well, that's the scientific explanation. Are there any questions?"

"How many Gs?" Snake calls.

"How many? Jeez, I don't know. A bunch."

"How's that wing now?" Mac asks.

"I don't know. I couldn't look. How many inches now, Jim?" the test pilot asks the engineers. "*Feet?* Jesus, you guys don't pay me enough. All I know is that it flaps now. We are going to look into that. Who knows? It may help. Attach oarlocks to the canopy rail, you know. What, Jim? . . . You don't believe me? Well, friend, here are the keys. *You* fly it."

He staggers around laughing and nodding, with more asides for the engineers, who are grudgingly smiling. At least forty, I'd say, and probably a houseful of kids. But we are watching him as though he were Achilles. I see now: he isn't fat, he's chunky. And I try to imagine his face as the white needle overtook the red.

Some men are different. The best hide their guts, don't take themselves too seriously. I realize that now. Well, he's welcome to his fifty thousand a year. On the stage he could make twice that much, but then he'd be just a famous comedian.

Me, I'll settle for being a glamorous fighter pilot.

Kirtland is a favorite refueling stop—going west, at least. You can always make it from there to George and, if the winds aren't too strong, sometimes to Hamilton. The major doesn't like that word "sometimes," so we file for George. Play it safe. I'm due for captain when the next board meets, and I need a Flying Evaluation Board like I need cholera. Not that I expect to make it. Promotions are so tight these days, and my record is pretty average—"singularly undistinguished," Ed says. In college, Ed was an English major. He's always seeing mythical significance in our lives. I don't know whether he's being funny or not. Maybe he's written so many term papers that he sees parallels where there aren't any. Once, when we're serious—drunk—he decides we are too weak and civilized. (At the time old Neil, who used to ride in rodeos, has grabbed this waitress and is sweet-talking her.) We're like the Athenians: we aren't disciplined, we aren't stern, we aren't *abstemious*.

So Ed and I are at Kirtland, in Albuquerque, and are taxiing out in these two hangar queens. They've been broken down in Oke City so long that one mechanic thought they were assigned there. They are real lemons. When we go coast to coast, they never get past Oklahoma City.

Being senior, I'm leading. We line up and run up to one hundred percent, which gives you about two hundred pounds of thrust on these queens. At seventy or eighty, I see this dog come out of the sagebrush from the left side. He's about half a mile ahead. Instinctively, I begin easing the throttle back and warning Ed, who is on my wing, but now the dog is continuing across. We're okay, I think, and ease the throttle forward again. We're skimming the runway lights on the left, so the dog, now well right of the centerline, should be okay. As usual, Ed has his wing overlapped.

At about 130, I notice the dog pause. He's seen us. Oh my God, he's panicking and reversing course. I guess he's heading home.

"Ease right, Ed," I call.

"I see him."

But the dumb dog changes his mind again and finally cowers on the centerline. It's a shepherd, almost. I'm straddling the lights now and moving into the desert of the high plateau. We're bound to miss him.

We're past and I ease us back onto the runway, Ed still close on my right wing. Altitude takeoffs must be gentle, and Kirtland is at five thousand feet. Skip, skip, airborne.

"You better check me, John," Ed says.

"Oh, *no-o*."

"Yeah."

*   *   *

June, 1950, and I am what? Twenty-seven, twenty-eight? I have to go back to 1923 and subtract. Half our squadron is gone, involuntarily returned to reserve status. The reduction in force—RIF is the dreaded acronym—had come without warning late last fall just as the stores in San Francisco were hanging Christmas decorations. With the Berlin Airlift out of the way, the politicians began making the usual noises about a standing army. It hasn't sunk into those opportunistic heads yet that we are living in a different age. They are busy logging points on the side of economy. But who can knock economy? We eat hamburger three times a week, Jenny and I; we don't look much like the fat militarists the liberal cartoonists depict. Once a month we live it up and have steak or lamb chops. We live in a cellar and drive a Ford. I'm beginning to despise congressmen. Their pork barrels are full, you can bet.

Feast or famine. Last year we flew a thousand hours in one month. This year we fly only on weekends with the Mobilization-Day Assignees. SAC absorbs what little money there is, and the fighter units have been halved. We've lost all our reserve officers. I understand that my old flight commander is selling vacuum cleaners. If he comes around, we'll have to buy one, I guess.

The M-Day Assignees are to fill the empty cockpits, so we have to check them out in our birds and keep them current.

"Won't you ever get a weekend off?" Jenny asks. "Sure," I reply, "only Tuesday and Wednesday will become our weekend."

She considers this plan as she pours the wine. The guy told her to serve a red wine with meatloaf, so we are having port. Gee, I wish she hadn't cut all her hair off—all that heavy blond hair.

We had our first big fight about that.

"There! and there! and there!" she shouted, opening issues of *Vogue*. "No one is wearing long hair now."

"Who cares what those skeletons are doing?" I retorted.

"I do."

Women. Show them some skinny corpse with her hip thrown out of joint, and they call it high fashion. I call it malnutrition.

"What about church?" Jenny suddenly asks. She has this smug look on her face as though she's just thrown a wrench into the machinery.

"No problem. Next Wednesday the colonel simply tells the chaplain it's Sunday. No problem."

I wake up to the phone. It is so dark that the dial of my wristwatch isn't even illuminated, but we can't have been asleep long. It's the base, I decide, so I hit the floor running, collide with a top-heavy clothes rack, step onto a fairly vindictive cat, and slam into a door facing. The cat has all four feet locked around my ankle and is sinking his teeth into my calf. I kick him into the kitchenette and grope for the phone. Convinced that there's an intruder, that I'm finally onto something big, our cocker springs from the bed barking. All his life he has waited for this moment.

"Lieutenant Copley," I pant into the mouthpiece. Above the barking I hear an excited voice chanting a single word. For a moment it doesn't register, and then it does. I can't believe it.

"Roger!" I acknowledge, and begin a sort of sack-race trying to get into my uniform. There seem to be more buttons than holes on my shirt. And it would help if the cocker would get out of the closet.

Slit-eyed against the kitchen light, Jenny rises onto her elbows. "Some old girl friend?"

I jam on my overseas cap, kneel to retie a shoelace, and break it.

"Y'know, sweet," she says, watching me, "maybe you're right. Maybe I shouldn't ever go up in a plane with you."

If you fly F-84s, you realize that a second represents twenty feet of altitude, so I don't even say good-bye. Instead, I hurl the snapping cocker away from the door and run up the stone steps to street level. Oh God, *fog!* Beneath the streetlights' halo, down the twisting hills, I gun the cold engine; then along the desolate waterfront I accelerate and, once on Highway 101, settle the speedometer needle on ninety-five. Through breaks in the overcast, I see the moon. It is June. Belvidere, Mill Valley, San Rafael, all asleep, drift by. At the gate, I switch briefly to parking lights and see the white glove motion me through. Within a minute I am in the locker room unbuttoning. My flying coveralls are clammy, my G-suit zippers especially obstinate. I try to slip in unnoticed, but the major is right there. Pointedly, he looks at the wall clock. I nod. He's right; Sausalito is too far away.

Most of them are present, milling around in their Mae Wests, nervously joking about how they really should take their turns in Mobile Control and as airdrome officer. My nameplate is hooked right beneath the colonel's on the scheduling board. I look around for him, hear his barking laugh, his cough.

There he is, still wearing his sport coat beneath his Mae West. Okay, that settles it; it's not a real alert, then. My tension drains away. I laugh, find a cup of coffee, look out at the busy ramp where tug headlights flash across the rows of silver birds with the armorers loading the ammo cans. Flashes of color: the yellow diagonal tail stripes; the red, blue and gold group insignia ("*Above the Foe*"). Above the chatter of the pilots, through the pivoted windows, I hear the auxiliary power units idling in little, governed surges. All for a drill, I think, except that those poor ground crewmen don't know it's a drill.

"All right, gentlemen," the major calls to us, "please seat yourselves as the scheduling board indicates."

The colonel is still telling some story, but he knows. Finally, he looks around and pretends to notice. Abruptly, he cuts it short, nods apologetically to the major who, I hear, was passed over for promotion last week by the board at headquarters, and tiptoes to his seat. His breath scares me. Slapping me on the knee, he asks, "Ready, Johnny-boy?"

"Yes, sir." I smile.

"Just us Irish tonight, right?"

30

Ready? I look again at the major's poker face, at the other faces.

"All right, gentlemen," the major says. "I guess you know by now why we're here. North Korea has invaded South Korea. What this means to us, we don't know. Remember that the last war began with Hitler invading Poland. Anyhow, Washington's taking no chances. Conceivably, this invasion could be simply a diversion, part of a master plan. But . . . well, let's play it as though this is what we've been training for."

He checks with his pencil down through his notes, then crumples them. "Well, the timing isn't ideal, is it? We've got the wrong birds for the job, and even they are grounded, half of them. But those people down there"—he jerks his head toward the city—"won't be interested in excuses if the Russians get through. So let's decide right now that they are not going to get through.

"If Seattle Sector picks up bogies, we'll assume cockpit alert, all of us. The controllers plan to scramble us in plenty of time and assign each flight a piece of sky to the north. Later, they may split us into elements, or even singles. It all depends on the number of tracks on their radar scopes. It could boil down to one on one. So it will be up to you." Here he pauses to blow his nose; he has a bad cold. "Gentlemen, I'm not going to tell you what to do. But I'd like to remind you what those cities down there will look like tomorrow if we don't stop them." Another pause.

Christ, I think, he's talking about *ramming*.

"Okay," he concludes, "you have live ammo. Preflight and stand near your bird."

I walk out with the colonel. His wife is still waiting in the parking lot. Baby-blue Cadillac convertible.

After kissing her, he waves and laughs. "Hell," he yells back at her as she glides away, "anybody can fly an airplane if he's sober."

He seems relaxed as we stride along, but I'm as nervous as a cadet heading out to a bird with a particularly hated check pilot. Some check pilot. He's practically dragging his chute.

"Hey," he says happily, "what did you think of that band? Great, huh?"

"Band, sir?"

"Jimmy Dorsey, Johnny. Jimmy Dorsey was at the club. Didn't you know? Whatsa matter? You don't like music?"

"Oh, yes, sir. I was just tired, I guess. I'd forgotten." (A lie.)

He snaps his fingers. "Oh, yeah . . . you're a newlywed, aren't you? Well, that explains it. Sex beats Jimmy Dorsey any day, especially when you're married to such a doll. She's a real beauty, your wife."

"Thank you, sir." The old lecher doesn't miss much. Forty years old, and he still notices the girls. He's always cutting in on us lieutenants at the dances.

"You got a flashlight?"

I hand him mine, and he shines it on tail numbers. There his is, tail striped with all three colors of the squadrons. "See you on Channel Able, if we go."

31

I borrow a light from my crew chief and set up the cockpit for a scramble. My fiberglass helmet and mask are already connected. I park them on the windshield arch, arrange the chute straps. Then the chief and I sit on the wing and smoke. Stars show above but there is fog on the bay, in the valleys.

"What's up, sir?" my crew chief asks.

"North Korea has invaded South Korea."

"Yeah? Where's Korea?"

"I'm not sure. Asia, I think. Near Japan."

"They're coming here next? Jeez, they should have left the hangars camouflaged."

"Not the Koreans. Maybe the Russians."

"Yeah? Really?" He's a young kid, and he's thinking about it. "Jeez, I hope they don't call off the big game this weekend. Oakland is gonna cream them."

Sergeant Gonzales arrives in the jeep with coffee, chugs over to the colonel's bird.

"Hey, Gringo-Colonel. How much night weather you logged so far tonight?" He hears the colonel running toward the jeep, so he guns away.

Cold finally, we flap our arms, move away from the birds and under a hangar floodlight, pass a greasy football. Jesus, he overleads me every time. Suddenly, out of the darkness, races the colonel to intercept my pass. He's still wearing that expensive sport coat beneath his Mae West.

"Okay," Henry the line chief calls, "let's knock off the goddamn horseplay. Oh, is that *you*, Colonel?"

At 0230, the Ops officer announces on the PA system that pilots may leave their gear in the cockpits and return to Operations. We converge on the coffeepot, rubbing our hands, stretching, pushing each other out of line. The major is talking on the hot line, nodding and gesturing as though the controller can see him. Then, still solemn, he lowers one hand to fend off the colonel, who is trying to tighten everyone's Mae West leg-straps and inflate their Mae Wests.

I sink into an easy chair, pick up an old *Time*. By coincidence there's a map of the Far East, a statement by Dean Acheson. The colored halves of Korea seem too far away to warrant this alert; the entire Pacific separates us. I pitch it back into the rack. In that same rack are twenty untouched copies of *Flying Safety Magazine*.

A roar of laughter, a mock wince of pain, and the major's Mae West collar balloons between his ear and the phone. He gives up and hangs up. A louder outburst: Mac, in turn, has pulled the colonel's CO_2 bottles. Laughing and coughing smoke, the colonel yells, "Attention, you bastard!"

Mac freezes, wipes off his grin with one hand. His eyes roll around comically.

"This court is now convened," the colonel declares. Grabbing several pilots, he lines them up. "Okay, c'mon, volunteer jury. One more, Johnny."

"I'm being court-martialed?" Mac asks.

"You're fuckin'-A. And shot. But, no sweat, it won't appear on your record. Okay, jury, report."

"Sir, all present or accounted for."

"Yeah, yeah, I know. I mean, what's the verdict?"

"What's the charge?"

"New foreman," the colonel mutters, and pushes us into a different order. "Now then, *report!*"

"Guilty, sir," I report.

"Absolutely. Good man, Johnny. Fuckin' Polack. Kneel, please." He taps my shoulder with the briefing pointer. "Rise. You're a fucking captain. Now, then, sergeant, issue me a sidearm, so I can take this Polack out back and shoot him. Articles of War, by God." He paces, nodding righteously, his hands clasped behind his back.

"Diane," the major says into the hot line, "give me Babyland."

Mac raises his middle finger along the side of his thigh.

"What's this, this obscene gesture?" The colonel, arms akimbo, stares grimly at the retracting finger. "Shooting is too good for your sort. The prisoner will stand for sentencing."

"I *am* standing, Colonel."

"Silence!" The colonel dons spectacles. "Three years in Mobile Control."

Entreaties, tears, nothing too imaginative. I barely smile these days. I yawn and turn away.

The major hangs up. "Okay," he announces, "we can assume Bravo Alert. Which flights, Billy?"

Our Ops officer shrugs. " 'A' and 'B,' I guess."

The major nods. " 'C' and 'D' are dismissed until seventeen hundred, but stay near a phone."

Still in my flying suit, I drive through the gate, return the salute, head slowly south along the dark highway. Beyond the bay, beyond Vallejo, first light. Battles used to begin at first light, with bugles and bearded men swarming through woods and over pastures. San Rafael sleeps, unaware that it has lain all night in danger. Perhaps the first morning papers with puzzling headlines and maps are skimming from bicycles across lawns to porches. A state trooper eases alongside, looks me over, moves ahead.

I am climbing in second gear to our street of tiered plots, of old shingled homes, past the dark movie theater and the Star of the Sea Church. Locking the Ford, I pause and let my eyes rove southward from the marina to the metropolitan glow, fading now in the general gray. For the first time I let my mind visualize the swift approach of one of their birds, the cockpit, the strange empennage. Closing, closing, already too

33

late to evade. . . . Could I eject at the last second? Would it matter in that fireball?

She opens one eye, watches me toss my cap and unzip. Inverted, flat on his back, our killer spaniel wags his stub but does not otherwise acknowledge my return. One night I'll tiptoe in wearing my helmet, mask and goggles.

"Some girl," she says.

"Average."

When I'm almost asleep, I realize that she's up on one elbow watching me. Welcome to the real Air Force, Jenny, I think, and then I'm gone.

4

LAS VEGAS

WITHIN TWO MONTHS the North Koreans had chased everyone all the way down the peninsula. For a while it seemed that Pusan would become another Dunkirk. But there was one big difference: *we* held the air this time. So the perimeter held, too.

Then MacArthur lands at Inchon, and the San Francisco papers are full of maps with broad pincer arrows enveloping whole armies. Our ground forces at Pusan break out of their perimeter, and everyone is careful not to get his logistic tail stepped on. Everyone except the North Koreans, whose tail has been flattened all along by our Far East Air Forces. During the first two months, the B-29s from Okinawa took out all the factories and airfields north of the Thirty-eighth Parallel and, from then on, Fifth Air Force tactical air—mostly '51s and '80s—worked the few roads and rail lines in classic interdiction roles.

This issue of *Life* magazine shows our jocks in Japan kissing their wives good-bye at the flight line and walking into their operations buildings as usual. The wives drive away to get the kids off to school and carry on as usual with housekeeping, shopping at the commissary and PX. At night they have the martinis chilled when the boys land from their last sorties of the day. With no enemy air opposition or flak to speak of, it must be a nice way to fight a war. But now the commuting to combat will end. Even if there's an armistice tomorrow, Fifth will probably move across the Korean Straits and occupy airstrips closer to the enemy. Their dependents will probably have to return to the States.

"So *you* won't have to go over there?" Jenny asks me with relief. She sets the dishes on the table.

I shrug.

"I mean, what would you do in the Far East after the war ends?" She removes her apron.

"Some of those guys have flown a hundred missions. Their tours will be curtailed."

"Someone will have to replace them." She sips her port and frowns while she considers this. "But Cartwright and all the other crazy lieutenants who volunteered—why can't they replace them?"

A dirty trick on the youngsters. Now, instead of accumulating their own Air Medals and war stories, they will simply sit there in the mud at forward bases and think of us back here at the country club. Unless the war *doesn't* end.

I lie awake thinking of this and listening to the foghorns near the bridge. It is October, and the hardwoods in Muir Woods were changing last weekend when we picnicked there. I am content, especially now that the war is ending, and my vague guilt at not having volunteered can dissipate. In her sleep, Jenny murmurs. She hasn't been feeling well lately and is already two days late with her period this month. I'm hoping that she's pregnant, but I don't say anything.

It is not until I'm driving to work the next morning, carpooling with Joe, that I hear a news announcer telling about the Chinese troops.

Chinese? Yeah, they've crossed the river. Too much speaking of "Police Actions" and "Limited War" by everyone except soldiers. Pat, who is a Pointer, says that Truman and the British and the UN should have kept their big mouths shut. Me, I don't know. All I know is that now that winter is settling in over there, it must be tough going for the crunchies. Napoleon's retreat from Moscow all over again.

By spring it looks as though everyone's digging in along the Thirty-eighth Parallel. There are bunkers and trenches, grim battles for higher ground, World War I stuff. Cartwright and the other early volunteers are halfway through their combat tours. Their letters are posted on our bulletin boards. To take out a tank with caliber .50, Cartwright says, you have to roll in from six thousand and high-angle strafe, aiming at the louvered air intake over the engine.

And now the MIGs have appeared. They come across the Yalu and are in and out like hawks. You've got to look around now, and God help you if you are slow to jettison your ordnance when they attack. Even then, you can't do much but try to outturn them, set up a defensive Lufbery. "They got old Clay two days ago," Cartwright notified us. "What we need are '86s," he adds, "for top cover."

"Gentlemen," our Ops officer says one morning, rattling his pencil between his teeth, "we have another levy. Wing needs fifteen replacement pilots, so I need five. Five brave volunteers to help drive back the Yellow Hordes."

Snake, hibernating, opens one eye. "Whores?"

"Hordes."

35

Snake closes his eye. The rest of us become lost in our magazines. It's the first time I've ever seen Mac read anything.

"Come, come, gentlemen," our Ops officer says, pencil and clipboard ready. "where's your gallantry? Your country needs you."

Mac sighs and lowers his magazine. "You are right, Billy. They are cowards and dreamers. I am ashamed that young men, young *bachelors,* aren't leaping up to volunteer. I volunteer Snake."

Flat on his back, without opening his eyes, Snake slowly raises his middle finger.

"C'mon, Snake," Mac laughs, "you've never heard a shot fired in anger."

Snake murmurs something, and Mac, his grin broadening, rises to bend over him. "What? A fucking what?"

"Training Commando," Snake says.

"Who, me? *Me?* Man, I have *seen* combat. Seventy-nine missions of sheer hell in the ETO."

"In Juarez maybe."

"I have scars I can show you. In Juarez? Why, you bastard, how would *you* know? You were in the tenth grade."

"They want one flight commander," our Ops officer says quietly.

Mac's eyebrows rise. "One who hasn't seen combat?"

"They didn't say."

Abruptly, Mac sits down and picks up his magazine.

Never volunteer for anything: that's Clausewitz. Not even for what promises to become a good deal. And air-to-ground certainly won't be a good deal now, not with all those Russian guns along the roads. It's going to become almost suicidal to go in on a bridge.

Poor old MacArthur. "Where did all these fucking Chinese come from?" he must be asking. Boy, now all those black arrows are heading south again. Somebody really goofed on an Intelligence estimate. Or maybe MacArthur had just assumed that, if China jumped in, Truman would have SAC atomize their asses. The whole country, I mean, not just Manchuria.

What's wrong, I guess, is that Russia has the Bomb now, and you never know what the hell Russia will do next. Look at the Berlin Blockade. And, even during the war, we weren't really sure whose side they were on. So I guess I see why Truman and the British are so nervous and why the UN is tiptoeing around.

"By noon, gentlemen," the Ops officer says. "Don't make me play God."

Luckily, I have to fly and when I land, it's already noon. I don't mind going so much—well, that's a lie, isn't it?—but I don't want to go air-to-ground. I've heard that Personnel is expecting an F-86 quota. May as well stick with a mission I know—air superiority.

"Me?" my eyes ask the Ops officer.

He shakes his head. "Five brave volunteers, John." I am ashamed at the degree of my relief. I hang my chute and helmet on the rack and ask the sergeant, "Who?"

Mac and Snake, Joe (my car-pool buddy), two new bachelor lieutenants. We are really hurting for bodies now. Filling the alert schedule requires the rest of us to meet ourselves coming and going, and then there's the Airdrome officer roster, Mobile Control to man, sometimes OD. But no one complains about seven-day weeks.

When the next quota comes in six months later, I'm in the base hospital, running 104 degrees. Mononucleosis, whatever that is. A kissing disease, my nurse says archly, and Jenny draws back to hit me. But I'm really out of it. When Jenny comes and goes, once even with a chocolate shake, I hardly know she's here.

By the time the flight surgeon releases me, there are new faces in Ops. Even our Ops officer is at Nellis getting checked out in F-86s. Only the major and three of the four flight commanders are left. I can feel my number coming up.

The war, predictably, is getting meaner. Mac has been shot down but rescued, Cartwright and Turnip killed, Clay is still missing. Snake writes that we should play it cool and volunteer for the Canal Zone, or England or somewhere. He says that they're switching to new F-84Es at Taegu and that, while the wings stay on the "E," everything else is bad news.

When the F-86 quota comes in, peace talks are underway, but, hell, they've been underway since midsummer, and now it's January, 1952. So I jump at it, and Jenny thinks that she understands.

"It's less dangerous?" she keeps asking me.

"That's right," I assure her. I don't tell her that our old Ops officer, Billy, is MIA. Billy's '86 went down on the river, so he's either dead or a POW.

"Besides," I tell her, "we'll be at Nellis six weeks getting checked out, then we'll have a month's leave in Indiana, then a week of processing at Camp Stoneman. By the time I get there, the war will be over."

Except for two footlockers, everything goes into the Ford. It doesn't take long. At the base, the major comes out to shake my hand and hug Jenny.

"Save me a bunk, Captain," he tells me. Yeah, I'm a captain now. I salute, and it occurs to me that I'm just beginning to understand what saluting really means. Still smiling, but with a certain gravity, he returns it, waves, and we're gone. The sweet old base, the blue sky, the golden hills themselves fall away as we climb eastward into the Sierras.

Nevada. Once you descend on the other side, you think you're on another planet, one melted to slag about the time that Lucifer fell, a place for him to land. No wonder the AEC conducts atomic tests here: the land has nothing to lose. Before we've been in Las Vegas two days, we wonder how you could tell if the town had suffered some unthinkable miscalculation in AEC's testing. The sunlight is always lightning-white, and the populace always seems as dazed as the survivors of some disaster, physical or financial. The old ladies who stand in supermarkets jerking on the slot machines are as tough-looking as carnies.

"Yeah?" the waitresses ask. Their cigarettes burn on the edge of counters. Their eyebrows are plucked, their hair usually peroxided. "You kidding?" one asks me. "Sure we got a liquor license."

"Keep Nevada Green," one automobile license-plate holder says. It's a relief to find a touch of humor, however bitter. The only green here is money. Well, a splash of lawn in front of the casinos. Their signs are probably visible from the moon and feature big names: Sinatra, Mel Tormé, Tony Bennett.

We find a second-story apartment a block off Frontier Street. There's even a token patch of lawn and a few willow trees. We are not to walk our cocker on the grass, the landlord gravely tells me. Low in one wall of our apartment is a big, boxed fan that sucks air through wet strips of cloth. If we keep the shades down and the single blind closed, the place stays reasonably cool, but so dark that it reminds us of a movie gangster's hideout. So we clown around about gats and molls. Jenny can do a pretty fair imitation of Ida Lupino. She lights one of my cigarettes and slinks around, hitching up her skirt to show off her gams, but finally starts coughing. Me, I need a shoulder holster and a vest.

"Yeah?" Jenny says. "Kid, you need more'n that." She blows smoke in my face.

"Yeah?"

"Yeah." Disdainfully, she looks me up and down. "Who ever saw Edward G. Robinson wearing a blue uniform?"

"Yeah? How about suntans?"

"Unh-uh, kid. Just pin-stripes."

"Undershirts."

She considered this, nods. "But not T-shirts. You wear T-shirts, kid."

To tell you the truth, I don't like our new blue winter uniforms, so I'm glad that they're packed. When we wear them, we have to avoid standing too near the doors of buses. I miss the old pinks and greens. Suntans are okay until you sit down the first time. Once the starch is broken, you look deformed.

Surprise! One of my neighbors finally speaks to me. We live approximately twelve hours out of phase. I'm coming in from a day of processing at the airbase, and he's just waking up and having a beer as an eye-opener. He deals twenty-one at one of the clubs.

"C'mon in," he says, "have a brew."

He opens the blinds, and I notice a woman seated by the window. She's a blonde, perhaps a natural blonde, but she's pretty far gone on something. Her eyes finally focus on me. Her shorts are too short. She looks like one of those girls you see riding on the back of a Harley-Davidson.

"This is Elaine," he says, then ignores her. She's humming to herself and trying to cross her legs. A book falls out of her lap, and I retrieve it for her. Foolishly, I stand there holding it out to her before I realize that she's not going to notice it. I lay it on the table.

"You got a cigarette?" she asks no one in particular. I offer her one, rebutton my shirt pocket. When I flick my old Zippo, she doesn't lean forward and tilt her head so I won't singe her eyelashes. Instead, she reaches forward and grasps my wings.

"Pilot," she says thickly.

"Yes. Would you like a light?"

Smugly she leans back and smiles. "Bucky was a pilot, wasn't he, honey? Your wings have a radiator on them, don't they? Did you know Bucky? He got killed." She inhales, and suddenly her eyes glisten. "He crashed and they couldn't get him out." She sobs and looks up at me.

"I'm sorry." I close my lighter and sit down.

"Has anybody got a light?" she asks.

I light her cigarette.

"You a pilot?" she asks.

"More or less."

"More, I'll bet," she says kicking one bare foot slowly. "You're cute." She winks.

"*Elaine*," he says; then, apologetically: "Don't pay any attention to her. She's, well . . . you know. So, how do you like Vegas?"

I nod and smile. Bouncing around as I do, I've learned that a grin and a nod usually suffice.

"A little . . . too dry?"

"Maybe a little, for my taste." I sip my beer.

"Where you from?"

"Indiana."

"Yeah? Jesus, honey, he's from Indiana. We're from Illinois."

Almost asleep again, she doesn't cheer much. In fact, as I watch, her cigarette falls from her lips onto the chair cushion. Quickly, he rises and retrieves it without waking her. Her jaw sags, her hair tumbles forward, she snores lightly. He shakes his head, stubs out the butt.

"Jesus," he breathes and slumps into his chair again. "I hide her lighter and matches so she doesn't burn the goddamn place down while I'm at work." He drinks his beer, looks at me.

"What?" he answers some child. "*No!* Eat some cereal. I'll be there in a minute." He rises to take my empty can. "Schlitz okay? We got Bud. No?"

"Say, Captain," he says as he sees me to the door, "if you would like to invest in a sure thing, I just want to tell you that now I know what I'm doing, okay? I mean it. It was an expensive education, but you work the house side of it five years, and you see what you were doing wrong. All I need is a little stake. Think about it."

The airbase used to be called Las Vegas Army Air Base. They trained aerial gunners here during the war. Now it's called Nellis Air Force Base, and it has become "The Fighter School." Williams is still in the T-Bird business, but Nellis has the fighters. When the Air Force gets a new fighter, it's put through its phase testing at Muroc and then suitability testing at Eglin. Finally in production, it goes to an operational unit and, simultaneously, here to Nellis. Nellis usually trains replacement pilots, and they do a good job of it. Even by the major's standards, the instructors are old pros, not in instrument flying, of course—there's no way a cloud can survive here—but in bending a bird around a corner and in ordnance delivery. That's about all they do, that and formation. Every month they fly fifty or sixty hours. That's a lot of time for a fighter pilot, a lot of Gs and a lot of takeoffs and landings. Every evening your butt's dragging. Jesus, you can't explain it to multiengine guys. They think that flying is all instruments and coffee. Half the time they're in the back, pissing on clouds, and then they ask you, "How many thousand hours you got?"

Anyhow, Nellis always wins the annual Air Force Gunnery Meet. Usually, it's one of the hot rocks from the Fighter Weapons School. And they should, because they wear out a few barrels every week. The last time I fired a gun was at March more than a year ago. After we got in the F-89s at Hamilton, we couldn't keep them out of the hangars long enough to fire their twenties.

I finish clearing into the base, formally signing in at Wing Headquarters, having my teeth checked, my last physical exam screened. I shake the chaplain's hand. Finally, my briefcase contains only my Form 5, so I report to my training squadron. The sergeant scans my pages of F-84 time and grimaces. He gives me a look. "Okay, sir. Report at zero seven hundred tomorrow. Room Three, down that corridor. Meanwhile, read these handouts."

I drive back to the apartment. We have a drink—we drink old fashioneds now instead of port—walk the dog, take in an early movie. Fremont Street is full of aimlessly wandering people. It's like the midway of a carnival that has stayed too long. All you can hear are the clatter of slot machines and the beat of jukeboxes. We enter the Golden Nugget, and I step up to a machine and reach for my change.

"Hey!" an old lady says, running to push me aside. She has a roll of nickels. "Play your own goddamn machine. I'm playing this one."

We leave, go home to bed.

At 0650 the next morning I enter a flight-sized briefing room. We are wearing summer-weight flying suits, and I scan the squadron patches and peg everyone right away. This guy is from Selfridge Field, that one's from Moses Lake, two more are Training Commandoes. Altogether, there are five of us. We nod, then sit silently in our folding chairs and light cigarettes. Over the blackboard, a blackboard still smeared with half-erased chalky curves and "X's," is a wall clock. We watch it when we aren't looking out the window at the flight line or turning expectantly when we hear footsteps in the corridor. I guess we expect to see Roscoe

Turner enter with his Sam Browne belt, riding boots and lion cub mascot. But nothing happens.

As the minute hand moves toward 0700, we silently compare our watches, stare more openly at each others' patches, and yawn. As the clock's sweep-second hand marks the hour, all of us turn toward the door. Nellis is famous for its professionalism.

At 0701, this pudgy, kinky-haired Training Commando sighs and shakes his head. "Big deal, huh? We get up in the middle of the night for *this?*"

"He's probably sleeping off a night on the Strip," this fourteen-year-old lieutenant says.

"Yeah," Kinky-hair nods. "Probably lost his ass and committed suicide." He shrugs. "Well, it just goes to prove what I've said all along. There is no such thing as a professional fighter pilot."

I sigh and cross my legs. A flight of F-80s is taxiing out.

Kinky-hair can't sit still. He fidgets, slumps into a chair, hums, slaps his thighs.

"Cigarette?" the lieutenant asks him.

"Oh, no. I don't smoke."

He should. His coverall zipper is straining even though his waist tabs are on the rearmost side-buttons. He's at least twenty pounds overweight.

"Anybody want to join me in looking for a coffee urn?" Kinky-hair asks.

We shake our heads. Boy, the last thing this guy needs is coffee. He's so nervous now that he will be ricocheting off us in formation. And he's a compulsive talker. There's nothing worse.

At 0703, Kinky-hair rises in disgust and leans out the doorway to see if anyone is coming. "Where's our instructor, Sergeant?" he calls.

The lean captain and I exchange looks and shake our heads. We watch him coldly.

"Nervous in the service," the lean captain mutters.

I nod, pat my pockets for cigarettes.

Kinky-hair returns, growling and pacing. Suddenly, he stops and his mouth opens. Turning stealthily, he examines our patches. "Well, well," he says, "there are only two Training Command patches here and the sergeant says that each instructor has only four students. So, since I know that I'm not the instructor, *you, friend, must be.*"

He is pointing to the lean captain sitting by me, who is either the world's greatest actor or really a T-33 instructor from Willie, as he insists.

"Ah, great, huh?" Kinky-hair laughs. "He really took us in. Jesus, and all along he's been sitting there watching me go bananas." He sits down, nodding appreciatively.

I am so suspicious now, however, that I no longer expect the lean captain, who really looks the part, to rise and concede his joke. Instead, my eyes never leave Kinky-hair. I start grinning, but Kinky-hair won't look at me. He is trying to get the lean captain to stand and "get this show on the road."

Finally, furiously, he leaves to report him to the Ops officer, but soon returns to announce that there has been a mistake.

"We have no instructor. My apologies, Captain."

But, since no one else wants the job, *he* will try to stay one day ahead of the class. He scans the cover of the manual, compares the picture of the F-86 with the birds on the ramp, nods, studies the fuel-system schematic ("This bird have a fuel-pump?" he asks doubtfully). Finally, he murmurs to himself, begins pacing, looking sidewise professorially at us as he paces.

"All right. None of you will admit to being the instructor, so *I* shall be the instructor. I have very little experience with monoplanes and none with jets but, what the hell, an airplane is an airplane, right?" He looks at the cloud on my patch. "Unless it's a balloon. You a balloon pilot, friend?"

He picks up a piece of chalk and sketches a blob. "Okay. Let's say that's the F-86." He draws wings and empennage. "Wing," he says, tapping it. "Airelons. Ailerons? I never can pronounce that word. For our purposes, let's just say 'tail.' The tail, you'll notice, is also swept back. Question? *Why* is everything swept back on the Saberjet? Well, that's a very good question." He muses. "I've never thought about it. Someone probably screwed up the jigs at the factory, and North American is bluffing it out."

Our laughter draws a crowd in the doorway. "How do you do it, Denny?" a Captain there asks. "My guys hate me already."

Denny—that's Kinky-hair's real name—has over two thousand hours in the F-86, and three thousand in the '80 and '51. He's a legend at Nellis, but he never concedes that he is our assigned instructor. ("Aw, I freelance, y'know? I skywrite a little, sometimes I dust crops if there aren't any good shows in town.")

"Where were we?" he asks distractedly. "Oh, yes. Well, the manual makes it look simple enough. There's a stick, a throttle, a gunsight—all easily identifiable—rudder pedals. An expensive P-51, right? Simple and reliable as a Zippo. My Zippo is broken and back at the factory."

If one of us asks him a question, his eyes widen with fear. "My God!" he whispers. "Does it ever do that?" Tentatively he smiles reassuringly, then, almost in panic, looks it up. "Page one thirty, John. I'm astonished that you, of all people, didn't know *that.*" Frantically, he comes to read over my shoulder. "No, see, you're thinking of balloons where you drop sandbags to climb." He considers this. "Well, I suppose we could do that. . . ."

We draw the fuel system until we can draw it from memory and the same with the electrical system and hydraulics. Every morning he pores over some possible malfunction, deducing what "might" happen. He's great at sound effects, especially explosions. Every afternoon, during ground school, an academic instructor simulates the malfunction using a mock-up to confirm Denny's "guess."

One morning Denny finally leads us out onto the glaring ramp. All the little silver birds seem tipped angrily forward with their feathers splayed. The parrot beaks are head-high, the wings waist-high. Landing gear fairing doors sag. The pavement is already so hot that shimmers rise from the busy, parallel runways. Beyond, like a mirage, lies the inevitable Mount Bust-Your-Butt. What happens is that people settle in valleys. Then later, when an airbase is built, it's necessarily out on the edge of the foothills.

Overhead, there is the constant whistle of engines. Denny pauses, head thrown back to watch in sheer joy a flight pitch out from tight echelon into the landing pattern. Overhead they sing, turn base leg in extended single file, settle with gear down into the final groove. Skimming the overrun, they flare and skate along the big painted numbers. A little tire smoke, their noses high, their canopies sliding back to increase drag. Beautiful.

"Okay," Denny announces briskly, "*this*, gentlemen, is the F-86 Saberjet. Good morning, Chief. May we dismantle your machine?"

The rangy mechanic, deeply tanned, wearing herringbone-twill coveralls washed almost white, laughs, then frowns suspiciously. He twists his baseball cap around as he listens to Denny.

"Bullets come out these holes, I believe," Denny announces. "Yes, you can see the muzzles." Shuddering, he recoils and draws himself together. "And this is the airscoop. Air comes in here, is compressed, and—well, read your manuals. Note—and this will be old hat to you, John, old balloon pilot—there is no propeller whatsoever. Great, huh?"

The sergeant must be new here. He stares at Denny, his concern obviously increasing.

"So much for the aircraft itself," Denny continues; "now let's get down to business." He rubs his forehead reflectively, nods to reassure himself, and produces from a parcel he's been carrying an ancient campaign hat. Broad-brimmed, with a yellow cavalry cord around its crown, it is clearly older than most of us. Donning it casually, he strides to the side of the fuselage.

"Mounting the Aircraft," he says officiously. "Mounting the Aircraft is very important, so watch closely, please." Rubbing his hands together and blowing on them, he reaches up, pauses, drops his arms, turns back to us. "Always from the left. You've been around horses, I'm sure, and realize what might happen."

"First, push this button." His head is up, his hat tilted rakishly. "Got that? Okay, now grasp this admirable little handle which has appeared." He raises one boot and places it on a kickstep. "Always the left foot first. Just like marching. All of you have marched, I trust?" But he has mistaken left from right, so now, as he rises, his left foot paws a yard away from the next kickstep. His smile frozen, he gropes for the step, is eventually cross-legged and almost horizontal.

"Now," he says, "here is where it gets tricky." His hat tumbles to the pavement, but his voice loses none of its assurance. An engine in the row ahead sends its blast back, buffeting him and drowning him out. All we can see is his head contorted toward us as his little mustache works and his lips frame unheard shouts. Finally, the chief, still puzzled both by Denny's contortions and by our hanging limply on to each other, helps him down.

"Questions?" he asks briskly.

In the air, he's like glass. No nonsense, not an unnecessary transmission. On his wing we float out to range and back. The mission is over before we know it. And what a *machine!* Coming off the tow-target, you can lay in the Gs and bend her up into a thirty-degree climb back to the perch. She's so sweet with her heady, impossible zooms that I actually feel tears in my eyes. The MIGs can't be better.

Solo, I climb to forty thousand, accelerate to Mach 0.9, and, leaving the throttle full forward, half-roll and let the invisible nose fall down through the horizon until we are vertical. Nine-six, nine-seven—a little wing roll—a slight hesitation at 0.99 and then, psychologically at least, there's a breathless little leap. Mach 1.01. I am supersonic. I'm streaming invisible shock waves that will boom through the hills. Although I realize that my altimeter, hopelessly lagging in its unwinding flicks, can't be trusted, I know that my eyes can. The pink-white desert is gaining its third dimension. I must be going through about twenty thousand. Jesus, the stick acts like it's no longer connected to the elevators. No resistance at all. Nothing changes except the desert. Hanging there, plunging to my death, I'm smiling—because I remember Denny's description of reversibility.

"All of you been compressed, right? You buffet, you act crazy because all the air molecules are screwed up. You get these shock waves, and all your surfaces lose lift. So the elevators don't elevate, and you start yelling and wishing you had bought the old lady more insurance. 'Dennis,' she tells me, 'you're such a lousy pilot, the least you can do is load up with term insurance.' "

"One potato, two potatoes," Dennis had said, "and *voilà!*" (only he pronounced it *viola*) "the old trim tab will save your ass."

My gloved thumb pulls the button on the top of the stick-grip and, viola indeed, the nose starts rising. A little more back-trim and I am leveling well above the beige dunes and white dry lakes, but still at an airspeed that would have been fatal in our old F-84s.

"Yeah," he had grimly acknowledged, "I know what you're thinking: you're wondering what if the trim motor fails, right?" He had paused in an exaggerated shrug. "Mon Dieu!" he had exclaimed and walked around for a while with no neck. "You speak Chinese?" he had asked hopefully.

44

I'm not worried; I'm confident. It worked this time; it will always work. I trust everything Denny says. Well, almost.

"You finks. You *rat*-finks. You lucked out, that's all. My goddamn gunsight was wandering completely off the reflector glass. If I'd pulled the trigger, I'd have shot myself. I needed a tail-gunner. All I had was this piece of gum." (He shows us the chewed wad.) "So now you're gonna tell everybody that old Denny can't shoot. *Me*—the world's greatest fighter pilot! I know you bastards. That's what you're gonna say."

For once, we had outshot him. This time the rag wasn't torn with his color. Just a few, maybe a single burst, but dead center. While his other students are celebrating his reluctant payment for drinks, I sneak off to the latrine—actually to the line—where I check his Form One. No gunsight write-up. He'd fired only thirty rounds.

5

KOREA

WE ARE OUT of the rubble of Seoul now, jouncing through open country, fanning muddy spray over darting pedestrians. I, the sole passenger, am manually sweeping the single windshield wiper of the jeep. The enlisted driver's arm gave out soon after we left K-16. Whoever designed the jeep was a realist; he knew about Murphy's Law. He just didn't know about arms—or springs.

I can't describe the landscape, but imagine Las Vegas after thirty days of hard rain and you'll be close. Even realtors would be hard put to make it sound charming. Still, somebody must want it, or we wouldn't be over here. Mud and erosion seem to be the key words. Puddles. Hub-deep puddles, and every moving thing slops through them—oxen, vehicles, old men with goatees and young women bowed under laden A-frames.

"Does it ever quit raining?" I ask the driver.

"Oh, sure. Sometimes it snows. In January this was all ice."

"What about the summers?"

"Hot. Dust."

"You don't plan to retire here?"

He smirks. "One more month, and they can take Korea and the Air Force, and stuff them. I'm going back to God's country—Oklahoma."

The base itself isn't bad. I guess the Army is right. You could put any Air Force outfit on a desert island—this base may become a desert island if it keeps raining—and within a month there would be all the creature comforts. That's because we fight from the same runway month in and month out, we retort. And because of our ingenuity. Here, our guys

45

have done everything you can do with packing cases. They live and administrate in the largest examples and use the smallest for tables and chairs. How did Caesar manage without plywood? Or sandbags? Even the birds are protected by sandbagged rivetments. As in the England of 1944 there are acres of tents and Quonsets.

From Personnel, I go to the squadron orderly room and then up to the BOQ area on the hill. The pilots are billeted in former warehouses, small stucco buildings with concrete floors. The jeep sloshes away. I cross the ditch on a wide plank, push open the door to BOQ Supply. A sergeant hands me blankets, tells me there is a mattress on the cot. No pillow, no sheets. War is a grim business.

"B" Flight has an end room. It's deserted; they are flying, I guess. I make my bunk and, having unzipped my old B-4 and hung it on a nail, I am unpacked. By each of the other cots is a little cloister of framed pictures—girls, women, children. Before entire walls of Varga and Petty pinups (all arching on their ridiculously long legs and high heels to show off their breasts and tiny waists, all smiling or pouting sexily in accordance with their captions) these ordinary faces from home seem reconciled. There are, among the pinups, a few old standbys, timeless as the Mona Lisa: Grable, Ella Raines and—God!—Rita Hayworth kneeling in her lacy nightgown on a soft bed, her long hair falling about her. Neither she nor I will outlive that photograph.

On the wall, too, is an acetate-covered chart. Names down the left column, missions X'd off beside each name. The flight commander has seventy. That must be nice. He's over the hump.

In the next room are two houseboys. When I enter, one of them quickly scoops up the cards, smiles. We introduce ourselves. One has an open face. The other is our flight's houseboy. He won't meet my eyes more than a second. He knows all the slang, all the jargon. Casually, he stubs out a cigarette.

"Ree," he says, importantly tapping his chest. Except for his eyes, he looks about fourteen. They measure me, flit away.

"Ree?" I shake his child's hand. His belt's a foot too long.

"No. *Ree!*" He writes it in the air: L-E-E.

"Lee."

A beam. He inhales proudly, leads me back into our room, tells me who sleeps where. It's stenciled on the various footlockers, but he keeps going. Then he shows me the stove which he stokes, the canteens he has to fill each day, the cement floor he has to scrub. The floor gives him away, so he directs my attention elsewhere. He is rich, I learn eventually.

From the swollen O. D. Lister bag, I draw a canteen of water. You can sometimes tell about a place by its water. I taste it. This place, I decide, stinks. But that's not fair either; the bag must be half full of halozone tablets. It smells like a rarely drained public swimming pool. While I'm screwing on the cap, a rangy, balding guy with a wholesome grin says,

"Great, huh?" Happily, he refills his canteen, swigs, refills it. He's Mormon, he says with immense satisfaction. "Everyone else drinks beer," he adds wryly.

That figures. I watch him. He nods pleasantly, strolls away to his building. Maybe he offers it up or something.

Back in the room, I notice the Coleman lantern hanging beside the bare light bulb. Do we really have electricity? I reach up and rotate the switch. The bulb glows feebly, brightens, dims. Yes, in the sense that Edison had electricity. While my hand is still on the switch, I hear a truck engine, brakes, men's voices. I freeze. Here they come. I'm a little nervous. It's easier when you're just a lieutenant; they don't expect anything of you then.

The door bangs open, and they pile up in the doorway looking at me. Then, almost shyly, they discard their webbed pistol belts, their caps, and approach to shake my hand.

"Hamilton? Oh, that's *rough* duty," they echo each other. "You bring your yacht?"

They know nothing about me, and yet I'm extravagantly welcome, I can tell. I'm not my predecessor; that's the difference. During the next week, when I ask about him, they just stop what they're doing and look at each other with spreading grins. Waspish, I take it? Unpredictable, perhaps even incompetent? They don't confirm my one-word guesses. All I ever learn is that no one except the CO and the Ops officer showed up at his farewell party.

"Oh, hey, everyone!" Scotty says. "Tonight's a big deal at the club. A movie star and her troupe. A real Stateside band. The old man wants everyone to wear his shirt." They groan.

"What do you mean?" I ask him.

Scotty looks at the other guys, then pulls something from the open, center section of his B-4, presses it to his heart with mock reverence, then dons it. A Western shirt of red and blue panels, with a white lightning bolt slanting from his right shoulder to his navel. Deadpan, he stands there, waiting for my reaction.

"You're kidding."

"Sure," he says, "Tim McCoy. But you'd better buy one, Captain."

Our flight leader is thirty-five, thirty-six. Salt-and-pepper, receding crew cut; big, broad face; a laconic manner. No one calls him captain. He's Cat Man, they say, and he leans back on his elbows and grins at me. "They give me rabble to lead," he says. "What can you do?"

He's not very military. His flying suit has no rank, no nameplate. Apparently, he doesn't own a hat. He'd been a test pilot at Wright Field. Maybe that's why he drinks so much. In the pitch-black at 0400, I hear an alarm go off and then a loud whack. When I flick my lighter, I see him lying there, eyes closed, beating at his clock with a boot. I close my eyes and, then, the other alarms start jumping around on the cement.

He's up. In his skivvies, he's peering out the dirty window, scratching and belching. Then he sits down on his bunk, slides something from under it, and I hear gurgling.

"Ah," he says. "Okay, girls, up! Today we have swimming and archery. C'mon." He claps his hands.

It's routine, I realize. They grumble, slide deeper into their sacks. So he shuffles around bumping the cots up and down, lights a cigarette, goes again to the window. "Christ, look at that moon! A perfect day coming up."

Under the blanket, I look at my wristwatch. Until I've been awake awhile, the hour hand seems to drift. But, hell, *that* many alarms can't be wrong. I go to the window. It's drizzling.

"You," he says to me, "can sleep in. You've gotta finish processing."

I make the administrative rounds, log a couple of flights in the local area.

They call him Cat Man because when he comes in at night, the guys in the next building start muttering. I see what they mean. In the doorway is his silhouette, lurching slightly. He's humming some old song, remembering a phrase every so often, and flicking his lighter. He must wear out a whole flint every day. It's like a sparkler, but there's no flame. So finally he hurls it and enters, stumbling over butt cans, sliding the chairs around. Muttering, he tries another lighter, and you can see his face slack with liquor. Lighting a candle is a two-minute effort for him. He's left his cigarette on the edge of the table, I realize. Stripping, he throws his flying coveralls in the corner, lies down and is gone. Scotty gets up to blow out the candle and stub out the cigarette. A good wingman, I'll bet.

When Cat Man goes to Japan on R&R, they say, he always returns with a sackful of imitation Ronsons. Lining them up on our table, he refuels each one, checks its flint. Then, rubbing his hands, he picks up each in turn and flicks it. If it lights, he sets it aside. If it misfires, he hurls it against the wall.

Scotty nods, sips his beer. "There's metal all over the floor," he says, laughing.

But, ah God, in the air, he's a dream. The contrast explains what he considers important. That two hours a day, maybe four, in the cockpit is all he lives for. Silence, not an unnecessary movement of the controls. He's always planning ahead. And afterward, there's no critique. We walk up the hill. He just leans back on his elbows, looks at us, and sips from his case of C.C. Maybe he'll wag his foot a little as he sprawls there; that's all. We understand.

He's been credited with three kills and a probable. With a little effort, Scotty says, he could have the probable upgraded. He doesn't bother. It wouldn't change the war.

There's no briefing either. He thinks we're bright enough to understand the group briefing officer. While the other flight commanders seat

48

their guys around tables and go down the checklist, Cat Man just lies on the Ping-Pong table and smokes.

I love flying element lead for him. He always establishes a definite bank and continues through ninety degrees as though he's on instruments. Above him two thousand feet, I slide across with Scotty, look down, and he's always there. I never have to touch the throttle. Last week I flew element lead for the colonel, and he was spastic. He'd get under me, then change his mind. I wore out both my throttle and Scotty, out in coffin corner. There could have been MIGs all over the place, and I wouldn't have had time to look for them.

Gil the Mormon and I are becoming friends. For a guy who doesn't drink, he makes a lot of sense. His religion does, too, when I'm medium drunk, except for all those gold plates and everything. But I respect him. He's really sold on it, and it shows in his life. He laughs us off, poses sobering questions sometimes, worries about Cat Man.

"Your body is a temple," he explains. "He's destroying his."

"Me, too?"

He looks at me, nods. "Why?" he asks.

I'll have to think about that. I don't know. My Irish blood, I guess. Something.

Our squadron commander and Cat Man were classmates, a fact that embarrasses the major more than Cat Man. Privately, they're on a first-name basis, and I know the CO wishes Cat Man had a hat and shined his boots. I guess he knew that Cat Man wouldn't buy the fancy shirt. But that doesn't stop him from dropping by the hooch for a drink of C.C. During the war, they were in the Pacific together, and they lie on our bunks and grouse about our dumb rules of engagement. We aren't supposed to cross the Yalu, for example, but most of the flight leaders do. Cat Man doesn't, and our CO knows that and respects it. It's not the idea of a possible court-martial that stops the Cat Man. It's just that, in some ways, he's a real soldier. Making ace would be nice for him, but one time when we could *see* MIGs down in the landing pattern at Sinanju, when we thought, "Now!" he simply kept turning.

"Ah, it's all a joke," he explained to me later. "You wanta clean up the MIGs? Okay, no sweat, bomb their bases at dusk, right? Catch 'em on the ground. This Richthofen stuff is a goddamn joke, especially since they don't want to come down to our altitude and mix it up. Naw, there'll be better wars with realistic rules. Meanwhile keep your nose clean. What if you lose a wingman over Manchuria? Is he a legitimate POW?"

I see what he means. It's a crazy war. We fly for a month and rarely see MIGs and, then, one day the sky is alive with them. Cat Man says it's their graduation day. Some Russian trains the Chink pilots for six weeks, then he leads them south of the river for a little cross-country flight while he calls out the sights. It's routine.

"Oh, sure," nods Cat Man, "and just try to get on the schedule day after tomorrow. That's when the next graduation occurs. Every wheel in headquarters will grab our birds and go after the new graduates. Down they'll come across the Mizu, stairstepped in trail from forty to fifty thousand. They'll fly down the Chongchon to Sinanju and then head north again. Regular as clockwork. Their Russian instructor probably tells them, 'And those silver aircraft down there, gooks, are F-86s. One pass each, and then pull up again.' You can practically hear him correcting them. Naw, it's a dumb war, guys. If I had any sense, I'd get out and become a farmer or a pimp or something."

"No," Scotty says, shaking his head. "You have an engineering degree." Scotty is a very literal guy.

"Big deal," Cat Man says. "Oh, *big deal. Most* pimps have engineering degrees. Naw," he says, "what I'd do, see, is open up a cathouse right outside the gate of every air base. Right here, the biggest. *Taksan jo-sans!* You guys could stroll out there between missions. I'd have a liquor license and real mattresses."

Cat Man is describing Yong-Dong-Po, situated immediately outside our gate. Black-market stalls and packing-case whorehouses. But most of us know better than to go out there. According to our flight surgeon, Korea has kinds of V.D. that aren't even mentioned in his medical books. Most guys simply hold on until they can get to Japan. But, to tell you the truth, I've decided to wait, period. I'm not especially religious, but I made this dumb promise to Jenny, who confuses sex with love.

The weather is lousy all winter. Usually, the steel matting is so slick with rain or sleet that sometimes I think my nosewheel steering is inoperative. We have to be very careful taxiing out. But the worst part occurs before we ever start engines. Wearing our helmets, we walk out to our birds with our raincoats draped over our parachutes. We look like four hunchbacks wearing capes. No one, not even Scotty, preflights his bird. Our crew chiefs open the canopies, take our raincoats, and help us in. Once seated, I wave my guy away, then grope for the straps and hoses. Now the canopy is closed, and I know exactly how a clam feels. Instead of machine guns, we should be armed with torpedoes. I shiver, signal for power, and wait for the VHF to warm up. Rain drums on the canopy. Under his poncho, the chief jogs and holds his hands in the exhaust of the APU. In the red flash of my left navigation light, he grins at me. I shake my head. Ten minutes until Start Engines.

This reminds me of those predawn takeoffs in England. At first light there would be a silent spinning of blades, then the first bark of exhaust, coughing, sending back smoke, finally smoothing until the props disappeared and the whole ramp crackled. In my mind, the slender noses swing and we taxi out, essing along, craning our necks to see ahead. Then, oh God, that sweet even drone of the V-12s as the colonel and his wingman roll. Finally, it is our turn. We lift from the shadows and skim the dark green of Essex. Eight years ago.

It is 0650. Overhead I twirl my finger and depress the toggle switch on the right console. The lights dim, the APU digs in, recovers. Behind me, hollowly, my engine hums, rising in pitch, finally drowning out the rain.

On the runway, overlapped in finger formation, my bird vibrating in Cat Man's wash, I scan my instruments, look over my shoulder at Scotty. He nods, I nod to Cat Man, and the first element rolls. As their blast and buffeting diminish, we can hear our own engines. Rudders fanning gently, the lead element sends back spray, becomes silent, distant. I tilt my head back and nod decisively as I release brakes. Slowly we accelerate. With luck, we can catch Cat Man before the terrain forces him to climb into the overcast. Rendezvousing on top is tricky, particularly when there are no tops.

Two hours of flying, and all we see are colored wingtip lights. I'm on Cat Man's right, looking along his leading edge, hypnotized by his green light. Sometimes, in dense cumulus, that light is all I can see. Unless I sneak a glance at my attitude indicator, I don't know where the ground is. I'm glad that I don't have a hangover. As it is, I have vertigo. Thank God I've done enough formation acrobatics so that vertigo doesn't matter.

Well, this is really glamorous, being a hypnotized clam and everything. Maybe Cat Man is right: we should have gotten out in '46 and gone with the airlines or become pimps. But not farmers; he's wrong there. I saw enough of that when I was a kid. You're a slave to a farm. The only time you can leave the place is when you take the livestock with you to the fairs. And there is no security. I was glad when they gave it up and moved into town.

Suddenly, we are out into blinding sunshine, into blue heavens. The ocean of billows races beneath, falls away, becomes almost static. Twenty-two thousand and clear above. Our forecaster blew it again. Cat Man yaws us out into tactical formation so we can relax and look over our engine instruments. It's great seeing the sun again. Those poor bastards on the ground. We test-fire our guns.

Moonbeam, our GCI controller, sleepily acknowledges Cat Man's report on the tops, then falls silent again. His scope shows nothing except us. In my mind, I can see him, isolated on his island, probably chained to his scope and wishing, with some justification, that *he* had become a pimp. A lieutenant probably, a former fighter jock who entered Personnel's pipeline when his stars were wrong. With worse luck, I could be him.

Peripherally, I see something wiggle. It is my oil pressure needle. It's in the green, but it's hunting. *Not now,* you bastard. I'll have to watch it. We should be over P'yong Yang. Ahead, the undercast seems to break off. Yeah, old Stormy really blew it.

"Blue, this is Moonbeam," GCI says. "I'm getting a paint now up near the Mizu, heading one seven zero."

"Blue," Cat Man acknowledges.

We are climbing through thirty thousand. Sun motes fill my cockpit. My oxygen blinker is the only thing moving. No, I'm wrong. Even as I scan, my oil-pressure needle starts ticking downward, settles on twelve p.s.i. Aw, hell, I'd better tell him.

But, as my thumb begins to depress the microphone button, Moonbeam calls excitedly that he has more tracks crossing the Yalu at the Mizu. It's a bandit train, he says. He means that there are multiple flights in trail formation.

"*Taksan,* Blue," Moonbeam shouts, then sobers. "Blue, I'm scrambling four flights but, meanwhile, Ginger Red is all I've got in the area. Red is seventy-five miles behind you, climbing through angels two zero."

"Blue."

"Blue, I suggest that you orbit and wait for Ginger Red before proceeding, over."

"Say again, Moonbeam. You're garbled."

Oh, bullshit, Cat Man. I sit dazed. I can visualize them: an entire squadron, stairstepped by pairs in two-thousand-foot intervals; big airscoops and barrel fuselages; fenced, swept wings; enormous tails. An unwieldy formation, but one unlikely to be surprised. The top of the staircase lies above our service ceiling.

"Blue, this is Moonbeam. How do you read me now?"

"Say again, Moonbeam."

Suddenly it occurs to me that perhaps Cat Man *does* have a bad radio. "Blue Leader, Blue Three, do you read Moonbeam?"

Two quick clicks of his mike button in affirmation. Oh, well, I decide. Christ, my oil pressure is down to five p.s.i. and ticking lower. But if I say anything now, who'll believe me? So I simply quit watching it, shut off all the little, professional switches in my mind, recheck my sight and gun switch. I'm a zombie—but a scared zombie. Somebody miscalculated. It's graduation day.

"Does anyone in Blue Flight read Moonbeam? If so, signal your leader to reverse course. I have two bandit trains in tandem. Acknowledge, please."

Scotty, conscientious, alarmed, relays. But Cat Man continues climbing right for them.

"Punch 'em off, Blue." His voice seems calm, but there's an edge to it. His drop tanks tumble, centrifuging fuel. I depress the red button, feel her lift and surge ahead. We're at forty-two thousand now, Mach 0.9, all of us at full throttle, no one leaving con trails. Cat Man eases right a few degrees into the sun.

"Blue, if you read, the bogies extend from your eleven- to your twelve-o'clock position. Turn starboard to one eight zero degrees. Acknowledge."

I focus my entire attention at eleven o'clock, increase the blast from my defrosters to dissipate the asterisks of frost. Then faintly, in my windshield quarter pane, like some dreamy constellation, a ladder glints momentarily, disappears.

"Bogies," I call, "eleven o'clock, Blue Leader."

Two clicks, and he begins a shallow left turn, shallow to preserve speed. They are dark specks now, an extended swarm of specks, sliding along my quarter pane. Their relative motion increases. Leaving the throttle full open, I play my turn, sliding over and slightly behind the lead element. Ah, Jesus, it's beautiful! The sun swings behind us, and we are closing. I estimate that we will hit the staircase at its midpoint.

Now it's as though I'm back at Nellis, curving in on the rag. My gunsight radar locks on, breaks lock, locks steadily. I have chosen the next higher step in the staircase. Silent as a shark, Cat Man presses in, streaming gray cordite smoke. At a range of fifteen hundred feet, just as I depress the trigger, my dumb radar suddenly breaks lock. Cursing, I twist the throttle grip, finally catch and manually adjust the drifting reticle, open fire. I hold the trigger down and finally drift the pipper through him. A few flashes along his pale blue fuselage, that's all I see before we're through the staircase and gone. Later, I turn slightly to look back. One MIG is burning, twisting down to the vertical. An element, leader smoking, is turning out of the formation. Serenely, the rest of them continue southward.

"Fuel check, Blue," Cat Man calls.

We read off our remaining fuel. I tell him I'm reading zero oil pressure, and he tells me to head home and take the lead position. When we join up, Blue Two—Norton—is missing. Cat Man tells me to orbit and he keeps asking Blue Two to check in. Finally, he alerts Moonbeam and we head home, settle into the undercast, land straight in. Either I'm a lucky bastard or these engines don't need oil.

Bittersweet. On his hundredth—and last—mission, Cat Man had gotten his fourth MIG, cause for a double celebration, but he'd lost a wingman. More as a matter of procedure than necessity, I have shut down my engine and allowed myself to be towed in. As we go by Cat Man's revetment, I see the colonel's jeep, the major's jeep. They're both standing on the PSP, arms akimbo, waiting for him to crawl out. There won't be any celebration, I realize.

"Empty," my crew chief says, holding the dipstick where I can see it. "It was full, Captain."

I nod, throw the shoulder straps back. It's quit raining, so I almost forget to collect my raincoat.

I open my eyes. It's almost seven. Rolling over, I look at Cat Man's cot. It's stripped. He's gone home and I didn't see him off. Every trace of him is gone: his footlocker, his B-4 bag, his single framed picture—a girl ' in her late teens, a girl with his frank eyes. On the table is his case of C.C.

Just seeing that case increases my nausea. We drank half the night to celebrate his kill and my probable kill.

I lie back and close my eyes. "You bastard," he had said, grinning. "Why didn't you tell me? How unprofessional can you get?"

Scotty relayed that Cat Man had told them that he had had to catch the next courier. He had run out of faithful lighters.

I'm acting flight commander for about two weeks. Up to the river we go, in the soup all the way. Five times on the better days we escort reconnaissance birds from across the field. Flak pops all around them, but they don't seem to notice. I guess they're too busy taking pictures. Once, one of them gets a direct hit, so we simply re-form and head home. A blank feeling. Sixty missions, I write Jenny. It's all downhill now, I tell her; with this February weather all the MIG pilots are lying in their bunks drinking sake or whatever they drink.

Finally, three new guys are assigned to our flight. All of them outrank me: two Marine majors and an RAF exchange officer of equivalent rank. Our Ops officer is a little apologetic about it; but he had to assign them somewhere, he said. I understand: the squadron's falling behind in kills. I'm comfortable leading an element. Date of rank puts the RAF guy in command over the Marines. Lean and startlingly blond, he lies on Cat Man's cot, a little aloof and out of place in his powder-blue coveralls, smoking an expensive cigar and sizing us up. Sometimes he looks steadily at us until we drop our eyes. He'd flown Spitfires during the Battle of Britain, we heard. I believe it. He's cool as hell in the air and, on the ground, he can watch the Marines clown around and not break up. Out comes the cigar from his mouth, a trace of a smile lights his eyes, then stone face again. But, gradually, he loosens up, accepts us.

Both Marines are from K-3, an airfield near the Sea of Japan. They'd put in a year there and then come over on exchange to sample air-to-air fighting. Flying F-9s they'd been working on the railroad, as they put it—the rail line between Wonsan and the Chongchon. Now they wanted to diddle with the MIGs. For a couple of missions, each of them flew wing. I felt like a fool leading them around, so after a while I told Jonathan—that's our RAF leader's name—I'd be proud to go back to wingman status. He studied me awhile, nodded, smiled, offered me a cigar. I'd solved his problem, I guess. Basically, I'm purely defensive, I realize now.

Mike and Spence, the Marines, have been together forever. "Since the Punic Wars," Mike says sorrowfully. Spence, tall and sandy-haired, had arrived first. From the first moment, he was one of us, laughing like a bastard when the Coleman lantern started wheezing and threatening to blow up. He shows us how to fix it. Mike, built like one of those tugs that tow our birds around, had arrived two weeks later. He walks in, sees Spence, says, "Oh, Jesus," turns around to leave.

Spence points to Roger's old cot, stripped for the past month, and

Mike sighs, drops his bag by it, and lies down to test it. Almost immediately, he sits up again to see what's breaking his back. It's Roger's footlocker, and I start looking around for another place to put it. But Spence catches my eye, shakes his head almost imperceptibly. He has this shit-eating little grin on his face.

Mike decides that it has to go and rises to move it, but Spence slowly shakes his head. Hesitantly, Mike looks at us, but we don't understand what's going on.

"You mean I've got to *leave* it there?"

Spence looks a little like an undertaker, cadaverous from his shoulders up. He inhales, looks at us hesitantly. "Well, Roger slept over it without complaining."

"Oh, bullshit," Mike says.

"These guys told me he didn't want it moved."

"Yeah?" Mike searches our faces. We turn away, biting our lips. Scotty starts shaking, but it could be from grief. Mike watches him.

"Well, Christ, what am I supposed to do, lie there and break my goddamn back?"

Spence has this eloquent shrug. "All I know is that Roger wanted it left there until we're sure he isn't going to turn up. Move it if you can't take it."

"Yeah, well, goddamn, Spence, you *know* I can take it, you bastard. What I mean is—"

"I *know* what you mean, Mike. And if I were you I'd pitch it right out into the snow." Mike nods, reaches down. "But then I didn't know Roger as these guys did."

We blink. Nobody knew Roger. He flew okay, he played good poker, he wasn't a lush. That's all we know. He didn't talk much for a second lieutenant.

Mike is wavering. I have my paperback close to my face, and I use my other hand to help block my face. Finally, he sighs, pushes it back, and lies down again. Somewhere in the past he must have really put it to Spence because this went on for four nights, with Spence wagging his head gently at us and placing one finger vertically over his lips.

Finally, one evening, after we'd blown out the candles, Mike jumps up, cursing, drags out the footlocker and falls contentedly back into his bed. Then he hears this snort of laughter from Spence.

"Spence! Oh . . . you . . . *sonuvabitch!* You . . . !"

Out they crash, the door banging. We get out of bed to watch them wrestle in the mud.

"Mike! Mike! I swear to God . . ." But Spence is laughing too hard to carry it off. Mike dumps him into a drainage ditch.

Leading the two elements, they are great. They single out some guy from the staircase, pass him to each other like two hockey stars, and then one of them puts him away. I saw it happen twice. But, more often, it's just the usual round-robin, the searching, the empty sky. When I see a kill now, I try to analyze how I feel. Not these guys. Or, if they do, they don't mention it.

Spence and I are the same age. I'm surprised to learn that. It comes out one night when he introduces me to martinis. They're like hypoxia; one minute you finally understand life, and the next you don't understand anything. I have to lean back on my stool to get him in focus. I'm asking him how he feels about killing, and he ignores me for a while. When I persist, he finally turns that lean sandy head toward me, and I recoil. I don't know this man. His eyes are as cold as this gin. He starts to say something, changes his mind, looks away.

"C'mon. I'm serious."

"John," he says finally, wheeling his stool toward me, "what do you *want*? You want *patriotism,* friend? You want the hand-to-brow routine? Just tell me."

"I want to know how you feel when you kill a man."

"I *don't,* John. I don't feel anything. Maybe I'm glad I didn't muff it. That's all."

"No," I say.

"Okay," he says. "You want horror stories? I'll tell you a horror story." He's tapping my knee. "You think I don't know the difference? Look, two months ago I was leading a gaggle of F-9s up near P'Yong Yang. We'd been briefed that a bunch of Communist leaders were going to meet in this courtyard. It was a pep talk or something. I went out to my bird and she's loaded with four cans of napalm. I hate the stuff, hate delivering it, but if it will shorten the goddamn war, I don't go hand-to-brow. The main thing is to get it over with, right? I want to go back to El Toro, and you want to get back to Hamilton. Where was I?"

"Four cans of napalm."

"Right. Okay, this wasn't any *orphanage,* see? It was a valid military target, the very bastards who started this fucking war. So off we go, and in we go through all this thirty-seven-millimeter stuff they've got around the city. Jonesy goes in—*bang!*—without a word, and the rest of us, skimming the rooftops, keep going. I see the square coming up, and then I hit the pickle button, just before the rooftops end. And, Christ . . ." His thumb slowly lifts off the button.

He's frozen, dazed, looking down at the floor.

"And?"

"And? . . . Well, there are all these faces turned up at me, see? You know how time seems to stop sometimes? They weren't what I expected. I saw young women in the crowd. Kids."

His eyes rise to mine. He nods. "*Kids.*"

I say nothing while he collects himself, looks around the room. Then, fierce again, he says, "So, you see, Johnny, why I don't lose sleep over some goddamned MIG jock—Chinese, Russian, whatever he is. They paid their money; they'll have to take their chances, like the rest of us."

His grin returns. "Naw, this is a good war you've got going here."

He slaps me on the back, and I fall off the stool.

Christmas Day. It's even snowing, instead of sleeting. Knowing that we had alert today, we'd opened our packages from home last night. One of mine, the one from my folks, had arrived in October. Mother has little faith in the U.S. mail and too much faith in cheap twine. Her box seemed to have been dropped from ten thousand feet. No matter how I'd set it down, it would roll. A bathrobe, cans of Dutch tobacco, some underwear, the inevitable brownies (crystallized now). Jenny sent me two books: Faulkner's *The Sound and the Fury* and Evelyn Waugh's *Brideshead Revisited*. She's still trying to educate me, and God knows I need it. I really like reading. But, not knowing who the important authors are, I read indiscriminately. I've got to get back to college some day. Next time I'll major in English. I know that now. There's no way I could have ever become an engineer. But I'm not sure about Shakespeare and those old guys. Jesus, I can still see myself dressed up as Silvius in *As You Like It*, with old Mrs. Morrow sweeping around the stage, telling me how a shepherd should act. Hell, if anyone had acted that way around *our* sheep, the flock would have run all the way to Evansville.

Alert has become an unpleasant chore. Ever since Fifth Air Force saw those photos of the IL-28s suddenly sharing the MIG bases in Manchuria, we've had to keep sixteen birds parked out at the end of the runway. It's getting difficult to find room to back up to the stove. There are hardly enough chairs to go around. Sometimes, hot as I am wearing this dumb innertube, I say to hell with this crowd scene and go outside to rake snow out of one of our lawn chairs. Bill, my crew chief, took a picture of me sitting out there reading.

It's 0600 now, an hour before dawn, and we have the first shift in the cockpits. Jonathan has never won a coin toss, not once. I sit there, all strapped in, and watch the snow come down. Ninety-seven missions, no confirmed kills. In another week, God willing, I'll be home. Jenny's letters are exultant, and they reflect my mood, too, I guess. Except that it *would* be nice to get one MIG—not the pilot, just the bird—before I leave. As it is, I feel as though nothing definite has been accomplished.

"Oh, *no*," Scotty had said before he left. "I don't feel that way at all. We've escorted the reccy guys so they could take pictures, we've screened the fighter bombers so they could bomb bridges, without seeing MIGs. And we've winged a few MIGs. Who knows? Maybe they went to the boneyard. Maybe we're aces."

Scotty's too much. You could throw him into a cesspool, and he'd make you think it was a good deal. Now he's instructing cadets. He's probably telling them how broadening it was, or something.

As the snow falls, as my fingers become too numb to turn the pages of my paperback, my mind keeps returning to my lack of kills, to specific instances when, unaccountably, I'd peppered a wing instead of the cockpit. And Cat Man's words gain significance, the last words he had spoken to me:

"The problem, Johnny, is you don't want to hurt anybody. Oh, sure, you aim—after a fashion—but there's aiming and aiming."

Practically what our flight surgeon, who was practicing psychiatry that week, had said one evening at the bar before he zonked out.

A gang comes rushing out of the Alert shack, but it's another false alarm. Some poor bastard had unzipped his many zippers and gone into the privy. It's a classic two-holer, tall and unpainted. I know how he feels. They wait for someone to slip in there and then come running out, yelling, "Scramble all sixteen!" Even if you suspect a joke, you've gotta flail around getting back into that immersion suit, because it could be real. Sometimes they even blow the klaxon.

The latrine joke was made for guys like Mike and Spence. They drive each other crazy with it. We hardly laugh now, except last time when Spence managed a variation. Knowing that Mike would keep sitting there, he even fired up his bird. We noticed the little building bumping around a bit then. Mike wasn't sure. We could almost see him struggling. And then Spence had several mechanics get under his nose and heave. As the nose wheel oleo extended, his jet wash lowered. Looking back, he applied as much power as the crew chiefs could stand. Finally, the privy toppled and out of it, bare-assed, amid streamers of toilet paper, Mike crawled. Gibbering and laughing, he held up his suit with one hand and shook a hairy fist.

The bases of the clouds shift. Light pours down, moves across the birds. Then it's gray again. Low tops probably, or layers. Up there on top, it's always great. It's another world. But that's hogwash about climbing up there and leaving all your cares behind. You simply leave a few, and gain others. I look around at the birds, the chiefs laughing at Mike's whispered plan for revenge. It all seems real—these men, this life, these machines—but it won't last, I know. Two weeks from now I'll be in the States with Jenny. Even as I depart, all this will begin to fade from my mind. If the soul endures, it's the mind, isn't it? Part of it, anyway—whatever retains memories. Even after bulldozers have pushed the earth around, I'll still be somewhere, like the humus from leaves. I'll be more than a little plot of grass. Meanwhile, you put in your time and try to maintain such dignity as a given situation requires. Having become an ace really won't matter eventually. What might matter, I think, is to have been someone your buddies could trust.

We're back in the hut, yawning around the stove. It's too hot here, but that isn't the only reason we're yawning. Last night old Bed-Check Charlie was around. At midnight he flew over the runway dropping his hand grenades. Finally, the siren down at Group Ops began howling. We could barely hear it. When I was a kid, I had one that loud on my bicycle. But we went outside and watched the orange canopy of caliber .50s light up the base. Those Army guys, manning their quad-fifties, were in their glory; but they were wasting expensive ammo. He was way out ahead of them, and higher. I thought of him up there, pitching his grenades, and wondered if he was laughing or whether he was rigid, committed as a Kamikaze pilot, whether he was me.

"Hey, those rounds are landing in Yong Dong Po and other villages, aren't they?" I asked Spence, and he had nodded. "Sure looks like it." But, later, when I mentioned it to one of the Army captains, he laughed. "No," he explained. "You're going by tracer burnout. We overshoot those villages." Bullshit. Poor goddamn whores.

It's noon, and we're all looking forward to the much-publicized turkey dinner. But we're in the cockpits again. The chow truck arrives, and we see a cook handing down the food, then the empty trays. I'm starving. I try to read Somerset Maugham's *Of Human Bondage*, but I can't concentrate. However lofty your aspirations, chowtime brings you back to earth. It's the perfect moment for some bored controller to see blips, I think; and, sure enough, the klaxon goes.

It was the usual thing: nothing. The MIGs had crossed the scramble latitude, that's all. We'd chased them, turned back.

After we're back on the Alert pad, I crawl out and ask about chow. Bill's rubbing his stomach.

"*Very* good, Captain," he says. "I ate yours; now you can have mine. When the truck returns."

I pick up Maugham again. My stomach's rumbling so loud that Bill starts laughing. He hands me my mail. Back into the cockpit I go. Ninety-eight, I think, and suddenly, she's there. I can almost see her. She's letting her hair grow again, she writes. It's at that awkward stage. All fall she helped her mother can. Now they're getting the cattle in for the winter. Her dad is better now; the operation really helped. Our cocker tangled with a porcupine. They never learn. He's seven now, but no brighter. She's mailed me some novels she read in college. I should have gotten them last week. It's been a long year, she concludes. "I'm winking at the meter man."

The mess hall is sending out another truck, Bill consoles me. He lies down beside the APU, dozes.

I feel it coming—the klaxon, another scramble—but I push it aside. There's the chow truck. Four trays, already laden, are handed down. Bill's on his way with one. I'm already reaching over when the dumb klaxon goes. He shrugs, sets it down, runs to the APU. Angrily, I hit the starter switch. The last thing I see is Bill looking at the tray and rubbing his stomach.

As we climb out over the bleak hills, we hear that the other guys have tangled with a bunch of MIGs. I uncage my gunsight, and the reticle slides right off the windshield. Only when it's manually caged do I have an illuminated ring and pipper. I'll have to use Kentucky windage.

The sun has set and, below, North Korea, snow-covered, becomes dark. There's not a light to be seen down there, yet it's bound to be streaming with trucks and troops. We test-fire our guns, and the sudden orange flashes are startling. Spence is leading the flight, I the element. It seems to me that this has all happened before. Properly I should relinquish my position to the new guy flying my wing, but he has flown only two missions and seems pretty nervous. Hell, I've told him: no sweat, these MIG jocks don't want to fight.

On the radio, we hear them going around and around, calling breaks and reverses. My wingman must be certain I'm a liar. Now we're conning and holding full throttle, coming on like a troop of cavalry. It's all happened before. Spence asks the controller if he's scrambled another flight and gets a negative reply. Ten degrees left, the controller adds calmly. I guess it's not real to him.

"Talley-ho," Spence calls, and I see little wisps of cons up on the river. We've punched off our drop tanks and are flat out. Right into the fight we go, and the surprised MIGs, like startled chickens, start zooming to safety. We follow, firing as we get a chance, but our main concern is to get them dispersed long enough so that the other flight can get organized. Then, we hope, we'll set up a defensive scissors, and all eight of us will work our way home. I don't know how many MIGs are around, but I've seen at least sixteen.

We head south, our flights crossing at a sixty-degree angle and then, gradually, recrossing. Two birds in the other flight are streaming fuel. They climb as high as they can, so they can glide if they have to. Spence takes his wingman up to escort them. We stay with the other element, essing above and behind. Now, I think, it's getting dark, so why don't you MIG jocks go home to beer call, and we'll do the same.

But not all of them do. They must be teetotalers or something, because four of them curve in. I jerk the nose around and hose off enough tracers to distract them. Up they go, and I see them glint goldenly. It doesn't make sense. The sun's down. While I ponder this, I see them going up after Spence and the fuel-streamers. One of the streamers lights up and falls, then a MIG blows up. It's really a sight at dusk, all that fire whirling down.

Somehow Spence's wingman gets slung off. I see both of them and then I see a whole flight of MIGs diving behind the wingman. I decide to break off escort, and we two curl down behind them. It's so dark now that I have trouble keeping them in sight. No matter how low I turn my sight rheostat, the red on the windshield blinds me. Only the brilliant orange flashes of the MIG cannon keep me oriented. For some reason my mind drifts back to childhood when my little brother and I were bicycling home, and this crowd of older boys let me past but stopped him. I hated to turn back, but I did and, seeing me coming, they laughed and let him go. Maybe they had just been testing me.

Anyhow, we close in, and I spray all of North Korea. I see little sparkles, which may be lucky hits, and then the MIGs break off. I get one glimpse of them silhouetted against the horizon and then they're gone. We gather up the wingman and head home. I ask him if he's okay, and he says the bird's okay, but he's starving to death. . . .

When we land, it is pitch dark, so we taxi back to the flight line. My crew chief hands me the tray of turkey. He'd kept it warm on the stove. He says that he's glad I've returned safely because he couldn't have eaten a third turkey dinner.

6

GEORGE

ONE HUNDRED. Without exultation, or even satisfaction, I watch them "X" the last square by my name on the mission chart. Jonathan musters a smile, warmer than usual, as he shakes my hand. Spence and Mike pummel me, chug-a-lug me, dig a case of beer out of the snow. My replacement is already here. They tell him that he even looks a little like me. He frowns, but I'm flattered. He is Dartmouth. I open a beer for him.

"Someday," I tell him, dramatizing it, "*your* name will be up there in lights."

After I've visited all the important packing cases—the flight surgeon's office, the finance office, the orderly room and Personnel—and gathered two columns of initials on my out-processing clearance, I'm no longer a member of the organization. Technically, I'm assigned to a fighter-bomber squadron stationed at George Air Force Base, California.

As I pack dirty laundry into my already swollen B-4 bag, I look up at the mission chart. The new name has already replaced mine. I remember 1944, when I left England. Someone erases your name, and it's as though you had never been there, that it was all a dream. Tomorrow, here, they'll paint over my name below the cockpit and stencil in his.

At midnight, medium-drunk, fumbling with the door like the Cat Man, I enter our room for the last time. On the blanket-covered table, a single candle gutters. Before I blow it out, I walk around like an old man and look at their sleeping faces. They brief at 0400, so I try to be quiet.

In his sleep Spence rolls restlessly, on the verge of a nightmare. "Get it up—*up*, goddammit!" he mutters in that hard voice I've heard only once before. When he rocks toward the candlelight, I can see his clenched teeth. Gradually, he subsides, his jaw muscles relaxing, his hands uncurling. He has reached some resolution.

Mike is lying flat on his back, his shoulders uncovered, his dog tags gleaming against his green T-shirt. Spence's voice had disturbed him, but now he's beginning to smile. As I watch, that big Irish face eases into an audible laugh. He swallows twice, is still.

In their corner, the two new lieutenants lie curled like lanky children, their faces slack and innocent, their breathing silent. From nails driven into the wall above their bunks hang webbed belts and loaded, holstered forty-fives, handy. "God help the North Koreans who infiltrate *this* BOQ area," Mike had said, laughing, while they drove those nails.

By the door, Jonathan sleeps in pajamas. Pale and blond, with those splotches of color in his cheeks peculiar to the British, he seems laid out for a stately burial, his long hands crossed on his chest, his aristocratic face centered on a makeshift pillow. I know nothing of his personal life—whether he's married, whether he has parents or children. If there are photographs, they are for his eyes alone. But *someone* regularly sends him those tins of stinking kippered herring.

Stripping off my shirt, I pause to say a little prayer for them, but I'm drunk, so I guess He doesn't hear me. Blowing out the candle, I go to sleep thinking of Jenny and that grim desert base which will become our next home.

When the alarms go off, I almost expect to hear a case of C.C. slide out. Instead, and almost as familiar by now, is this weary British voice saying, "All right, lads, up now. Come on. The Boche are coming, right?" He's mellowed. We love him.

Gradually, I realize that I don't have to get up. The courier bird doesn't arrive until 0900. What a luxury! Against the mounting candle-power, despite all the stretching and fumbling, I shut my eyes determinedly. I'm lying here, listening to them for the last time. As usual, Spence throws a shower clog at Mike, who grunts and lies there rubbing his big chest.

One by one, they collect their toilet kits, their O.D. towels and head for the latrine. I can imagine Jonathan wielding his straight razor; Spence making faces in the mirror; Mike taking his Spartan cold shower; the two new guys watching them while they pretend to shave.

Then, before they leave, I hear them coming, individually, to look down at me. Without opening my eyes, I can tell who is standing there. Their breathing, or something, gives them away. I want to drop the pretense of sleep, rise up and hug each of them, but I just lie there. I know better than to open my eyes and embarrass them. We said our good-byes last night.

The battered door closes for the last time, and I open my eyes to darkness. Considerately, they'd blown out all the candles. It's a real tribute, better than a medal. They're gone. I'll probably never see them again.

Up north, the weather is supposed to be good. The MIGs may come up after the F-80 they're escorting. The two new guys aren't ready for the rough stuff. Russian instructors will notice them right away. I hear their shouts, their voices straining under the G-loads. Wide awake, sitting up in bed, watching, I realize that I may as well get up.

Very businesslike, most professional, the courier pilot stands in the waiting room. It's the first flight briefing I've heard since Nellis. He wears glasses shaped like our sunglasses and he goes down his checklist importantly. You'd think we were going over the Pole to Paris. His flying suit is pressed, his boots shined, his scarf just so. For him, this is a big deal. He's based in Japan, but on these courier runs, he gets credit for a mission, maybe two. He'll draw combat pay, collect Air Medals.

"Emergency Procedures," he announces grimly, holds up his clipboard. Light reflects off his glasses. Christ, he's got *four* engines. What could happen? The jock sitting beside me gives me this sick look and crosses his legs.

It's a bucket-seat configuration, webbing supporting canvas down each side of the stripped fuselage. We sit facing each other. Everything's vibrating and jingling. I look out the little window, see the power being expended to lift us. A last skip, and the vibration ceases, the engine noise diminishes. Black pavement, the dirt overrun, fall away. We're banking, and I watch the single runway, the ramp, the raw building area, all dwindle to unimportance. I can't let them go so easily. There should be time for reflection before the next thing happens. As I watch, I see two elements on takeoff roll. The first two are already lifting from their shadows, yellow banded and fierce looking in their determination, their smoke trails lengthening, flattening. Already they're doing three-eighty, I know. Within seconds, they're passing through our altitude, the second element closing. They dwindle, vanish into stratus. A little smoke lingers.

Thirty days of leave. From Japan I have brought Jenny real pearls. For a while she wears them even in her mother's kitchen when she's cooking. They look great over her wonderfully mounded sweater. We're still a little shy around each other. I have to woo her again, but it's a short courtship.

Cockers have poor memories. He's slow to come around. Maybe he enjoyed having all the affection. Through the snow we hike, the three of us. His feathers are fringed with snowballs. Panting, plunging, often breaking through the crust, he pulls us along. He remembers me now, I think. No, when we return to the fire, he crawls into her lap and growls at me. *He's* the male in our home.

We buy a Jaguar. Four thousand bucks. Our entire savings. But it's more than transportation, we keep telling each other; it's a way of life. Ever since one casually went by us on a hairy mountain curve, our old Ford straining at its limit, we'd been saving for this moment. It's so low that Jenny's taken to wearing slacks. That long, narrow hood, those rearing fenders! Behind, there's nothing—a token trunk. We've rigged a little dog seat. With us, he leans into the curves and has visibility around the clock—when the top's down (only once so far during this crazy winter of alternating seasons). When the top is up, all we can see are the hood and fenders, pavement racing beneath them. But the sound! From an unusually steady idle, it becomes, under load, a hypnotizing moan, finally *whoom*.

Once, alone, on a road I know, I open her up, wind her up tight in each gear, even in fourth. One-twenty, one-twenty-five, one-thirty. She's steady—no wavering, no protest. I wait for more, but that's it. I let her wind down. At seventy I'm crawling.

From his high pickup truck, her father looks down at me. I've never made any sense to him. This car confirms it. He tries it, shifting uneasily until he's in high. Then he pushes down hard on the accelerator, lets up at fifty, shrugs. I'm crazy, that's all. She could have married Jim Burdett and done well by herself. He doesn't drink, he doesn't smoke, he's a good farmer. He takes care of his folks. He stays near home and looks in on them regularly. I've met Jim, and I like him. A good, solid man. Maybe her dad is right.

"No," she says, kissing me. "He's a bore."

A *rich* bore, I think, then almost forget him. What's wrong is that she's crazy, too. She flings that poor Jag around, laughs, looks at me.

Then, one day, my leave nearly up, we're off. Westward we go, the cocker between us surveying everything with murderous intentions. Route 66—Oklahoma City, Amarillo, Albuquerque, as Nat Cole's song explains. We know half the old motels, try the few new ones. Five bucks a night, and they don't even allow dogs. On we go, usually back to the old ones with the roses right outside the door, those with the Tourist Court signs. Old, but freshly repainted.

Exhausted, dead, and in heaven, I roll away, look at the dark ceiling. Her blond hair, long again, lies near one breast. We're breathing hard and listening to the diesels rasping past. On the floor, disgusted, lies our dog.

In the cool mornings, alternating driving, we speed past timid convoys of cars, shifting into high at eighty-five, and watch the tiny mirror. Up into the mountains we climb, drifting down as easily again as one does a Falling Leaf in a training bird. It's all rhythm, I realize. You find the natural rhythm of a machine and go with it. We make Albuquerque before sunset.

"I remember you," the old man says. "You stayed here before. You had a cocker spaniel and a pretty wife."

"I still do."

He looks out the window. "Isn't that a different car?"

"Yes, sir."

"Get good mileage?"

"Fair."

"I need something more economical to operate."

So much for the Jaguar's impact on America. Well, the young love it. As we unpack, they shyly circle it. We are celebrities, one girl decides. She recognizes Jenny.

"Ask for her autograph," another girl whispers, "so we'll know who she is."

The boys murmur about the length of the hood, the heady numbers on the speedometer. "Twelve cylinders?" one finally asks.

"Six."

"*Six?* Even my Ford has eight."

Ticking, the engine cools. I raise the hood so they can see the aluminum camshaft covers, the twin SUs, the procelain exhaust manifold. They quit talking.

Marriage. It's like rolling and rolling through cumulus. While I lie on one elbow watching, she brushes her hair in long, sensuous tugs. The dry air makes it crackle. In the mirror her eyes meet mine, and her brush falters. She colors.

"Quit staring," she says. "I feel like Nefertiti."

I feign sleep until her bedlamp clicks off. Then, laughingly, I roll over and grab—the growling cocker. She is a fiend, this woman.

Gradually, the real world of jumping alarm clocks and clammy cockpits recedes, and I move around in the dream that I cultivated in Korea—Jenny and the Jaguar. Beauty and the Beast, as it turns out. Racing along the roller-coaster dips of two-lane blacktop near Grant, New Mexico, we notice water droplets hitting the windshield.

"Rain?" Jenny asks. "Out of a clear sky?"

"No." I watch the coolant temperature and the exhaust, finally pull over. Wrapping the dog's towel around the smoking, deadly radiator cap, I remove it and pour in one of our two burlap water bags. The hoses are okay, but there is water on the oil dipstick.

"Blown cylinder-head gasket," I tell her.

Slowly we proceed, stopping wherever possible to refill our water bags. Garage owners shake their heads. I buy more bags. In Indianapolis the dealer had assured us that Arizona is full of Jaguars. Maybe he meant mountain lions.

"What do we do? You have to report in at George day after tomorrow."

In reply, I swing us off Route 66 and head for Phoenix, well to the south of our course. God is good. We find a Jaguar agency there. The salesmen affect British accents, but the mechanic is a competent Okie. He smirks and nods.

"Do you own a Jag?" I ask him.

"You crazy?" He points to a 1946 Studebaker.

The salesmen, their hands clasped behind their side-vent sport coats, peer under the hood. One frowns at me. "Like a steam locomotive, you say?"

*   *   *

Somewhere between Indiana and California, we calculated later, Sam was conceived.

"We don't even know where," she muses.

"Before the gasket blew, certainly."

"Albuquerque, then," she decides.

Just north of the Los Angeles basin, protected by mountains from both smog and high-density air traffic, lies Victorville. It's right on the edge of the Mohave desert. From Daggett and Barstow, Route 66 curves sharply, descends through the cement dust and smoke of Victorville's sole industry to the Cajon Pass and San Bernardino. Low buildings flanking the highway for a quarter-mile, a few gas stations, a single old motel with a precious quadrangle of lawn, two restaurants and a car lot—that's all a traveler sees.

The base itself is of World War II vintage—the usual two-story, white clapboard barracks, mostly peeling and unoccupied, with tumbleweed piled up along their windward sides. Whitewashed rocks around the flag-pole. How, I wonder, had this one survived the postwar closings? Then I remember the long runways. Ed and I had landed here after he had hit that dog. Once a B-17 training base, George had long runways. They, and probably some congressman, saved it. It will become an important base. Two TAC F-86 wings and an ADC squadron—more aircraft and per-sonnel than I have ever seen at a single base—will be stationed here.

"Oh, look at the *housing!*" Jenny exclaims, pointing.

Although it is dusk, I can tell that the quarters are new—low, California ranch-style quadruplexes, with real lawns, enclosed patios, and dogs. Outraged, our cocker narrows his eyes and begins barking steadily into my ear. The pack of dogs freezes, then looks in all directions. Finally oriented, they give chase. By the time they fall back, I am deaf and the cocker is hoarse and emotionally exhausted.

"What?" I ask Jenny an hour later as we unpack in the Green Spot Motel.

"*I say*, where do you think we'll stand on the housing list?" she yells.

"Fairly high. We won't be in this motel a year."

After dinner, we walk the dark town. In the moonlight everything looks better. "But where do you shop?" Jenny wonders.

I lower the rough stationery and try to absorb Spence's words. Jonathan is down—KIA probably, MIA officially. "Semper Fidelis and all that, over," Spence had ended.

Somewhere, then, in North Korea there lies another corner of a foreign field that is forever England. Already burning, a MIG pilot, perhaps dying, had watched Jonathan zoom and ess overhead to kill off speed. Then, with the last of his own airspeed, the MIG pilot had pulled up and simply kept pressing his trigger. He had just hosed the air, and Jonathan had flown right through it. Later, during a routine Intelligence briefing, I actually see it. Jonathan's wingman had taken a turn firing after the MIG had begun its short zoom. His gun-camera film shows the MIG climbing steeply and opening fire. Suddenly, from the upper right-hand corner of the screen, an F-86 appears. At this second the Intelligence briefing officer stops the projector, then slowly hand-cranks the film through. "*There*," he says, cranking and pausing on a frame. "Note the white puff at the wing root. Probably a round of thirty-seven millimeter."

In successive frames, silent and ghostly on the grainy film. Jonathan's wing breaks off, the fuselage rolls toward us, continues to the inverted position, gradually disappears to the left. It is all unreal. Now the screen shows only sky.

I think of him in his blue flying coveralls, standing by the doorway of Ops, sungrinning; or I think of him lying on his bunk, eating those kippered herring from a little British tin. ("Queasy stomachs, lads? Come on, try one.") I remember an old snapshot he once showed me: mottled, corcaded Spitfires aligned in lush grass, Jonathan standing before them, his blond hair awry, the long fingers of his right hand holding a cigarette. Carelessly dangling from his left hand is a leather helmet with huge earphones. His Mae West is open, his stance tired, his face almost serious.

All through the late summer and fall of 1940, he had fought over England. Now he is dead, finally brought down by a dying man in a last instinctive spasm. An Oriental? Or an experienced pilot, conceivably an old adversary from one of the Communist Bloc countries—say, East Germany? Wars have a way of going on.

I'm still a stranger here. You'd think that, out of some two hundred pilots on this base, I'd know someone; but I don't. Most of the old heads are former Air Guard P-51 pilots with hardly any jet time activated because of the "Police Action" in Korea. They've been together for years and move in cliques. Everyone's friendly enough ("Welcome to the Rag-Tag Militia," they say), but I can imagine what's happening behind the scenes. Personnel doesn't know where to assign me. Each squadron has already named its flight commanders, and I'm too experienced to be used just anywhere. Finally, the colonel asks me frankly if I'd be good enough to be patient for a while.

"Several guys are due for Korea any day now," he says. "You'll get a flight. Meanwhile, here's what we really need: we need you—all three squadrons need you—to conduct maintenance test hops. No one else has enough time in the bird to be put on test orders, you see?"

"Yes, sir."

"It may be a little hairy, at first, Captain—what's your first name? John?—okay, John, it may be hairy, I warn you. Our crew chiefs are still looking for the propellers." He laughs. (*Jesus*, I think.) "But they're learning."

To learn a subject, teach it, as the old saying goes. To learn a bird inside out, test-hop it. Test several a day—freshly reassembled after major inspections, possibly with new, untried engines, or controls—and you learn quickly. Once, as the spring days lengthened, I tested seven birds in one day. Emergencies were common: an engine failure during takeoff roll; a chilling, flame-out landing (I stayed in the cockpit a little longer than necessary after I was towed in because my knees were actually shaking) and a fire in the aft section when a tailpipe clamp gave way. Each evening I'd drive back to the housing area and fix a stiff drink, maybe two. Jenny says I drink too much; all she usually drinks is a glass of wine with dinner. In Korea I'd written her about Cat Man, and she'd replied that he sounded like just another drunk.

Our neighbors on the left aren't career-types. He's a doctor fresh out of medical school, and they never stay in the service long. On our right are the Sands—George and Laura. When Jenny read their nameplate by the door, she began laughing. "He must be a nurse," she said. "They must be lesbians."

"Why?"

"Forget it."

George and I like to tinker with cars. Considering the Jag's nature, it's a good thing I do. On weekends, we stay out in the string of carports behind our building and get greasy. One of our cars is always up on blocks. I've bought a shop manual and some tools. Thank God I can buy Jag parts in San Berdoo. George has a new Chrysler sedan with the big V-8. With grease still under our nails, we slouch on the patios in deck chairs, lowering our beers occasionally to rise and check the steaks. Jenny and Laura are in the kitchen discussing recipes and kids. Out of the morning sickness stage now, Jenny's getting briefed on the next hurdles of pregnancy. Laura is a veteran.

George says that the base is really named for him, that that guy's portrait in the club doesn't mean anything. "Over the gate," he says, "the *s* has been left off. 'George's Air Force Base,' it should read."

"You're smashed, honey," Laura says, coming out to sit on his lap. "Go check on the kids."

"Careful," he says. "You're sitting on my new *Road and Track*."

"Is that *all*, sugar?" She kisses him, smiles archly at me. "I'm not bending anything else?"

One Saturday afternoon when we'd gotten into an argument about automobile suspensions, George shows me this great S-curve just south of Jerry's Oasis. Jerry's sits right off the western end of the primary runway. You'd think that pilots would know better than to go there. Some evening a guy's going to lose power right after gear-up and take out that little building. Anyhow, this two-lane macadam road heads south along some unimportant meridian, then, abruptly, in a remarkable concession to the determination of some property owner, bends ninety degrees left, then right again. There's just time to get all crossed up in a drift before it's time to head south again. What's great about it is that the ditches on either side are really shallow. If you leave the pavement, they won't flip you. Equally important, you can see oncoming traffic. There's never much.

After several runs, George and I, in his Chrysler, have worked up to about seventy-five as we enter the first curve. In the Jag, eighty. But, after a while, we notice what the macadam is doing to our tires. Later, in the club, when we mention these curves, a few other jocks get interested. Before long, there are two MGs, a Cadillac, and a Buick Century out there squalling around. Bill, one of the first lieutenants, owns the Buick. He's a wild man, but I can't believe him when he says that he's gone in at eighty, not with that flabby suspension. So I have to ride through with him. Hell, we go bouncing right across the ditch into the desert and leave this long cloud of dust. Those sporty portholes in the fenders hadn't helped much.

"See?" he says. "Eighty."

But I'm not the champion. Oh, no. The record is held by Harvey in a modified Jag coupe, the new XK-120 M. Harvey's not even in the service, but he looks service—crew-cut, sneakers, something ("Crazy?" Jenny suggests). He runs a small filling station in Victorville. Anyhow, he says he's been through at ninety-three, and all of us believe him, especially this highway patrolman who chases Harvey a lot and who (unofficially) holds second fastest time through the esses.

What's terrible is that Harvey is going into Naval Aviation. In fact, he's at Pensacola now. Maybe he's just trying to insure that he's never stationed in the desert.

What do you know? After only a decade as a pilot, I'm a flight commander. At this rate, by the time I'm sixty, I'll be a squadron commander. ("Fifty-five," Jenny calculates.) Anyhow, I love it. For the first time *I'm* the most experienced guy in the flight, so I feel comfortable leading them. What I don't like about it is all the paperwork—writing effectiveness reports, for example.

Even before I signed in here, our wing was designated a fighter-bomber wing. Which explains why they're hanging bomb racks now—so we can get used to their drag. Little by little, the F-86 is losing the very characteristics that had made her great. It isn't even the same bird we flew in Korea. To permit the safe installation of ordnance stations, the wing itself has had to be beefed up. So it's a heavier machine now, a thousand pounds heavier. True, the engine is more powerful, but increased thrust can't compensate altogether for extra weight. Then hang on these racks, which play hell with the aerodynamics, and what have you got? It's like dancing with your wife when she's four months' pregnant. Not that I do much of that.

Tactical Air Command doctrine has it that, once a fighter bomber has delivered its ordnance, it becomes a fighter well able to defend itself. I'm sure that the guys at TAC headquarters know better, but when your assigned missions include interdiction of an enemy's supply routes, you've got to have these dumb ordnance stations. Besides, Congress likes the idea of a dual capability, naive as that concept is, and they hold the kitty. I've even heard—and I don't even like to think about this—that we're eventually going to have an atomic bomb hanging under each bird. "A bigger bang for a buck," as our secretary of defense says. But no one up in Wing will confirm it. All they pretend to know is that, once our wing is fully manned, we will move en masse to Europe. Hot damn!

Summer moves in on the desert, the cool, clear mornings quickly giving way to shimmering haze. Lying as still as a crocodile, his feathers fanned by our gurgling evaporator, our cocker won't even raise his head from the cool tiles. When I come in each evening, his stub of a tail wags a couple of times, and that's it. For them it's a long day. Jenny won't go to the pool anymore. So after dinner we sit out on the patio until dark and listen to records. Wagner's "Liebestod" played on our tiny record player through a little radio–alarm clock. With the first stars, the incessant wind becomes cool, and our crocodile appears in the doorway with his leash. Wriggling, he slithers from my hand to hers, but he won't drop it. Around the housing area we go, fending off German shepherds and boxers. It's like escorting a reccy bird, except that the cocker, all hackles and bladder, does the essing. Jenny strides along, swinging her arms like a British guardsman, while I, rubber-legged with fatigue and scotch, am jerked here and there by the leash. Jenny's supposed to walk about a hundred miles a day. Her doctor is one of those exercise nuts. But, of course, he doesn't throw himself at the ground all day dive-bombing.

The worst part about this air-to-ground stuff is the ground. It really rushes up at you, especially in a sixty-degree dive. There isn't much time for smooth tracking. And the *Gs!* We'll have to change our insignia to a hemorrhoid. When I lay in five or six Gs for the twentieth time of the day, I feel just like a funnel. "Yeah," old Spence had warned me, "you'll see. In about a year some surgeon will stick a big knife up your tailpipe and spin you around on it. Ask any Marine aviator."

But I'm getting the hang of it. The other flight commanders, especially Dan and Whit, are coaching me. They've been in this fighter-bomber game all along. Kneeling on the ramp, Dan flies his hand down to a pebble on the pavement. Between the war and the "police action," he drove a Greyhound during the week and flew with his Guard squadron on Saturdays and Sundays.

"What you're doing, John," he says, his blue eyes fixed earnestly on mine, "is settling into a chute that doesn't compensate for wind, right? Then you have to crank her around at the last minute and get into the proper chute. That's no good. So instead, pick an aiming point, precalculated—say, two hundred feet at ten o'clock from the pyramid— and forget everything else." He pencils the ground track on the cement, then scratches his cropped hair in puzzlement. Whit, shaking his head, squats and draws another line. "Here's your drift angle, Johnny."

A shadow looms over us. It is our squadron commander. "Okay, who's got the dice?" he asks. He watches for a moment and then says, "Aw, for chrissake, Dan, Whit. You're both fucked up. Gimme the pencil." Then he jumps back, laughing and clapping his hands. They rear back and grab at his ankles.

Dan inclines his head toward the major. "The major can't even hit the dry lake. When I'm in the range tower, I pray like a bastard every time he rolls in."

"Oh, bullshit!"

"Yes, sir. That's a fact. Jesus, you should have seen his rocket passes yesterday. I was *running* after his first pass. Running and praying."

Delighted but pretending to be outraged, the major howls, grabs Dan's neck from behind, shakes him.

"Yeah? *Yeah?*" the major taunts. "Last week! . . . last week, Dan, where did *your* rockets go, you bastard?"

"Dead center, sir." Dan cowers away, giggling. "Right on the pyramid."

"Oh, bullshit!" they chorus, beating on him.

"Okay, okay. They were maybe twenty feet off."

Another howl and, weak as drunks, they begin stretching him. Dan rolls over and looks at me. His grin broadens. "Where was I, John?"

"God knows."

Exhausted and happy, our eyes all seem to come together for a moment, and I know I'm home again.

Indistinguishably, the long days of summer, all dusty-gold, all filled with flying, pass. In the dead of night, dreaming, I wing over, plummet, watch the desert revolve and steady out while I, hanging light on the seat, bend to the sight. The altimeter hands flick around, the circle grows, gains a third dimension at its bulldozed rim. I depress the red button on the stick grip. *Pickle.* Then, heavily, the Gs come in, the earth sliding under the racing reticle until I am blind and lost in the sun flashes. Rolling out on a tight downwind leg, I hear old Dan exclaim, "*Twenty* feet at nine o'clock!" I look down to see the gray puff of smoke obscuring the pyramid.

Within a week this dream becomes real. I'm beginning to hit the target regularly.

"Uh, Dan," Whit calls, "we've created a monster."

Homeward we go, angling down through the hot sky, so close together that the thermals jar us as one hunk of metal. Dan's yellow helmet turns toward me, his face hidden by the dark visor and mask. He jerks his head sideways. I nod and sink, sliding beneath them so closely that I feel their suction, hear their exhausts. Bobbing up into echelon, I look along their helmets, then back at Bill who's settling in. We have perfect faith in each other, we four. We are like a family troupe of acrobats.

Back in Ops we unzip our G-suits and walk around with their bladders

71

and pockets flailing like chaps. Whit, the low scorer, keeps feeding nickels into the Coke machine, beating on it while we accept the frosted bottles and sprawl back on the couch. I have never been so content, I think. Never.

"Thanks," I tell them seriously. "Thanks for everything."

Their eyes fall away. Embarrassed, they shrug and look out at the parking lot. "Oh, oh," Dan says, quietly nudging Whit. "Here comes trouble."

An armada of new convertibles is wheeling in and parking. Behind each windshield there's a young second lieutenant with a mustache. They slam doors, yell happily at each other, lift their trunk lids. In they come, feisty as gamecocks, laden with flying gear, and pile up in the doorway.

Pete, our Ops officer, comes out of his office to greet them. "Welcome," he says dismally, nodding to them, waiting for them to switch hands so they can shake. "This way, gentlemen. For now, just grab any empty locker."

"*Fifteen?*" Pete counts. "We were supposed to get only ten." His handsome Greek face darkens, and he leans over the counter for a phone. "Fifteen will bring us to full manning. Goddammit, I *told* them I'm not running a Boy Scout troop."

"Hold it, Pete," the major says as he enters. "I know what you're gonna say, but . . . c'mon, let's go into your office."

While the sergeant collects their uniformly thin flying records, Whit beats a Ping-Pong paddle on the table until, distractedly, we begin a game of doubles.

From the office Pete's voice leaps, then gradually sinks, muttering in reconcilement. "It's *your* ass, Major," I hear him say. Smokey, old L.A. fireman, loudly chats with the lieutenants, trying to screen Pete's voice. He buys them Cokes, slaps the machine, asks where they are from.

When Major Slocum and Pete reappear, it is obvious that they remain in complete disagreement. Which doesn't mean much in the military, of course. A major outranks a captain so, automatically, he's right. Pete slumps at his desk and considers the list in terms of the flight boards.

"Pay attention!" Whit shouts as he slams the ball at me. In avoiding it, I trip, drop the paddle, and collide with the major, who says, "Okay, get out of the way, John. Let me show you a little championship form. Serve, Dan, goddammit."

Weaving from side to side, his eyes alight, his face as rosy as a baby's, Major Slocum dances back at the crack of the serve and comes up from the floor with backspin. Maps and gloves fall unnoticed from his unzipped coverall pockets. "Hey!" he calls in sheer joy, then jumps aside from Smokey's wild return.

"That was yours, Dan," he admonishes, laughing.

"Possum," the other two squadron commanders call him, more

because of his appearance than his shrewdness. He is loved but not admired. His present gamble in loading up with green pilots explains why: his neck is out a mile, and so is Pete's.

Noisily, four lieutenants relieve us, expertly cutting the ball, moving with the reaction time of chickadees. One, a tall redhead, easily outclasses the others and, later, when Pete hands me my list of names, I realize that, for better or worse, Red is one of mine.

Jenny is going through the dill-pickles-and-ice-cream stage now. Peanut butter. No alcohol, because Art, our doctor neighbor, suspects that alcohol stupefies fetuses. Art tries to cross his fat legs, scratches our cocker's ears, leans his head back against the cushion to loft cigarette smoke.

"*You* drink, smoke, never exercise," I remind him.

"Sure." He shrugs. "But I'm not pregnant."

"Ha!" his wife Irene exclaims, poking her finger into his paunch. "What's *that*, then?"

"What, indeed? You shoulda asked me last week when I was base obstetrician. This week I'm base psychiatrist. Ask Irene; she was an OB nurse for three years."

Although Jenny gets along with most of the other wives, she has no close friends. She doesn't play bridge, and now she refuses to be seen in a bathing suit ("I look like a sea lion"). Once she went to a Wives' Club luncheon, but left early.

"All they talk about are their kids. And recipes."

"That's their life."

"Well, it's boring. Can't a service wife be a little intellectual? Show a little cultural interest?"

"Okay, Bennington, don't be a snob. What's wrong with having been a nurse, or a stewardess, or a schoolteacher?"

"Who taught school?"

"What's her name. The redhead."

"Catherine? She's a college graduate? I don't believe it."

Now she is getting to *me*. "What," I ask coldly, "is so great about being a college graduate? If I had been 4-F, I might have a degree in animal husbandry, and . . . Listen, Jenny, Irene probably never heard of William Blake, but if your water breaks in the middle of the night, who are you going to need, Irene or your Bennington class poet?"

Ah, Christ, she's crying. She's never even mentioned Bennington to anyone, she sobs. Besides, who here would have ever heard of it?

"Okay, okay, you aren't a snob."

I hug her, apologize, listen to her big news. She *has* made a friend, she sniffles, finally smiling. Someone really interesting.

"A college graduate?"

"I have no idea. Please, John."

Her name is Betty Camston, and she lives right across the street. I've seen their nameplate. He's a major, a wing wienie who flies the base C-47 once a month for pay purposes.

"And she paints, and she reads, and . . ."

"Cute?"

". . . she has all these absolute treasures they brought back from Europe. *Yes,* she's cute. You've seen her. She's a doll. Anyhow"—she pushes me away—"will you listen? Get away, or I'll call Art. Their house is a museum. Really. Paintings and sculpture, Oriental rugs . . ."

I am mixing drinks, trying out my new soda siphon. It uses outdated CO_2 Mae West cartridges, which I scrounged. Actually, it blows all the scotch out of the glasses, and we scrabble around with paper towels for a while. In those old movies Ronald Colman made it look so easy.

"Who did you bomb today?"

"The pyramid."

"You *hit* it?" She sits and tucks her feet under her.

"Almost."

"It seems a grim thing for me to praise. Should I be proud?"

"There's a trick to it."

"You aim or something?"

"That's part of it."

"And?"

"You hiss."

"Hiss?"

"Sure. Like the kamikaze pilots in the movies."

"American dogs, you die?"

I nod.

She shrugs. "Well, of course. Give me the seltzer bottle, idiot." Splash, splash. No big deal.

"How'd you do that?" I ask seriously.

"I'm landed gentry, and you're an Irish peasant."

"Half," I amend. "Half Irish."

"You're half Irish, like I'm half pregnant. Since you obviously have nothing to say, shut up. I have an announcement. No, not yet. Are you listening? We are invited to dinner tomorrow evening at the Camstons."

"So?" Actually, I'm impressed. "No problem. Tomorrow is Saturday. No flying. We can make it."

"Right. Now, then, follow me." She leads me into the bedroom and pulls a dress from the closet. "I spent the entire afternoon letting this thing out, but . . ."

"It still doesn't fit."

"I got it down to here."

"Well, you'll be a crowd-stopper. Okay, you need a new cocktail dress. A tent?" I watch her replace the dress and pull out my sport coat. Silently, she lifts one cuff so I can see the frayed edge.

"You," she says firmly, looking at me as though I may try to bolt and run, "are *not* going to wear this. The Salvation Army won't have it."

"We are going to San Berdoo?"

"Bright and early."

"Uh, how about, say, noon? George and I are replacing his shocks tomorrow and—"

Sweetly, she keeps shaking her head. "No, you're not. How much cash do you have on you?"

I consult my wallet. "Thirty bucks. Thirty-one. But I have to buy thirteen quarts of oil. That's what the Jag takes. Thirteen."

"Next month."

"Jenny, it's *been* sixty days, and the manual specifically states—"

"John, I don't *care* what the dumb manual says. *My* manual says I need to get out of the house every sixty days. So, with your thirty bucks we can barely make it. Payday is Monday."

George takes it pretty hard. Sunday, I tell him; we'll install the shocks Sunday. "One more day won't make any difference."

"Laura has big plans for Sunday. So-o, I guess we'll just bounce along *all the way up to Bakersfield and back.* Or I could try installing them myself."

I really feel like a dog. We drive down to Berdoo, buy the dress, buy the dumb coat—sidevents, for Pete's sake—get her hair done, and return. I hold the Jag on a hundred all the way in from Cajon Pass. Great car, putting out like that on such dirty oil.

What I like about Jenny is that she enjoys speed, too, even now when the dips could cause the baby to do an Immelmann or something.

On my knees, with pins between my lips, I sight along her hem-line. She's looking sideways into the wavy, full-length mirror.

"Isn't it too short in front now?"

"No," I say. "It's exactly the same as in back."

"That's not what the saleslady said."

"What does she know? She wears glasses. I'm a pilot."

"All right." She nods, and I whip the dress over her new hairdo. She squeals, looks in the mirror, and pats the elegant coil. Then, frantically, she races to her sewing table. By the time I've dressed, she's finished hemming it and is standing in the chair again. I ignore those lovely calves and look up at the mirror: a poreless, tanned blonde's complexion, heavy, sunstreaked hair, now intricately arranged; the new dress loosely elegant. I'm stunned, humbled. She shakes her tiny watch, consults mine.

"We're late!" she exclaims.

In the military, arriving late is not considered fashionable, but rude. One rings the bell exactly at the appointed time. In fact, we are three minutes late. I like my sports coat; it's houndstooth, she says. But I could have bought two four-ply Dunlops for the price.

Eric answers the door. He's a big deal, I can tell from the first second. Cuff links, blazer, old school tie, even a squadron patch with Latin on his breast pocket. Cordial. Stepping back, he watches Jenny's bare shoulders

75

as he takes the wrap she has worn seventy-five yards. An old lecher, even if he's only about thirty-five. His grip, soft, long-fingered, catches my hand so that it can't function at all.

"Nonsense," he says, shrugging off our contrition, "you're not late." He's tall, I realize, six-two, at least. Wavy hair at the temples, regulation headquarters pallor, a little puffy-faced and weak-chinned, he might be described as handsome, or at least distinguished. But not military, not athletic.

Jenny's right: this is an art museum. There's no other way to describe it. I'm afraid to step on these Orientals; they ought to silk-rope them off. And the walls are warm with oils. Jenny goes flying to one of them.

"This is the one, John," she says. The little frame light makes me look at her face rather than the painting. Reluctantly, my eyes turn to the scene where bright daubs of paint suggest a crowd, with wet pavement reflecting everything.

"You like art, I see." Eric nods. "Wonderful. Did you also study art in college, John?"

"No, sir. All I had was mechanical drawing for one semester."

"You don't paint then?"

Who ever heard of a fighter pilot who paints? "No, sir. Jenny paints."

"Please," he says, "let's drop the military courtesies. I'm Eric."

I nod. I decide not to call him anything.

The next painting is England. Essex, probably. I know it the minute I see it, all green and dreamy with the morning sun burning off the fog. A cottage, a few sheep, some pale willows overhanging a brook. The artist probably stood right where we used to turn initial approach. I really like it, and I raise one finger to point to something until I realize that Eric is hypnotized by my grease-filled fingernails. His smile is frozen. Quickly I put my hands behind my back and taper off with some banal observation.

"Um-m," he says, nodding vaguely.

Jenny, amused but a little defensive of my Cro-Magnon grooming and education, explains that, although I don't paint, I can draw.

"Airplanes." I shrug. "When I was a kid."

"Even as a child," Jenny says, "John seemed to grasp perspective instinctively."

"Oh? You knew him then?"

Oh, boy, here we go: the whole long story that she considers romantic. I walk ahead to avoid it. It always ends with her expressed regret that I don't try to continue my education. I have "so much potential," and all that.

"I'm sure of it," he murmurs. He's almost yawning. He pats my shoulder and guides us to his favorite.

"Corot?" Jenny asks in awe. "An early Corot?" She bends to the signature. "No, I can't make it out."

Eric smiles, shakes his head. "Well, it doesn't really matter, does it?

He's not anyone you've ever heard of. Nor will you hear of him. Clearly, he admired Corot. He had Corot's eye, but something"—he shrugs, stares at the painting as though it's a fake—"fire? is missing. He's dead now, I believe. Once we had high hopes for him."

"Oh, I *like* it," Jenny says. "He came so close."

"Yes. Yes, he did." This more sadly yet.

"Perhaps a little more white here, for sharper illumination?"

Pleased by her observation, he bends to me. "Your wife *does* know art. Betty said she does." His voice is just loud enough for Jenny to hear.

"This one"—Jenny nods—"reminds me of Utrillo's *Abbey of Saint Dennis.*"

"Exactly. It is good, isn't it? But they're all good; they are simply not *great*. They'll never amount to anything. He never achieved importance."

"Still," and Jenny smiles with satisfaction, "they are yours to love."

"Well, let's say that, however poor they may be as an investment, we got our money's worth." He pauses and smiles. "Two cartons of Pall Malls for each painting," he tells us in quiet triumph.

Jenny's smile falters. "I don't follow you."

"No? Then you weren't in Europe right after the war. Of course you weren't; you must have been a child then, a high-school girl. Well, let me tell you that in nineteen forty-seven two cartons of American cigarettes would buy almost anything on the Continent—the best china, whole sets of it, authenticated first editions of Goethe, silverware . . ."

Jenny frowns, quickly refuses his offer of a cigarette. He flicks a tiny gold lighter and his eyes on her seem genuinely puzzled. Jenny has a strong sense of justice. Eric has spun in and doesn't realize it.

Now, out of the kitchen comes this doll carrying a tray of hors d'oeuvres. She looks about twenty, so she can't be Betty.

"Hi!" she says. Quickly she sets the tray on the coffee table and extends her hand to me as a man would. She's Irish, I can tell. "I'm Betty and I'm running late." She looks me up and down, nods and rolls her eyes at Jenny. "Uh-*huh*," she says, arching toward me momentarily, then swinging away. "Where's my drink? What the hell?"

"Oh!" Eric closes his eyes, winces, vibrates his head. "Drinks! I'm sorry." He snaps his fingers then inclines his head for our orders.

Scotch. *Great* scotch. He leaves the bottle on the table so we can admire it. Twenty-five years old, the label says. Probably cost him half a carton. Expansively, we sit back drinking it. Eric shoots his cuffs, crosses his tailored legs. He's charmed by Jenny; his eyes rarely leave her bare shoulders, her full breasts.

I look around. Over the dining table, set with heavy silver on thick linen, hangs a crystal chandelier. That is *not* standard issue. And books, a whole wall of them, expensively bound with lots of gilt, the complete works of . . . everyone, it seems. Not a paperback among them.

Generously, Eric pours more of his ancient scotch. For several minutes he has been trying to finish some story, but he can't get the girls' attention. They are examining Jenny's new, surveyed dress.

"You should have seen him." Jenny laughs. "Pins in his mouth, sighting and cocking his head. My fierce jet fighter pilot."

"Elizabeth," Eric says for the third time. He has his hands poised to resume his anecdote, but his smile is almost gone. Women would chatter right through an earthquake. The San Andreas Fault could let go right now and swallow this whole side of the room, but they wouldn't even notice.

"There's only one way," I tell him. "Start telling me about some cute secretary up at Wing."

"I heard that," Betty warns. She composes herself. "Yes, love?"

Eric sighs, lower his hands.

"Oh, I'm sorry, sweet." Betty laughs. "Look at him. Aw-w, poor thing. We got carried away. We were acting like civilians or something." She looks at Jenny. "What are we? *Are* we civilians?"

"Military dependents," Jenny says in her officious voice. "Camp followers."

"If I could get in a word edgewise . . ."

Betty shushes us, then sits respectfully at attention but on the verge of exploding into laughter. She wipes off her smile and bats her eyelids at Eric.

"I was *telling* you about the colonel," he says finally. "I had drafted a letter for his signature, and he came into my office asking what 'penultimate' means."

"So?"

"Well, it's a commonly used word. I mean, can you imagine a full colonel not knowing—"

"Sure." Betty nods; "What *does* 'penultimate' mean?"

"Betty, please . . ."

"Eric, most of us went to Fresno State or the equivalent. My folks were slack-jawed Okies. . . ."

Silently, white-faced, he rises and excuses himself to check on the meat.

After he's gone, she shrugs and swings her legs from beneath her to the floor. "I'm sorry about the scene. It's me, I guess. I must be going into menopause or something." She hefts the table lighter and snaps it, deeply inhales her cigarette. "Eric does all our fancy cooking. He's really very good at it. I bought him a chef's hat not long ago. As you might gather, he doesn't think I'm funny. He digs all this seasoning and basting. He should have been a *French-a-man*. Me, I couldn't care less. I make fantastic hamburgers, period. My idea of sauce is A-1. Hey, John, I love your Jaguar. It moans so sexily when you go by every morning. Or is that *you* moaning? But, my God, where do you all sit? With the dog and everything? And where will you put the baby?"

"Oh," Jenny says, "no problem. John has got it all figured out, haven't you, Ace? I am to hold the baby, of course, and sometimes the dog, if the top is up—correction, if 'the hood is erected'—is that right, John? I get the hood and the bonnet and the boot confused—while *he's* over there driving. I'm covered with dog hair, my hip is dislocated, and I'm holding a wet baby while he plays—who is it?—Ascari, Nuvolari?"

"That's your *only* car?" Betty asks. She is beginning to realize that I am crazy.

"That's it."

Betty exhales, leans over to pat Jenny's knee. "Kid, you are a trooper. A real sport."

Eric returns. "So far, so good." He checks his gold Rolex, sits beside me and reaches for his drink. "Seriously, John, you should try to finish college. There are two colleges within an hour's drive. Check on their evening classes."

Oh, sure. I come in dragging my tail from dive bombing, change, wolf down supper, and drive fifty miles to sleep through Plato or somebody.

"It's been too long, I'm afraid."

"Oh, nonsense."

"Ten, eleven years."

"So what?"

"I don't remember anything about math or physics or—"

Holding up one hand like an AP, he stops me. "Your major was what?"

"Engineering, but I completed less than—"

"Forget engineering, forget anything technological. Such curricula are too demanding. All you want is what the Air Force wants, right? A *degree*. Any sort of a degree is better than three and a half years of nuclear physics. The promotion boards handle hundreds of folders a day. 'Does he have a degree, yes or no?'"

This makes no sense to me, but Eric has probably sat on promotion boards.

"Listen," he says. "You've got management experience. You're an *officer,* for heaven's sake. Some colleges recognize this and automatically grant credits for certain introductory courses, perhaps enough to add up to a whole year's work. Okay? Now add that to what you've completed and *voilà!* You may reenter as a *senior.*"

"In what?"

He shrugs. "In whatever your counselor suggests. And in whatever comes easily for you."

His food is easier to digest than his advice. We compliment him, and he shrugs. "It's simply a matter of selecting the right cut. You can't patronize the commissary for this sort of thing. The meat must be of the right age, the marbling must be perfect."

Snifters of Courvoisier with our coffee. Jenny smiles across the candlelight at me. We are full and content. I am a little giddy at the thought of some kindly godlike professor waiving all academic obstacles. As the brandy warms me, anything seems possible. I am grateful to Eric for his advice, and I tell him so.

"Well, I'm glad." He claps my shoulder. "Ladies, did you hear that? John's going back to college."

Jenny gives me this skeptical look and, without comment, continues her conversation with Betty who briefly holds up one thumb in acknowledgment but never shifts her gaze.

"Well, now that we've assured your success in the Air Force, perhaps you can help me with *my* career."

Laughing comes so easily now. "Certainly. Anything."

"I warn you"—Eric smiles,—"I'm serious."

"Speak."

"I want to get checked out in the F-86."

"No sweat. Talk with Pete or the major."

"I have. You see, I've never flown fighters. I've never flown *any* sort of jet."

"Oh." Jesus. No wonder.

"Pete suggested that I go through the program at Nellis."

I nod.

"But that's a long, drawn-out course, as you know. And, after all, I have four thousand hours."

"In multiengine?"

"Yes, in multiengine aircraft. But surely there's enough correlation that . . . I mean, fighters can't be *that* difficult to fly. Is the F-86 unforgiving? Is it dangerous?"

"It flies itself."

He smiles. "Exactly."

"It's not the bird that's dangerous. It's the sort of flying we do. We're crazy."

"John, I simply want that F-86 checkout on my records for the same reason that you want a college degree on yours. Career-wise, it's important. I won't be flying much with the squadron. Just round robins and short cross-country flights, all straight and level." He smiles.

"Why?" I ask bluntly. "I mean, okay, you get checked out, but to get the F-86 suffix on your records, you have to become combat ready, don't you?"

"We'll see," he says mysteriously. "One step at a time. The important point to remember is that we are assigned to Tactical Air Command. And if someone hopes to move upward in TAC someday . . . well, you see?"

"Why not SAC or MATS, where multiengine experience counts?"

"Slow horses, John. Slow. And *nervous*. In MATS I was simply a poorly paid airline pilot. You fly the line. Railroad seniority. And SAC's star is waning now. They've had their heyday, their spot promotions. Besides, who wants to stand alert and play their silly games day in and day out?

No, John. At the moment TAC is *the* place to be. New wings, new birds on the way, new blood. Rapid expansion provides opportunities."

Anger is building within me. Christ, this guy plays the Air Force like some guys play the stock market. *Sell MATS, buy TAC.*

"So," he asks quietly. "What about it?"

"I don't know," I tell him. "I'll talk with Pete, but I'm nobody."

7

GEORGE

As soon as I throw back the covers, I know it's one of those one-percent days. Out of three hundred and sixty-five, there are usually three and a half days of unlimited visibility. I'm not talking about what Weather calls "Ceiling and Visibility Unlimited"; here, half the days are, theoretically, CAVU; but there's a real difference. Climb to forty-five and you can see not only all of L.A.; you can see the outskirts of San Diego. *That* is "visibility unlimited," and it's as rare here as it is in England. Everything has to be just so, and God can't seem to manage it often.

Jenny, as unglamorous as she ever gets, hair awry, no makeup, is leaning on one elbow.

"What?" she asks irritably.

"Nothing," I say, and lower the shade again. She drags my pillow over her head. Usually, I want no breakfast—just coffee and orange juice, Danish pastry when it's fresh—so there's no point in her getting up at six.

Whistling, I shave and ram my feet into heavily starched suntans. Last night I changed my brass to this fresh shirt, the silver captain's tracks, the senior pilot's wings. My low-quarters are gleaming, my overseas cap new. After walking the dog, I vault into the Jag, switch on the pump, bring the sexy engine to life. As I drive past the Camstons', Betty, pulling her robe together, leans out their front door to wave. Laughing at her pretension of swooning, I blip the throttle and wave back.

I have a test hop, no big deal now that the mechanics know which hose connects to which. A surging regulator, a leaking hydraulic coupling, once a split-flap landing when one of the flap motors failed *and* the connecting shaft sheared. But no more flameouts or fires or elevator-actuator cables off their pulleys. I guess the crash crews are getting rusty, playing checkers, dreaming up improbable situations.

The bird is cleanly configured. I taxi out. It's chilly, and there's a twenty-five-knot wind down the runway. A good, sweet engine. The first bird of the day to release brakes.

"Hey, give us a thrill," calls someone from Mobile.

So I rotate her into a steep climb and am at traffic pattern altitude before I'm over the far end of the runway. I know that all over the flight line, everyone has stopped to watch. They know that it's no trick, that I'm not showing off *my* abilities, but simply showing off the bird. I'm treating them to a few seconds of real beauty. I wish that I could make our Flying Safety officer understand this. ("You'll have all the kids trying it," he says. Yeah, he's right.)

Up to forty I go, avoiding airways as I climb, and level momentarily. Every five thousand, I have to record engine instrument readings. I cruise-climb her up to forty-five thousand feet, then let the Mach build. Forty-six; forty-seven. I wonder whether she can go higher. I've never been so high before. God, the *view* from up here. By simply twisting my head, I can actually see Bakersfield to the north and—is that *San Diego* to the south? Leaving the throttle full forward, I ease her up to fifty thousand, but that's it. My fuel is down to a thousand pounds. If I try the least little turn, she stalls. My mask flutters. Down to forty-five, and I half-roll her for the required terminal-velocity dive. She's so sweet. Just a little wing roll going through Mach 0.97. I wait as we silently plummet. If there's ever been a bird that will exceed 1.1, this is it. Obviously, she came out of the jigs at Inglewood with a perfectly aligned frame, and the flaps and ailerons were installed at exactly the optimum droop angles. Mach 1.0 comes immediately. She's one in a thousand, a real love. At twenty, I'm level and at 0.93 when I see this flight of four ahead. I overtake them and decide to race beneath then pull up to rock them with my wash. In fact, I'm beneath them before I notice the colored bands around the leader's fuselage. The Old Man! So I break down and enter the acrobatic area where, pleasantly, I tire myself before landing.

"Best bird I ever flew," I compliment the chief, but when Dan walks out to ask how his bird had checked out, I tell him she's a real dog.

"Yeah. Fuck you," he says, grinning.

As I hang up my chute and helmet, the crash phone rings. Pete and the major plot the coordinates on the wall map. Everyone gathers around. It's very quiet. We hear the Rescue chopper go fluttering and thumping off to the northeast. The Old Man's flight and another have joined the search.

"Who?" I whisper. I look at the scheduling board. I can't place him. Dark, as I recall, and short, one of Smokey's new lieutenants. As I hang my G-suit in my locker, I look at the lieutenants. They are pacing.

Kids take chances. It's that simple. No planning, no second thoughts. If they live to be twenty-five, they're over the hump. Ask any automobile insurance company. In the fighter business, we say five hundred hours. By then they've usually scared themselves enough to settle down to business. They've gotten it out of their systems—buzzing, flying under bridges and wires, acrobatics on the deck, pushing marginal weather too far. Everybody goes through it—every young fighter pilot, at least.

Maybe the multiengine guys get their kicks synchronizing props or something.

This isn't the last one, I know that much. With fifteen kids, we'll probably lose three or four. That's why Major Slocum was dumb to accept so many. It'll cost him his job and limit his future promotions. The worst gambler in Vegas would back off from his odds. That's why the other two squadron commanders keep slapping him on the back and buying him drinks.

That evening, after Rescue had followed up a highway patrolman's tip and located the wreckage, strewn along two miles of desert near Bicycle Lake, the major calls a meeting and gives everyone the word. He figures the lieutenant was buzzing, and he's probably right. On the deck at speed, the altimeter is a little off, and desert terrain, like water, is deceptive. Buzzing isn't professional, he says.

I guess we flight commanders were lucky. At the age of these kids, we'd had the challenge of combat and therefore didn't need any extra excitement. But all these clowns have is that machine and the desert, and I expect the two will continue coming in contact at an alarming rate. So we cancel solo flights and we brief every move we'll make in the air. That's what the major wants. We must exercise "adequate supervision," he tells us with growing concern. At Selfridge, he reminds us, he'd had no problem breaking in second lieutenants, and he'd raised a squadron of real tigers.

"First-class flight commanders!" He nods meaningfully. "*That* was the difference."

Two days later, one of Whit's guys loses control turning a tight final approach, so Whit's in the doghouse, and so is Dan, who was in Mobile Control. They don't say anything, but they slam their locker doors harder than necessary. Jesus, what can they do, fly every aircraft in their flights? We brief and we critique, but it's water off a duck's back. The kids keep sighing and looking out the window. We're preaching to the choir.

In time our squadron's accident rate sets a new peacetime record. We've lost three guys and four birds within five weeks. They're crashing F-86s faster than North American can build them. And, after every accident, Ninth Air Force calls the wing commander back to North Carolina to explain his managerial deficiencies. If the colonel hadn't been an ace during the war, the general would have canned him long ago. It's crazy, because while the colonel's back East, we lose another one.

"Imagine that!" he tells the major in our presence. "Here I am, see, crawling around on the general's carpet when the phone rings. He writes something on his pad and hands it to me. 'Another accident,' it says."

Out at the air-to-ground range, we have had a new foul line bulldozed two hundred feet farther away from the strafing panels, and further, we have established higher release altitudes for dive-bombing. At the base, Mobile Control now has to be manned by one of us four flight commanders. (Oh, the *cheers* from the first lieutenants!) Our traffic patterns are so loose now that even the Flying Safety officer sighs.

"What else can we do?" Pete asks us one evening. "Are we forgetting something?"

As it turned out, we were. A month later, while the squadron is night flying, I lean back in the rickety chair in Mobile Control. The four-ship echelons seem to climb as their red-and-green navigation lights approach the pitchout points. In single file they rustle around overhead. All I can see, even when I'm standing outside and peering through binoculars, are lights, especially as they turn final approach and switch on their landing lights. If the interval is too close or someone is making a widow-maker final turn, I can radio him to go around, but I can't check the position of anyone's landing gear until they're flaring over the runway, and then it's too late.

While I'm considering this, I do a double take on this bird floating past. My God, no gear! I yell into the mike, fire a red flare, but it's too late. *Whoomp* go his empty drop tanks as they flatten and send rooster tails of sparks back. I may as well shoot myself with the flare pistol.

I tell the whole world to go around ("I can't," mutters some clown in the tower), grab the biggest fire extinguisher in sight, and start running, only to trip on the long mike cord and go sprawling. Maybe I should go into vaudeville; no, comedians have to be in better physical condition. Before I've run a hundred yards, I'm wheezing and practically dragging this giant foam extinguisher. They ought to fill them with helium or at least mount them on golf carts. Ahead, the sparks have stopped, and his navigations lights have gone out. He must be climbing out. Headlights are streaming across the ramp, the fire chief's pickup leading. I hear the bellow of the foam trucks, see their swirling lights. To save time, the red pickup jounces straight across the desert and beats me to the bird. His spotlight hits the cockpit, then me. The cockpit is empty. There is no fire.

I'm walking now but still dragging the extinguisher. The fire chief is laughing. "Jeez, Captain, for a minute I thought you was another belly landing."

I can't talk; I just stand there panting. As the foam trucks arrive, their spotlights play over us and the bird. I squint around against the glare.

"Where is he?"

The fire chief jerks his thumb over his shoulder. "He's okay." The lieutenant stands on the edge of the lighted area.

Pete and the major drive up in a jeep. Pete's jaw is set like a sheriff's. Without a word or a glance at the bird, he strides towards the kid, who acts as though he may resume sprinting. I fall in beside Pete.

"Easy," I say.

84

But Pete, old Training Commando that he was, isn't going to use the mule-training technique. His half-bunched fists are simply for face-to-face intimidation.

"Wasn't the horn working, Lieutenant? The red light?" Arms akimbo, his eyes terrible, he waits.

"I don't know, sir." The lieutenant's face swings helplessly toward mine. He notes my heaving chest, looks down.

Without another word, Pete turns toward the bird. The crane from the motor pool is a long time in arriving. We decide to switch to the northeast-southwest runway, and I use the major's radio-jeep as Mobile. Once the other birds are safely down, I return to the accident scene. Only one foam truck remains. The crane has raised the bird, the landing gear has been lowered and down-lock pins inserted. Later, in the hangar, with the bird on jacks and the hydraulic mule connected, they'll wear the landing gear out raising and lowering it. If a pilot really believes that he experienced a malfunction, he'll be there watching. If he knows he goofed, he won't. That's the way I decide about a guy.

Amazingly, there's little damage. The drop tanks, the landing light and the flaps—that's all. "Maybe," suggests our maintenance officer, "the flaps can be, uh, *straightened,* if you know what I mean, Major."

The major nods ecstatically. "Drop tanks are expendable, right? Landing lights . . . well . . ." He shrugs. "This isn't an accident, Colonel; it's an *incident*. Maybe the general doesn't even read incident reports."

I'll never forget the colonel's expression, that of a father who is trying to explain *Winnie the Pooh* to a particularly literal child.

"Have you ever met the general, Possum?" the colonel asks.

"No, sir. Not that I can remember."

"You'd remember."

"He reads all the message traffic?"

"Every word."

"What have we got to lose?"

Smiling grimly, the colonel pats his own bottom.

Everything really hinges on the condition of the flaps. Our Maintenance officer and the civilian from the sheet-metal shop slide their hands around like they're working an Ouija board. No big deal, they agree. The major whoops.

"*What* accident?" He laughs. "Show me the corpus delicti. That's what you can tell the general. John, go erase the tapes."

Even the kid is grinning. He throws up his arms and whirls around, lights a cigarette, nodding conspiratorily. Pete stares at him. Apologetically, he field-strips it. Pete's tongue rolls around in his cheek. His eyes never waver.

Pete claps his hands and tells us to assemble all the little bastards in the briefing room.

"It's time," he says grimly, "that they learn the facts of life."

"At ease, gentlemen," Pete calls futilely.

We make shushing noises and steer them around like children.

"SIT DOWN, GODDAMMIT!" Pete yells.

They sit. There is absolute silence. Not since their early cadet days have they heard such fury. Composing himself, Pete begins. Initially, they're attentive. Later, it's water off a duck's back. Their sighs suggest that he's still preaching to the choir. *They* hadn't crashed, had they? So why the big lecture? As in most classrooms, the clowns always choose the back row. We are seated in random order, and we should be seated by flights. Like parents, Bill and I need to be where we can separate the troublemakers. Of these, I seem to have drawn the most. Only Charles, my fine-looking New Englander, who is both older and quieter, seems mature. Obviously, he is bored with his Nellis classmates, with us and with our laxity, perhaps with the Air Force way of life. His eyes follow a restless pattern and finally quit returning to Pete's face. Instead, he watches a flight of red-tails, shimmering in their exhaust heat, as they line up on the runway. When they've departed, his eyes gradually swing toward mine. Neither of us drops his gaze. He is looking thoughtfully at me as though he's trying to decide something. We end up smiling in frank commiseration. It's amazing how quickly you can establish rapport with certain people; but, in a whole lifetime, you find just a few. Already I trust him. He and I should, in fact, be up there flying together instead of hearing Pete's litany of his former students who are dead now; killed by their own lack of discipline.

Along the back row, they are watching Red palm cards. He shuffles quickly on his knee, lets a skeptic cut, then snaps the aces out. Above their faint murmur of admiration, Red's weimaraner eyes sweep happily until they settle on mine. He shrugs, nods, collects the cards and puts them away, finally and attentively raising his chin toward Pete.

It's a delicate thing, this business of raising fighter pilots. *Teamwork,* we preach. If they've played team sports, it's easier. Some guys have to block, some guys get to shine. I guess I've always been a linesman, but I suspect that, in Red at least, I've got a quarterback. It's a precious quality. It's important. You want to nurture it. But you can't nurture dead things.

Pete calls us four flight leaders in. Feet propped on his desk, his dark hands rotating his Zippo in unconscious somersaults, Pete explains again. "We're used to older heads, right? You tell 'em something; they do it. Now we got a tribe of teenage Apaches, and we are politely suggesting that they not ride their ponies so fast. Right?"

Exactly.

He laughs. "Yeah, Jeez, I know. I remember looping bridges, but now . . ."

In the lounge, they are yelling and smashing the Ping-Pong ball. Suddenly, the five of us feel old. We have become mother hens. Pete shakes his head. "Well, you've got it. I can't do it. They're your Apaches, right? Calm 'em, but don't tame 'em. Do I have to say this? No. You know what I mean. What we want is simply a fighter squadron." A palms-up shrug. "No, I know, *not* simply. We want a *good* fighter squadron; we want tigers, but we want tigers who respect regulations. You are to create such animals. Somehow. Questions?"

For two months we play Training Command. I keep them at a formal distance and wait, but it's not working. I approach Pete.

"They're getting time under their belts, aren't they?" Pete leans back in his chair and tilts his head. "No accidents. We're getting there. Some of your guys have almost three hundred hours in the bird now."

I rise and grasp the doorknob. Pete stands, too, and comes around to lay his hand on my shoulder. "Okay, John. But *easy*, for God's sake. And *keep it high*."

I am a poor dogfighter, and I know it. With another two hundred hours of experience, they will beat me, some of them. Red, at least. He especially thinks that we captains are all old ladies, that as fighter pilots we are worthless. Records and ribbons don't impress lieutenants; they have to try you. I guess it's natural. I remember that I wasn't content to fly old Ken's wing in the P-51 until he had humbled me—the old dog, teeth bared, standing over the almost-grown pup. It is as primitive as hell, this dominant-male business. But once you have whipped them, they will listen to you. It's sad that kids are so immature, but that's life.

I take them on, one at a time, beginning with Red. The two of us climb to thirty-five, and I pump the stick. As he slides back into trail, I rotate my G-suit valve to maximum and ease into a turn. I try a couple of the tricks I learned at Hamilton, but I can't really move him ahead of the abeam position. We've lost ten thousand feet. Finally, canopy-to-canopy in a scissors, I outplan him and slide behind. Like a wild horse, he goes crazy trying to shake me. Finally, during a split-ess, he dives into the ground. The ground, we had decided during briefing, would be elevated ten thousand feet.

Up we go again, and this time I pull old Cat Man's favorite "stunt" on him. You're in a chandelle, and you keep feeding in rudder. It's really a controlled one-turn spin with a follow-up, high-G barrel roll. I screw it up, but it works against Red—*this* time.

And the others are easy, especially Charles. I'm going to have to work with Charles. He's really too bright to be a fighter pilot, too sane, too methodical, even less aggressive than I.

There's respect in their voices now. I doubt that Red still calls me "Mother Copley" behind my back. So I relax the pressure a little, ignore small infractions, get Pete's permission to let them fly in pairs, first on practice instrument missions, later on air-to-ground, finally on air tactics. I pair them with judgment—Charles isn't yet ready to fly with

87

Red, but Al is; Hank and Joe won't try to kill each other. I think they're over the hump now; they saw Bob Hoover's airshow the other day, and now they realize how far we all have to go to be great. Afterward, Bob gave his usual modest talk, telling how many times he'd screwed up as a test pilot.

8

GEORGE

HEY, WE'RE HAVING A PARTY! The lieutenants have invited us old couples up to their chalet for dinner. The entire squadron will be there.

Jenny is hesitant. She's in her ninth month now and has Nothing to Wear. Laura loaned her one of her largest maternity dresses, but it's silvery.

"I look like the Goodyear blimp," Jenny decides, turning before the mirror.

"No," I say, "your sides would say 'Goodyear.' "

Not funny. "Okay," I console her, "we'll send our regrets."

"*You* go," she says bravely, then reconsiders. Through the wives' intelligence network she has heard about these bachelors and all the girls up there. You can't discount this intelligence. I swear that if I crash-landed on the tundra and was rescued by a beautiful Eskimo girl ("Ha!" Jenny says), Jenny would know all about it within an hour.

"Absolutely." She nods. She begins sewing, her new Singer portable whining away, her face a girl's in its little light. "You are *not* going stag."

Most Air Force parties are a real drag. Same old thing. The wives gather at one end of the room and talk about their kids; the men migrate to the private bar at the other end and talk shop. Occasionally, from fifty feet away, Jenny will catch my eye and wrinkle her nose at me. Questioningly, I hold up my empty glass. She elevates her full one, shakes her head.

But this party will be different—in lots of ways, it seems. For one thing, no one seems to know the date, much less the approximate hour. For another, no one seems to be in charge.

"BYOB?" we flight commanders ask. "Should we bring food, casseroles, salad?"

Charles shrugs. "Don't ask me. I no longer live up there. I live in the BOQ."

Joe says that Horse will know. Horse is in charge of refreshments because he really likes to eat. "God, yes!" Dan says. "We had my flight over for dinner last Friday. Locusts!"

"No sweat, man," Horse assures me. "We've got it. Just show."

I'm not sure how I feel about a second lieutenant calling me "man." But he means no harm; all of these bachelors use this jazzy slang among themselves. They mimic dance-band musicians, pretend to admire the crazies down in L.A.

"Hey, Tim, dig this record when the brass comes in again. *Ten* of 'em, man."

Bachelors aren't very organized, I'm afraid. "Ah, *when?*" we persist.

"When?" Horse considers it, turns to Tim. Tim grins. "Not Monday."

"Anytime," Horse decides, and turns away.

"Well," Whit calls after him, "Friday?"

"Friday's usually pretty dull. Saturday might be better. We'll really be going by then."

"Friday, then," we old men quickly agree, although Dan would really prefer seeing the party after it becomes an orgy. "Say, 1900?" Whit suggests. "Depart Wherry at 1815?"

"Why not?" Dan says, "Scooter said to come whenever we get the Call."

"The Call?"

Dan laughs. "The Call of the Wild? Hell, I don't know."

"Shouldn't Whit be leading?" Jenny asks, poker-faced. "I mean, he *is* 'A' flight commander, isn't he?"

"Okay," I say.

"I mean, isn't there a *regulation* or an SOP concerning vehicle convoys? Is this a professional Air Force, or isn't it?" She shifts uncomfortably in her bucket seat. "Laura is right. Sport cars are ridiculous when you're pregnant."

One weak scotch and water, and she's a little drunk. That's what total abstinence does to a person. This baby is bound to be born a grouch. All the way up the mountain she's been needling me about our "uniforms" —our side-vent sport coats, our beige slacks, our loafers. Men lack imagination, she says, cocking her head at me so that Whit's headlights illuminate her batting eyelids.

"Okay, Blue Four," she yells into an imaginary microphone. "Let's close it up back there. The Professional Air Force doesn't operate sloppy convoys, you know." And when we pull up before the bachelors' ski lodge and automatically align our cars in echelon, she leans out to motion Dan a few inches ahead. "Let's dress it up, Blue Three," she calls.

"Oh, very well," Dan nods, and eases forward. "How's that?"

With the engines dead, we can hear the deep beat of the music. Stan Kenton at full volume. It holds back the forest. Smokey claps his hands and dances around. "Hey!" he calls. "Let's have an orgy." Grimly, his wife pursues him, swinging her purse at his head.

"Chocks!" Jenny says in mock alarm. *"You forgot to chock them."* No more for her tonight. I don't know, maybe it's the last phase of pregnancy, a sort of hysteria as the pain approaches.

The lodge is alight and pulsing. It reminds me of that evening in 1945 when I took this nurse dancing at the Palladium. We nearly got killed by the jitterbugs. The last thing Jenny needs is a hard body-block, so I open the door cautiously and prepare to run interference.

Amazingly, the large room is deserted. Then one of the doors along the mezzanine opens, and a pixie wearing a TWA stewardess's uniform hurries down the stairs.

"Hi," she calls, and flashes us a grin. "Sorry, but I'm late." Smokey tries to help her with her bag. "No, thanks, I'm used to it. Go on in. Booze in the kitchen."

Not to be denied, Smokey exits with her. Smokey is our lover, a quiet, effective wolf. His Valentino eyes melt loose women at every airport. But not this stew, apparently. He returns immediately, a little flushed, a wry expression acknowledging the rebuff. Stews know how to handle wolves.

Upstairs, a girl screams, a door flies open and a half-naked brunette runs out onto the mezzanine. Chasing her, popping a towel, is Tim, wearing only shorts.

"Oh!" she gasps when she sees us. Pushing him inside, she retreats, one hand to her mouth, her eyes amused. Tim catches the slamming door and waves to us. "Be right down."

Smokey, Tim's flight commander, returns the mock salute, then rubs his hands before the fire. "Hey!" he says. "Did you see that brunette?"

Tim's head reappears. A girl's hand is pulling his hair. Straining to keep us in sight, he yells, "There's booze in the kitchen. I —"

"Boy! Boy!" Smokey beams at us.

"This is ridiculous," his wife snaps. "Let's go."

"Now, Mother . . ."

"Oh, come on, Kitty," Dan's wife says, "don't be a prude. After all, there was no set time."

Around the entire mezzanine behind the closed doors young voices, male and female, compete with the hiss of showers. The music has stopped; a record has hung up on the spindle. Whit corrects the malfunction, lowers the volume.

"Stop it!" a girl's voice demands. "Quit!"

Jenny has become pale. She was strictly raised, the Bible prominent in her home; her father still questions my intentions.

"How you doing?" I ask her. Her intelligence estimate had not exaggerated the amount of sin here.

"Our dorm wasn't quite like this."

"How do you feel?"

"Like the fat lady at the circus." She looks up at the timbers of the lodge, frowns at the wild laughter. "The Circus Maximus."

Two lieutenants, Scooter and Joe, enter with a hundred-pound bag of potatoes. They nod to our wives during our introductions. "Welcome and so forth," Scooter says. "Potatoes." They dump most of the bag into the fire. Ashes fly.

"Good," we say, our wives biting their lips.

They police up potatoes, poke the fire. "Why don't we cook them here?" one asks the other.

"What? The steaks?"

"Why not?"

"What'll we do with all that charcoal?"

"You're right."

They disappear, reappear with bottles and glasses. "Drinks? Drinks, anyone?"

Hands rise.

"Bourbon or gin?" Joe rubs his hands. "How about gin? There isn't much bourbon."

"Gin."

They pour enthusiastically, half filling each tumbler.

"Mix?" we ask anxiously.

"Mix?"

"Tonic? Collins mix? Anything. Vermouth?"

They open the refrigerators, frown. "Let's see. Milk? Orange juice?"

"Orange juice. Ginger ale?"

"Orange juice."

The bottle is almost empty.

"How about ice?"

"Oh, yeah. Here." He hands me two cubes, bangs encrusted trays against the sink, obtains one cube per person.

"This isn't on my diet," Jenny says to me.

"Just nurse it," I whisper. "We won't stay long."

But we do.

Soon, we hear a mild explosion outside the lodge. The sound approximates that of a hot start on an old F-80A, a sudden ignition of pools of fuel. *Whoompf!*

Yells and confusion, the two lieutenants reeling back from the charcoal broiler and, suddenly among them, this beach goddess, wearing a revealing terrycloth robe. Anne. She holds their hands under cold water, pushes wet towels on their pink faces. Under her hands, they tremble like children, their mustaches, their eyelashes and eyebrows singed. Aghast, they feel them, consider their loss.

"You're okay, you're okay, you *idiots*," she croons. "Keep your hands in the water."

Later, her head still turbanned from the shower, she settles among us by the fire like a daughter, and dries her hair. Then, catching a brush thrown down to her from the mezzanine, she brushes it. Watching a woman brush heavy hair hypnotizes me.

Anne is Brad's fiancée. She is the only girl I've ever seen who is more beautiful than Jenny. But then she's only twenty-two or -three. She flies for American—I can imagine her, her hair pinned up, trim yet buxom, smiling from between the rows of First Class. "Bye! See you." A different world, I guess. Where a captain is important. And one that Brad will soon enter, unless their screening system is more rigid than ours. Brad can fly, but his judgment is terrible. He will pitch out hard, mechanically, into a thirty-knot cross wind. From Mobile I had to send him around twice yesterday. Flying is a lot more than coordination. Anne had pointedly asked Dan about Brad's competence, and those of us who had heard her had quit talking to hear Dan lie.

"Aw, well," Dan had said uneasily, "he's not Lindbergh, but how many of us are?"

"Will he be a good airline pilot?"

"How should I know?" Dan had laughed. "*I* wouldn't, would you, John?"

At midnight when we leave, the tempo seems to be accelerating.

Jenny is exhausted, and I'm a little drunk. "Not so fast around these curves, John."

We descend onto the desert floor, and I poke along because those headlights behind us might be old Second Fastest himself. They're closing rapidly. They pass. It's Smokey's Cadillac convertible. I decide to catch him.

"Don't, John."

"I just want to clock him for a second. He says it will do one twenty."

"Please don't. I feel woozy enough now."

I ease off; the gap widens. Kitty's probably raising hell with him. She's always raising hell about something.

"What did you think of Anne?"

Jenny looks at Smokey's dwindling lights. "Very nice," she finally replies.

"I couldn't find anything wrong with her," I say in admiration. "Not even her pacifism."

"Well, you certainly spent enough time looking. All you old men did."

"Of course, she's wrong about Korea. The U.S. didn't have a thing to gain by entering that war. She should read Dean Acheson."

"You have, I suppose."

"No, but Pete has. He's taking Command and Staff by correspondence, and they get into geopolitics and foreign policy. Pete says that we and the UN behaved selflessly."

"This is at Maxwell, this Command and Staff School?"

"That's right, but—" Jenny's dry laugh stops me. She can be pretty cynical. Washington has more con artists than Leavenworth, she had agreed with Anne, but quickly changed sides when Anne, a history major in college, remarked that *all* soldiers are mercenaries, in a way.

"Why, then," Jenny had asked me, "aren't we richer? Do you always accept the low bid? What were the MIG pilots making? Next time, don't jump at the first offer." Anne had begun blushing and her blush had deepened when Jenny had praised the patriotism of the poor airline pilots who have to eke out an existence.

"Hear, hear!" Charles had grimly applauded. To me he had whispered, "All soldiers are mercenaries as all women are whores." Charles and Anne, I gather, are intellectual enemies. They seem to have a love-hate relationship.

Ahead, I see the split-beacon flash from the base, then the green wink indicating an operational runway. Somewhere in the black sky a guy may be viewing them with relief.

"And what do you think of Charles?" I ask.

"I may leave you for him."

"I have a Jaguar. Charles doesn't."

"One more reason." Jenny is almost asleep.

Gently I swing the esses, looking for dust and perhaps an overturned Cadillac.

As I turn eastward from Jerry's Oasis, I see the unlit cruiser float out of the darkness. So I hold the Jaguar at fifty-five all the way to Wherry. Probably old Second Fastest. But, like us mercenaries, he is a comfort to have around when you're in danger.

The Air Force's Burn Treatment Center in San Antonio is, they say, the best in the world. That's where they sent Brad after they pulled him out of the cockpit at Kirtland three weeks ago. During takeoff roll, Brad had called that his brakes were dragging. Maybe so, but he was keeping up with Dan. You always use a lot of runway at Albuquerque because of the altitude. I remember that time in 1950 when Ed hit the dog there. Anyhow, Dan won't say much for fear of influencing the board, but I know what he thinks. He thinks that, to avoid falling more than a plane-length behind, Brad had jerked her off the ground and prematurely retracted the gear. Stalling, he had fallen onto his full drop tanks, ruptured their thin skins, and deposited twin streams of oily flame along two thousand feet of pavement. Once the aircraft had quit sliding, it was engulfed in fire. For some reason, Brad hadn't blown his canopy but had simply tried to open it electrically, and it hadn't fully opened. Then, still wearing his backpack, he had tried to squeeze through. That's where the firefighters found him, screaming and cooking.

Changing to our blues at Kelly, we took a taxi to the hospital.

"Five minutes, ten at the most," the nurse, an old major, says.

On the white sheets lies a lean Negro, naked except for a small towel over his groin. We suspect that she misunderstood the name, so Dan whispers it again to her. She nods and looks at us. Dan's eyes widen. *My God,* I think. Now we notice a strange smell in the room. The dark body lies flat, as though laid out for burial. Tubes feed and drain it. As we advance, we see the blond hair and the areas where the helmet and mask had preserved Brad's identity. Suddenly, the head rolls in pain, the face contorts.

"Lieutenant Bradley!" the nurse sings brightly. "You've got *compan-ee!*"

With effort, the swollen eyelids crack open, close again.

"Lieutenant Bradley! Honey! You've got company. Wake up, sweetheart."

"Forget it," Dan whispers.

"No. He should wake up now anyway. His morale is our main problem, I think." She keeps calling his name and gently running her palm over his hair. "He'll be angry with me if he doesn't get to see you."

The dark frame writhes, the chin lifts. In little stages, the eyelids open, the pupils glint, move over us, soften.

"Dan . . ." So faintly. "John."

"Hi, Brad," Dan replies brusquely, moving to his side. "How ya' doing, boy?"

The blond head nods weakly; the cracked lips try to smile, form words we can't understand.

Briskly cranking up the head of the bed, the nurse lifts her flabby arms to adjust the IV flow, then lays her hand on his forehead.

"Well," she smiles, "I do believe your fever is down, Lieutenant. Do you feel like talking for a minute to these young men? You do? *Fine*. Now not long, y'hear? Just for a few minutes," she warns us. Her eyes smile, but her manner is distracted. Nurses treat everyone except doctors like children. She leaves, and the door silently closes.

For thirty seconds there's a hush. Brad, like a brown, dying fish, wriggles upward, trying to get comfortable. He's coming and going, forcing his eyes to remain focused, swallowing hard. When he raises his pink hands (the gloves had helped), they tremble.

"I . . ." he finally begins. "I'm sorry I . . ." His lips form "screwed up." Suddenly his eyes are wide open, imploring.

"No," Dan and I say practically together, "*you* didn't screw up, Brad." Dan looks at me. "It was your engine," I decide. "You should see the turbine wheel." I look at Dan.

"Yeah," Dan lies, "it's a good thing you aborted. That bird was sick, Brad."

"Engine," Brad says in wonder.

"Was failing, Brad," I say much louder than necessary. For all his problems, he's not deaf. "The bearings were seizing." I nod as though I'm talking to my aunt who hasn't heard anything for twenty years. With my hands I even try to depict a bearing seizing a shaft until I realize how pornographic it seems. "No question about it. You *did* the smart thing: you chopped the throttle and aborted."

He can't seem to remember. His eyes examine the ceiling as though he's reading a striped-bordered emergency checklist being projected there. Finally he nods and whispers, *Throttle off. Landing gear up.*

"Right!" Dan nods.

"Perfect, Brad, boy," I add.

A grotesque grin. His eyes lower to survey his body. "Boy? Don't call . . . *boy.*"

We laugh appreciatively and tell him we'll send old Philbrook, who is naturally black, down to see him.

"Phil." He nods, coughs weakly. Unaccountably, his mind returns to the accident. "Fire!" he whispers, wild-eyed, as though it's a secret.

Dan quickly reaches down to pat his shoulder, freezes. Then, like the nurse, Dan strokes the singed hair with his wide, stubby fingers. "Yeah. She caught fire, Brad."

"But the fire's *out* now, Brad. *Out*. You're okay now." I can't control my voice.

"Canopy!" He hasn't heard a word. His eyes dart about. *"Fire!"* He grasps my arm, almost pulls me down onto him before I can regain my balance. *And I don't know what to do,* except push the call button clipped to the sheet.

Instantly, she's here, cooing reassuringly, easing me away from the bed, grasping his hand. Her voice is simultaneously soft and chastising; by now it must sound to him like his mother's. She holds a hypodermic syringe up, squirts a few drops. "Let go of the captain, honey," she says easily in her southern-belle drawl. *"I'm* here now, and I'm going to make you cool and sleepy, okay, sweetheart? Now, then, can you just roll over a little? Fine. That's it. Relax . . . *good*. All right, you'd better tell them good-bye, hear? Tell them to come again."

I'm not sure that I can move. It's as though she has hit *me* with that horse syringe of morphine or whatever it is. *O my sweet Christ, spare us this.* My childish mind has panicked. I try to calm myself, to breathe evenly, to reaffirm that *I* wouldn't be trapped by my own stupidity as this empty-headed boy was. Imagine *anyone* trying to crawl through such a narrow gap while wearing a parachute. Stupid, stupid, *stupid!*

"How is . . .?" He begins coughing and the phlegm terrifies him. Dan holds a Kleenex to Brad's parched lips and guesses, "Everyone?"

"Everyone." Like a child's, his nods are exaggerated.

"Fine, Brad," Dan says. "Busy though. Same old thing. Dive-bombing and LABs up at Inyokern, strafing and rocketry at Goldstone. Old John is hogging all the flying time while I sit in Mobile."

"Bullshit," I murmur. Brad's eyes smile. The shot is getting to him now.

"Everyone," I say, "wants you to hurry up and get better." He wants another Kleenex, but the tubes restrain his reach.

"Can't cough it up, honey?" She is back with us, checking his pulse, quieting him. "Well, I'll give you a big shot of Jack Daniel's" (winks broadly) "to loosen that old phlegm, sweetheart."

Brad grimaces at the taste, regains control, tries to see around her. "Dan?"

"Yes, Brad?"

"Do you think . . . I could ever . . . ?"

"Ever what, Brad?"

95

"Fly," he whispers finally.

The nurse laughs. "Why, honey, *of course* you can. But first you have to be discharged. And to be discharged, what must you do?"

"Get well." He nods.

"And then?" she asks archly.

"Date you." He is very sleepy now. He grins.

She winks again at us. "I know you fly-boys. Promises, promises. Want to lie on your side now, sweetie, and get a little sleep?"

He resists her. He is, I realize, still awaiting Dan's answer.

"No question about it," Dan lies. "In fact, we went down to Inglewood last week to pick up your new bird. They're probably painting your name and 'American Airlines' on it right now."

"No date, no discharge. *Remember.* Now, then, gentlemen, I think he needs a little rest. You tell that little stewardess that I am not going to let her beat my time with this sweet thing. No, sir."

Expertly she rolls him onto his side, and we see the skin-graft dressings.

"Can we bring you anything, Brad? Besides Anne, I mean," Dan calls, grinning at us. "Your motorcycle?"

Brad is asleep.

"Well," the nurse says after we have walked a few yards down the hall, "his skin grafts are coming along just beautifully, but his kidneys . . . they are always the problem."

We wait, but she just gives us this tight-lipped smile and squeezes our arms. "Write to him. I'll read your letters to him." She pats our arms and goes back into Brad's room.

Two weeks later Brad dies. Horse escorts the body to Alabama. At the base chapel, the chaplain runs through the usual memorial service.

We line up with the steeple and ease down to three hundred feet. Joe is tucked in on my left, Hank is two plane-widths out to my right. The element leader's slot is empty. We are slow and easy, right on time. Beautiful Anne is probably standing on the chapel steps with Dan's flight. There they are, looking up. I doubt that I'll get to see her after we land.

Jenny is beautiful nursing Sam, but the crazy kid may have to go on a bottle, her doctor says. This week Art is the base pediatrician, so he is reading like mad trying to stay ahead of Sam.

Now, having no further excuse to avoid enrolling in evening classes, I drive twice a week down to this small college in San Bernardino. The English class (Twentieth-Century European Fiction) is worth the round-trip mileage on my bald Dunlops, but I can't stay awake during Economics even though the prof hops around a lot to prove how dynamic his course is. That's my fault, I know, because where would the world *be* without economics? It's just that I can't get too excited about the Taft-Hartley Act and all those bar-graphs in our textbook. This prof is probably a little insane because he's so smart. He keeps waving his hornrims around and dropping them when he rushes to the board. Once he broke both lenses and thereafter nearly killed himself crashing into his desk and falling across the podium. No wonder he considers teaching such a challenge.

When the English prof, who sometimes acts a little strange too, becomes dreamy and poetic with his eyes a bit out of focus, he catches me up into his mood. I like him, especially for not laughing when I asked about the symbolism of the snowstorm when Hans Castorp has this vision. He doesn't wipe you out as our English Composition prof did at Purdue.

This tootie (as the lieutenants would call her) in *The Magic Mountain,* Claudia Chauchat, said something which I found myself mulling over yesterday at Fort Sill. She said that the essence of morality consists of exposing one's self to danger and sin. I guess, by that standard, our squadron is made up of *saints.* We had been out most of the night in Oke City and all of us had such hangovers that we were blacking out at two Gs. You could almost hear old Whit's gang groaning during the pull-outs from dive-bombing. Dan's flight had it easy—just a flat napalm run on a column of burned-out tanks—or it *would* have been easy if they had immediately lined up with the proper clearing. (Everyone was a little concerned because the bleachers, loaded with graduating cannon-cockers and VIPs, lay in a clearing, too.) I thought we'd get to strafe "enemy troops," but Smokey drew that slip out of Pete's hat. So, Jesus, we drew the skip-bombing, and the aerobatics. Well, the delay fuses worked, and the five-hundred-pounders skipped and blew up the enemy command post, or whatever it was; and no one flew through a tree or shrapnel. But the aerobatics were really sloppy because no one wanted to pull Gs. When I made the high-speed run past the stands (nearly clipping the FAC's whip antenna) and pulled up for the vertical rolls, I blacked out cold and had to guess when to lay in full aileron.

I'm glad everybody survived that circus, and that the Jag started this evening, because I don't want to miss class again. It's May, and final exams are next week.

While I'm driving along in the foothills and thinking all this, I see in my mirror a familiar black-and-white machine pull out from a side road and begin closing. I let up on the accelerator until I'm legal and pretend that I don't see him, that I'm startled when he comes alongside. Man, he's *coming!* I can tell from the dust rising off the macadam behind him. Alongside now, he waves me over, and I shrug righteously and comply.

He gets out, and strides straight to me, leaving his clipboard in the cruiser. It's old Second Fastest himself and, as usual, it's a pleasure to see a man who has enough pride in his uniform to maintain sharp creases and gleaming leather.

"In a hurry, Captain?" he asks me. Good memory, too. I'm in civvies. It's the car, I guess.

"I wasn't speeding, Officer."

"I didn't say you were." He relaxes his erect posture a little, and tips his campaign hat back. "Hear about your buddy Harvey?"

"No."

"He's dead."

Everything stops. "No."

He shrugs, smirks. "Okay, he's not, but they buried him this morning."

"How?" I don't believe him.

"Airplane crash. Up at Moffett Field."

"Takeoff?"

"Landing pattern, they said. Probably going too fast around the corners, as usual."

No, I think. Probably too *slow* for the angle of bank, if anything.

"Well." He nods pleasantly, and turns. "Thought you'd like to know."

I nod. "Thank you, Officer. It was good of you to stop me."

"Well, you're the only Jag around now." His grin is wolfish, his eyes hidden by silvered sunglasses. The sun is almost down. For some reason he removes his campaign hat and his glasses. I'm startled. It's *me*. Almost. Our eyes search each other's.

He sighs and looks back down the road as though he expects to see that white speck raising dust, materializing out of the shimmer, booming toward us. But there is nothing except the wind.

"See you." He nods brusquely and strides back to his hot Olds.

The Economics prof is explaining this beautiful graph and looking with increasing enthusiasm directly at me. I guess he thinks my eyes are misty because I'm caught up in the beauty of the Federal Reserve System.

9

DOVER

WELL, WE'VE FINALLY got our orders. France, by God, to augment our NATO forces. We'll never get there, of course, because it's December, and we're scheduled for Fox Able. Fox Able is the North Atlantic route, the one established by the Ferry Command during the war—

Labrador, Greenland, Iceland, and Prestwick, Scotland. During the green months you can hop right across within a day or so. Piece of cake. But *in winter?* Well, you simply don't schedule Fox Able during the winter. The points of departure and destination are rarely open at the same time. No alternates, of course. So—especially when you're the sixth squadron moving in a ridiculous daisy chain, one squadron to a base along the route—you laugh a lot and count your green.

Three weeks ago, I drove Jenny, Sam, and the dog eastward to Jenny's folks in Indiana, hitching back to the base on a goony bird. As I wander through our house now, strange in its semipacked condition, Betty Camston knocks, asks how it went—the trip to the Midwest—and, well, I invite her in for a drink. Eric shipped over with the advanced party about a month ago. They sailed aboard one of those old troop ships.

"Everyone is entitled to one mistake," she says later as, silently, we sit listening to a record. "And Eric was *my* mistake."

She says this so brightly that I laugh. But then she looks directly at me, and I quit breathing. She squeezes my hand.

"You love Jenny?" she asks.

"Sure." I think about it, nod in confirmation. "Yeah. She's great."

"Yes," Betty says. "Yes, she is. Just checking." Then, without warning, she lifts my drink from my hand, sets it on the coffee table, and kisses me. Blindly, I roll her in and feel everything rising. Abruptly, her lips close, her sweet-smelling head tilts back, and she pushes weakly against my chest.

"Hold it!" she commands, easing away. "Just checking, see?"

"I'd be easy, wouldn't I?" I say this in awe.

"Yeah." She kisses me lightly on the forehead, rises, smooths her skirt. "A piece of cake, I'm afraid. Now then, one of us had better leave posthaste—postchaste?—*immediately,* else we shall never again be able to look our respective spice in the eye. Not that I want to. Is there by chance an underground passage? No? Must I cross the street like a brazen hussy?"

"We could rig up a disguise. We could go in horse costume."

"You, sweet child, aren't going anywhere. Thanks for the drink, the—everything. If I don't show up in France, if I decide to stay in L.A. with my mother for eighteen months, give my love to Jenny. Literally," she adds drolly. "Otherwise, who knows, kid? *C'est la vie,* meaning 'Repent at leisure.' Be careful. Or is that bad luck?"

"What?" I unclip my mask and hold my helmet away from my ear. "Say again." Our engines mask Betty's voice.

The desert wind whips her short hair across her face. "I say, it's just like all those cavalry pictures—the yellow scarves and gloves." Her megaphoned hands fall and she waits until I nod, then quickly reaches up to touch my hand. She's crying. *My God,* I think, what's happening? I feel so tender toward her.

Suddenly, Whit's flight lunges almost in unison out of the diagonal row of birds, swings into shimmering trail. Along either side of their yellow taxi-line, wives, stews, crew chiefs wave. The pilots' gloved hands rise briefly, the helmets nod. As they approach, Whit sees Betty by my bird, unclips his mask, grins at us, then shakes his head in mock severity. Pouting, then laughing, she blushes and waves him away while he bounces in that exaggerated pantomime indicating laughter. He buttons up again.

When we line up and advance our throttles to one hundred percent, I try to get her out of my mind. My eyes flit aimlessly around the panel, turn toward Red and Al. Red looks back at Joe, then nods. We roll and, within fifteen seconds, as peripherally the little colorful area near Ops flashes by, I think, Aw, to hell with Whit; I'm glad she came down to see me off.

We lift, raise our gear handles, and watch it all fall away—Betty, George Air Force Base, scenic Victorville, Route 66, Daggett, Barstow and the dry lakes to the north. Ahead, angling down in wind-blown snakes, are the smoke trails of Whit's flight. I link our trails with his. We climb.

Those impossible Frenchmen. If they had finished our bases last summer, as agreed, we could have gone then. But, as old Eric had written Betty, they're in no hurry. As always—and I guess they exasperated Caesar's soldiers, too—they come to work with a goatskin of wine, some bread and cheese, and they work about four hours a day. When they aren't eating, they're smoking and shrugging. What I can't understand is how they could have put up all those cathedrals with concrete that lasts a thousand years, and yet can't build a runway that will hold up a little seven-ton fighter. According to our new group commander, Colonel Bronton, who looks like that Egyptian premier Nasser, some guy from Germany made an emergency landing on our new runway last month and his wheels broke right through. Obviously, the French contractors are crooked. When they think it's important, they can pour better concrete than anybody, but when they're building airbases for the dumb Americans who save their asses about every twenty-five years, they probably drive one mixer at sixty miles per hour down the runway, then spread it around.

As for the flying, I'll say this for my guys: they've played it professionally so far. Clouds, turbulence, sleet, crap, whatever—every time I've looked up from my instruments, they've been right there, right where I told them to fly—back a tad farther than usual, and loose so they can bounce with the gusts. We even had freezing rain when we let down here. A mean inversion. That's the worst—freezing rain—that and thunderstorms.

We've gotten as far as Dover (Delaware, not England), a MATS base, but now our chain of six fighter squadrons—there's another whole wing of birds committed to NATO, and they're backed up from Scotland along Fox Able—is bogged down. Weather. And you can't push a chain; even Ike and the Pentagon know that. But TAC does wish we'd clear out of the States so they can get back to monitoring the formation of our replacement wings. They'd like to pitch us to United States Air Forces, Europe—USAFE—and wash their hands of us. Meanwhile, Christmas is almost here and our families are scattered all the way back to California. Every time the mail catches up with us, my father asks how I like France. Even Jenny is confused. It's just beginning to sink in that we might not reach France until we are doddering old men. The Lost Legion, or something.

Some Christmas. In my wallet I've got, what?—thirty-five bucks. In my overnight bag are two wrinkled uniforms, a few blue shirts, some underwear already yellowing from hand washings. That's all I could cram into the radio bay, that and a few paperbacks. Faulkner and Hemingway.

Everyone is getting a little restless. We keep checking the weather up ahead. I'm glad *I* don't have to make the decision. That's why Nasser and our wing commander draw such big salaries—Nasser, actually, because the Old Man's going to leave us now that we're bogged down. He's got to get over there and kick some French asses. If Nasser goofs, there'll be seventy-five fighters up in some snowbank or bubbling at five hundred fathoms. But he won't goof, because he wants to make brigadier. Oh, no, he'll wait until we can *see* France from here before he says okay.

The club isn't much. At 1700 when the bar opens, we go in, and we're the only ones there. All the Military Air Transport Service guys are home assembling tricycles or something. They're mostly old guys with green instrument cards and big butts. It takes them about a month to fly nonstop across the ocean. They've got these Noah's Arks—C-124s with two or three stories—and they sit up there over the wart-nose drinking coffee and making one-degree corrections on their autopilots. Maybe they go down in the hold and jog to break the monotony, I don't know. One time I caught a ride out to the Coast on one, and this captain told me to go ahead and try the controls. Flies like a fighter, he'd said. I'd shrugged and twisted this wheel and, about five minutes later, up comes the right wing. And then it takes about three of us, straining hard, to keep the ark from capsizing. The bastard had obviously never flown a fighter.

Someone finally talks the motor pool officer into giving us a bus and driver so we can see the town of Dover and eat some of the famous seafood. We keep piling into this little bus so it almost stops between gears. Then it takes this seafood restaurant about a week to prepare all the clams and lobsters. When they bring out the lobsters, Callahan, who's from Boston, jumps up and gives a little lecture on how to dismantle lobsters. He's very serious. I guess he's afraid we'll just try to bite off the claws and tail and form snap judgments about seafood.

"You've got to suck the legs," he says, but it doesn't seem worthwhile.

By the fourth evening, with Christmas only two days away, we decide to have a party. We talk to the bartender. Air Force bartenders are usually moonlighting crew chiefs, and all we have to do is make them honorary members of our squadron and they'll mix up some kickapoo for us. To make anyone an honorary member, you simply pour some Chivas Regal over his head, quote our Latin motto, and give him a squadron patch. Charles is really impressive when he does the anointing, because he pronounces the Latin with such authority. The words take on a power of their own.

"What do they mean?" we once asked Charles.

"Oh, fight the weak. Something like that." He mustered a sick little smile.

Occasionally, he and our two West Pointers get all hung up in the dumbest arguments: whether Clausewitz still makes sense, whether Lee was greater than Grant, whether—get this—whether *Beowulf* is an allegory. That's when Whit looks at Dan, and they move on. Finally, I can't take any more and follow them.

If that's what you learn in college, who needs it? I mean, hell, we learned all about *Beowulf* back in high school, when Miss Roberts would lunge around, cackling like Grendel's mother. She even had this big wooden sword which the shop teacher had made for her. *Hrunting,* she called it and, Jesus, she'd slash around. She could even read *Beowulf* in Anglo-Saxon when her dentures weren't giving her trouble. A few teachers thought she drank, but she didn't. She was just crazy.

This bartender is a natural victim. The guys keep buying him drinks, and now he doesn't even bother to hide his glass. Within half an hour, he decides that he once crewed fighters. F-80As, by God. Thumbs up all along the bar.

"Shit," he says fondly, "I knew you guys were fighter jocks the first time you walked in here."

"Aw, c'mon, Fred. How'd you know?"

"How'd I know?" Fred reels back, pouring. "Why, just the way you walked in. You look everybody right in the eye, y'know? You act like you own the fucking place. You're lean and mean, and you all kinda move around in formation. How's this?"

Hank samples it, rolls it around on his tongue, slaps the bar with the flat of his palm and falls off his stool flat on his back. It's a trick of his; he never hurts himself because he slaps the floor like a judo expert. "Maybe a little more vodka," he calls from the floor.

Anyhow, they've got this bartender believing he's a member of the Lafayette Escadrille or something, and his jigger begins boiling over like a fountain.

"Here's to the I-16, Chief!" I yell on an impulse.

He looks blank, so I know he never crewed F-80As, but I don't expose him. Charles gives him our secret formula for kickapoo, and he listens conspiratorially, wincing every now and then. The name is corny, I know, but it's really wicked. Not too many bars stock the high-proof vodka.

"You say you got this recipe from the *Russian* Air Force?"

"Shhh!"

"Yeah?" Dubiously he begins pouring into an aluminum GI boiler and noisily throwing the empty bottles into the trash. When the crème de menthe goes in, smoke begins rising.

Charles backs away. Hank tests it with a dipper and does his fall again. "That's it! Now for the frog legs. Where can we buy some frog legs?"

"Jeez, you got me," the bartender says. "Maybe the kitchen has some drumsticks."

"No, no, you'll ruin it if you put anything but frog legs in it."

It's 1800 and pitch-black outside. From the BOQ rooms upstairs, our guys are descending, their hair still damp from the showers, their eyes taking in the younger wives in the next room. And, conscious of all this attention, the wives start behaving unnaturally, squealing and laughing, flouncing around in the dumb winter fashions of 1954. I'll simply never understand why women like calf-length skirts. They look like little girls wearing their mothers' dresses. If you're a woman with nice legs, why cover them up?

This cute brunette with her hair in a ponytail can't get through the front door with all the clothes she's carrying. Old Smokey, our lover, hurries to pick up some slippers she's dropped. He leans against the doorjamb and feeds her his corny line. We laugh when, knowingly, she cocks her head at him, waves a slipper, and keeps moving.

This club is like a library; we can't seem to get it off the ground. At George by now there'd be drunks lying on the floor. But this is a family club. The dining room is geared to kids in high chairs. I can just visualize all the MATS guys and their wives wondering whether to order wine with their dinner. Well, in a way, it must be nice to fly their air-line schedule and know you're going to have so many days off between runs.

We are halfway through a game of Horses, and I was high man until Dan and his clowns muscled in. I can see it now: the way they're rolling sixes, I'm going to end up paying. And then Joe starts kidding me about how slow my bird is. Well, I guess so, I tell them. Look at the tail numbers; my bird is a little older.

"A *little?*" Joe laughs. "Hell, it's Rickenbacker's old SPAD. You can see where the top wing used to be."

Dan leans over my shoulder. "Hey, lover," he murmurs, "what say you and I slip out and see what's doing in town, okay?"

I shake my head and talk about going to bed early. "That's what I mean, lover. Or are you holding out for Betty Camston?"

"Dan," I grab hold of his arm, make him look at me. "*Nothing happened.* Honestly."

"Of course not, lover. Hell, I saw her practically jumping up into your cockpit."

"Dan, I'd believe you."

"Well, you'd be a goddamned fool."

"She's not that sort, Dan. She's a lady."

"Yeah. Okay, John. Okay! Now let go of my goddamn arm before I get gangrene."

In the middle of the floor Red and Major Slocum are Indian wrestling. Red has about a yard of reach on him, so he wins every time. Not even Nasser can take Red because Red's so limber and has such good balance. He's like a big orange spider with a mean sense of humor.

I'm bored with Horses. I may even be bored with drinking. I'm going back to the BOQ and read Faulkner. It helps, I think, to have reached a certain alcoholic plateau when you read Faulkner. It's easier, then, to slip into his rhythm. I know one thing though: Miss Roberts wouldn't think much of his run-on sentences. It wouldn't matter to her that he'd won the Nobel Prize with them. She'd graded papers for so many decades that even when she was reading a book, she'd blue-pencil in proofreaders' marks. Shakespeare was the only writer she admired, and she held reservations about him. She wouldn't read his sonnets because they are dirty.

Charles has promised to guide me in my reading, so I won't waste any more time with Ellery Queen and Agatha Christie. I like going to the library with him because he walks straight to the right shelves and begins handing me books.

"You'll like these two," he says. "Read them. They're literature." He's usually right; I do like them.

What's great about Charles is that he is modest—not about literature, but about his looks. When he walks into a room, all the women nearly faint. It's that lean, aristocratic face and dark straight hair that lies so perfectly along the contours of his head. "No," Jenny once assured me. "It's his *manner*, his courtly manner and those pale blue eyes." It's true: when he looks directly at someone, they simply quit doing whatever they're doing.

All this seems to pass right over Charles's head. Well, not always; sometimes he blushes and seems irritated. Like now, when the guys want him to make one pass through the fashion show and lead all the women into the bar. He is explaining some of Faulkner's symbols to me, things I hadn't particularly noticed, like the bear.

"You thought the bear was just a bear?"

"That's right," I tell him. Jesus, he'd find symbols in Air Force regulations. Still, I really like him. He's far and away the most mature of the lieutenants. In fact, I believe he's more mature than I am. Jenny once said that our dog is, but she was kidding, I hope.

Hank likes to ride Charles. "What ya' reading?" he'll ask Charles, leaning over his shoulder. "Where are the dirty pictures?" I doubt that

Hank has ever read a book. He grew up on a ranch in North Dakota and before his dad finally made him go to college, he drove a rotary plow two winters for the highway department. The only time Hank ever holds our interest is when he's telling blizzard stories, like the time he had to take a doctor through ten-foot drifts to this ranch house where a woman was having twins.

"And it was some kind of *cold*, gents. Sixty below with a forty-knot wind. When I hit that starter an hour later, the old diesel barely kicked over. That's when I got religion. That's when I quit drinking." He bangs his glass on the bar. "Innkeeper!"

"Hell, you never drove a plow, you lying bastard," Joe says, corking him.

"I didn't? You drag your Polish ass up there some January, and I'll show you." Hank throws Joe halfway across the room, then picks up the mess-hall dipper. "Is the kickapoo done?"

"It's still boiling," Fred says, looking at his watch with unfocused eyes.

I'm hungry, so I decide to ease out before it's too late. That stuff is like venom. But I can't get past Red. I feint right, then run left, but he grabs me. I'm Indian wrestling. Red is laughing so hard he's weak. No matter what I do, he nearly falls down laughing. I like good-natured drunks. Still, he can't stand to lose; something in him never gets that drunk. If I ever luck out and beat him, he'll drive me crazy for a rematch. So I wave him off and try to break away, but the squadron commander sees us and yells, "Get him, Johnny! Throw him on his ass. Show him how the brown-shoe Air Force handles punk kids."

Jesus. Did he have to phrase it so strongly? I sigh and grab Red's hand in earnest. Poor bastard. He can hardly stand up. Finally, watching his gentle eyes, I realize that he's out of it. He's gone. So I simply relax my pressure, and he starts snoring, his drink crashing to the tiles. I catch his head just before it hits the floor, and we park him on this long couch. Major Slocum's laughing and writing on a paper place mat: "KIA in fair combat by John Copley, 21 December 1954, and witnessed by: Possum Slocum," and a dozen other names.

I enter the dining room and see Scooter moving tables around. He's doing his elephant routine, holding up a limp arm from his chin and shrieking and trumpeting.

"Okay, Elephant," a concerned wife says, "let's move this one against that wall."

Scooter's really got elephants down pat. Somewhere, months ago, we saw this movie *Elephant Walk*, in which this herd pushes down a palisade wall and then tramples all the huts in the compound. That really got Scooter. He came back to the BOQ and began moving around with realistic ponderousness, shrieking and pushing our double-deck bunks around. Once, during maneuvers in South Carolina, he almost pushed our tent over. But you never know with Scooter. Sometimes he's a White Hunter wearing a pith helmet, flying boots, and a water pistol on his hip.

"Trader Horn," he will say, shaking hands. Strangers don't know what to make of him.

"Don't push it. Pick it up." The girl is exasperated. "You're going to break the legs."

Scooter pauses, lifts his head. "Lady, don't you know *anything* about elephants? Logs and natives we pick up. Sometimes pretty girls. That's all. Tables we push."

I wonder what set him off this time. Probably those squealing C-124 brakes. You can hear them for miles.

Near the MATS families, I find a table and sit down. Chores done, Scooter joins me. He's smiling his dopey smile. Scooter. No one knows how he got that name. Once he had been a professional musician, a trumpeter whose hero was Chet Baker. The first time I heard Scooter play, I thought he'd won the horn in a poker game. He had trouble hitting C. Later, I learned that this is the way Chet Baker plays. It's considered very cool to muff every other note. Like his hero, Scooter plays "Body and Soul" after the first time through as though he had no conception of the melody. We decided that he had better stick with airplanes until one evening when he did a classical takeoff on the cornet you hear at bullfights. True and stirring, the notes rang through the building, and you could shut your eyes and practically see the crowds and the pageantry. That's when Red tore a blanket from a bunk and used it as a cape. Throwing his trumpet aside, Scooter suddenly became solemn, stamping his heels rhythmically, trilling his tongue and slowly turning under his upraised hand. Then, ritually, he charged Red's blanket while we shouted, "*Olé!*" Soberly, expertly, Red put him through the various passes until Scooter ignored the blanket and dumped Red.

During cross-country flights, Scooter sometimes carries his trumpet in the cockpit. As he turns off the runway at a strange field, Scooter lifts his trumpet bell up over the windshield and, unheard in the singing of the engines, "plays a little tune for the natives." I never heard it, of course, but it may have been important as some sort of statement.

Now he pitches the menu aside and rubs his temples. Hovering over him, pencil poised, is our waitress. Scooter looks briefly at her, then gazes around restlessly.

"Do you have," he finally asks her, "a menu for elephants?"

She looks quickly at me. I shrug.

"*Elephants,* sir?"

"That's right," Scooter says, regarding her with his serious gray eyes. She's becoming nervous.

"I'm afraid not. At least, I haven't seen one. The special tonight is shrimp casserole, and it's very good, sir." Scooter's eyes never waver from her face. She inhales, giggles, looks around helplessly. "I don't know what elephants eat. We don't serve hay or peanuts, if that's what you mean."

"No hay?" Scooter holds her with his poker face. "Vines, then?"

"*Vines,* sir?"

"Sure, vines. Elephants *like to strip vines.* You must know that."

"No, sir. I never had much education, sir." She's really uneasy now, so I lay my hand on Scooter's arm. "We have steaks and shrimp casserole," she says. "I could bring you a big salad."

Scooter slumps. "All right. A big salad."

"Is that all, sir?"

"No, a New York, medium rare. I'm carnivorous when I'm starving."

After dinner we return to the bar. There they are, right on schedule, the lovers huddled around two old nurses, the clowns trying to imitate the acrobats, a full bottle sailing as a football overhead, Major Slocum reasoning with the humorless club manager. Smokey is dancing to the wrong rhythm with some drunk girl—woman, I see now as he swings her into the pavilion-like lights—who seems to enjoy his increasingly obvious grasps. Unnoticed, lying on his back beside their feet, is Billy, demonstrating the backstroke as it was taught at Ohio State. At the bar are Charles and our only other intellectual, a Southern boy who did graduate work at Vanderbilt. I gather that they are discussing God. Behind the cash register, conscientiously operating the machine and wearing an apron, is Hank. A MATS couple comes in, and Hank mixes their drinks, pockets the tip.

I glance at my watch. They're good for at least two more hours, unless the skeptical manager finally decides to call the OD. You can tell that he's undecided. He sees Hank playing it straight at the cash register, and he notes the record attendance. No one, it seems, knows what happened to the regular bartender. I slip out.

Hemingway's *Farewell to Arms* is supposed to be one of his finest novels, but I'm having trouble getting through it. The dialogue in the love scenes makes me laugh. Hemingway would probably shoot and stuff anyone he heard say that. Anyone who takes himself as seriously as he does can't tolerate ridicule. Well, I'm sleepy, and God knows there will be no sleeping later. If the weather breaks, we'll need sober flight leaders.

10

FOX ABLE

LIKE A CARRIER PILOT, nose-high, blowing snow off the overrun, I touch down on the hidden numbers, hold the nose off, and open the canopy. On this slick surface—an inch of fresh powder over ice—aerodynamic braking will be our only hope. At Loring we learned that these winter tires with the wire embedded in the tread can't perform miracles. More rudder! She's still trying to weathervane. How a cross-wind can dip down into this ten-foot-deep channel through the snow, I can't imagine. I feel like a bobsledder in his chute, and I would settle for that if there were some way to bank this bird around that wall of snow at the end. Brakes—easy, *easy!* Okay, an optical illusion: I still have two thousand feet to roll out.

As I turn off and close my canopy against the burning subzero wind, I look back at my flight, all three more or less under control, hangovers notwithstanding. Bunch of pros. Right behind them though is Whit's flight, and Whit's wingman loses it at about the four-thousand-foot marker, gyrating, overcontrolling, finally sliding sideways, then backwards. Everyone makes way for him. Ah, he's *smart*—he has advanced his throttle. Reverse thrust. Nevertheless, into the snowbank he goes, tail-first. Whit notifies the tower, then tells them to disregard, for out of the snow the wingman comes, generating his own blizzard, laughing on the radio.

Blindly, following the little signs stuck into the walls of the snow maze, we rock along in single file until we break out onto a long ramp, where a thirty-knot wind has our parkaed crew chiefs, scattered like lost Eskimos, jumping to stay warm. Boy, I'd settle for a parka right now. This inner tube I'm wearing is no good now, and in the January Atlantic it would simply prolong the agony by another minute or so. I decide to leave my helmet on and my mask loosely fastened.

Goose Bay is an American airbase situated on Canadian soil. The O Club is throbbing to the juke, and the young Canadian waitresses are glad to see new faces, however frostbitten. Colonel Bronton has a girl bring him a pitcher of martinis. He drinks straight from the pitcher, then goes into his old George routine, a truly impressive "ox demonstration," moving the bar. Colonel Bronton—Nasser—*is* an ox, a smart ox with a mustache. It is a matter of will, he explains. You could do it, Art, if you believed you could. With each lunge, Nasser shifts the massive, immovable bar another inch.

"Jesus, Colonel, you're a *locomotive*," Art says in apparently frank admiration, then to us, "I hope the big sonovabitch has a heart attack."

Later, his vitality restored by a sirloin that overhangs its metal platter, Colonel Bronton demonstrates how a strong fist can beat holes at cadenced intervals in the beaverboard of a BOQ hallway—until he hits a stud. All of us bite our knuckles.

Down the white corridors bearing street signs almost topped by snow, we walk—to Finance, to the PX, to the weather counter at Base Ops, despite Colonel Bronton's warning that we not keep bugging the forecaster.

"After all," he reminds us, "no one is going anywhere until I say so, right? *I'll* check the weather." With that, he zips up his parka, raises its hood, and, like the Minotaur, plunges out into the white maze.

Another blizzard of those fine flakes produced by stratus, a sustained storm. The roads come and go with the rotaries. The runway, we hear, is kept open—somehow. After thirty-six hours, our birds show only vertical tail fins aligned amid the drifts. Nevertheless, solemnly, we brief each morning, half drunk, only partially encased in our immersion suits.

On the twelfth day, however, no more sober, indeed, with books still checked out of the library, astounded to find our birds uncovered, we depart Labrador for Greenland, more or less at the direct order of the ranking officer at Goose. That gentleman, a West Pointer and former cavalry officer, told Nasser, we hear later, that he did not consider us a military organization.

BW-1

As the winter sun at its low zenith sparkles off the dark water below, we make landfall on Greenland. What at first appears to be an unforecast shelf of alto-stratus proves to be the Great Ice Cap and, as we close to within one hundred miles of the coast and begin a shallow descent, I recall our briefing. The major showing the color slides was a ferry pilot who had flown Fox Able many times. He wore no wedding ring, I noticed.

"Emergency procedures," he had said. "Now, then, let's say that when you arrive, both BW-1 and BW-8 are socked in. You don't have a good instrument letdown, you don't have GCA or ILS, and you lack the fuel to return here. What do you do? Yes, you *pray* a lot but, while you're praying, you simply land wheels-up on the ice cap, okay?" He flashed a movie star grin at us. I heard Scooter's squeal of terror from the back of the room.

"Seriously," the major continued, "*it's been done.* And the crew was picked up in good shape."

"Rather than simply crash, sir," Al asked him, "why not bail out?"

"Anyone want to give the lieutenant the answer?" the major asked us old heads.

"Survival Rule Number One," Dan shrugged.

"Right. *Stay with the bird.* Don't ever forget that. They'll find you quicker."

I filed it away, then lost interest. If a guy worries too much about outside chances, he's no good as a fighter pilot. He's too safe and professional to get in a fight.

"Gentlemen, in places that ice cap is eight thousand feet deep," said the major. "Neither spring nor summer fazes it. So let me repeat: track outbound on this heading, establish three-hundred-feet-per-minute rate of descent, jettison your canopy, lock your harness, insert your seat-pin, and wait. Impact should be soft. There may not even be serious damage to the aircraft. Questions?"

"You can recover the bird, too?" Nasser asked in awe.

"No, sir."

"So it doesn't matter."

The major smiled wanly. "To the pilot it does, sir."

Well, what the hell, I didn't blame him. You can't brief a squadron as though they are kamikaze pilots. You've got to provide them with *some* emergency procedure, some hope. Never mind that landing on the ice has been done only by blimps and Fokker Tri-motors, that we, at 135 knots or better, would stick up like darts in a dartboard.

As in a dream, we descend and see the dark cliffs beneath the white frosting, the blue-green icebergs shed from the cap, the deep-set fjords leading to the glaciers. A thousand feet beneath our noses lies the old shipwreck. We curve into the nearest fjord—*Tunugdliarfik,* the briefing officer has casually printed on his blackboard—and descend until the cliffs on either side are above us. I pump the stick to signal trail formation. Gradually, they assume landing interval and we follow the windings of the fjord. Our destination lies at the dead end, where the mountains and the glacier rule out overhead traffic patterns and choice of landing direction.

Snaking around the final bend, we see it—BW-1, Bluie-West 1, a single PSP runway. Dropping gear and flaps, we drag it in and land uphill, setting the steel planking into an uproar. Our crew chiefs are the ones we last saw at Dover. They leapfrog bases in C-124s.

"So how was Goose?" they ask.

"Ever been to Sun Valley?" Dan begins, and we pick it up from there—sex-starved women, free booze, skiing.

"Yeah?"

Scooter does a little riff on his trumpet, but it is too cold. A guy could lose his lip, he explains. It is only 1330, but the sun will set in half an hour. Around us the mountains are darkening as we watch. Oppressive, too foreign, it's like being on the moon or something.

Much later, numb with alcohol, we stand outside the little club—the Hudson Bay Trading Post, Whit dubbed it—and watch the Aurora Borealis. Our up-turned faces change colors with the skies.

"The Valkyrie are riding. They're coming for us," Charles explains. "Their armor sheds this strange, flickering light." His face is green.

"Oh, bullshit," Red says, and gives him a shove. Red is a very literal guy. We get a lecture about solar flares, electrons and ionized particles. The sky loses its interest.

Stamping our feet to keep warm, we gradually retreat to the bar, where a sign states that the ice used in our drinks is a million years old. The bartenders make a little show of stepping out the back door to chip more ice off the glacier. So much for the entertainment. It is easy to understand why the big birds overfly Narsarswak. And why, since they carry all the film, the movies here are a million years old, too.

I go to sleep watching my window change colors. It is well below zero. Only a month ago, our skins dark from the desert sun, we were drifting the ess-turns south of Jerry's Oasis. Crazy.

KEFLAVIK, ICELAND

It is late dawn. We climb steeply out of the fjord. In this subzero air our engines are superefficient. One heady circle and we are already angling upward through ten thousand feet. Below, the base, unreal again, falls away. Looking down, I see the glacier pushing against the little club, held off only by the icepicks of the bartender, and then it is all consigned to memory. The Ice Cap, the fjords, Cape Adelaer—all are lost in the blue distance. Except for the white cons boiling behind us, we, too, seem frozen in the January sunlight. Stars of frost speckle my canopy and, through this pattern, I see the yellow markings of the other three birds against the line where the natural blues meet.

Delighted to have escaped BW-1 so easily, we are a little loose with radio discipline. Finally, Colonel Bronton, twenty miles ahead—I can pick out his con—tells us to hold it down. So we shut up. There isn't much to do, though. Our drop tanks are feeding evenly, our oxygen blinkers and pressures are normal, our engine instruments are registering in the green arc segments of their dials. As for navigation, all we can do is track outbound, and the white needle of my radio compass is stable at three degrees left of my tail. I can't check my groundspeed because there aren't any checkpoints, not for another ten minutes, when we come abeam of the Coast Guard ocean station vessel.

Below, the Atlantic is dark blue, marbled with white. If the sea is as forecast, the waves are sixteen feet high, the water temperature so low that our rubber immersion suits would be useless. If my engine flames out, I am dead. Somewhere down there is a Rescue amphibian, but what chance would he have in those swells? It's better not to think about it. Trust in God and those bespectacled General Electric engineers who designed our single engines. I couldn't be a Navy pilot. They don't have to worry much about mountains, but I understand mountains. I don't understand how they can live with that cold water. I think I'd get used to the catapult and the arresting gear, but I don't like all that water. Charles says Man came from the sea, that we were once sharks. Maybe so, but it has been awhile. Every jock in the Air Force hates to see land drop below the horizon. I can't make myself read the ditching instructions. Old Daedalus was the first jock, they say, and if he hadn't had that warm, flat Aegean extending to the horizon, he wouldn't have released brakes. As it was, he lost his wingman.

Joe is taking pictures of us, weaving around, hands off, easing out to roll the film and change filters. The way he slides in toward me so recklessly, one of his color slides may survive to make the cover of *Life*. I can see us tumbling in fire and smoky silver. Dark, his short hair ruining what might have been a heady resemblance to Paul Muni, Joe is a second-generation American, whose parents emigrated as children from one of the eastern European countries. As he talks—always loudly—his mind and his eyes wander distractedly. The only time he seems to concentrate is when some clerk asks his name. No longer does he bother pronouncing it; he just begins spelling it and anxiously watching the pen. But he flies good wing—after he runs out of film.

To my right, Red is rolling to relieve the boredom. He holds the bird inverted while Joe snaps his picture. Red has a one-second attention span, unless he is shooting pool or watching some girl. Farther out, Charles, motionless, nods his head. Okay. Ahead ten miles, Pete leads Hank in a composite flight. They glint against the vast blue, disappear. The sun warms me; I yawn.

When my watch tells me we've passed the point-of-no-return, I stuff my Greenland data and map down beside my seat and unfold the map of Iceland. It isn't exactly studded with runways. Keflavik has, in fact, the only decent runway. If the weather moves in, there's nowhere else to go. Theoretically, we'd descend to one hundred feet with GCA guidance, and if we were still on instruments we'd climb, recross the homing beacon at twenty-five hundred feet on a specific heading, and eject. A nice theory, it's the only one they dare put in writing. But I know what I'd do: one hundred feet would just be another call along the glide slope. If I was stabilized and the guy in the radar van kept calling the same heading, by God, I'd land. I've had to do it once before. Sometimes the fog used to roll in over at Fairfield-Suisun when we'd divert there from Hamilton.

Red has the Reykjavik radio range station two degrees to the left on his radio compass. He must be right because I see the cons ahead are ever so slightly curved to the north. But my birddog is hunting now. It's pointing everywhere. Joe says that his is pointing to Bermuda, so why don't we just go there? Colonel Bronton tells us to shut up, god-dammit.

We are the third flight. Behind us are three more, with call signs—Chartreuse, Green and Yellow. By twisting around in my seat, I can see their cons. We are six flights of four stretched out over a hundred miles.

Whit is leading Green, and Pete is leading Yellow. I hear Green Flight running through an oxygen check. Bunch of drunks, Green. Their radio bays are crammed with bargain whiskey. They pale at the thought of hard landings or turbulence. Whit is saying something about oil pressure.

"Whatcha got, Green Leader?" Nasser calls.

"Green Leader has fluctuating oil pressure," Whit replies calmly.

"Okay, get out your checklist."

The colonel, in a terminal dive, would consult his checklist. He'd still be turning the pages when he hit. The rest of us know what little advice the checklist offers regarding fluctuating oil pressure: you hold cruise power settings and you watch the needle. A prayerbook would be more useful. Whit knows that I had once returned the two hundred miles from the Yalu with the needle ticking near zero, knows that jet engines are different. I keep quiet.

In my mind, though, I can see him weighing the odds. One night when we were reminiscing, he said that he'd once brought a burning A-20 back across the Channel from France, so suspense isn't new to him. An old pro, so cool now, he's not going to say anything more until it hits zero. At a poker table, he's the same way. He'll smirk at you through his prescription glasses, and bluff you right out. His metabolic rate is so low that he always seems half asleep. When we'd remain overnight at Las Vegas (on the slightest excuse), he'd sometimes win or lose a thousand in two hours and never mention it the next day. He has the Western rancher's long-range view of life.

When I hear him tell his flight to go to Guard Channel, I know he is near zero. Without switching our receivers, we can hear Guard.

"Green Leader," Whit calls calmly.

"Two, Three, Four," they check in.

"Okay, this is Dragnet Green Leader with a MAYDAY, MAYDAY, MAYDAY."

There is a quarter-minute of silence, and then we hear two voices responding, cutting each other out. Then, clearly: "Roger on your MAYDAY, Dragnet Green. This is Duckbutt Alfa. Transmit for ten seconds, please. . . . Okay, we are west your position but will turn at this time. State your estimated distance from Keflavik, please."

Ah, Christ, they're going through the motions as though it matters. Either the engine keeps running or it doesn't. And, if it quits, Whit will be gliding at twice the speed of the amphibian. Still, if I were he, I'd be glad that someone is trying to help.

We're thirty minutes out, so Green must be at least thirty-two. Still, the dumb engine keeps running. Through a residual oil film, metal seeks metal; thank God, it's not like the old Merlin.

Twenty-five minutes out, and still no vibration. Twenty, and Whit reports slight vibration but no change in rpm. Fifteen, and she's beginning to pound. The tachometer is slipping back. Thirteen and, just before she seizes, Whit pulls the throttle to Off and establishes a glide. He's coming down, holding 185 knots indicated.

With this tailwind, he can make land; maybe not the runway, but land. Ahead, there are big holes in the stratus.

Fifteen thousand. I rock my wings, and my guys converge on me. We skim the gray top of a snow shower. In my earphones, I hear the steady tone of a beam leg. Approach Control clears us to continue our penetration.

High Cloud bases. Good. Whit will have a little maneuvering room after he breaks out. We circle east of the airbase to insure that there will not be any traffic pattern congestion. Scooter is giving Whit course corrections. Without his defrosters, Whit can't see much. He is just watching the irrevocable unwinding of his altimeter.

"Range, Green Two?" he calls.

"About twenty miles, Green Leader. Two degrees left."

GCA has him now and takes over. They are angling him toward final approach.

"Okay, Green, no heroics." Whit mutters. "Move farther out."

"Ah, no sweat, Lead," Scooter says. "I'll just insert my old trunk up your tail pipe and push a little."

"*No*, goddammit, Scooter! You'll just screw us both up. Now, get out to the side."

I doubt that his engine is windmilling, so I say a little prayer for his battery. Without it, he will have no flight controls, no windshield defroster, no flaps. Even now, he is probably scraping frost with his hunting knife and fingernails.

"Okay, I have the runway," Whit says. "Green Leader is pulling his emergency gear extension. . . . Okay, Green is down and locked."

I see them now on a high final. Like wary ducks approaching a pond, they delay committing themselves. Whit tries a few degrees of flaps, then waits for everything to assume the right perspective. A hero if he makes it, a fool—probably a dead fool—if he doesn't. He still has a few seconds to turn away and eject. No one would criticize him, but everyone—especially old Nasser and Major Slocum, both on the ground now—is using body English to help him.

He is steeper now. The others can't stay behind. Full flaps and slipping. He's got it made. Yeah. *Beautiful.* Over the end, leveling. Little puffs of tire smoke. Perfect. Thank God—literally.

Everyone's yelling, "Way to go, Whit!" Everyone except Colonel Bronton. Maybe he is, too, silently at least; but he will reprimand us all for poor radio discipline and then, I suppose, we'll have to hear again about that guy at Langley Field.

Same song, third verse. At Dover and Goose we outwore our welcomes. Here at Keflavik, *no* American is even initially welcome. Situated thirty-five miles west of Reykjavik, Kef is not properly considered a military airbase. It is an international airport with military tenants whose stay is conditional upon heavy U.S. financing of the base and a low American profile. We are as welcome here as the Clanton boys were in Wyatt Earp's Tombstone.

Thank God there is a finance office. Without partial pay, we can't even eat. My wallet is empty. When the clerk asks where we are permanently stationed, we say France.

"And the base?"

We shrug. We show him our orders.

"But," Red adds mysteriously, "we aren't going *there*."

The clerk quits typing, regards us suspiciously. "Where, may I ask, *are* you going?"

"Toul. Maybe Chaumont. We don't know."

"Oh-h, it is *classified* information?" He becomes conspiratorial.

"That's right," I decide quickly.

After checking the weather, we gamble by putting nearly all our clothing into the laundry or cleaners. Safe enough, as it turns out. When Kef's weather improves, Prestwick's deteriorates. At best, the ceiling is like a seesaw pivoted over the next ocean-station vessel.

One morning when we file into the air terminal's dining room, the place is almost filled with BOAC passengers whose Constellation is a ghost in the driving snow. Whenever I see the English handling knives and forks, I become hypnotized. They never switch their forks from hand to hand, and they pack food onto their utensils with such assurance that we wonder at our own relative delicacy. This particular group of passengers is so typically British that they, like character actors, seem to be deliberately exaggerating their peculiarities. Here, I decide, is a Rolls salesman, eating alone—dignified, aloof, imperious in his manner of summoning his waitress. His mustache twitches as he chews. Apparently he regards us as some sort of chain gang. Crowded together at the next table are mere executives and civil servants, their coat sleeves too short, their elbows patched. A few Prince Charleses peer earnestly at us from beneath their mops of hair. Their cheeks look rouged.

"Excuse me," a tweedy old maid asks, "are hamburgers eaten for breakfast?" I shrug, defer to Charles, who replies, "Not usually."

"I see. Well, I must try one anyway so I can tell my sister that I have."

At the BOAC captain's table—he reminds me of the chauffeur in the movie *Sabrina*—sit two rather plump stewardesses and a steward. Around them circulate trim, blond, Icelandic waitresses.

Never have I seen so many pipe-smoking men in one room, all fondling shell-black Dunhills or Barlings and rolling up oilskin pouches. "Umm," they reply to each other's comments regarding the dismal weather. They stand, rocking on their heels before the windows, their hands clasped behind their backs.

Surprisingly, we don't ruffle them much, not even when Scooter pauses in the doorway to lift his gray rubber sleeve and trumpet. A few raised eyebrows, a shift of pipes from one side of their mouths to the other, an indulgent smile here and there. In their eyes, I suppose, Americans have never behaved sensibly. And, as Jonathan used to say, the Anglophiles among us are the worst—hypocrites in that we rebelled against the Crown; we had our chance to be gentlemen and muffed it. These passengers seem relieved to hear that we'll be going on to France rather than remaining in England. They remember the last invasion of Yanks.

By BOQ standards the hotel in the terminal is plush. An Icelandic girl works at the desk. She is a Communist, she tells us bluntly, adding "The sooner you leave, the better." She stares us down. We hear that the old Icelandic policemen who hang around the terminal are also Communists. Clearly, they hate Americans, especially after they get to know *us*.

"Well," Hank shrugs, "they aren't armed and we can outrun them. And they *are* Communists."

"Yeah," Joe says, "but we are building up their wind."

I am sure that these old men pray to the Norse gods to let the weather break every evening when we, boozy and obscene, return from the O Club, finally beaten by the slot machines, and consult our watches to determine if we are sleepy. With darkness coming in midafternoon, our internal clocks are confused. Typically, we sleep from 0400 until 0700, endure the formality of an 0800 briefing, then, after breakfast, sleep until dark. When Scotland is lost in drizzle, as it is for days at a time, only the flight commanders must rise to attend the briefings. When we return, the lieutenants questioningly open one eye.

"If you had been up and ready," I tell them, "we could have made it."

"Bull," they sigh, and sleep again.

Four hours of daylight, five when it's clear. No wonder these Icelandic girls are so fair. In Yuma, they'd die like mushrooms. Prisoners, we have become resigned and almost intellectual. Illiterate intellectuals, Charles says. His sinuses are giving him hell, but he won't go to the dispensary. "It's chronic," he explains, "which is *verboten*, right?" His fingertips are white as he presses his eyebrows, his eyes tightly closed.

"Are you sure it's sinus blockage?" I ask him.

"No," he admits. "It may be a hangover."

All the lieutenants have college degrees. We old dropouts can simply listen to their more serious arguments and pick up a free education. Which counts for nothing in our records, of course, but is still important. One night, Charles, who perversely, in trying to fight off a sinus attack, had drunk too much, begins something with great irony, something about reading much of the night and going south in the winter.

"What?" Al cocks his handsome collie head, amused.

"Nothing."

Spiritual dryness, no regenerating beliefs, Charles explains later. The nose drops haven't helped, nor has the scotch. "Let's go to the dispensary," I say.

"Forget it."

"Well, you oughta find out what's wrong at least."

"You got any scotch, John?"

I pour some into two tumblers. "Suppose it's migraine?"

"Then this will help." He nods, and downs it.

Snow hisses against the dark window. It's 0230. The Icelandic cops prowl the hallways. Earlier we had heard the Tasmanian Devil go past.

Don is the Tasmanian Devil. Somewhere in Florida last winter we saw a Bugs Bunny cartoon. Of all the rabbit's adversaries, Don considers the Tasmanian Devil most worthy.

"Oh, sure," Don says. "It's not even close. The Devil has character. He's right out of Homer."

"Philosophically," Charles conceded, his painful smile becoming a laugh, "you know where the Devil stands: *everyone* is his enemy."

As the days pass and the boredom level rises, Don becomes all too explicit. He rotates, literally, in furious revolutions. It is funny until about midnight, as a rule. Then, and I know when I hear him coming, I've had it with the growling and the upraised claws. Usually I'm trying to write Jenny through his screams and whiskey breath.

Don's father is a captain in the New York City Police Department. In joining the Air Force, Don had disappointed his old man.

"Can you see *me* as a cop?" Don asks us. No, we concede; a robber, maybe.

Sometimes when he's drunk, Don walks around batting full glasses out of our hands. You can get mad and start quoting *The Universal Code of Military Justice*, or you can take him on, or you can simply laugh. All of us, even our old Egyptian giant, Colonel Nasser, brush the liquid beads off, and laugh. But I'll always remember that first time when, like a striking snake, Colonel Bronton's hand had grabbed Don's shirt and dragged him up nose-to-nose. A little lightning there, a flow of electrons, a final, terrible potential. Seeing it, the colonel had gradually relaxed and, while he had continued, good-naturedly, to maintain a little steel in his eyes, we could tell that Don's mad grin had finally unnerved him. At George, in a dog fight, I sensed its meaning, chillingly, after we had scissored down to the tree tops. Thank God I'm only half Irish, only half insane.

Each morning we walk down to the line to preflight our birds. Bleak country, this—a cross between Las Vegas and Moses Lake, Washington, in January. As for the flight line itself, well, all ramps look pretty much the same, especially with our birds aligned in familiar order along them. It warms me just to see them, these sweet old '86s. In a way, they are our only reality. I think of all the ramps where we and these machines have sat and waited for something to happen—in Arizona, their canopies had to be opened an inch; in Oklahoma and Florida, closed against the rain; at Mountain Home, even the wings and horizontal stabilizers had to be covered with tarps. And, everywhere, the red intake and exhaust covers and the red-streamered downlock pins angling with the breeze like the telltales of sloops.

Duck-walking beneath the low wing, my boot soles scraping, I check the accumulator pressures, examine the pavement for evidence of leaks, click the fairing doors against their microswitches. She has been pushed two feet so that the flat spots on the tires are on top. The engine was run up two days ago. Leaning into the dead cockpit, I let my eyes run over the switches and circuit breakers. I don't have to think about them individually; anything wrong would catch my eye. I am like a hostess surveying a set table.

Ha! This morning the rudder pedals are fully extended. Someone crawled in for a little snooze, probably after a beery night at the NCO Club. Otherwise, she's secure, ready to go. My helmet and mask lie on the seat, my chute harness is arranged. I reach in to set the altimeter to field elevation, and note that the Kollsman window indicates 29.86, a rise in barometric pressure. I close the canopy, retie the tarp, and walk away, looking back occasionally. Dan falls in beside me.

Soon. Soon now. I can sense the break coming. We are like sailors listening for wind. Everything is drier. It is already dusk. This evening we'll see a few stars. Others join us as we stride back to the BOQ. Happily, they look up through the sliding layers of cloud to the highest deck, still sunlit. No one says anything. We are afraid of jinxing it.

I go to sleep thinking of that crazy Marine, Mike, who in Korea would awaken every morning crippled by that footlocker. Yesterday I met a Navy pilot who had known Mike. He told me that Mike had been killed a year ago in a chopper crash. It is always stunning. I had pictured him wearing a silver leaf and holding down a key slot somewhere.

11

PRESTWICK

ONCE WE SWING Stornoway, we relax. The North Atlantic lies behind us. Lindbergh flew across in about thirty-three hours. We, in our transonic jets, needed a month. So much for the giant strides aviation has made during the past twenty-eight years. Well, we beat Columbus—I think.

From seven miles above the Hebrides, we can see the Highlands. Bill Wallace who, up ahead, is flying Colonel Bronton's wing, can't maintain radio silence. If you want to hear someone gibber, just tell Bill that you didn't know Wallace is a Scottish name. Anyhow, he's practically falling out of his cockpit pointing out a hill named Ben Nevis, and Loch Lomond.

"Never heard of them, Red Two," the colonel says. "Now let's keep it at ease."

After drab Iceland, the Highlands *are* impressive. My eyes are hungry for color. Coasting in, our windshield defrosters ruffling our discarded instrument let-down books, we soak up the beauty. Blue estuaries lead into the green hills, fishing fleets are everywhere. Out on those moors somewhere are Ivanhoe, Heathcliff, Sherlock Holmes and Watson.

Leveling at five thousand, rustling along in loose finger formation, I notice the rocks. Yeah, that's why there are so few farmhouses, that's why they emigrated to America. The Carolinas are still full of their descendants. Even sandy coastal soil and red clay beat rock. But someone stayed. That *canal!* It seems to go right across the county to the North Sea.

I crank in Prestwick and listen to the Morse. My birddog needle swings without hesitation to the twelve-o'clock position. Sliding toward us from the horizon is a pall of smoke: Glasgow. Where are the famous shipyards? Adding our negligible trails of smoke, we are over the Clyde before I see them.

Ahead now, standing out clearly in a comparatively pastoral setting, is Ayr and, beyond it, the runways of Prestwick Airport. No more rocks. Instead, there are meadows, and great trees overhanging the roads. The land reminds me of New England. Even the airport seems old and civilized, with no raw earth anywhere. Groomed lawns slope right up to the runway edges. A few miles to the south lie the famous links of Turnberry. Ike has played there.

Our BOQ is seventeenth-century Tudor, half-timbered and slate-roofed, situated on the hill. All it needs is Ronald Colman and a groom to lead his horse away, maybe a couple of collies. Scooter shows Hank how to touch his forelock. From the lawn we look across a token wooded preserve to the runway and, beyond it, the civilian terminal. Everything is already catching the last sun—after all, we are still above fifty-five degrees North Latitude, as far north as Hudson Bay—and the perimeter road flashes with automobile windshields. Between the road and the runway a crew of workmen is busy. There the grass is disturbed over a wide area. We learn that a transport carrying diamonds recently crashed there. (We have to restrain Scooter, who has become a vacuum-cleaning elephant.)

The hush of the mansion subdues us. We hear a majestic clock ticking, see the easy chairs and the fire. Wood paneling, thick carpeting. Here Ronald Colman would lay down his crop and gloves, perhaps greet C. Aubrey Smith—no, *Olivier,* Don corrects me—and then absently accept a smoking jacket from his valet. A little fancy work with the soda siphon, a bit of slitting and speed-reading of the mail, eventual mulling over the situation in India.

Charles strolls around, his hands naturally clasped British fashion behind his back, examining everything. The patina of the wood, the waviness of the small panes set in lead, the general luxury—all combine to set an appreciative smile on his face.

Upstairs, however, there are GI bunks, metal lockers, a communal shower room, but modern toilet booths. Most of the guys are happier with this familiar environment. Hank laughs, slams his locker door, and we assist each other in getting out of our immersion suits. One of the most satisfying experiences in life is to step out of these sweaty inner tubes. In Korea I used to kick mine the length of the PE room. Now I fold it thoughtfully and hand it to a sergeant. Somehow I realize that I will never wear one again. You know when you are doing things for the last time.

Wearing wrinkled Class B uniforms, our hair still wet from the showers, we descend the grand, wide staircase, past continuous paneling to ground level.

"Gentlemen," the American Club officer nods. "Welcome."

Having hosted another entire wing (in segments) and our lead squadron, he is understandably wary. In ROTC or OTS they had told him that officers behave as gentlemen; now he knows better. In guarded asides, he discusses certain precautions with his NCO. I gather that our vanguard behaved approximately as Attila's usually did, that this pale, bespectacled lieutenant is actually a veteran whose position has been overrun four times. Now, possibly to test us, he smilingly announces that the bar will open at 1700. It is now 1630.

Without warning, Scooter trumpets his rogue-elephant shriek right in the lieutenant's face. When the latter's eyes are again visible behind their fogged lenses, they register alarm. Dan leads Scooter aside to calm him. After one questioning shriek, Scooter subsides.

"No," Dan says firmly, shaking his head.

Fortunately, at this moment Major Slocum, wearing his navy blazer and slacks, his yellow flying scarf tucked like an ascot, descends the stairs as the master of this house must have descended them a century ago.

"Gentlemen," he nods to us, shakes hands with the Club officer. "Well, where's the bar, Lieutenant?"

Scooter's trunk rises, but Dan restrains it. There is a general muttering reminiscent of the crowd scenes in *A Tale of Two Cities*.

"Uh, perhaps I misunderstand," the major concedes regally. "Certainly you cannot mean that you won't bend arbitrary club rules for *this* occasion. After all, how often does a fighter squadron fly the Atlantic in winter *nonstop?*"

"Another half hour, sir." He looks at the old clock with its stately pendulum beat. "At the strike of five, we will open our bar."

"Oh, *well*," Hank shrugs. Once the Club officer turns his back, Hank opens the clock's case, moves the minute hand through a whirring, striking half-revolution.

White-faced, through clenched teeth, the lieutenant informs him that the clock's hands have not been touched for several years. From his tones I gather that the very planets will likely be affected in their courses.

I can feel it coming, and I'm just drunk enough not to care. No one is rolling any aces now. The poker dice clatter along the old bar, and twenty-five guys roar incredulously. Tim makes a big show of examining the dice. "Red, these aren't *your* dice, are they?"

They are the house dice, the old Scottish bartender assures us. Well, *they* also deserve to lie on a glass-encased pillow in the Desert Inn. We are rolling till some sucker rolls the twenty-first ace and gets to drink the pot. The seventh ace had fallen to Dan, who wildly ordered a shot from every bottle on the top shelf. I had rolled the fourteenth and almost emptied my wallet. And no one has rolled an ace since. Down the bar the leather cup goes, each guy rolling, then thoughtfully gathering them up. What are the odds?

"*Bang!*" Whit jumps back. They are howling. I can't see. "What?"

"*Three* aces!"

Okay, four to go, and eight guys must roll before the cup again reaches me. I calculate that I'm safe. I watch the old Scot pouring jiggers of different-colored booze, and I shudder. He looks up at me, recomputes the cost of this shakerful, winces, sweeps all my money except for one dollar.

As the dice cup approaches Dan again, he begins laughing hysterically. There is now a good chance that he will roll the twenty-first ace and have to drink his own poison. Two to go, and there are five dice in that cup. Dan rubs his freckled face, killing time, prolonging the suspense.

"Dan, you bastard," the major says. "I *order* you to roll two aces."

"Oh, very well, sir," Dan nods, bangs the cup inverted, and steps back. The major lifts it, shouts. No aces. Dan accepts several congratulatory hands, while the major fumes and rejects the cup.

"No, honestly, fellas," he says, "I've got to go." He consults his watch. "The Old Man has called a staff meeting for eighteen hundred."

They drag him back and force the cup into his hand. He loves it; everyone can see that. He's *hoping* that he rolls the twenty-first. A real actor, he rolls up his sleeves, his chipmunk face pink, his receding blond crew-cut alight.

"Dan, you bastard," he mutters. "If I roll them, you will spend the next *year* in Mobile Control."

Bang! I can't see anything except a pyramid of heads. He lifts the cup and does a triumphant back flip, almost landing on his feet. One to go.

Tarzan, who weighs less than one-twenty, is next, and we are all secretly relieved when he escapes—perhaps literally—death. A rare grin from old Tarzan.

Then Tim, who, until this moment has been especially enthusiastic about the game, slowly accepts the cup. "Oh, all right," he says, his grins and frowns coming in quick succession. "I need a drink, right? And here's a free one."

Oh, no, I realize. Suddenly, I *know* that he is safe, that the cup will miraculously pass through the remaining three men and return to me. And it does. Sometimes I can glimpse a little of the future—never important events, never good fortune—and while Tim is still shaking the cup, I can actually see myself holding that huge glass. When the vision is fulfilled and I raise the violet bubbling mixture, so near its apparent flash point, I am strangely unconcerned.

"Good night, gentlemen," I tell them solemnly.

"Hold it!" Tim yells. He runs to the fireplace and begins heating the poker.

Charles and Hank lean near me. "Don't chug-a-lug it, John. Remember Socrates and his hemlock. It's too dangerous." Hank shakes his head. "Stupid goddamn game."

While the poker is heating, I look around at that marvelous old bar. In the lounge, the clock is striking six. I'm glad that it's not striking eighteen. Through the imperfect glass in the windows, I see a distorted portico and, beyond it, flailing shrubbery. It is dark. The cold front has arrived. A slight groaning of timbers catches everyone's attention.

"A bad omen," Tim says from his kneeling position on the marble hearth. "And the only way to fight evil spirits," he explains, rising and bringing the glowing poker toward me, "is with cleansing fire. That's why we must observe this ceremony. Right, Johnny?"

"Absolutely."

I set the shaker on the bar and everyone except Tim, who is shielding his eyes, retreats. He thrusts the poker into the liquid. There is a minor explosion which blows hissing drops everywhere.

"Okay, John, *quick!*" Tim shouts. "Down the hatch! Here's to John, he's true-blue! . . ."

The very fumes of the thing make my eyes water, and it tastes as potent as it looks. Thank God, a good third of it lies in droplets about the room. Still, there's too much of it remaining to chug-a-lug. Despite their singing and their yells of encouragement, I need a full minute to get it down. When the shaker is empty, Tim beats me on the back, grabs the glass, and hurls it into the fireplace.

"For he's a jolly good fellow!" he sings, and gets them going. Throughout my body I feel an awful numbness spreading. *This is going to be something,* I think; and, unaccountably, I start laughing. I feel *great.*

"Okay, next round," Tim calls. "Everyone to the bar except John. John, go sit down somewhere."

"Why 'except John'?" I ask him. I decide that I'll show these kids how an old fighter pilot can drink. I slap the bar with the flat of my hand. "Roll 'em, Hank."

I can't figure Charles. He regards me with disgust, then leaves the room. Well, to hell with him. Hank asks how I feel.

"No sweat." But I can't keep my tingling foot on that railing.

"You look sunburned, Fearless."

When the dice cup gets to me, I roll the seventh ace. "A little revenge, gentlemen." I can hardly quit laughing long enough to order a shot of everything on the top shelf, mostly liqueurs.

Charles is back, and he's arguing with Tim.

"No problem, Charlie," Tim grins. "In any case, what are the odds?" He winks at me.

Lightning *can* strike twice; I believe it now. The Laws of Probability bear closer study. So do these dice. Toward the end, my buddies are *trying* to roll the twenty-first ace. I have no vision this time; perhaps my brain cells are all dead or something. That's why I'm so stunned when I roll three aces, including the twenty-first.

Tim saves me. He heats the poker until it is almost white hot and blows that mixture of reds and greens and yellows all over us. We are a shambles. Everyone's laughing his ass off, I most of all. If I can stand still long enough for them to wipe my hair and face, I can easily chug-a-lug what's left. Goddamn wet glass keeps slipping in my hand, so I have to use both hands.

"Don't chug-a-lug it, John," the major orders. "Just sip it, hear?"

"Aw," I reassure him, "I'm *fine,* sir. We old brown-shoe aviators gotta show 'em, right?"

"*Sip* it, goddammit!"

After two big gulps, the glass gets away from me. Tim catches it and throws it into the fire.

Triumphantly, I stand there beaming at them. *Greatest bunch of guys who ever lived!* Reaching out, I hug a couple of them to me and, as though on signal, they keep their arms around my shoulders and start walking me to the door. How ridiculous: they think I'm blind drunk when, actually, I'm just beginning to see them.

"No," I say, and pull free. "I can walk."

And I do, with immense dignity, even though the floors slope so that my feet fall an extra few inches. A new warmth is flooding through my body, tumbling little gyros (some indispensable, I realize), causing my hand to reach for the stair railing. Up I go, sweat breaking out on my sticky forehead, each riser higher than the previous one. What little peripheral vision remains tells me that they, my faithful wingmen, are flying close formation.

"Thank you, gentlemen," I nod, and lie down on my bunk. "See you."

"Okay, John?" Charlie asks.

"Fine." I wave and close my eyes.

They switch off the light and close the door. Instantly, I realize that I am spinning down into a frightening vortex. I struggle to my feet, find the doorknob, stagger down the hallway, ricocheting off opposite walls, to the latrine. Once inside a toilet booth, my control disappears, and I spew horrible colors into the bowl. I am actually hugging the bowl, listing and recovering, consciousness fading.

"No, by God," I say to myself. "*Up*, you bastard." I will not be found on a latrine floor.

Somehow I make it back to my bunk. Everything keeps whirling even though I leave the light on and one foot on the floor. Hard right rudder, I think, and stick slightly forward of neutral. Here, my mind pauses: *what* am I flying? No two birds respond the same way. It has to do with the relative placement of control surfaces. I spin in.

Every morning we awake to low stratus and drizzle. Little Tarzan, lying in bed and looking up at the ceiling, says that he had a dream in which God directed him to build an ark and load the squadron aboard it.

"Yeah?" Don asks. "What about women?"

"No women. No procreation. We're to be the last of our species."

"What about our birds?"

"He didn't mention them. Probably because they're already submerged."

"Or He knew you couldn't build an aircraft carrier," Don said. "What did He say about liquor?"

"Liquor's okay."

Charles rolls up on one elbow. "In other words," he summarized, "you are simply to put a hull under this building. Our present bleak existence is to continue indefinitely." He lies back and picks up a paperback.

In the great banquet hall of Edinburgh Castle we stand before the suits of armor. They would not fit any of us except perhaps Tarzan who would, in any case, have lacked the strength to move about under that weight.

"So who needs to move?" Tarzan says. "I'd just prop myself in that corner and let all you big bastards wear yourselves out, and then I'd just raise my old halberd and—"

"You couldn't," Hank says, pointing at one.

"Could you?" Tarzan asks him.

The suits are too small, the weapons too heavy. We let *that* sink in. They had been tough little men, we realize.

Outside, we examine Old Meg, her green muzzle commanding the eastern approaches leading up from the city, and try to imagine what it was like to defend this castle five hundred or a thousand years before the airplane. On three sides Castle Rock drops straight to the valley below. We are at traffic-pattern altitude. Only to the east would there be a problem.

Shivering in our raincoats, we scan the ridged backbone of the Old Town. Charles, Scooter and Don are pointing. For once, they are serious. Except for the rain, it is quiet. We can hear a clock striking faintly, the mutter of traffic. I try to visualize it: a calm dawn, fog limiting visibility, the Northumbrians waiting with their grim weapons, all the pipers silent, everyone listening. A distant jingle of metal, voices rising. *They are coming.* Hank stands by the touch-hole of Old Meg. Below a glimpse of color, motion—the ridge is swarming with men. Behind, a stirring, an animal growl rising. Bright shields are lifted. The pipers' elbows squeeze inward on leather bags, and the skirl lifts the clansmen to a single sustained cry of defiance. A bright clap, and smoke rolls. Reload. The enemy writhes, falls back temporarily, swirls around their human heaps.

Thoughtfully, we turn away. The ridge is empty, the castle stands. Bill Wallace looks at each of us, and we nod appreciatively. King Edwin had known his business. A piece of cake, defending this castle.

Are we really leaving? Last night a cold front moved across Scotland and cleared out all the stratus. Sunlight warms us as, packing, we collide with each other. We have been here two weeks, but we are leaving.

The forecaster isn't so sure. Apologetically, he taps the lows, lets his pencil drift along the troughs, moves his palm across Chaumont and Toul-Rosières. He kills us with little remarks. We can expect snow showers throughout the Moselle Valley. As for alternates, Orange down near Marseilles, and Fürstenfeldbruck near Munich. Intermittently, both Chaumont and Toul will be above minimums.

The two squadron commanders are in a huddle with Nasser, who keeps shaking his bear's head. His eyes roam over our faces, and he inhales deeply, but he remembers what happened to our first squadron. On just such a day, they'd flown to France, arriving just as all bases were going below minimums. At Toul the GCA operators, accustomed to slow-moving transports with their radar-reflecting propellers, couldn't adjust quickly enough to the faint, darting blips of jet fighters. They were lucky not to have lost more than one bird. All of us know that.

"No," he says in a voice we can hear. "We've come this far without an incident. The Old Man trusts me to play it cool. I'm playing it cool."

But we can fly locally, he decides. The birds need it, and we need it. We are all getting flat spots from sitting. But take it easy, he warns us; we may not realize how rusty we are.

Ah, God, it's good to be airborne again. Up out of the green hills we curve. I know I'm grinning like an idiot, but I can't help it. And, just from our joyous, rolling check-in, I can tell that the others feel the same way. Long before I've completed a one-eighty, I see Hank and Red come smoking in, all banked up, their speed-lines curving inside ours. Increasing their angle of bank to kill excess speed, they slide just beneath our wash and reappear on my right, frozen in close formation. Nice.

We climb past fair-weather cumulus, and then everything—the narrow streets, the blue estuaries, the deep green of the land—falls away, flattens and becomes unimportant. At twenty thousand, we level momentarily. I settle them in with lazy-esses, the element edge-on in the vertical banks. When they quit bobbing, I take them past vertical a few times and then, as I used to do at George, I hold what I've got and we roll. Easily and gracefully as a boomerang, we soar and swing back, become indifferent to the horizon. We are one, a firm metal phalanx lying back, hushed and inverted at the top of a loop, our oxygen valves the only noise. Now we plummet. There are no section lines; I have to use the gyro compass. Cuban-Eights, cloverleafs and, as our drop tanks empty, some high-G trail. Lufberies, squirrel cages, crazy, evasive stuff while each of us tries to keep his gunsight pipper on the bird ahead. We work at it, sweat.

I am exhausted, my G-suit bladders hard as plaster, my stomach muscles weak from exertion. It is our only exercise. We squint through gloved fingers into the sun. Sometimes I am already plummeting while Red and Hank are still arching up like salmon against the blue.

Will I never tire of this? I waggle my wings. I am panting and laughing. In they slide, with momentary extensions of speed brakes, until we are overlapped again. I nod my approval. *Not* so rusty, after all. Charles hung right in there.

We are over Edinburgh, I realize. The Firth of Forth lies just beneath. I yaw them out so they can look down.

"There's the castle, Blue," I say, "ten o'clock."

Their helmets tip downward.

"Piece of cake," Red says.

12

FRANCE

TWENTY-THREE DAYS and ten briefings after we had first arrived in Scotland, we hear the forecaster, still scholarly, still sliding his palm impassively over the Continent, say that we can go. Because he wears his usual expression, we are slow to react. I am almost startled when Hank starts beating me on the back.

"Fearless Leader! We're *going!* We're going to France."

As the rising murmur drowns him out, the forecaster finally shows us that he's human. He grins and bows. "Thank you, thank you."

Well, *finally.*

"Jesus," Dan says, "I've forgotten where we're going." He starts shaking his two nocturnal prowlers, who have just returned by train from Glasgow. They hold their heads and protest. Their eyes are hollow with exhaustion.

"I warned you, didn't I?" he says with satisfaction. "Tomcats always end up in trouble."

The flight itself is anticlimactic. Over Chaumont we circle to burn off excess fuel. Some of the landmarks, especially the Roman aqueduct, seem familiar from my P-51 missions during 1944. In widening circles, I take my flight northward over Nancy and Toul-Rosières, as far north as Pont-à-Mousson. From there, we can see Metz and several new airfields still under construction, among them our eventual, permanent destination.

On the ground at Chaumont, I find two old friends from my Korean days. They command flights in the '86 wing based here. We reminisce awhile and are surprised to discover how quickly we run out of common memories. We can't even remember all the names. After introducing each other to our lieutenants, who are on their best behavior, we pull out pictures of our kids. The lieutenants disappear.

Although the blue-tails have landed up at Toul, there are still too few BOQ rooms. Therefore, our squadron is billeted in the town of Chaumont, twenty minutes from the base. We are delighted. Our ceilings are so high that no one can make the celebrative champagne corks (and chewing gum) stick to them. Champagne being both expensive and of limited appeal to confirmed gin drinkers, we switch to *vin ordinaire*—pronounced repeatedly for Callahan's benefit by Scooter, who insists that the fingers must be held just so, thumb and forefinger touching, when ordering. "*Vin ordinaire,*" we repeat with equal care to the bored waiters and are relieved when a carafe of wine appears. And *cheese.* We slice through the crust of mold into a whiteness almost liquid. Frank smears it frantically on torn chunks of bread and chews ecstatically. So much for his resolution to trim weight for his coming wedding.

"*Je désire un chambre avec un grand lit pour deux,*" Scooter tells the proprietor's wife, who apparently likes bread and cheese, too.

"*UNE chAMbre, UNE chAMbre,*" she corrects him and smiles at us.

"Oui, *UNE chAMbre.*"

She replies, "Non, messieur," and rattles off something ending with "*très jolies mademoiselles.*"

Scooter pauses, leafs through his book. His lips move. A slow smile. He raises his eyes sidewise to us. "She's a cat," he says.

The old town is crumbling onto its sidewalks. Our Scottish boots are dusty with mortar. Through unshuttered windows we peek in, hoping to see France. Usually our eyes meet those of old women, who smirk. Generations of us have passed through. Perhaps they lay with our fathers. Now their eyes are cold. We are up to no good; we seek their daughters, their granddaughters. Here comes one girl, her head down like a nun's, brushing the side of the building to avoid us. The lieutenants smile, are slow to make way.

"Mam'selle," they say huskily. She ignores them.

Rebuffed, Al grimaces. It is a new experience for him. Some women find his Teutonic, collie face irresistible. He pulls off his silver-braided overseas cap, reflectively runs his fingers through short blond hair, gazes after her. What do they *want,* his shrug suggests. I laugh, and he blushes.

"Well, they loved me in Vegas."

"The word gets around," Hank says.

Here comes another—tall, such black hair, such a fair brow. Al smiles, sweeps his cap off in a bow. She wheels her bicycle past. There is a long loaf of bread in its luggage carrier. Al pinches off the end. She stops, surveys him until his eyes fall. *This is my town,* her gaze says. *Why are you here now that the Boche have gone?*

We have walked all the way out to the aqueduct, we realize. There are only fields. Above, the Roman arches curve to keystones. Sections of the dark structure are intact but, abruptly, the aqueduct ends in rubble. The military is not new to Chaumont.

At dusk, en route back to town, we notice that the encrusted shutters are closed. We shall never see France. During our week here, we have walked all the streets, even those which begin grandly but end in farmyards full of manure; we have seen all the local girls we are likely to see; we have worked our way through the hotel's menu. With increasing frequency we find excuses to return to the base. It is not Hamilton; it is not even Dover. Pipes run through BOQ rooms instead of through the walls; aesthetics be damned, the French contractors must have decided. But it *is* an airbase, and our birds are there.

No, we hear, our home base is not quite ready to accept us. The runway has developed cracks, and the parking marguerites haven't flowered. This is a joke, the French explain with exasperation: *the dispersal areas haven't been poured.* A few trailers have been trucked in for the advance party, whose families slop around in the mud. The earth is gumbo; it has been churned by tanks as well as bulldozers. Nothing, our engineers report, is up to expectations, much less specifications. We shall have to consolidate our wing at Toul-Rosières and wait, simply wait. Grim smiles. We are experts at waiting.

As we burn off fuel to reach landing weight, we curve around the triangle formed by Nancy, Metz and Verdun. It is the famous sector patrolled by the SPADS of the 1st Pursuit Group in 1918. In a few fields near Verdun, there are still the faint impressions of trenches. Almost a whole generation was harvested down there. From Metz westward to Flanders the annual plowings still turn up metal and bones, they say. In another twenty years, all traces will be gone, the survivors will be dead. The Great War will exist only in *L'Oissaire*'s million skeletons, in history, in uncompromising national attitudes.

Letters. That is the great reward of arriving at Toul. A few had been flown to us while we were in Scotland, but now there are bundles. Like dogs with bones, we slink away with them. Snapshots of Sam on his first birthday, of the cocker on his ninth, of Jenny in the Jag, of Jenny's father under the hood of the Jag, of the farm after the two-day blizzard. "Dad put the Jag in the barn. Said it might make a good chicken roost, but he couldn't think of much else it's good for." She loves me, she writes— almost as much as she loves Montgomery Clift. Did I receive the cookies? (Yes.) Were they edible? (Frank thought so.)

Ground school in nuclear weapons, actual flights with dummy weapons. We are gradually learning the area, widening our round-robin patrols. Fortunately, we sight no Fokkers.

If we wish to send for our families, the colonel tells us, we must do so at our own expense. Until there's a trailer designated for them, the government won't pay their fare. Nor will the Air Force pay per diem for living on the French economy. Still, we send for them. Jenny, Sam and the dog will come "steerage," Jenny decides. "It will not only save money to sail across—steam across?—especially if I can stay in the kennels, but we (Sam and I) can promenade around the deck *avec le chien* like Myrna Loy. The Jaguar started today, for some reason. With luck, we can duplicate this miracle next month in time to deliver her to the port. I think she misses California. I do."

The bachelors are beginning to act a little wilder. Maybe it's because they know it's all over; soon our wives will be here and, well, where does that leave *them*? "With all these cute mademoiselles!" we retort, but it doesn't sell. They're despondent and are already pulling away from us. I notice it in Charles, who has become a little cool. We've quit discussing literature, but we still go the the better movies together.

One Sunday morning Frank wakes me because he wants to discuss his wedding over breakfast, which he never misses. "Go wake your own flight commander," I had muttered, but then I got to thinking of bacon and eggs, and staggered up and out. Coming back, we find a muddy sport coat lying on the steps of our BOQ. Just inside the door lies a sport shirt. I recognize it as Scooter's. It is printed in a pattern of little golden trumpets, and it had been expensive in Ayr. Scooter's trail, as Dan had warned us, should be followed all the way. Up ahead, he could be lying in a puddle and drowning or something. Along the hallway lie little clues. They lead to a door ajar and, opening it, we find unrecognizably muddy shoes, socks and, asleep and uncovered on his bunk, the old elephant, boyish in sleep, clutching his muddy trumpet. He's breathing easily, so he hasn't swallowed his tongue. I cover him with a blanket, and he sinks deeper. Right through the day he lies there in state, his trumpet on his chest, right through the fire extinguisher fight that evening, right through one Jackie Gleason and two June Christie albums played at near-maximum volume. (Red has a new hi-fi which must be audible throughout Europe—and distortion-free, as he insists.)

"Scoot?" Dan shakes him. "Jesus, he's not asleep; he's unconscious."

"No, I'm not," Scooter says, eyes still closed.

We gather around him. Don tests him with a Tasmanian Devil growl. Feebly, the trunk rises a few inches.

"What time is it?"

"Noon, Pacific Standard Time," Don says. Don refuses to change his watch from California time.

"The dining room closes in thirty minutes, Scoot," Charles says.

That did it. Scooter is ravenous. After showering, he decides that life is worth living. While he eats, he explains his "dishabille." Medium-drunk, Scooter had heard that a dance-hall band in Nancy needed a trumpeter, so he headed for Nancy, inadequately clothed for the temperature, walking and hitching. But it was late at night, and there wasn't much traffic. One Peugeot did stop, and in gratitude Scooter played the driver a little tune. Wide-eyed, the driver pulled away before Scooter could get in. Then, freezing, he tried to hitchhike in either direction. Meanwhile, he began walking back to the base, finally cutting across fields, following the split-beacon "as the Wise Men did the Star."

So that dance hall in Nancy *still* needs a trumpeter. And, as Dan reminds us with concern, elephants never forget.

In retrospect, it's probably a good thing that Scooter's chief sent him off with a bottle of Courvoisier.

The earnest, foaming tugs shove the *Mauretania* against the pilings at Le Havre. Thousands of faces smile down at us few greeters along the dock. It is April, and the tourist season has begun. My eyes skim the tiers of waving people. She's not there. I work my way upstream through the last of those disembarking, my internal birddog needle finally steering me to the kennel on the top afterdeck. There she is, with Sam and the cocker.

"Hi," she says, kneeling there and hugging them. She is as pale as I ever have seen her. A big embrace, then tears. She's not quite here yet, I realize. And getting here was *not* half the fun.

It had been a terrible crossing, with the ship rolling to near-record limits. She had been too ill to visit the dog, could hardly raise her head to tend to Sam. The propeller shaft, almost immediately below her berth, pounded incessantly.

We will fly home, I assure her. She will never again have to go by boat. She nods and wipes her eyes. Sam stares at me with no sign of recognition. He and the dog had fared better; neither had missed a meal.

The boat train takes us to Paris, a taxi to the hotel near L'Etoile. She practices her French on the porters, the maids, the waiters. They love her, cluck at the baby, pat the growling dog. Her color and appetite return. A third honeymoon. April in Paris is true. The artists don't exaggerate this city. Sam we park in the nursery, but the cocker can go almost anywhere. He becomes blasé, frowning from taxi windows, threatening poodles in restaurants. We don't, however, take him into sacred buildings—Notre Dame, Les Invalides, the Louvre.

In Nancy we share a duplex with a French couple who work at the base. They are warm and kind to us. Do not shop there; this is a good wine for the money; ignore the landlord's promises.

A few of the guys buy cars. We cannot rely on the bus schedules. Often we are late for work. Don's wife arrives. He buys a German Ford. It looks like a roller skate, Frank tells him. "No, it's on casters," Don says.

"What does the name mean in English?" we ask as we inspect the emblem over the grille.

"Lemon," Don replies.

When the Jaguar arrives, minus mirrors, minus tools, filthy inside and out, I am despondent. The white headlights must be changed to yellow Marchals. On quartermaster gas, she pings. I drive across France vainly looking for a carwash. Jenny winces at the sight of her.

"Well," she says, "I know what she's been through."

But we are together again, the five of us.

13

GERMANY/LIBYA

MIDWAY THROUGH THIS summer-long May of 1955, we learn that an F-86 has landed at our future Alsatian base without leaving furrows of broken cement. The French contractors smile and shrug modestly. They adjust their berets, gesticulate with their cigarettes (I am always hypnotized by their fingers-up way of holding them). Americans are too impatient; cement does not become concrete overnight. This runway, they inform us, is poured of the same cement as the Maginot Line.

USAFE sends an F-100 down to test the pavement. The F-100 is a newer, heavier fighter that can go supersonic in afterburner while straight and level. It lands like a falling elevator. We are supposed to be equipped with them next year. The F-100 hero shoots several landings while we wince and the firemen gun their engines in anticipation. No problem. Everyone smiles. The runway *is* like the Maginot Line. There is a whole morning of handshaking.

Two weeks after we move in, an F-86 lands at an altitude of three feet and drops in. The Maginot Line cracks. Eventually, the contractors reappear in their muddy Citroens and caution us against making hard landings. Kissing one palm against the other, they demonstrate the proper technique.

"Once more," Tim says. Slack-jawed, he watches their hands, then follows us around imitating them.

It is no secret that the French government is adamant in its refusal to permit nuclear weapons storage on French soil. On the contrary, Paris wants this prohibition to be well understood by Russia. Maybe they have a point. God knows they have seen enough war during the past century, but where does that leave us? We must have quick access to our nukes or revert to a conventional role.

Why couldn't France have announced this restriction several years ago before we built all these expensive bases? Perhaps they needed new bases for their air force, Charles suggests with a cold smile. No, I say, I don't think that. Charles shrugs.

Well, in any case, what we have now is such a comically unworkable situation that the Soviet agents must suspect a trick. Let's see, they must be saying, their existing airbases in Germany are already crowded, so USAFE can't move nuclear delivery wings there. But France trusts them not to slip nukes across her borders . . .

Our best bet, it seems to me, would be to smile and let the Russian planners go insane trying to reason it out. Clearly, *our* planners did; they are seriously discussing staging us through German bases already multiply targeted by the Russians. We are, in fact, establishing an Alert detachment at a large base near Trier in the Eifel. This detachment will maintain a dozen birds on alert and, further, will be manned to load nukes on all remaining aircraft as they stage through. Who was the optimist who said that a poor plan well executed is better than no plan at all?

Commanding this detachment is a slim West Point major, quite senior, who has recently served at Sandia weapons center. When I heard this, I guess I expected him to glow in the dark, or something. Because of his seniority, Personnel had been pitching him around like a hot potato for weeks. The three squadron commanders were, of course, delighted to see him leave.

Major Allen will have permanently assigned to him an Operations officer, an Armament officer, a Supply officer (who will assume custody of the nukes), and about forty enlisted men. I regard the Supply officer—a volunteer—with awe. In terms of money, the Louisiana Purchase was less significant. If even *one* of his line items can't be found during subsequent inventory, they won't simply ask him to sign a statement of charges and dock his pay so much a month. They'll ask him whether he wants a blindfold. I watch this pudgy lieutenant ease around and wonder what sort of patriotism or naiveté could prompt an Iowa farm boy who does not even draw hazard pay to assume accountability for all these sleek, unimaginably costly weapons.

"Well," he explains, "there's no problem. If we get down to nuclear employment, we'll all be dead anyway." He grins. "Besides, once they are hung on your birds, guess who signs for them?"

"Ha!" Tim says. "If I sign for one, I won't expend it. I will not go along with your silly accountability system. I'll hide it in my closet."

The Alert detachment in Germany will be a seven-day-a-week operation, holidays included. Twelve birds and twelve pilots. We cannot leave the base. If we go to the barber shop, we must sign out. No heavy drinking in the evenings, midnight alerts, no dependents except for those of the cadre. Each pilot in the wing will serve in vague rotation, a month at a time. It is an opportunity to settle into the realities of our new mission, we are told, to learn the weapon and its monitoring system. But, we counter, there will be limited flying, just enough to exercise the machinery.

"Like firemen." Don shrugs. Smokey, old L.A. fireman, nods. "You get good at checkers and philosophizing, at girl watching."

On the plus side, you can escape the mud of France for a month or so each year. And whoever is chosen as Operations officer will have an apartment in the housing area of this plush airbase. The mission is a drag, admittedly confining, but . . .

Major Allen calls me aside. Am I interested? I don't know. No weekend jaunts in the Jag; not much flying except for periodic TDY to North Africa to practice gunnery and "special" weapons delivery. On the other hand, I'd pick up an Ops officer's specialty code and that helps when (and if) promotion time ever comes around. The board might even decide that such experience balances my having dropped Victorian Poetry.

Jenny, Sam and I are living at an expensive hotel in Metz—there seem to be no inexpensive hotels for Americans—and we are near the bottom of the captain's waiting list for a trailer. We talk it over while Sam and the dog listen.

"Yes, sir," I finally tell Major Allen.

I am curious to meet the Germans, the fiends who permitted Buchenwald and Auschwitz. My God, *how could they?*

For a month we will have to live in the hotel in this German village near Bitburg Air Base. I stare at the smiling owner who seems such a gentleman, watch the middle-aged maid as she makes up our bed.

The town was eighty-three percent destroyed during the war. The maid speaks a little English, Jenny (whose grandparents emigrated from this country) a little German. Had I served during the war? There is a terrible hesitation in her framing of the question. Jenny answers for me.

"*Ach, Gott.*" The maid nods, her eyes unfocused on the view from the window. She murmurs *schrecklich* and then something I can't understand.

"What did she say?"

"She said that if there is another war, she hopes that the first bomb kills her."

In Indiana an agent from the Office of Special Investigations is asking our neighbors just how American I am. My teachers—retired now, I suppose—may have trouble remembering me, but my Scoutmaster won't; he gave me my first ride in an airplane, a drafty little Taylorcraft with a marvelously strong landing gear. The agents in Southern California have even checked with Jimmy, who is a big deal at North American now. "What have you done *now*, you crazy fool?" Jimmy asked in a letter.

What I've done now is applied for a Top Secret Security Clearance. It is required of all our officers. The process begins by completing this book-length questionnaire. Are you now, or have you ever been, a member of a subversive organization? Well, let's see, during the Thirties I sent off those big threes from the Quaker Oats boxes and became a member of Little Orphan Annie's "Secret Three" Club. We had rings with message compartments, invisible ink, and we even knew code, as I recall. Then there was the Roscoe Turner "Heinz 57" Club, but that was all aboveboard.

"Get serious, Copley," the major in Personnel warns me. "This is no joke."

Okay. "Have I ever visited a foreign country within the past ten years?" Yes, Korea.

"Purpose of visit?"

"What if," Tim asks the major, "my parents still live in Moscow—is that okay?"

"Just fill out the questionnaire, wise guy."

"Right," Tim nods, "better dead than Red," he adds, and jumps away from Red.

My old flight volunteers for the first month of Alert. I will need their guidance, Hank tells Major Allen. Not being from North Dakota, I am irresponsible and flighty. Further, my automobile is unreliable. In case of an alert, I will need a lift.

Major Allen calls us together, officers and airmen. Henceforth, we are so classified that we cannot reveal our mission to anyone—not even our wives.

"Not even the forecaster?" Hank asks.

Major Allen shakes his head. Our practice missions, he explains, will range into France and Belgium. The forecaster will provide the winds and temperatures aloft over those countries.

"He will think we're going to attack France and Belgium?" Hank is incredulous.

"No." Major Allen smiles. "He will suspect that you may some day attack targets within East Germany. But *don't confirm it*. Okay? Tell him that you are sports balloonists." (Laughs.)

He wears no class ring, never mentions the Academy, but he's the real article. His obvious competence and dedication are not, of course, entirely the result of his privileged education. He was born the real article. One of our duds wears the ring. He goes around telling arthritic old crew chiefs not to step on the drop tanks.

Major Allen has to begin from scratch. Few of the NCOs know how to load and check out the weapon. It is a complicated procedure and requires religious use of a lengthy checklist. A mistake is unthinkable, even when the loading must be done at night and in driving rain. Major Allen is out there with them, his flashlight playing over the connections. He poses questions to his armament officer about abnormal checkouts on certain circuits. What if *both* safeties fail? Is there still a possibility of proceeding?

"I think so, sir," the captain nods.

"Captain, I don't ever want to hear that word 'think' again. Is that clear?"

We pilots get the same treatment. There can be no mistakes; there are no shortcuts. We study the enemy's order of battle, plan our penetration routes, select our Initial Points. He sits down with us at our tables, suggests that we not count on using an abandoned rail line (shown on maps five years old) for our final alignment. Lazily, he leans back in his chair.

"Suppose it is overgrown with weeds? Or the track has been ripped up? Would it, in any case, be easily found at dawn or dusk?"

He had graduated sixth in his class, we learn. The words "study" and "polish" are beginning to take on awesome dimensions. There are few compliments during those first months. I learn that it is possible to encourage without complimenting, to criticize with silence.

"Well," Red says, "preaching is easy, but perfection comes hard. Here's a little practice-target folder I'd like to see him try. It's at the same radius and it has the same sort of run-in as my real target."

"Which Major Allen has approved?" I ask.

"Which Major Allen has approved."

"Then he could fly it," I assure him.

Red holds out his hand. "Ten bucks?"

I shake.

A week later, as he and the major are hanging up their parachutes, Red silently thumps with his middle finger a wadded ten-dollar bill at me. To his chagrin I unfold it and show it around. It is possible then. We have been challenged.

Okay, who is second best? How can we tell? Easy, a young Academy first lieutenant says. And necessary, he rightly maintains; competition (and sex) hold one's interest. He devises a point system. One-half mile off-course costs you five points, a mile ten; each knot off the precalculated run-in airspeed docks you a further point. And so forth. A sharp guy, Mike. In ten years he will be famous, I predict, and not simply because he's the founder of Operation Chickenshit, as we call it.

The weeks pass, and the scores are conspicuously posted. My name is near the bottom, Red's near the top. Mike is second-best, actually best because the major rarely gets to fly now. He is usually putting out fires elsewhere, arguing with the home office about maintenance, with the housing office here about obtaining a few more sets of quarters. Cartoonists don't understand command. They depict generals as fat, pompous asses. Cartoonists play to the groundlings, Charles mutters, and jerks his thumb at Hank and Joe.

"*We* fly," they protest.

"Well, so did Shakespeare," Jenny reminds Charles at dinner in our apartment. "Play to the groundlings, I mean."

"But not *all* the time," Charles replies. "Granted—an adversary relationship is expected and, to a certain degree, healthy. But a *little* credit for work well done doesn't indicate that the press is abrogating its responsibilities."

Down the inked lines we fly, carrying concrete-filled shapes simulating special weapons, our shadows rising and falling like hurdlers', over the dripping black conifers of southern Germany, over the sunny estates along the Loire and the Rhone. In the summer there is haze; in winter, mist. Visibility is rarely more than five miles. Our course lines are ticked off in minutes. Set course, punch a stopwatch, hold an exact speed, descend to the trees and skim the hills. Where cloud becomes fog, climb to clear all obstacles by one thousand feet and proceed, using dead reckoning. Avoid airways and airport control zones.

Winter is coming. Rain streams back along our canopies. There are no windshield wipers. We race along between stratus and trees, leaning forward in our cockpits, searching for a particular road or rail line. Often towns with high steeples lie to either side. No one has authorized this joyless buzzing, but there is no other way to learn low-level navigation. If we are to penetrate enemy radar defenses, there is only one way. The generals would quickly disclaim us, would pretend to be appalled. We understand. That is their role, this ours.

Route Nationale Three, poplar-lined, string-straight. A snow shower to the south, a black steeple against a white sky ahead. Charles is chasing me and grading.

"Jettison drop tanks *now*. Push up power," I call. We jettison nothing.

Dreamlike, past the yellow headlights of the chevroned Citroens and corrugated 2CV Renaults, the Initial Point appears and quickly slides beneath. Over it, I change course, leave pavement for rail lines. A second later, abeam a crossing, I push the red button on my stick grip.

"Hack!"

"Roger," Charles acknowledges.

I am indicating 480. I nudge the throttle. The rail lines curve away. Now I must trust our mapmakers. I hold my heading, hold 486 knots. It is an act of faith, like swimming out into the darkness. A light on my instrument panel glows.

"Pull-up Point."

"Roger."

But we don't zoom into an escape Immelmann. An airway lies above. Instead, we climb to the cloud bases and see the pitifully insignificant bridge slide under my nose.

"Piss-poor," Charles says.

Beneath my mask, I grin. The tension ebbs. I unclip my mask to light a cigarette. We climb from beneath the shelf of clouds, follow the Moselle northward. It is almost dusk.

To have linked all the details into one flowing operation *is* professionally satisfying. Not that we will ever drop real nukes, of course; this is just a game we play for drinks. Perhaps, on gray days when the world seems dead anyway, it might be possible to take out a bridge or a marshaling yard without remorse. But not if they lie within cities. On a sunny day, no matter how often Major Allen taps with his pointer the drawn components of the cutaway bomb, I can't imagine really employing it against a whole Soviet fighter wing.

"You can't, huh?" Major Allen asks softly. "Well, what do you suggest? A jousting tournament? Reorganizing the Lafayette Escadrille? We are outnumbered five to one. Do you imagine that *they* will hesitate to launch their nuclear IRBMs if that day ever comes? Look at their ground order of battle, the number of divisions billeted just beyond the border. Our targets are *valid military targets,* John."

I consider this. The cleansing white lights that might give NATO a chance to hold, a partial restoration of parity.

"You *must* imagine it, John. Otherwise, *why are you here?*"

Good question. Is, in any case, employing tactical nukes worse than dumping napalm on them? God, I don't know. But I'm here now, as a deterrent. The nuke is simply another weapon, except that its employment requires presidential approval.

"Everyone goes through this," the major says, sighing. "I did. We cannot afford the luxury of irresolution, as scientists can. They can create something, then say, 'Oh my God.' But we are stuck with the fact. I *believe* in deterrence. I *believe* that without our nukes there is a much higher probability of war."

I nod, finally.

But Frank is deeply troubled. In college he minored in philosophy and now, on principle, he resigns his commission and takes his bewildered bride home. He will try for an airline job. Without rancor, Major Allen shakes his hand. A man must follow his conscience, he tells Frank.

"Frank is about four years late," Charles says laconically. "Call it integrity if you like."

"Well," I rationalize, "we'll never get off the ground anyway. Our first indication of trouble will be a blinding white light over the base."

"Maybe. Maybe not. They want to hit our SAC bases in the States at all

137

costs. We are small fry. There might be enough time. Our DEW Line will see their bombers coming, but . . ." His voice trails off. He smiles and nods hopelessly at our field phones. "Yeah."

In the dead of night, often in the autumn rain, our loading crews stream in grim headlit convoys from the storage area a mile away to our revetments in the woods. Tarps hide the training dummies, security curtains shield the floodlit planes. Men in olive-drab ponchos blow on their hands and guide the dollies back under the wing pylons. They leave the canvas covering as much of the slim weapons as possible. It is like surgery, except that access panels replace incisions. Heads bend over the vitals while the supervisors read their checklists. It has become routine.

Beside me stands a young Air Policeman and his huge shepherd, Wolf. Over the months I have come to know Wolf. I can tell from his expression that he is not vicious unless you are a yelling, padded trainer thrusting a gauntlet at him. Absently, I reach to pat him, but the AP, shocked, jerks him away.

"Sir!" he says warningly. He is afraid that if the secret of Wolf's gentleness reaches his superior, the dog will be destroyed. I understand. Wolf doesn't. He smiles at me.

Now the weapon is nakedly silver, symmetrically beautiful beside its fat drop-tank companion. The drop tank is gray with age, the pampered weapon like chrome. Blood-red streamers form its panache. From the cockpit an airman reads off light indications as he clicks a knob on a continuity tester.

"All right," nods our big armament officer. He consults his stopwatch, compliments the loading team. "Bunch of pros." A slow grin. "Okay, *download*." They groan.

Yesterday in an earth-covered, sandbagged igloo behind guarded steel doors, I checked off serial numbers as the supply officer read them off. We were both tired, and there was a page to go on my clipboard. I leaned back against one of them and wished I could smoke. You can get used to anything, really, because the mind has its own security curtain. All I was thinking about was Sam's fever. At 0200, when Jenny tortured him in the bathtub of tepid water, it was 104 degrees.

By the time the Suez and Hungarian crises develop, our wing is reasonably combat-ready. Every one of our seventy-two pilots has trained here in Germany for at least two months. The headlines become black, and the practice alerts become real. We pace around the field phones and sleep in Ops, on the floor, on the Ping-Pong table. Or try to. It's too late to evacuate dependents. Meanwhile, our dull fear spreads into the housing area—"Little America," it is called. Jenny hears the big flatbeds deploying equipment to dispersal bases. I think of her and Sam and the dog as blindly I recheck the forecast for East Germany and post the winds aloft. In the woods the APU exhausts periodically rattle us awake. It is a grim time. Oktoberfest passes unnoticed. We dare not fly.

Crew chiefs run up the engines; armament crews recheck the weapon circuitry. The covers are replaced, and the fall rain drums on the aluminum.

The hot lines ring. We tense. Our duty officer, a roster-designated pilot, answers them: "Ready to copy."

We watch his face and his coded scribbles. Tim cheers and waltzes me around. I recheck the code for the day.

Stand down.

They are yelling, and I am having a hard time remaining impassive as I crank the phone to Maintenance, to Armament and repeat the code words. I can hear their cheers, and I pause to listen before hanging up. The push-to-talk switches are frozen open with frankly human paralysis. The best training is that which soaks your marrow, and the catalyst is fear.

The sun is warm and bright, the air clean. I am chasing and grading Major Allen in a sort of renewal of faith in the system. Typically, he has not spoken since takeoff. We are skimming the highway between Milhausen and Belfort with its ruins of old forts.

"There!" he exclaims in his quiet instructor's voice. "That's where it began."

"Say again, Lincoln Leader."

"The Western Front," he explains. We lapse into silence again but, as he advances the power and turns his IP, I see again the old, grainy photographs—the dead, lying face down or on their backs, already swollen and fly-ridden. We make no sense. But we make no important decisions. Statesmen agree that war is far too serious to be left to generals. Like most soldiers, comfortable with their barracks routines, generals are far less fond of war than statesmen. Look at the record: General Von Moltke tried to dissuade Bismarck, his nephew tried to warn Kaiser Wilhelm II, the German General Staff argued (briefly, true) with Hitler. *Ambition,* however it is garbed, *causes war.* From my recent reading I have gleaned this.

"Am I right?" I ask Charles.

"I don't know. I was a lit major."

"C'mon."

He shrugs. "I'd guess you're at least half right. But beware the simplistic approach, John. Nearly everything is complex. Certainly we aren't blameless. If nothing else, we demonstrate possibilities."

"Which politicians exploit."

He nods.

"We should stick to polo?" I ask.

"I don't know."

Wheelus, beige and barren, isn't much like George. I don't know why, but it isn't. Both are desert airbases, both are often airborne as dust in the Santa Anas (ghiblis or siroccos, these winds are called over here), but there is a basic difference. Maybe it's purely geographic. At George we knew that we could drive for an hour and be in what passes for civilization in America. Drive for a *day* from Wheelus and you are still nowhere. Nevertheless, twice a year (theoretically) we must visit scenic Wheelus, the gem of "Exotic Libya" (here many boos and elephant shrieks)—for gunnery and practice in atomic weapons delivery, acronymed HABS and LABS (High Angle, or Low Angle, Bombing Systems). In short, European population density and weather being what they are, USAFE—United States Air Forces, Europe—has its Weapons Center in Africa.

Twice a year, for six weeks at a time, every fighter pilot must requalify in his weapons specialty(ies) at Wheelus. Or what? Well, nothing. Regulations deal with dreams, the dreams of idealistic generals who, when the budgetary chips are down, have to face facts. As Ops officer of the detachment, I cannot be spared for two such trips each year—thank God.

Across the fabled Tyrrhenian Sea, towards the rough, bloody arrowhead of Sicily we climb. Again we are the despised clowns of Fox Able, off on a new holiday from responsibility. Radio discipline is pretty raunchy. Sliding in close, Hank guzzles from a leather wine flask for my benefit, slides out again, wavering. At forty-two thousand feet, we are fixed between blues, motionless in a sailor's grid of parallels and meridians. Behind, almost forgotten, lies the giant, deformed boot kicking the stone. We leave no cons. Only the curvature of the earth limits our visibility. Over Palermo we could see Malta; over Malta, Tunisia and—too faintly to be certain—the coastal rim visited by Ulysses.

We throttle back for the long descent. Ahead, a foamy sliver becomes a freighter veeing her bow-wave back. She, also, is headed for Tripoli, but she is still ten hours out, we are only ten minutes from touchdown.

I signal channel change and call the tower for landing instructions.

Down the golden line we fly, each alone, fifty feet above the desert, flashing over holes shielded from the sun by shabby cloth. Arabs live in those holes. No wonder they hate us. We wash our sudden exhaust over them, make their babies scream.

Dead ahead, poised on a ridge, is a small white dome—the Sheik's Tomb. It serves as our IP. As I skim it at 503 knots, I depress my pickle button, and my intervalometer begins its countdown. When an amber light illuminates, I begin my Immelmann, keeping the delicate, wavering needles centered, holding exactly four Gs. At forty-five degrees of pitch, a gyro releases one of my six-pound practice bombs. We separate, arching in opposite directions. Up into the powder-blue I strain, vertical, past vertical, finally inverted over the run-in line. I half roll and curve down to the east, watching over my shoulder for the white puff of the spotting charge. There! A little long. I must have been a half second slow in attaining four Gs.

"Three hundred feet at twelve," Scooter calls in his pitchman's voice from the range tower. "No cigar. Step right up, folks. Who's next?"

In the afternoons, when turbulence makes low-level a real kidney-jarrer, we dive-bomb.

"Leader's in," I call from base leg at twenty thousand.

"Hold it, Blue. We have Arabs in the circle."

We take turns as range officer. With the range officer is a mounted Libyan policeman. His horse is, well, Arabian. Beautiful, with his shiny skin flickering, the horse wheels nervously. The range officer points, the policeman spurs away. From twenty thousand, pilots can see his stream of dust enter the circle and curl around. He is good with a quirt. From above we see the dots scatter and run for the earthern rim.

"All clear, Blue."

I do my half gainer and reverse, establish the prescribed seventy-eight-degree dive angle.

"Leader's in," I call.

At fifteen thousand, I pickle and pull out. Although it could lead to fried eyeballs some day, this insistence upon feedback following performance, I look back. *Puff.* Two hundred at three o'clock. The winds have picked up, I rationalize.

Within a few minutes, the dots swarm back into the circle. It is like looking at an especially puzzling microscope slide. They are digging up our six-pounders, metal we consider expendable. Some, we know, have their spotting charges intact. In the markets of the Old Town, these casings fetch a few piasters. Melted down, our bombs become pewter trays and bracelets, occasionally incendiary, I imagine. (Imagine heating cordite.) Well, it beats starving. As range officer, I have seen them—heads thrown back, arms beckoning the planes in—through binoculars, and roused the policeman. Fatalism is not my philosophy. I am not even Presbyterian. Oh, certainly, the odds of being hit within a nine-hundred-foot circle are small. Of being blinded, better, I suppose. Of being knifed by a close competitor—oh, *yes,* the police officer smilingly demonstrates with his saber—excellent. Still, one must try to be first to reach the bomb.

The police officer has conferred dignity. He takes his time mounting. He smiles at our naiveté. It doesn't matter that he understands little English. He sees our eyes, and our pity amuses him.

"The world," I begin one morning while watching him smoke one of my cigarettes, "cannot go on this way. *Compris?*"

He smiles as he exhales smoke.

"You know what I mean?"

He smiles and stretches as Cat Man did when we philosophized in Korea.

"No?" he asks, laughing at me. He goes to water his valuable horse.

The score sheets have become a joke. The plots are clustered at three and at nine o'clock, because the Arabs were at nine and at three o'clock respectively. Hits near the pyramid are considered bad form. Some of the guys crayon strings of Arabs below their canopies, but I know of only one fatality. An old man tried to catch a lobbed bomb. He did. The range officer didn't think to plot its final impact. The mounted police officer laughed.

Letters from Germany. She's in love with her gynecologist, she warns me. She should have married a doctor; I'll never be rich *or* loved. But I wouldn't swap jobs with him. That would ruin sex for me. She likes being pregnant. That's crazy because it's painful and dangerous. It's a girl, she writes. She can tell how differently it moves around—languidly. The slinky hormones are already in motion. What's my schedule? Should she push or contract? We really must beat the tourists to Switzerland, she suggests. The Jag? Oh, she's sick again; she's done very well, considering the octane rating of QM gasoline, but she's making this funny noise. "A pounding?" I write. "A metallic knock?" No, she replies, a rattle. My God, I think; she's *dying*. "No, under the chassis, and the exhaust is very loud." I relax.

Yes, it was the muffler. But Kurt suggests that we sell the car. Kurt (our Mercedes agency mechanic, a limping, haranging veteran) has the most practical of philosophies: in America, buy a Ford or Chevrolet; in Germany, buy a Mercedes or a VW; in England, a Ford or a Mercedes. "The English," he explains haughtily, "do not understand *anything*." He is very positive about this. One evening, he and his *Frau* come to our apartment for dinner. She is a delight, an enthusiastic diner, a person unchanged by wine, a scolder of frank mechanics.

"Oh, the British!" she concedes. We visit them and see photographs of the town lying in the streets. Slowly they hand us the old prints, gravely they maintain silence. I cannot tell whether bombs or artillery shells caused this damage. If artillery, then it was the U.S. 12th Army Group. (I have read Omar Bradley's book.) Montgomery's British passed much farther north. But I say nothing.

Over Kurt's workbench is a framed certificate bearing the Mercedes star. He is a graduate of their mechanic's school in Stuttgart. Beside it is a large poster, a telephoto shot of Fangio and Moss driving their silver W196s, both calmly drifting, goggled and helmeted, their wheels almost interlocked: Silverstone, Nürburgring, Monaco. . . . Kurt always calls my attention to it, tapping the star and nodding as he finds wrenches which might fit the Jaguar's balky carburetors.

"Jaguar," he smirks. "Le Mans."

Better than long-distance bombing is our old ritual, air-to-air gunnery. In the nuclear age, it is an anachronism, I suppose, and yet it defines us. Even the generals are sentimental about it. Each year they applaud the winner of the USAFE Gunnery Meet. It is a rite.

From Homs to Misurata along this surfless coast, we take turns towing the banner. Its nylon translucence often renders it invisible until an attacking pilot reverses his bank in the pursuit curve. Initially, one must use the tow-ship as his basic reference and trust that the rag is still behind it.

This morning, my empty stomach rumbling for breakfast, still half asleep, I am towing. The sun is just clearing the horizon, and light off the water is painful. My left hand has become a sun visor. I am searching for Dan's clowns as I set course. Usually, Dan has checked in by now. I have the whole Mediterranean to myself. The tow-bar, for a wonder, is absolutely vertical, the rag perfect, the air still—but that bunch of drunks has slept in.

Whoomp! An F-86 races beneath me and pulls up through my path. I jar and flail through his wash. My heart has stopped.

"Wake up, John." It is Dan's giggle, the bastard.

Inevitably, the other three bump me, too. My bird is almost uncontrollable at this speed.

"I just lost the rag," I tell them.

"You better not have," Dan laughs, "because old Red Leader is in, *hot,* and *I'm gonna shoot at something.*"

Bastards. I drank with them until midnight, catching up on all the scandals in the trailer park. Dan's wife is our gossip columnist. Her letters should be classified. Bill's wife, she writes, caught him in bed with their French maid, and you could hear her screams in Etain. In retaliation, she took off for Paris with the Greek god (a red-tailed bachelor who is the Wing Stud). And remember the two blue-tailed lieutenants who had bragged about visiting the Old City? Well, they've got it bad. And when a certain major's wife heard about it, she turned white and practically *ran* to the clinic. There was a party at the O Club last Friday and Mickey, strictly blind, pinched Nasser's beautiful wife. "Nasser picked him up like Tom does Jerry in the cartoons and threw him out into the snow."

Elegantly, steepening his bank like a bobsledder, Dan closes. His scoop becomes ravenous. Cordite smoke trails him. A flick of his wing, and he's gone.

"Leader's off."

"Two is in." Tarzan plummets from the perch, arrests his fall abeam me, rolls evenly from left bank to right in terrible beauty.

Rhythmically, they curl around me in a lazy sine wave; Three is off, Four is in. Perfect interval. The sun rises and heats me, their calls lull me; I lie within a cocoon of their sine waves.

Dust from the coastal road. Here, a single vehicle can be detected from fifty miles away. I watch it as our little circus moves past and think of the immensity of the brown pall, laid to leeward as though it were mustard gas, by the *Panzerarmee*'s mottled tigers and half-tracks, slewing on their treads, racing ahead of Montgomery's Eighth Army. Rommel, gentleman enough even in defeat to compliment Auchinbeck's grim opposition in the face of British doubt, was the professionals' professional. The Fox was finally caught, but not by the Allies, not when retreating toward the airhead in Tripoli, not in European battles. Any soldier would have shaken his hand, would have gone beyond saluting.

I awake with a start over the Gulf of Sirte. How long have I been daydreaming? I make a quick one-eighty and nudge the throttle. Like an old man, I have been lost in time.

"Roger, Yellow," I concede to Whit. "I was off base. Sorry. You are cleared in."

"Well, I should hope. Hold still so I can shoot you."

When Yellow Flight leaves, the rag is a shambles. I ease back the throttle and begin the long descent. Puttering along at prop speeds, getting nowhere, suddenly I raise my visor, unclip my mask, and search my eyes in the mirror. *That is me?* My God, Red is right. I *am* an old man.

When I see the target stretched on the frame before our Ops Quonset, I realize that it, like a record-weight marlin, will never be forgotten. It is spattered with seven colors, a different one for each pilot, like some wild artist's drip canvas. I note the three-inch-long green holes. Joe avoids my gaze.

"Joe," I say.

"Yes, sir. I'm sorry. I couldn't seem to let go of it."

Smiling, I grasp his throat. "Funny," I tell him, "I can't seem to let go of *you*."

I release him. "Tomorrow you tow, and I'll shoot."

Dan had shot *seventy* percent, Whit fifty. Fantastic. Four guys had qualified.

Dan grabs me in a bear hug, lifts me off the ground. "Johnny, you fuckin' Irishman, you're my good luck piece."

"So take me to Vegas."

"By God," he nods, "I will. Get your chute and helmet."

I have the sergeant throw the target over the wall. It's no longer the virginal cloth the Arabs hope for, but it's a gesture. In time we may establish trust. And there are, in truth, lots of targets almost untouched. These embarrassments they receive in record time. Sometimes I kid myself that all the world's problems can be solved so easily. We waste so much, we Americans. And what do they do with the nylon cloth? Why, make silk purses, of course, and their handiwork is surprisingly attractive. I sent a purse to Jenny, and she didn't understand until I showed her the blue semicircle edging an interior seam.

In the Old Town where I bought this purse and two camel saddles ("Please, sweetie, no more camel saddles; we are fresh out of camels"), one mustn't look at the veiled women, and cameras are *verboten*. No sweat, I can live without *these* women. And vice versa, I suppose. Ideally, we millionaires should just buy out all the shops and go away. Hatred is so clear in their eyes. But how many purses, how many camel saddles, how many brass trays (caliber .50 shells) and pewter ashtrays is one in good conscience obligated to buy? Poverty is always bad, but when an industrious people cannot feed their children, it is heartbreaking. I look at the waiters in the club, so polite, so afraid for their jobs, and I don't know what to do.

Twice a week our wing goony bird arrives with mail and parts. While its props flutter to a stop against cylinder compression, we grin at the wing wienies in the cockpit, meet them at the door with cold beers. They aren't really leprous.

"Where are we? Greece?" Happy asks.

"*Oui, monsieur*," Tarzan bows. "You want to see the Acropolis?"

"First, I want to see your latrine, Tarzan. Then I want to see that Greek blonde" (hums "Never on Sunday").

Some of these multiengine types are *ex-pilots,* to use their phrase— former fighter jocks, who with age and too many staff jobs behind them, sell their souls for flying pay. They man the desks all week and "free men for combat" (a slow smile on Happy's tough face). Eric Camston flies the goon, too, especially if it's going up to Norway or Denmark. But he's not like old Happy here.

"Did Eric ever get checked out in the '86?" I ask Happy.

"Shit, no. Why would anybody want to check that prissy bastard out in anything?"

"Has Betty joined him?"

"You kiddin'? She's too smart a girl to leave mama for that clunk."

"How is he taking it?"

"Crocodile tears and a stiff upper lip. Let me tell you something: Eric is in no pain—ever. He's in Sweden right now, and he ain't there for winter sports."

I provide Happy and the other goony bird wienies with beer, chow and beds—three of the four necessities, as Happy says; but where is Merlina?—and since all of us are still wearing flying coveralls, we patronize the Seabreeze, our screened, one-bartender waterfront club where we riffraff hang out. "What say we have a couple for the perimeter road, shower, change and go to the club for a steak?"

Happy shrugs, absently crumples a beer can.

"Hey, easy," I warn him. "Don't bend them too much. The Arabs don't like it."

Happy smirks. "Fuckin' A-rabs." He nods, rubs his back. I hand him a fresh can.

We walk down to the water. Tarzan points northeast. "Look, *monsieur,* the Acropolis! Ten drachma, please. Hey, good flick tonight, troops. Giant crabs invading New York."

Happy has a paunch now. Desks and goony birds don't generate enough Gs to keep the bellyband tight. He chunks rocks; some of the flat ones skip. After ten throws, he is winded. He slumps down beside me, unzips my sleeve pocket to extract a cigarette.

"You stationed down here?" he asks me.

"When? What do you mean?"

"During the war, dummy. I *know* you're not stationed here now."

"England."

His head goes back, his smile rolls away. "Oh, *tough!* You were up there with Gable? Fuckin' Hollywood Air Force. No bombs, just film. You shoulda been down here with us and our muddy P-40s. This is where the war was."

"You're talking about World War Two?"

"*The* war. The big one."

"Who were you fighting, the A-rabs?" I ask him.

"All I know, friend, is this is where King Arthur came, not England."

"King Arthur."

"Sir Arthur *Coningham?* Air Vice Marshal Coningham?"

"Never heard of him."

He is appalled. "You're kidding."

I shrug.

"*Everyone* knows about him. My *mother,* for chrissakes, knows about Coningham."

"Your mother knows about Gable, too."

Tarzan is out of it. I keep him balanced on his barstool, but he's gone; his head is on the bar and his limbs are dangling. Happy accepts the dice cup, grimaces as Dan's iron claw grabs his neck. I twist in time to block Whit's rabbit-punch.

"Anyhow, you know the Army," Happy continues. "They thought we were still part of the Signal Corps so they had us circling the flagpole. Old Army field manuals are big on air umbrellas and barrage balloons. Purely defensive. The *Luftwaffe* thought this was great. They never had to worry about where we were, about their birds getting caught on the ground. Then King Arthur comes down and tells Patton—Old Blood and Guts—to go fuck a duck. Patton had Two Corps, see?"

"King Arthur?" Dan puzzles.

"Yes sirree."

Dan's eyes open wide. "The *real* King Arthur?"

Wheeling away in exasperation, Happy stands to leave. "Thanks, John. Thanks for the brews. When you going over?"

"What'd I say?" Dan asks, his palms up.

"King Arthur was seventh century," Happy says through gritted teeth.

"But he was magic or something? Don't get mad."

"Jesus Christ, John. I can't take any more."

I calm him down with another beer. He explains that Air Vice Marshal Sir Arthur Coningham was *the* Mister Tactical Air of World War II, and that if we had never heard of him, we must have all been in the seventh grade or prison or somewhere.

"I've heard of Sir Ar—" Whit begins, but I clap my hand over his mouth.

"Okay," Happy says finally. "Well, then things picked up. We went after the Krauts and showed the crunchies what air can do. We were busy. I wore the same flying suit for a month."

"I believe that," Dan says.

"I didn't need guns."

Somebody has to light Happy's cigarette. His Zippo is out of fluid. He shows us where the fluid went, unzipping and lifting his undershirt to display the red blotch. "It felt great," he says, "just great. If I had overfilled it, I could understand it. I mean, if you can't trust Zippo, who *can* you trust?"

"Me," says Tarzan, lifting his head from the bar.

Happy sweeps him towards him. "Yeah," he grins. "Probably so. Where was I?"

"Flying P-40s down here for King Arthur."

"Right. Okay, visualize it: a bright Sunday morning, a whole flock of flying Quonsets—JU52 transports—and not much escort. We had full cans of ammo and lots of gas. It was sickening. Goddamn slaughterhouse. We just, you know, fired out. Our cans went empty. And they were flopping around, skidding and slipping, trying to get away. It was sad, you know? I was crying finally. Can you believe that? *Me? Crying?*"

He is almost crying *now*, fourteen years later. Starkly, I see the grainy gun-camera film clicking: the whole camera aperture vibrating, smoky lines converging, tracer rounds slowing with distance, every fifth round a tracer, and the clumsy birds hanging there in silent disintegration. I have heard of the Palm Sunday Massacre. He was there. It dwarfed all of gangland's massacres, but few civilians ever heard of it.

"We were in a feeding frenzy, like sharks. Only there was plenty for everybody. Their crossed controls didn't fool us any more than side-kicking fools a shark." Briefly he looks at us, then down again at this beer can he's crushing. "You know how API lights up when it hits metal? Well, their wings were as thick as railroad bridges, so you couldn't cut 'em off like tree limbs, but you could work on the tail, except then you were hitting meat. They were evacuating troops, you know. For some reason I'd aim at the engines. It had three, but if you knocked out the side engines, he had to try to ditch. I guess I thought—you know, give 'em a chance. But they'd somersault when they touched down."

Now Whit and Dan are seeing it. They raise their heads.

"For some reason, I'd always begin with the left engine—that's how military you can get—and then when it began backfiring and smoking, I'd slide over to the right. Once a whole cowling came tumbling right over my canopy and banged into my vertical stabilizer. That was the only danger—debris. After that, I was almost afraid to shoot. That was the only problem, that and limited ammo—*and the stomach for it.*"

He is as cynical as Wilfred Owen, whom Charles has got me reading, about war. For God and Country and all that. And yet—*and yet*—Owen went back to the Front to die. And not simply to die passively but to continue the fighting he despised. Posthumously, he was awarded the Military Cross. And he would have despised that, too, except insofar as it proves that he did his *duty,* that he didn't run. That, in other words, he was *honorable*. It seems that we have two of the three words of West Point's Motto. For Country? That old lie: *Dulce et decorum est / pro patria mori.*

"*Jawhol!*" Happy smirks, "*für der Vaterland.* You know where I learned to speak German? In Ohio at my grandfather's knee. Correction. At my grandfathers' and grandmothers' knees. Count 'em; that's eight fuckin' knees. Anyhow, these guys died for their Fatherland, and nobody cares. No one even remembers."

"Rolling and rolling there/ Where God seems not to care. . . ."

My mental film is still running. Ugly machines hang in a froth of debris, sparkling and smoking into ignition. They smack the water and stop too quickly or cartwheel. Silence. The film runs out into white light.

"How many did you get?" Dan asks. The question is expected of one of us.

Without raising his head, Happy holds up three fingers.

"How many total?"

Happy shrugs. "Sixty? We claimed seventy, so sixty." (Laughs) "Plus whatever escort the Spits got." He pats my pockets, finds my lighter, extracts it. "Goddamned slaughterhouse. I couldn't do it now. But, then, *I don't have to do it now,* do I? I'm a wing wienie."

We put him to bed. It was necessary.

I'm sorry that Red and Hank missed this story. To them, wing wienies aren't simply has-beens; they are our poor white trash. But what I should try to remember is their seeming ignorance of and contempt for the entire past. Korea, Schmorea. Udet? Who was *he*? Roosevelt? Which one?

None of these clowns with GI driver's licenses knows how to double-clutch, so I climb under the wheel and away we go. The six-by-six bellows its song over the salt flats, and I deliver a beer-soggy truckload of crew chiefs to the airmen's tents, then proceed around the perimeter road to the officers' area where most of our tents lie collapsed by the brief ghibli. In my headlights I see Major Possum Slocum, curled in misery like some wartime refugee, struggling to erect a tent pole. I leave the lights on and dismount to help him.

Canvas weighing more than lead, there is no way two men can erect an eight-man tent, but we do; like two guys in a horse costume, we rise individually to our feet, suffocating and panting, straining to kick the poles upright.

"By God," Major Slocum nods as we tighten the guys.

The hot wind stings us with sand. We try to catch our breath. Amazingly, there is still electrical power. Even more unlikely, the dangling bulb works.

"Hey, Triple-A!" Possum laughs. "Thanks, John. Y'know, I just don't understand why anyone in his right mind would do this for a living, do you?"

"No, sir."

"Maybe we're crazy," he says thoughtfully, then begins flapping sand out of his blankets and remaking his cot, hospital corners and all. There remains a half case of cold beer in the truck. I switch off the headlights, find a church key, and open a couple. It's all I do these days.

He lifts his in silent appreciation and wearily sits on his cot. "Y'know, I was just thinking—sit down, John, there on Pete's bunk—I was just thinking: I own *two* four-bedroom houses and I rent a GI trailer up in France. Can you tell me why, after fourteen years in the Air Force, I'm still living in a goddamned *tent*?"

He is grinning, and yet he is serious. He shows me an envelope. It is from a Colonel Sam Jordan and the APO is Wiesbaden's.

"Read it."

It is a job offer: Flying Safety Office, Headquarters USAFE. The job offers an attractive blend of stability and short inspection trips. No tents at all, and he would be home every weekend. A T-Bird for transportation. I fold the letter and hand it back.

"What do you think?" he asks me.

I am flattered. Majors never consult me. "Sounds good."

"You know Sam?"

"No, sir."

"You've heard of him though. No? Well, Sam would be a great boss. We were cadets together, for Christ's sake. And now he's a full bull, and I'm still a major." (Laughs) "Don't get me wrong. No sour grapes. He's good. He's no ass-kisser, you understand? Why are you smiling?"

"Flying Safety."

"Yeah," he acknowledges, and looks down in embarrassment. "I know. Who needs it? Don't forget your seat-pins, use your checklist, don't crash. The only thing a Flying Safety officer is good for is to investigate accidents and tell us what happened. But now they're trying to sneak out from under that. They want to *monitor* the board and make sure the right papers go out on time. It's all paper now."

"Oh, I don't know. They gig people for unsafe practices."

"Yeah, and I'd certainly gig *you* fat cats up at the Alert detachment. You've violated so goddamned many rules I could stay there a month compiling discrepancies. I'd be like the fox in the henhouse."

"We'd bribe you with booze." I am laughing now. "Besides, Major, we maintain Visual Flight Rules at all times . . ."

"VFR bullshit. Why, I'd fill up two clipboards in ten minutes."

"Oh, no. On paper, we look legal as hell and, while you were there, we would play it right by the book."

"Okay." He reaches over to tap my shoulder. "Then I'd gig you for just flying or something. It's not safe." He laughs and slaps his thigh. "Well, you're pretty cagey, aren't you? You still haven't told me what you'd do."

I was hoping he wouldn't notice. "I'd take it," I tell him. "I'd jump at it." I can tell that he's already decided to go.

"No, you wouldn't."

"No." I smile, and he corks me. "But *I* haven't filled in all the blocks at squadron level. You have. You've commanded two squadrons and . . ."

He holds three fingers in front of my eyes. "*Three* squadrons, Johnny. Two at Selfridge and this one. Eight fucking years of getting my ass chewed out. I am a *professional*—a *career*—squadron commander. And that's all I'll ever be. I'll make lieutenant colonel, probably on the last go-around, but not full bull. They'll never let me command a wing or anything."

I shake my head in feigned protest.

"Oh, bullshit, John." But he's pleased. "I know that, and you do, too. Right?"

Loyally, I shake my head.

"Oh, for God's sake, John. I'm just a jock. I'm not *Allen*, see? I'm just a tired old jock who was standing behind the door when God was passing out brains."

Abruptly he stands, folds his spare blanket, and places it carefully across the foot of his bed, adjusting it as fussily as a cadet. In his turning to sit down again, I see his age. Two years ago, he was back-flipping off the bar while holding a drink. He is what—thirty-nine?

To change the subject, I ask him if he knew that Happy flew P-40s down here.

"Happy? Aw, yeah, but I didn't know him then. I was over in Algeria until I got wounded. Decapitated. Incapacitated? *Castrated*, Margaret says. Well, North Africa is North Africa. And we also had P-40s. Tell me, who *didn't* fly P-40s down here. Roosevelt? And you? You were probably still in the seventh grade. England? No kidding. You and Gable. Glenn Miller every night. NAAFI girls. Well, I'm afraid that I'll have to reflect that in your OER. Right now I've got you listed as 'Fair, almost dependable.' England automatically makes you 'Piss-poor.' "

He is shoving me around, making me go get the last of the beer. We are both laughing like bastards. He's not Irish, but he may as well be for the little sense that he makes.

"You never flew a P-40? And you call yourself a *pilot*? Never happen, GI Spamcans, right? You flew Spamcans with Gable. Big deal. Well, we finally got 'em down here too—your castoffs, I suspect—and, to bring them up to our standards, we threw sand into their carbs and smeared mud all over them. That was easy: just taxi for thirty seconds. God-damnedest place you ever saw. Blowing mud. Then, Jesus, what?—Korea, I guess; I lose track, don't you?—and Spamcans again and more goddamned tents." Dismally, he looks around, settling his gaze on the swinging light bulb until it becomes the symbol. Silently, smiling crazily, he points at it. Then, becoming stern, he stares at the ballooning canvas, rises, and begins throwing things around. He doesn't meet my eyes again for a while.

"Margaret is sick of it, too, I'll tell you. We've been apart more than we've been together, not to mention the wars. One night last spring we sat down and figured it out on paper. We've been married thirteen years and, if you add up all the TDYs and the overseas tours without dependents, we've been apart seven years. I was surprised myself when we stacked all the orders and per diem vouchers" (sly smile) "together. Seven years, minus about three months."

He shoves a page from one of Margaret's recent letters at me. It describes the trailer park during the subzero weather. No lights, no heat, no water, and no telephone to use in reporting these outages. The base was dying. Mothers set their children before the open doors of propane-fired stoves. Men with blowtorches crawled around under the trailers try-ing to thaw pipes. *Time* reported the good life of the GI family in Europe.

"You are lucky that your family is in Germany." He nods. "Lucky as hell."

"Yes, sir."

"Within a month, mine will be, too."

And he was right. Possum Slocum is gone. Margaret and the children are in Wiesbaden. We try to absorb this. Four years isn't forever, but in the service it is a long time. We remember his confidence in the concept of a young squadron at George, his country-boy ridicule of the colle-gians among us, his back-flips off the bar.

Tomorrow, I'll write another of my self-pitying letters to Jenny, asking how she'd like it if I resigned my commission and went back to college? Last time she replied that I could get out, but she was staying in.

"I like to eat," she explained and then dismissed my threat as ridiculous, as "ghibli fatigue." Yeah, she's right. Who in his right mind would quit after almost fourteen years of active duty? Six more, and we can retire on half our base pay. Jenny is sensible.

And, now, again in her eighth month, she has enough problems without hearing my moans. She can barely squeeze under the wheel of the Jag and flatly refuses to carry its heavy battery indoors at night or jiggle the frozen pistons in the SU carbs.

"Put Dry-gas in the fuel tank," I write her. "It's the QM gas."

*   *   *

151

Scooter hears the call of the wild. It always occurs near the end of the fifth week down here. Sailing his paperback at Don (who, as a matter of pride, doesn't bat an eye), Scoot trumpets and disappears. Then, Don, who has been lying absorbed in a Mickey Spillane for two hours (while feeling beneath his cot for his beer), finishes his paperback and hurls it at Hank. Hank examines the nude lady on the cover and lies back contentedly to read it. Such is our recommended reading list.

Dan strolls in and announces that he is slumming. He picks up my copy of Proust and reads awhile, sitting finally on the foot of my cot. Suspiciously, he cocks his head at me.

"What's *with* this guy?" he asks finally.

"What do you mean?"

Charles closes his eyes.

"Why, he's queerer than a two-dollar bill," Dan says matter-of-factly. Bus drivers can spot a queer right away.

"So?" I am mimicking Charles, who is beginning to smile.

"Whaddaya mean 'So?' So bullshit! You don't want to encourage these guys, see? They are bad news, believe me."

"He's dead, Dan."

"Yeah? Well, good riddance. One less fucking queer in the world." Dan pitches the book aside. So much for Proust.

"How's Jenny?"

"Pregnant."

"Yeah. What is it, another boy?"

"A girl."

"You hope."

"I know."

"Yeah," he smiles, "girls are fun but they'll con you. Where's the fucking Mick?"

We shrug.

He looks around. "Where's Whit?"

"Movie."

"Where's Scooter?"

"Probably with Don."

"Hey, *wake up,* don't you guys recognize trouble when you see it? Is his trumpet here?"

At all times Dan is the responsible flight commander. His concern becomes contagious. We prowl the base and finally locate Don in the O Club. No, he hasn't seen Scooter. When the movie lets out, we search the faces. Whit strolls out.

"What's up?"

Dan explains. "Okay, Whit, he's *your* boy. So Scooter is loose. *You* borrow the major's jeep. I borrowed it last time. Tell him we're tracing missing government property."

Westward into Tripoli along the palm-lined shore, sitting so erectly that we hope to be taken for Air Police, we drive. It is midnight and the

British Officers Bar is closing. Usually we pause here and run through the numerical sequence of Pimm's Cups, but tonight we are Elephant Hunting. Through the relatively clean New City, with its store windows protected by grids, we continue, with Dan, old Greyhound driver, at the wheel and Whit riding shotgun, one hand resting on a lugwrench, the other training a flashlight on shadows. Our search pattern carries us out into the suburbs of the Italian community where the houses are familiarly Western with lawns and hedges. In Mexican patois, Whit questions an Arab. No, he has seen no *loco gringo*.

Then, resignedly, knowing that Scooter never makes it easy, we drive through the ancient gate into the Old City. The sleeping buildings press close. Once, while Dan races us in reverse out of a particularly spooky dead-end alley, I see a body lying beside a building, but it is an Arab, asleep or dying. His eyes open and stare dully into my flashlight. He is a skeleton.

A cold wind has risen, blowing scraps of paper through the deserted market. Moonlight chills the vistas. Nothing seems familiar. Sometimes I think that we are lost, that we will run out of gas in some particularly dangerous maze, that men with knives will spring from the shadows, leaving no trace of us or the jeep.

"Let's get out of here, Dan," I whisper.

"Yeah," Whit nods. "My flashlight is playing out, and I am cold as a witch's teat."

Reluctantly, pensively, Dan steers us back through the walled gate and investigates a parallel route back to the base. With first light, the wind dies; the palms become silent, gain color. I am shivering and hunching in my L-2 jacket.

Ahead is the Main Gate. In the floodlit area beside the Air Police shack stands a camel, and sitting on the camel is an Arab wearing a sheik's burnoose and leaning on a hump. The Arab turns in his saddle and sees our jeep, now showing only parking lights. He waves us by. It is Scooter.

"Jesus," Dan sighs. Relieved, we begin laughing.

The Air Policeman returns our salutes. Scooter doesn't seem to recognize us. He is blind-drunk.

"What's the trouble, Airman?" Dan asks the AP. "This Arab is one of ours. He's okay."

"He wants to take this camel onto the base, sir."

"I see. He can enter, but the camel can't. You suspect the camel, is that it?"

"It's against regulations, sir."

"Show me regulation," Scooter says blearily. Apparently he has been repeating this for some time. He is hoarse and exhausted.

"Right here, sir." The young AP holds out a loose-leaf notebook to Dan. It wouldn't have done any good to show it to Scooter.

Dan reads with the help of our flashlights. "Well, *is* it a vehicle?" he asks. "Where would you *put* a decal?"

"S'not a vehicle," Scooter murmurs righteously in his hoarse voice. "S'a pet."

The AP looks at us and rubs his eyes. Then, nodding, he turns the pages to that regulation. "Very well. Pets. 'All pets must be registered, and owners must produce, upon request, evidence of current vaccination against rabies. . . .' "

"Right." Dan nods. "He'll comply first thing Monday morning. Camels don't catch rabies anyway."

The AP is nineteen, maybe twenty. He studies our poker faces.

"Show me regulation," Scooter intones without real interest. He leans precariously out of the saddle. His head sinks, rises again, droops.

"Sir. *Captain!*" the AP implores me. He laughs at the absurdity of the scene, then immediately becomes serious. His desperate gaze settles on my face. "Look, sir, I *can't* quote the lieutenant any specific regulation, but *you know it's not right.* Don't you, sir? I'd catch hell from my NCOIC and the provost marshal. They'd have my stripes."

"Yeah," I nod finally. "He's right, Dan. C'mon, Scoot, let me give you a hand."

Scooter reins away indignantly, and the camel shows his teeth, makes a weird noise, farts.

"Hey, Scoot," Dan laughs. "C'mon. Turn the poor beast loose. Where'd you get him?"

I can tell we're not getting anywhere. Scooter has shown no recognition of us. It takes Don to convince him. "They'd shoot him, Scoot. He'd become camelburgers in the snack bar."

Now it's light enough to see Scooter's eyes. They are red slits squeezing out tears. His lips tremble. He lifts one sleeve to cover his face.

"Aw, *naw.* They wouldn't . . . *shoot* . . . him, would they?"

Elbowing each other, we do a little crowd scene, nodding and muttering about the general callousness of the Air Police. We even get the puzzled AP to nod and pat his pistol butt. Finally, Scooter offers Dan a foot and climbs down. He sobs uncontrollably, pats the camel's side and tells him to go home. The camel kneels clumsily in the roadway and settles himself.

When I land at 0730, I go straight to our new CO's tent. I knock on a tent pole until he opens his eyes.

"Yes?"

"Sir, Scooter has been booked by the Air Police on two charges."

He looks at his watch. "How could *anyone* have gotten in trouble this early in the morning?"

"Last night, sir."

"I see. Why didn't you wake me?"

Good question. He's getting paid for this business of guiding errant junior officers. I shrug.

"Captain Copley. John? John, never hesitate to awaken me. That's my job. I'm a bail bondsman, among other things. What did Scooter perpetrate?"

I tell him.

Aghast, he slaps his forehead and covers his head. "*You* handle it. My God, what do they expect of us poor COs? No wonder Possum threw in the towel."

"This is no big deal, Major. Nobody was raped. You just go down for a tongue-lashing and then you lash a little."

Scooter becomes his legal ward, so Charles and I relax. Our CO has to scrape and bow more than Possum would have. Possum would have reminded the provost marshal that this base exists for us, that fighter pilots who are totally rational aren't fighter pilots. It's a matter of stance.

These two majors stand there, one belligerently running his thick finger down the page, the other nodding incessantly, apologetically. Provost marshals are never so indignant that they're speechless, and this one is in full song. The logs for the month are brought out, and our unit designation almost monopolizes one column. The charges become a litany, with the major's responses unheard: driving without GI licenses, creating a disturbance in the O Club, urinating in the salt flats, engaging in flare pistol fights on the beach, creating a disturbance in the club, assault and battery, obscenity (nude bathing) at the beach, conduct unbecoming an officer (vomiting in the potted palm), entering an Off Limits area.

"What's *this*?" Our commander frowns. "'Creating a disturbance in town.'"

"In the harbor. The civilian police reported it. A gook reported one of your officers, the same one who played Sheik of Araby last night. He's bad news, that guy. Paid some Arab to row him out to a freighter anchored in the harbor."

"Why, for God's sake?"

"Ask God. Ask this eight-ball. Don't ask me. Anyhow, he didn't have enough money to pay the fare . . ."

"What was he doing out there?"

"Major, I don't know and *I don't care. Compris?*"

Scooter recollects little. He had tried to drum up a chess game at the British O Club, and no one was interested. So he'd hired a punt.

"Why?" the major asks with real curiosity.

"Well," Scooter says calmly, "sea captains play chess, don't they? As a rule?"

It is *Fastnacht*—Shrove Tuesday—and we are lost (but making good time) on a tertiary road, nominally paved, somewhere northeast of Prum. Jenny, slim as a teenager again, studies the map by flashlight. She cannot believe that we took the wrong road out of Munstereifel. Our new Porsche pounds along the rough pavement, its high beams searching for the next switchback. Kurt, our German mechanic, is right: this *is* a good German car. The suspension ripples through the frost heaves; the engine sounds like a light plane's. We love her—almost as much as we do Becky, our ten-month-old daughter, whose maintenance schedule roughly parallels the Porsche's. Both are due at their clinics next week for a checkup. In my sleep, though, I hear the Jag's lost, sweet moan.

Ahead, the road seems to end in conifers. No, it's another switchback lifting us farther into the mountains. We are in the clouds, but at least the rain has ended. There are just a few spatters from the old trees.

It's a good thing that we left the kids with friends. They'd be ravenous by now. All through Switzerland and northern Italy last summer Sam kept asking when we were going to eat.

Jouncing until the shocks bottom against the suspension stops, although we are now creeping along in second gear, we emerge from the forest onto a plateau of tilled fields.

"Is that a vineyard to our left?" Jenny asks. "If so, we must be near the river."

It is a vineyard, but we are not near the river. We are not on our map, or at least this road isn't. We are west of the Mosel and east of the old Roman road leading southward to Prum, Bitburg and Trier.

"Lights!" Jenny exclaims.

Into a nameless village we drive, making the transition to relatively smooth cobblestones as the Porsche's exhaust begins thumping off the buildings. From darkness we come straight upon gaiety, strings of colored lights draped across the road and people in peasant costumes dancing in the streets. The sudden contrast between the spooky approach and this improbable scene reminds me of some old fairy tale. We are safe now from the witch or dragon.

Reluctantly, the dancers fall back to let us pass. They stoop to smile in at us, knock on the glass and laugh at our ferocious cocker. Around us whirl couples of all ages, the men shouting and colliding, a polka band sending their heels to new heights. We are trapped. No longer dare we creep in first gear.

When the polka ends, a young, exhausted couple collapses against our car. They laugh; they speak no English.

"Oh," the girl suddenly understands. She bends to my open window, and I try not to stare at her heaving, perspiring cleavage. "*Ja, ja. Prum!*" She pronounces it differently and, pushing back strands of hair, she nods and points vaguely ahead.

"*Nein,*" the young man laughingly indicates a slightly different direction.

"*Gerade aus und denn rechts?*" I ask.

"*Nein, nein,*" they both laugh.

"Just *gerade aus,* I think," Jenny murmurs and frowns as she restrains our cocker's murderous lunges. "The road must curve to the right.

156

Here, hold *this*," she tells me and hands me a huge glass of wine. At her window, the mayor and his *Frau* are welcoming us. A new polka begins. Suddenly, our doors open, and we are all three out on the hay-strewn street. This Brunhilde of a girl is spinning like some giant humming top and I, locked to her, am getting dizzy. Where is Jenny, where is our dog?

Toward midnight, I have either learned how to polka or am so drunk that I think I have. I can also speak German. Brunhilde is a forceful teacher. Lately she has been behaving coyly and steering me into the shadows for a kiss or two. I gather that her whispering about *Fasching Kindchen* is a blatant invitation, but I don't believe that old saying. She laughs and places my hand on her breast. At midnight a cold wind rises, and the dancers whirl away. The street is empty. Jenny and the dog are asleep in the Porsche.

I start the engine. It is all a dream, and yet in my mirror I can still see the colored lights. We emerge from the fairyland, gain a familiar road. I have the feeling that I could never find that village again. By day, in any case, Brunhilde—I never did learn her name—would be a coarse, horny-handed farm girl, like some I knew in high school. The villagers are snoring now in happy exhaustion. At dawn they will rise, ready to face bleak Lent, and walk to the church for their ashes. One thing is certain: they are exactly like us, these hardworking Germans. How could we have engaged in such fratricide?

Hans listens to my account of that magic evening, smiles tolerantly, and skims my clearance with his pencil.

"You are very naive, Captain."

During the war Hans flew ME-109s. Now he works as a civilian dispatcher behind the counter at Base Operations. He is blond and cadaverous. I suspect that he is seriously ill and knows it. "To hear us talk," says Hans, "all the Nazis are dead, yes?"

Smirking, he initials my clearance and hands it to the sergeant. While he clips his pen inside his shirt pocket, he lets his eyes settle on me. "Well, I will be frank with you. I was a Nazi. How could I have served in the *Luftwaffe* before the war and not have belonged to the party? You tell me."

I fold my clearance. Hans's smile reminds me of Cat Man's. They would be close, those two cynics. Last month Hans had Jenny and me into his home for dinner. He is a bachelor and an excellent cook. I gather that he was once married. Holding his glass of Mosel up to the old lamp over the dining room table, he inspects it while he answers my questions about what it was like being a German fighter pilot in 1944.

"You know Buchel?"

I nod.

"I was based there for a while. Yes. We flew from that little strip. There were no radio aids; and, well, that February was so bad, you know. Already when we took off, we knew that we would have to parachute. Yes, I am telling the truth. We had no fuel. We had to lead new pilots who were children. You did not have to shoot us down when the weather was bad."

He smiles wanly, sips his wine, painfully recrosses his thin legs.

"*Five times*. Yes, I parachuted five times. Does this mean I am an American ace?"

The weeks become months, the months years. Like confused birds, semiannually we migrate southward to Tripoli, always returning with our internal sexual clocks bonging like Big Ben, our vee formations stretching and quacking joyously on UHF. Our tans are the envy of our wives.

Leave. Most years you lose it, in whole or in part. Wars and rumors of wars, as someone of importance once wrote. War games, if nothing else. This year we are the Reds, the villainous aggressor forces, so things are looking up. Except that the Canucks are the Blues.

No squadron adjutant can seriously post a leave schedule; so, to avoid ridicule, they laugh as they post them and write "Dream Sheet" across the top. Every week the schedule has to be revised. Last year I almost got canceled because I hadn't completed an altitude chamber refresher course. It's stupid; I can recognize hypoxia. On test-hops, losing pressurization at altitude isn't that uncommon. Pete, back at the Squadron, who still maintains my Form 5, teases me.

"Yeah," he says solemnly, "but you didn't remove your mask and turn pegs on a board until you passed out."

"So?"

"So you've got to prove to some sergeant's satisfaction that without oxygen you pass out. Now start packing and I'll have the orders cut."

"What about leave? When do I get leave?"

Pete shrugs. "You had your chance last January."

Actually, we swung a little deal. I could go on leave the instant I got a current altitude chamber card. I could sign out for Wiesbaden, and we could proceed roughly in a clockwise circuit around Europe from there. Major Allen got on the horn with Pete and worked it out.

"Oh, yes," Kate Allen remarks. "He's great at seeing that everyone else gets leave."

"Except you."

"Right."

"He's very dedicated," I inform her.

She spills her bloody mary on her cocktail dress and reels around laughing hysterically. I obtain a wet cloth from the bartender and, as she scrubs, she gradually regains control. "Yes, John," she says. "Yes, he *is* dedicated. He's a regular George Washington."

It is July and we are having a record heat wave: 84°F, according to *The Stars and Stripes*. Germans are dying of heat exhaustion. They wouldn't believe Las Vegas in the summer. Our cocker, head bowed by the fastback of the little coupe, sits panting and eyeing the Allens' beagle. Sam is crushed in beside our dog.

Kate Allen stoops to peer through the cab. Even with two suitcases strapped outside, we are crowded. "I can't see daylight, so you must have everything." She laughs.

I ease out the clutch, which, as always, seems to be connected to the cocker's voice box, and away we go. The beagle leads the pack of chasing dogs.

This July sun, so feared by the Europeans, has dried off the Continent. A warm breeze strokes the meadows. In the chamber at Wiesbaden, I do not wait long before acknowledging that I sense the first symptoms of hypoxia. For me, it is not blue fingernails or lightheadedness; it is always a flush, an unsatisfying inhalation of air reminiscent of those ten-mile cadet cross-country runs when the air became too lean to erase the black specks. I would keep going, but my mind would leave, would go blank. Afterward, I would stare at people without absorbing what they said.

When I got my new altitude chamber card, we set off. The food! It seems impossible to find a tasteless meal. Why do we Americans consider ourselves privileged? And even the house wines are cheaper than gasoline. But I'll take American beer. However appalling Germans may find this, it is my honest preference. I find their beer acidic, and the same is true of European coffee. But in every other respect, I quickly concede European superiority.

Jenny wants to see all the cathedrals and galleries; Sam, tow-headed and wearing *Lederhosen*, all the *Gasthausen;* and I, all the automobile factories. Porsche and Mercedes permit cameras; neither Ferrari nor Alfa do. In Modena, there is knee-high row of red, fish-mouthed Ferrari roadsters. I move a gear lever, try the big wheel. The service manager smiles briefly, then returns his serious attention to Jenny.

From listening to those musical rivulets which merge at Chur to become the Rhine, we slide the Porsche around the switchbacks of St. Gotthard's Pass to a high meadow where goats graze. This scenery literally forces one to stop and admire it.

"Listen!" Jenny whispers. Faintly borne by the gentle upslope breeze is the sound of church bells. Clouds hide the village itself.

These marvelous days blur by. Is it joy or simply luncheon wine that floats us tirelessly through Austria and Italy into France? There is no itinerary, there are no reservations made or needed. Where possible, we avoid the American tourist traps. Follow the German tourists, we learn; they know where the better *pensions* are. Through grand French doors opening onto a balcony, we view the pastels of the Riviera for five bucks a night. Never mind that our pink luxury hotel was abandoned two decades ago by the smart set for newer, Las Vegasy hotels nearer to the beach. We still have the best view in Cannes, and the quality of our tennis courts doesn't matter. Grass near the base line and decaying nets provide me with needed strategy against lithe Jenny.

On the famous beach, while Jenny naps in her new bikini, I, slit-eyed, watch a girl remove her halter. Pouting at my now-frank gaze, she tilts her head in amusement at me before lying face-down again. I sigh aloud.

"Can we go swimming now?" Sam whines. "C'mon, Dad."

"Perhaps you *had* better cool off," Jenny murmurs without opening her eyes, "*Dad.*"

"Keep your shirt on while we're gone," I tell her.

At dinner in a three-star, four-spoon hotel near Lyon, the waiter rubs his chin and tries to explain in English what langoustines are. He makes pincers of his hands and undulates.

"Belly dancers!" I whisper, to Jenny's disgust.

"Lobsters? *Like* lobsters?" It has become a game of charades, with the waiter eagerly nodding and pointing at her. "*Mais petite,*" he warns.

Crayfish. Crawfishes, we called them when we were kids. Only a Frenchman would try to eat one. Gamely, we experiment with the utensils. There is a claw-cracker, there are tiny forks, a sauce. It reminds me of biology lab, and I never was good at that. All over the restaurant waiters are nudging each other and smiling. The sauterne is too dry, and this marine mutilation is pointless. There is a huge mound of them. I look hungrily at Sam's little steak.

From the Arc de Triomphe immense tricolors billow like spinnakers. Paris's grand avenues and perspectives compel us to stay longer and spend more than we had intended. We give the Louvre two whole days this time. Degas's ballet dancers and racehorses deserve a day. Corot. Monet. It is a feast that leaves us dazed, overcome. Jenny is stunned; she says nothing. Outdoors, standing where they must have stood, she gazes for minutes, then nods to herself. She is oblivious to the lurching Citroens, the ubiquitous Renaults.

Germany, the real phoenix, risen new and clean around such miraculously spared landmarks as the Cathedral at Köln, the Frankfurterhof, the *Rathaus* in Munich, has recently lost some of its charm for me. It has to do with shock as well as callousness, I suppose. I doubt that I could live here indefinitely. This new coolness on my part rises straight from a single incident.

A motorcyclist had hit a shepherd dog and a crowd had gathered. Obviously broken-backed and paralyzed, the huge black-and-silver animal lies grotesquely twisted on the cobblestones. Only his staring eyes suggest the hideous pain. There is no collar. No one knows the owner. The jackbooted *Polizist* examines the bent front wheel and fork of the motorcycle and writes in his notebook. The young motorcyclist seems only concerned by his hard luck. No one looks twice at the dog.

"Officer," I call. "Shoot the dog. He is in great pain."

The officer quits writing for a moment. "Is your *Hund?*"

"No."

He shrugs, completes his report, drags the dog by his tail to the gutter, half salutes me, and strides away. Livid, I feel the tears coming, my rage rising. Jenny is crying.

"Doctor? Where is a doctor?" I ask two men. They look at each other, then noticing my eyes, quickly lead me to a corner and point. When I rap on his door and hear a dog bark, I know that he will help. As I lift the shepherd's rigid foreleg, the old doctor inserts his needle into the vein and presses the plunger. The great body sags in relief. Gently, he closes the dog's glassy eyes and nods at me. We rise. He refuses payment.

"Thank you, Doctor."

"Captain," he says. "You must understand. There were dead *children* lying in the street. It changes you."

Leave over, back at base, I am completely taken with my daughter. Becky was born with Jenny's lashes. I nuzzle her. Three weeks is too long to be away from this doll.

"She *is* my child, isn't she?" I ask Jenny. "I see nothing of me there."

"Who knows?"

"You had better." I set my drink on a table.

She swings away from me, opens mail. "The Italian, then. We were in Menton, Kitty and I, and you were bombing Arabs. Does she look Italian?"

"Menton is in France."

"So was he." She shrugs. She hands me a bill.

During my absence, Dan has held down Ops. He laughs with Jenny, whirls the ice in his empty glass until I take the hint. Jenny leaves to check the roast. Dan wags his head sideways toward her. "She's too good for you, Copley."

"I know it."

"Of course, Betty Camston is a looker, too," he murmurs and retreats giggling. "We old bus drivers know about that. That *strange stuff!*"

Every August, at the Nürburgring, some fifty kilometers to the north, there is the *Grosser Preis*. For me, it eclipses even Monaco. Around the fourteen miles of the course, campers have pitched tents. The crowds know automobiles, follow the fortunes of each driver throughout the seasons as do American baseball fans their favorites. They do not come to see accidents. Many carry stopwatches.

We hurry down to the Hatzenbach. It is the closest area where one can observe distinctions in driving style. Along the rustic railings, a mile from the grandstands, we listen. Distantly, we hear an engine, hear it indirectly through the public address system.

"*Fangio!*" the announcer exclaims. "*Fangio kommt! Weltmeister Fangio.*"

Indeed, he *is* coming, flat out in high gear. There is only the sound of his Maserati; he is that far ahead of the pack. Crazily, unintelligibly now in the roar of the packed stands and the Doppler effect of the exhaust as

161

Fangio passes and downshifts for the South Curve, the announcer calls the lap time: nine minutes, thirty seconds, I translate. Impossible.

Now we hear his engine directly. He has already reached the North Curve, and the engine soars in long surges up through the gears as though the esses do not exist. We look at each other. The engine has taken on such a hard frantic note, constantly swelling in volume that, instinctively, most of the spectators begin retreating from the railing.

Out of the shadows, blood-red against the trees, the Maserati appears in a drift and Fangio slaloms down to us. Using the blacktop where practicable, the grassy shoulders where not, his engine barking crescendi through the downshifts, his multicolored airscoop sniffing the quickest way, he descends. Cording his forearms against the kickback of the steering wheel, he leans his famous brown helmet into the curve. From fifteen feet away, hypnotized, we catch a glimpse of stern eyes. Otherwise, his face registers relaxed confidence. There is even the hint of a smile. Then his goggles flash in the late sun, and he is gone, lost in his concentration and noise.

Our color slides are becoming blotchy. I made the mistake of mounting them in glass. Mildew is breaking them down into red lights, an expert tells me. Nothing can be preserved. It seems that even colors in the stasis of emulsion become bored. No longer do we show them to friends, but sometimes Jenny and I become nostalgic over brandy and drag them out: Fangio poised at the wooded crest; Moss, leaning back elegantly, his white billed helmet banked into the curves; Collins, jaw belligerently outthrust, wild-eyed behind his goggles, dead now. All stopped in time, all still important but, inevitably, decomposing. The printed word, the engraved trophy, will probably survive longer.

Ah, God, it's all going anyway, I guess. During our last alert weeks in Germany our old cocker, deaf and almost blind, made his last visit to the vet. I buried him in the woods near graves of German soldiers. I can't explain his absence to Sam, who is four now, much less Jenny who had finally acquiesced. His moans in the night had become ours.

"Maybe he has a soul," I say sentimentally, hugging her. "What the hell do preachers know?"

Despite frequent deluges of detergent and wax, our Porsche loses its glitter, develops Teutonic, and probably expensive, idiosyncrasies en route to shipment from Bremerhaven.

Finally, our old birds, their skins dull with corrosion, are given to delighted Pakistani pilots. Now the revetments lie empty. It really hurt to see them go. I watched the last bird until it was a speck. The end of an era in so many ways.

As the guys and their families ship home, I inherit buildings and furniture at the German base. It is a little like those days in Texas after World War II. I walk around Ops, opening and slamming doors of empty lockers. The building is deserted, the safes empty. Everyone is gone, the wing disestablished. It has all been a dream. The pilots have gone to become B-47 co-pilots, radar site commanders, civilians, airline pilots. All the targets—those horrors we'd dreamed about—have become the responsibility of other wings. I check down the inventory with my heir, a suspicious Porky Pig of a Supply officer, watch airmen load the lockers on trucks, then the safes, the desks, finally the parachute rack. On the floor rests our hot line. Suddenly, it rings. Hesitantly, I answer it, using our defunct call-sign. It is some French girl counting, "*Une, deux, trois, quatre*—testing, please. You are reading me, *monsieur?*" It is a charming voice.

"*Oui, mademoiselle.* You are loud and clear."

"*Monsieur*, this phone is *not* disconnected?"

"Yes. I am a ghost." Porky Pig grins.

All I have is a handful of receipts. I heft them; they are about the right weight. We step outside and Porky locks the door to the building. We shake hands.

Lying near the walk is our old mascot, our old scrounger of hamburgers, a giant schnauzer. We had inherited her from a reccy squadron and made solemn promises. Seventy-two pounds she weighs. An inveterate fugitive from the AP dogcatchers, the mother of a hundred Eifel mongrels, she always met us when we taxied up into our wooded hardstand area.

I open the Porsche's door and fold the driver's seat back. She looks at the dead building and then at me. I'll never forget her expression of that moment. Gingerly, she rises and climbs in. Out to the housing area, past her rabbit-hunting fields, we drive, her whiskers tickling my face. Occasionally, she looks at me in an embarrassingly direct way. I guess she's sizing me up, trying to decide.

Jenny wipes her hands and kneels in awe to hug her. "Does she have a name?"

"Sure."

"What is it?"

"Dame. *Da-muh.*" The shaggy tail thumps.

"Lady?"

I shrug. "Hans says that's not her real name. No German would name a dog Dame."

"We are going to take her to America?"

"It's up to you," I lie. None of us has any choice. Free will is a joke. Jenny is crying and laughing, Dame is panting. From Luxembourg she, unalarmed by the engines, flies to New York. We catch the afternoon train for Paris and take off from the field where, three decades ago, Charles Lindbergh had landed to swarming floodlit adulation.

In transonic fighters, we'd been seventy-two days in coming from California. In an ancient, MATS-chartered, propeller-driven Constellation we will be in New York within a day. Dozing, I sink back into my plush seat on the aisle and feel the long porpoise fuselage rise and fall.

163

The engines drone on, just slightly out of sync, resonating, fading, each revolution of the props pushing the invisible sea and Europe behind.

The cabin is dark, everyone is asleep. Jenny holds Becky in her lap. Their long lashes are closed. Sam has his thumb in his mouth, his knees lifted in the fetal curl. Overhead, the aluminum racks vibrate as the resonant period comes and goes. We are in midocean, effortlessly crossing converging meridians.

Somewhere to the north, not far, lies Fox Able—Iceland, Greenland, Goose. For a full minute I stare out the black window.

Gently, a hand touches my shoulder. It is one of the stews.

"Okay, sir?"

I nod, puzzled.

"I thought you might have a touch of airsickness."

"No." I smile. "I'm fine. It was just a dream."

She nods, straightens, continues to the cockpit. I watch her legs in the glow of the aisle lights.

PART TWO

14

WASHINGTON

IT WAS ONCE the world's largest office building. Someone told me that it was originally intended to be a government hospital, that it has ramps for wheelchairs everywhere. In one way or another, people have been lost inside it for years. Which explains why I'm still standing out here in this ten-degree, twenty-knot wind. I'm freezing to death, but I can't make myself walk fifty feet and grasp that outsized handle.

Ah, God. My mind reels back, my eyes lift instinctively to the airliners curving up out of Washington National. Their turbined propellers sound like locusts high in the trees.

"How many years did you spend in the Pentagon, sir?" I had finally asked old Nasser one evening in France. It was that same evening at the club that he had given me that phony, but well intentioned, pep talk about the inevitability of every Regular—every lifer, as the more cynical young airmen dub us—having to serve time up the river, meaning the Potomac.

"Well, John, there is no way out," Colonal Bronton replied, ignoring my question. "We go together like taxes and death. It's just part of every Regular's career." He claps his big hand on my shoulder and studies me. "Aw, I know what you're thinking, because I remember thinking the same thing. . . ." His bear's head had assumed a demonstrative, frantic expression. "Three—maybe four—years out of the cockpit. I'll never get back. Right?"

167

Absolutely. I had curled down over my martini. "You served two tours there, sir?"

"Two? Who told you that? God forbid. But, let me, in all honesty, say this: *one* tour is good for a man, especially for an idealistic young major like you." He shrugs, sips his drink. "Why? Because it teaches you the facts of life. You go in there believing in the purity of Old Glory and that the fucking storks bring babies, right? That's where you are now."

I had bought us a round, and he had nodded approval.

"Okay," he had continued. "What are the alternatives? Suicide looks bad on your record, so that's out. Command and Golf School? You don't play golf. In any case, it's always there, like the Rotary. Old school ties count only ten points anyway. So that's out." He becomes conspiratorial. "*OER's*, John. 'This young officer walks on water,' signed by any two-star. *That's* holy water."

"But I can't walk on water, Colonel."

"Sure you can. Listen to your lieutenants, Johnny. They love you, man."

That's when everything had stopped. By then I had realized that Nasser—Colonel Bronton—had never served a Washington tour, and I just hung there with those words echoing: *They love me.*

Nothing so touching ever comes directly; it always comes obliquely, from Singapore or somewhere.

"You didn't know that?" he asks, watching my expression, laughing. "Aw, come off it, Johnny. All I've heard since I joined this dumb wing is what a great flight commander you are. They think you are Moses. Seriously, you didn't know that?" He had quit twisting on his hidden bar stool.

Pushed along through the numbing wind by this remembered joy, I make it to the massive door, so symbolic in its resistance to my pull, and am blown inside the building. The door sighs, clicks shut. I remove my hat and tuck it under my left arm, shuck off my gloves. My cheeks must be frozen. But, inside, I am still warm, still glowing, after six weeks of hearing that echo.

Down the corridors I stride, past tall windows alternated with portraits, my hair clipped closely, my gray gloves in my right hand swinging six to the front and three to the rear, my slim black briefcase motionless in my left hand. I am your basic aviation cadet fifteen years later. And, then, just as I pause at Pershing's portrait, I visualize old Cat Man, tongue-in-cheek, watching me. So I knock off the West Point stride and try to get my bearings.

I'm still on "A" Ring and am approaching a particularly noisy radial. It trembles like a stockyard chute. Cautiously, I lean forward to peer around the corner and am immediately swamped by chattering women.

Back against the wall I go, and side-step as though I'm on the ledge of a building until I find refuge in a doorway. Jesus, I don't know what I expected to find inside the Pentagon—a bunch of generals smoking cigars, I guess—but certainly not a stampede of women. At sluice-gate speeds, they stream past, the shorter ones leaning forward and pumping their arms like marathon walkers. Suddenly, the door I'm leaning against opens, and I have to twist like a broken-field runner to regain my balance. Glaring over her shoulder at me, a young lady hurries out into the mainstream.

"Help you, Major?"

Smiling, motionless, a gray civilian sits cocked back in his office chair, his hands laced behind his head.

"Some kind of alert?" I ask, closing the door.

"Much more serious. It's the morning coffee break."

I show him a copy of my orders.

"Aw, gee," he says, "that's a tough one. There's no such office, or if there is, you can't get there from here. Go back to Europe and start over." He sighs. "Well, next corridor on your left and two rings over. You'll know when you get there. Goddamned Air Force has all its clocks stopped at the hour of Billy Mitchell's death. Bunch of headhunters. How'd a soldierly-looking guy like you break away from the Signal Corps?"

On his desk is his name block. Carved into the block is the Combat Infantry Badge with a wreath and star. His grade is colonel. I wince and come to attention.

"Sorry, sir."

Amused, he rocks forward, stands, and shakes hands. "Donovan. Good luck, buddy. See you on KP. I'll be flying the China Clipper with you. It beats pots and pans."

I salute and, wryly, he returns it.

"Come and visit. I'll tell you my combat stories."

Processing, lost, I wander through the maze, climbing to airy, plush offices featuring good-looking secretaries, descending to stark, crowded offices with old biddies. Everyone wants four copies of my orders. Usually they discard three. In Personnel, on the fifth floor, outer ring, efficient, middle-aged secretaries make their typewriters hop and slither through processing forms. On their desks are family pictures and small flower vases. They have a helluva time saying "out" and "about," but they are warm and very professional.

Intelligence. Jesus, spooks are all alike. They give you this big act, nodding omnisciently, looking you over as though you're blue-collar help, as though your wings are a charming anachronism preserved by the Air Force to maintain its early image. A pudgy, pink little man leafs through a folder, stops, lifts his eyebrows in wonder.

"Sit down, Major," he says with sudden interest. "Sit down, please."

There is no desk sign to reveal his grade. "Umm," he says, "Harvard and Georgetown. Well, my friend, you can't beat that, can you? Well, we can certainly use you. Frankly, I'm fed up with cow-college graduates. Geopolitics under Kaiserling?"

"No, sir."

"Millikan?"

I shake my head.

"Good," he says grimly, "Millikan is an ass."

"May I see that folder?" I ask.

"No." He smiles and continues reading. After a few minutes he closes it and nods with satisfaction. The door opens, a secretary leans in. "Colonel Potter is on the phone, Major," she tells him. Reddening slightly, he stands to shake hands. I expect the Little Orphan Annie secret shake.

"We'll be in touch, Conley," he nods. Slitting his eyes, he lifts the phone and cups his hand to guard his transmission.

Having completed processing, I walk until I find my office. When I enter, the lady at the farthest desk is the only person to raise her eyes. She squints at the nameplate above my right pocket, smiles, and lets her hands fall off the keyboard onto her lap.

"Well! Major Copley! We are so glad you are joining us." We meet in the middle of the room. She offers her hand. Surprisingly, it is a young hand. "I am Minerva Caldwell." For a secretary, she has an easy authority. "I declare, you must be smart. Usually, it takes two days for a stranger to find this office. Why don't you hang your coat here and let me introduce you to these gentlemen? Major Copley, Major Smith."

"Smitty." He grins. Freckles. He wears a business suit. I am beginning to get the picture.

"John."

There is a second major. "Monk." He hands me a cigar. He has just been selected for lieutenant colonel. "It's true," he says happily, "it's possible to make LC without knowing nothing. In fact, that's the *only* way to make it. Otherwise, the colonels consider you a threat to their jobs."

"Right," an older man says, as he comes out of his cubicle. "Getting him promoted was the quickest way to get rid of him. Up *and* out. Sit down. What's it like out there in the real Air Force? You a civil engineer by trade?"

"No, sir. I'm nothing."

"Good. We can use you. But, as a matter of curiosity, what misfortune sent you here, for God's sake?"

I hand him a copy of my orders. He scans them, then my record.

"Okay. I get it now. You're Ops, but down in Ops they're sitting in each other's laps. Last year it was famine-time down there. And you had a year of engineering in college. That's what did it. Good old Personnel. The pipeline is either full or empty. Actually, they use Tarot cards. Well, no sweat. Minnie here knows this job upside down and backwards."

"No," she corrects him, "I know this job right side up and forward, but certain co-workers here do not."

"Minnie, Minnie," they chorus, holding up their hands.

"I simply meant," the colonel says, "that you know this job so *thoroughly*, so . . ."

She waits, tongue-in-cheek. She lifts a ruler.

Smitty giggles while the colonel searches the air. ". . . so *perfectly*, so . . ."

"She's been here since Grant," Smitty yells, and the ruler smacks her desk. "She began with—" Smitty backs away and circles the desk to keep on the side opposite her.

"Cavalry posts!" the brevet LC says, and hurries out the door.

They are all laughing. A happy shop then. I lucked out. She wipes her eyes and settles herself at her machine.

"Don't believe them, Major Copley. They are not gentlemen. They will tell you anything. They have absolutely no respect either for the truth or for womanhood. Now, there is one other officer whom you won't meet until after the holidays."

I look at the desk by the window. Its glass is polished, its paint new, its baskets empty. The name block bears a silver leaf and a civil engineer's transit. The name itself is inscribed in Chinese or something. He is a character then. But, as she mentions his name, gloom seems to settle in. Smitty gives me this sick look and pulls at his nose; the colonel signs a letter.

"Settled?" he asks me. He also wears a business suit. It is like a law office. I understand: too many uniforms in Washington, too much service parochialism in the building.

"Motel, sir."

"Property prices are unreal, aren't they? You can't buy anything for less than twenty-five. A four-bedroom will run thirty. It's insane."

"I know."

"Terrible. When Minnie came here, you could have a string of polo ponies on what a colonel makes. Now I can't buy my daughter a single horse."

There is just the slightest lull in her typing. Then she rips through a few more lines, making the machine hump up and down through the signature block, pulls the paper from the roller, deftly saves her carbons and rises to place the original in his In-basket. Her spectacles fall until arrested by their cord and, haughtily, she murmurs something about a string of jackasses. He slaps the desk and laughs.

We have the bases, he explains. Those safes are full of base folders, filed by region, alphabetically. "Hamilton" appears on the tab of one especially thick folder. We work closely with the Requirements people and the Major Air Commands. The Requirements shops analyze roles and missions, then look over existing base capabilities.

"There's a lot of deadwood, of course, which Congress won't let us shut down. . . . Ah, God, here I am, already infecting you with my cynicism. I'm supposed to tell you that God designated these bases or

171

something. But you know better; you read the papers. Every year Congress shudders at the defense budget, so, okay, strike some obsolete bases. Then they *really* go apeshit—excuse me, Minnie. You know, save money, but don't do it in *my* state, in *my* district. Podunk Air Force Base is the cornerstone of our national defense, right? We gotta keep this payroll or these people will be impoverished, and they're *my* constituents. Aw, hell, Smitty, *you* tell him. I'm a cynical old bastard. When I came here, I believed in God. I even believed in the integrity of senators and congressmen, if you can imagine. I was like a Mormon missionary— you a Mormon, Copley? No offense; I'm talking about enthusiasm, not religion." The colonel throws up his hands and goes back to his cubicle.

Dutifully, I listen to Smitty and follow him around. He's not much help. "It's like he said: if you recommend a base closure, look out. Some senator and some congressman are going to start *eating* the poor goddamn Secretary of the Air Force. That's his job, to be served up as hamburger when those cannibals come around. Sometimes they call here or the Command Post. We don't speaka da English, see? We give them L and L's number which, of course, they already have."

"L and L."

"Legislative and Liaison. The Geisha Guys. Anyhow, the Navy has it even worse. For a century they've been trying to close down this little shipyard in Boston which still builds frigates like John Paul Jones's. No way, old buddy."

Mrs. Caldwell looks over her spectacles at him until he lapses into silence; then, in disgust, he bursts out, "Okay, Minnie, *you* brief him. *You* set him straight. Give him the old official line."

She nods. "Thank you, Major Smith. I shall try. Please, Major Copley, have a seat, and I'll try to correct a few of the alarming misconceptions I've heard presented to you." She removes her glasses and leans back in her chair.

Like a strong actress, she knows how to command my attention. Without her glasses, she can show me her eyes. Suddenly, I understand: she is our real boss. Not officially, of course, but actually. A sort of faculty member, part of the cadre. We officers come and go, the real hierarchy remains.

"Now, then, may I restore some of your perspective with a simple question? Whom should a senator or a congressman represent?"

I see. It is not a simple question. There are two levels of obligation, there is a dual loyalty.

She waits until I nod. I like that. She assumes that everyone is bright until he proves that he isn't.

"I concede," she says wryly, "that often their emphasis is misplaced and, yes, there *are* absurdities—pork barrels, in the lexicon of the journalist—but any large, loosely integrated system lends itself to exploitation. Nevertheless, there are men of integrity in Congress and more than a few, I believe."

"Ha!" Smitty exclaims.

Without shifting her gaze, she waits for his apology.

"Sorry," he says finally.

"In many cases, there are humane considerations which may override the operational or engineering aspects. There may be, for example, a sizable force of specialists employed at a given base—highly experienced mechanics, sheet-metal artisans, master machinists—a pool of Department of the Air Force civilian employees not readily absorbed elsewhere, especially within the same geographical area. Given another emergency, on the order of Korea, let us say, they might prove invaluable. Now, usually, we are dealing with an older group of civilian employees who—"

"We are dealing with sacred cows, John," Smitty interrupts from across the office. "You can't move civilians around like us ordinary cattle."

". . . who have lived in this particular area all their lives or at least since the outbreak of World War Two. They have attained such seniority in our GS system that one cannot callously dismiss them, nor can one—"

"It happens all the time in civilian industry, Minnie," Smitty calls. "Move or quit. That's what my brother was told last year."

". . . expect them to relocate at their age. Beyond their plight, consider the economic impact on a small community. In one way or another, the federal government would have to expend funds to assist them."

"But this comes out of the Air Force's hide, Minnie. It comes out of *our* budget, okay? Money we could spend for new airplanes, for runway lengthening at important bases."

"I am quite aware of that, Major Smith, but may I remind you of the ultimate cost of Secretary Johnson's economy cuts just prior to Korea?" There is quiet triumph in her voice. It is an old argument, I suspect.

"Hey," he says, coming over to hug her, "you know I love you, don't you?"

Coldly, she suffers his arm around her for a moment. "Now, Major Copley," she continues, "don't misconstrue what I have said. You are a pilot, an Operations specialist, and you must view each base purely in terms of operational capabilities and requirements. That is your job. Others will consider the extraordinary circumstances. Eventually, the chief of staff will make a recommendation to the secretary. If it represents a compromise, do not become bitter. Remain detached and professional."

Always, promptly at 0800, Mrs. Caldwell enters smiling, full of warm good mornings, and hangs up her coat. From a wrapping of damp waxed paper she removes a single flower and places it in her vase. Then she unhoods her machine, checks the ribbon, cleans the keys, and, this morning, looks over at me sitting at my desk reading the manual she gave me yesterday. "I saw three interesting houses for sale listed on the Concourse bulletin board."

I nod. "Twenty-one thousand was the cheapest."

"Unless you are willing to commute twenty-five miles, I doubt that you will beat that. But I am talking out of turn. Do you find your reading absorbing, Major Copley?"

"Heart-stopping."

"Perhaps it will make more sense after you have read a few base folders." She goes to the safe, returns with a thick folder: Shaw Air Force Base, South Carolina. It is an old reccy base, one of many military bases in that state.

Later, when I ask her *why* there are so many, Smitty bursts out laughing, and she has trouble limiting herself to a smile. She refuses to look at him.

"Oh, my friend," Smitty says finally, "you are a dumb Yankee, but even Yankees have heard of Mendel Rivers. No? Really? You don't know who Mendel Rivers is? Have you ever heard of the House Armed Services Committee, old buddy?"

I am wearing my new brown Ivy League suit with its vest and narrow lapels. Thank God the civilians have finally learned not to ruin trousers with pleats and cuffs. But it is eerie wearing civvies to work. I can't take them seriously.

"Don't worry," Jenny assures me, "no one could mistake *you* for a civilian. Where did you buy that suit—Uniform Sales?"

After a few days Mrs. Caldwell—she is a widow, I have learned—takes me around and introduces me to her counterparts within the Air Force bureaucracy.

"Why, I am just so pleased to meet you, Major Copley," these Daughters of the Confederacy say. They touch their hair, tug their skirts down as they look me over. "I certainly hope that you like it here. We are just one big family, you know."

When, however, I meet the general, our colonel does the honors. Generals, I notice, wear uniforms. He is a big man.

"Hi, Copley." The general grins. "Welcome. What'd you fly? '86s? Oh, for chrissake, another fighter jock. I'm outnumbered. You play handball? No? Well, you oughta learn. I take my frustrations out on that little ball."

I ought to learn to write, too. Every time I hand Mrs. Caldwell something I've drafted, she begins reading it with her usual pleasant expression. By the time she has finished, however, she is breathing deeply, her lips are tightly pursed, and she seems to consider a long time before looking up at me.

"Formal writing, Major Copley, requires a certain *tone*. I had hoped that, while reading those regulations and manuals, you would uncon-sciously acquire something of that tone. It is probably more complicated than that."

While studying the folders, I have seen aerial photographs which send my mind reeling back through time, patterns of runways, romantic old hangars—Langley still has one emblazoned "The Third Pursuit Group" —ramps I've walked. I have to force myself to concentrate. One problem is my growing conviction that I *am* malassigned, that I should be down in Ops. But that's even more of a maze down there in the basement. Here, at least, we have two windows, one in the colonel's office, the other where his absent second-in-command has his desk, which I occasionally use for its better light.

"Ever feel like that Athenian youth down in the Labyrinth?" I ask Smitty one day.

"What the hell are you talking about?"

"That story of the Minotaur."

"The *what*?"

"Forget it."

When the Minotaur does show up, I don't recognize him. I'm reading by the fading daylight when this heavy package falls on the desk, startling me. I look up into a grimly smiling moon face. The eyes seem pleased by my surprise. I had not heard the hall door open, believed that Smitty and I were the only two in the office.

"You are Copley. I recognize you from your official photograph."

His accent I can't place; it is not quite German. He is certainly not Chinese, even if he is built like Charlie Chan.

Having opened a drawer and found Kleenex, he eases me aside to rub out the coffee-cup circles on the glass and empty the ashtray. I look over at Smitty who has his hand over his eyes but is otherwise at attention.

"Sorry, old buddy," he apologizes later. "He returned early. I should have warned you. That desk is an altar. It is never used."

The next time the LC appears, he's jovial. I suppose he had a couple of martinis with his lunch. Unbuttoning his vest, he strolls around, compliments Mrs. Caldwell on her dress, and pauses to sit on the corner of Smitty's desk. He lights his pipe and laces his hands over one knee. Smitty refuses to sit again.

"Say," he leans toward Smitty, "I heard a good one at SHAPE Headquarters last week. Do you know General Dibrell? No? Well, you know *of* him. It seems that this priest and this rabbi went into a house of ill repute in Harlem. Have you heard it? No? Well . . ." he murmurs, with one hand channeling his voice. His Irish accent is the standard tenor and much like his Jewish accent. At the punch line, Smitty comes apart, whooping and slapping his desk. He reels around gasping for air. "Where does he *get* these jokes?"

On the way out at 1600, His Nibs tells Mrs. Caldwell that he won't be in tomorrow. If Senator Russell's office calls, transfer the call to him in the Secretary's office. Before my desk he pauses while he buttons his handsome topcoat. "Copley, we'll have to have a chat soon. I like to know my people through and through."

I nod, fake a smile, and sit again as he leaves.

Smitty rises to imitate him, but the door opens again. "Mrs. Caldwell, tell the colonel I'll set up a meeting with the general for Wednesday."

I wonder why he doesn't step into the colonel's office and inform him directly. The colonel is at his desk.

Maybe it is the sudden absence of the black topcoat, I don't know; but the room seems brighter again. I look at Mrs. Caldwell and, gradually, she begins smiling as she types. She arches her back, and stretches in a ladylike way. At his desk Smitty looks up long enough to wave his hand in disgust at the door. Eventually the colonel appears in his doorway and exchanges looks with Smitty and Mrs. Caldwell.

"I give up," he announces. "I can't think anymore today. I'm going home."

"Good night, Colonel," we say.

Smitty and I work until 1700. On the sweep second, he bangs his folder noisily, rises, and grabs my folder, stuffing them both into the safe. "Anything to go in here, Minnie? No?" He slams the drawer and twirls the dial.

Striding around, buttoning his cheap topcoat, he says, "Minerva, I won't be in tomorrow. I have to go skiing in Switzerland with the Secretary of Defense. If the President calls, tell him I'll see him at tee-off time Saturday. Get your coat on, John. Let's go get smashed. Buy you a drink, Minnie?"

We buck the wind, now lifting the cars in North Parking and, as I stop by the old Porsche, he tells me to meet him at the bar in the Marriott. When I arrive, he pats the stool beside him. A martini is already waiting.

"Bring us some popcorn, Margie." He sighs. "Hey, I heard a great joke this afternoon, John. Want to hear it?"

"Was it really funny?"

"Maybe during Harding's administration."

"What's with this guy?"

"You've heard of the Devil? Well, he's the Devil, my friend."

"Evil Incarnate?"

"Absolutely. Better start two more, Margie. Margie, this is General Copley. He owns that big building across the street, so you'd better be nice to him. Take him to bed."

"Major Smith!"

"Well, at least give him some popcorn. I'm not shittin' you, John; Fat Stuff is bad news." He nods. "*Real* bad."

"He doesn't seem dangerous."

"Neither did Billy the Kid, friend, until somebody crossed him. He will wipe you out."

I smile. "I'm not in the habit of crossing lieutenant colonels."

"Neither was I. But with him it doesn't take much. Just fail to laugh at one of his jokes."

"What can he do? The colonel is our boss."

"No, friend. *Fat Stuff* writes our effectiveness reports. You get the picture now?"

"I thought the colonel wrote them."

He shakes his head sweetly. His freckled face beams a fixed smile. "The colonel *signs* 'em. Fat Stuff writes 'em."

"But the colonel won't sign them if he disagrees."

"Won't he? He'll sign whatever Fat Stuff puts in front of him." He waits for my outburst, then raises his hand. "He can't help it, John. Fat Stuff has important connections upstairs. He grew up at Offutt and worked a few miracles for SAC. The wheels think he hung the fucking moon. Just thought I'd warn you, old buddy."

I hand an abbreviated staff study to Mrs. Caldwell for approval. As she reads it, her eyes momentarily lift to mine. "Better. This is better, Major Copley. You've caught the right note of formality." Deftly she transposes fragments to correct the syntax. In time the paper looks like a diagramed football play.

"Smoother now?"

The door opens, and Fat Stuff enters. "Minerva, I wonder if you would do me a great favor? Here are three letters I'd like typed right away, and please use official stationery. That's my girl. Now, I've got to run. Just leave them in my basket."

He squeezes her, pats my shoulder, and leaves again. She ignores the letters and continues reading my staff study. "Well, you can't introduce new material at this point. Is this a fact or an assumption?"

While I ponder it, she skims Fat Stuff's letters. Then, without a word, she rises and walks over to place them in his In Basket. Smitty picks them up, shakes his head, reads aloud: "Dear Sir, your bill for the month of October contains several errors of such gravity that I intend to report you to the Better Business Bureau. My records indicate that we did not dine at your restaurant on the evening of the nineteenth. Either there is confusion regarding the date or my signature has been forged. . . ."

Smitty drops the letter back into the basket and smirks. "Well," he says. "You didn't expect it to be official business, did you, Minnie?"

She remains silent.

"Aw, c'mon, Minnie. Don't make waves. You could bang 'em out in ten minutes."

"Yes," she acknowledges.

"He can fix you, Minnie."

"Then let him," she says firmly. "Now then, Major Copley, this is really an assumption, isn't it?" She taps my report with her pencil. "A reasonable assumption, but not a fact. Therefore, you may want to emphasize other points in your discussion." Her eyes are clear and unafraid. I feel her strength flowing into me.

On the following morning I have to go out to Andrews to get checked out in their T-Bird program. It's routine: some acro, some patterns and landings, a couple of GCAs. The IP is a nice kid. We enjoy each other and even take turns spinning the bird. When I return to the office that afternoon, Fat Stuff's letters are gone, and Mrs. Caldwell is calmly typing away. Smitty rolls his eyes at me and whistles soundlessly.

"Who won?" I whisper.

"I don't know. I think she did, but we'll see."

The year flows away, and another begins. One morning while I'm writing away, lost in the wonders of Lowry Air Force Base, I notice this expensive black loafer easily kicking near my chair. Fat Stuff is ponderous, but he comes and goes while your mind is elsewhere. One minute Smitty and I are the only two in the office, the next he's sitting on the corner of my desk. I never heard the door open, but I'll admit that I'm a little deaf now.

I begin getting to my feet. Smilingly, he shakes his head and waves a flat hand. Add a hundred pounds to Mona Lisa and you'd have his smile. Just as I decide that he's smashed, he says, "John-boy, it seems that we have mutual friends."

I sit back in my chair.

"Did you know that?" he asks. "Aren't you going to guess?"

"No, sir."

His shoe quits swinging. His smile is fixed, but his eyes narrow. He looks around to see who is listening. Smitty becomes a dynamo, opening and slamming safe drawers, riffling pages while, with a pencil between his teeth, he frowns in absorption. Slowly, Fat Stuff eases his big butt off my desk. His eyes are fixed on mine.

"The Camstons," he says in a voice quiet with rage. "Eric and—*Betty?* —Camston."

That figures. Eric, I mean; not Betty. When I think of Betty . . . well, I try not to think of her. I also try not to think of Eric—"Old Cuff Links"—except now I'm wondering whether he goes crazy trying to out-dandy Louis the Fourteenth here.

"We, Moira and I, ate dinner with them last evening at the Orleans. Have you eaten there? You haven't? Well, you must."

Fat Stuff, Smitty explains later, married money. Moira's father owns half of Geneva and Montreux. Is Fat Stuff Swiss? No, well, perhaps he was born there. He is New York City and Georgetown. They maintain town houses in both areas, drive matching Cadillacs, have a maid—a uniformed, live-in maid.

"You should see his ripsnorter of credit cards," Smitty adds. "He strings it out to scare his general buddies who accompany him when he takes congressmen to dinner. The generals—the younger ones, anyway—are fascinated. They live in those crummy 1920 brick quarters at Bolling, see? *They* can't afford the Orleans. They ride the boat to work while this LC glides across the Potomac from Georgetown in a new Caddie. Where did they go wrong? they wonder. Why didn't the Point warn them?"

Back home, wealth is measured in acres and tractors, and it comes hard. No one in my family knew or knows how to make money. God knows I don't. But who needs it? In the Air Force we have security. Fat Stuff can't hurt me. The system wouldn't permit it.

Fat Stuff and I have little chats. Why haven't I completed college? Why am I not enrolled in some evening program in management? I tell him that I am going to George Washington two nights a week. Then why am I studying English when I could be learning something useful? I should reconsider.

Mondays and Thursdays. Those are the evenings when I try to sneak out of the office a few minutes early, wolf down dinner, and be on campus by 1830. It's an urban campus rather than a real one, but I like my profs. One whirls around like an especially tippy pepper-grinder, but he knows his Shakespeare, and the other is a woman. Neither has to rely much on notes, and both have good senses of humor. I enjoy them. It beats watching TV and, more importantly, I'm collecting six more credits toward a B.A.

I sit next to this little blonde who needs a hearing aid. She really does. She has to lean across the aisle and copy my notes. When she's absent, I slip a piece of carbon paper in my spiral and make a copy for her. Over Cokes after class, she calls me John, and I, almost old enough to be her dad, feel young again.

"Are you an English teacher?" she once asked me.

"Lord, no. I'm a GI."

Jenny has warned me that I'd better act my age or I'm going to be a *dead* GI.

Fat Stuff insists that we must get together with the Camstons some evening. He wants to meet this Jenny he has heard so much about. And *Betty*—here, suspicion lights his eyes—she, too, is "very attractive." "And I think she has the hots for you, you lucky fellow."

"Yeah?" Smitty says later. "Well, be that as it may, let your old GI guardian angel provide you with a word of advice: one drink, see? No more. I am serious. Hey, and butter up *Moira*—Mrs. Fat Stuff. Jesus, what a shoat she is. She looks like a big, expensive boiler ready to let go. A giant pink sausage wearing four girdles and the Tiffany window display. Whatever you do, don't relax and be yourself."

"You did one evening?"

He closes his eyes and nods.

Mostly stratus and rain this winter, occasionally a few inches of snow. There doesn't seem to be a snowplow south of Pennsylvania. The

Porsche stays filthy, a muddy little turtle. So does Jenny's new wagon. I try to wash them once a week, and the dog once a month. The cars, at least, hold still.

Abruptly, it's summer. Maybe a week of spring so everyone can photograph the cherry blossoms and buses over by the Jefferson Memorial. Well, that's Washington, everyone assures me—a sloppy winter, a token spring, and a five-month, debilitating summer. But fall! The falls make up for the rest of the year.

In April, in Brentano's on the Concourse, I feel an arm drape across my shoulders and hear a familiar whisper. I force a smile. Eric Camston promenades me around. How is Jenny? Still beautiful? Have I seen the Air Force art exhibit? No? Well, I need not bother. The artists should stick with calendars and magazine covers. It's ridiculous to commission such junk. Aircraft are simply not artistic subjects. And the commissions!

I'm his long-lost buddy. He steers me around the second floor, introduces me to minor members of the Joint Staff. You'd think we'd fought together in the Lafayette Escadrille. He claps my shoulder and smiles down at me. I am a *real* fighter pilot, he tells everyone. Although my lunch period has ended, I must see his office upstairs and meet a few of his colleagues.

"How do you do?" they say, and look at my suit. I guess they can tell that I didn't buy it at Raleigh Haberdashers.

"How is Betty?" I ask when I can get in a word.

"She's fine," he responds. "Never better. Mean as ever. What are you flying now?"

"T-Birds, like everyone else."

"Why don't you swing a deal with the Guard? They're getting Deuces, you know. By the way, I go down to Craig next month for jet upgrading. How *about* that? Finally. We'll have to fly the T-Bird out to George, for old times' sake."

I had forgotten that he's one of those who doesn't let go after you shake hands. Every so often, he pumps away and gives me his Sincere Look.

If Eric thinks he's going to do some real flying now, he's in for the biggest letdown since the Tacoma Narrows Bridge collapsed. Down to Maxwell, up to Scott or Wright-Pat, and back to Andrews. Two refueling stops, two hamburgers, four cups of coffee and a pack of cigarettes. Track outbound from one station and inbound to the next. All straight and level, all absolutely boring unless the weather stinks. I don't understand how airline pilots can do it year after year. Money, that's how. Eight hours and twenty minutes is our monthly allocation. One hundred hours a year, but only one can fly at the controls because there are two pilots in each bird. Even if you shoot a few GCAs and ILSs, you get rusty. I made a stupid mistake during my last instrument check.

"Try to fly more than one weekend a month, Major," this young captain suggests. "Split it up. Short cross-countries with lots of instrument pattern-work at the distant end."

Well, he's right and he's wrong. My proficiency would last longer, but during this tour flying isn't my primary responsibility; pleasing Fat Stuff is. And, being nonrated, Fat Stuff doesn't get all choked up about flying requirements. Flying must not interfere with staff responsibilities, he had written in one of our Office Instructions. Not only does he disapprove of our being out of the office on weekdays, but he also seems to resent our being beyond his reach on weekends. Twice now, on Friday afternoons, he has sat on my desk and asked if I'd mind helping Smitty prepare a talking paper over the weekend.

"It's deliberate," Smitty says. "I don't need any help."

"So I needn't cancel my flight?"

"I didn't say that." He smiles.

"I don't follow you."

"He telephones the office and asks to speak with you."

"Bastard."

"Sure."

One person I am not keeping happy is Jenny. If she plans a weekend, something spoils it. A flying buddy desperately needs a cockpit filled, or I have to study, or something goes wrong at the office. The madder she gets, the more I drink. Some evenings we hardly speak. By the time Sam, in his pajamas, reads me a funny passage from *Wind in the Willows* and I read Becky one of her stories, Jenny is absorbed in a book or some TV show. So I sit down and try to catch up with old Strether's doings in *The Ambassadors*. But Henry James requires concentration—the prof warned us to look for patterns within patterns—so I never get far before I slam the book and take our old schnauzer for a walk. Some evenings we walk to the Potomac and back, about five miles. Often, when we return, Jenny is in bed with the pillow over her head. Somehow I'm going to have to make time for her. I think she cries a lot; it's beginning to show in her face.

"How old are you, Daddy?" Becky asks as I shave. Her hair is tied in pigtails with yellow ribbons that match her robe.

"I'm eighty-two, Becky."

"Is that old?"

"For a pilot."

"Tina's daddy is only thirty-five. How old is Captain Kangaroo?"

I rinse my razor. "Well, let's see, he's a captain, so maybe thirty."

"You are *not* eighty-two. Is a major higher than a colonel?"

"No. A major is not higher than anything. Have you eaten breakfast?"

She nods. "How old are you, Daddy? Quit teasing."

"Old. I don't know. I have to examine my teeth. Now, please run along so I can get dressed. Go brush the dog. She looks like Pooh Bear."

I scowl into the mirror, suck in my gut. A little gin flab above the towel. Too many martinis. They show in my eyes, hasten the general disaster. I have to squint to read the charts now. Like the Porsche, I'm beginning to rust out. Thirty-seven, and three to go for twenty. With luck, lieutenant colonel before then. At twenty, I can draw a pension and become a garbage man.

Downstairs, Jenny is standing before the stove and stepping over the dog. "Go lie on your bed, you thief." She points.

"Good morning," I say, and hug her from behind. She is wearing the robe I gave her at Hamilton.

"Good morning," she murmurs without turning. A few gray hairs. Frosting her hair last year was a mistake. "What's the temperature?" I ask. No answer. I lean out to check the mercury. "Another hot one for September."

Jenny puts my breakfast on the table, pours coffee. Sam is gathering his books.

"How's the fourth-grade play coming along?"

"It stinks."

"Do you like your new teacher?"

He shrugs. "She's okay. See you." He kisses Jenny and bangs out the door. He used to hug me.

"Well, Major Copley," Mrs. Caldwell says, "I've never seen Hamilton, but it must certainly be a nice base."

She is halfway through a mess I wrote yesterday. It is not a model of objectivity.

From her desk drawer she pulls a tissue and delicately blows her nose. "I may cry," she announces. "All these *heavenly* descriptions, these golden words. Perhaps with a choir, we—"

"All *right,*" I say finally. "I *know,* I *know.* Give it to Smitty or Monk. I should have disqualified myself."

Monk takes over the Hamilton Folder, reads what I've written, and hee-haws. He quotes sentences to Smitty. "How sweet!" Smitty's face shines. "Sounds like a realtor's ad. You own Hamilton, John? Hey, look, relax. Nobody wants to close Hamilton except realtors and developers."

On the way out to the Porsche last night, instead of the swollen, muddy Potomac, all I could see were the golden hills and the vast blue bay, with those fragile old F-84s lifting from their shadows and skimming the dike. In the distance were the sailboats, white against Angel's Island, and the misty towers of the bridges. I saw our Irish colonel's face, broken-nosed, jocose, ruminating about Chennault and the maneuvers of 1933. And that night I dreamed of old Will going in without a wing.

I'm supposed to spend this evening studying for our midterm in Shakespeare. Instead, I have to run through a dog-and-pony show in preparation for tomorrow's briefing. Fat Stuff wants each of us to rehearse his third of the bases. He's practicing to become a general; therefore, we can't just sit and discuss the folders in a conversational manner. I have to prepare a formal briefing. He wants to sit back and shoot at my visual aids and, of course, at me.

My first mistake was in assuming that an aerial photo is an acceptable briefing aid.

"It's not," Monk says. "Nothing but thirty-five millimeter. That's the way SAC likes it. Even the Bible has to go on thirty-five millimeter."

"Well, it's too late now," I tell him. "What's wrong with standard Air Force aerial photography?"

"For your information, John," Monk says, "SAC ain't the Air Force; SAC is SAC. And Fat Stuff was SAC. Got it?"

"No, Copley! No! No!" Fat Stuff shouts, "For Christ's sake, man, what are you doing? No aerial photographs unless they are thirty-five-millimeter color."

"I'm sorry, sir."

On his fingers, he ticks off the no-nos: "No opaque projectors, no butcher-paper drawings, no flip charts, no blackboards. Thirty-five millimeter, or it's not professional. Is that clear?"

"Yes, sir."

That was last time. This time I've got Graphics working their cans off. We are going to "dress this up," to use Fat Stuff's phrase. I may even throw in some slides about chariot racing.

It goes over big. I know what he wants now: he wants horseshit, so I lay it on thick. When I've finished, the colonel, who has emerged from his office, casually mentions that the general he will be briefing likes aerial photography. I must be sure to include some.

Smitty sticks his head into a filing cabinet drawer. Mrs. Caldwell laughs outright. Monk, who usually laughs only when Army beats Navy, having already made lieutenant colonel, lets go with his hee-haw. Still facing a red-faced Fat Stuff, I try to control myself, but, what the hell, I too laugh. It's suicide, but I can't help it.

Under these circumstances a human being would laugh at himself, but Fat Stuff is not human. He's a natural villain if there ever was one. A prototype. For a few seconds, rage immobilizes him. Then, wheeling in his chair, he marks each of us for perdition. Even the colonel gets the hot-eyed treatment.

"What'd I say?" the colonel asks. "I was trying to be helpful. Did I say something wrong?"

This convulses us again, all except Smitty, who is staring at a staff report as though he might eat it. No loss if he does.

Later, Smitty tears imaginary epaulets from my shirt and drums me out of the service. A little rehearsal for the real thing, he promises.

*   *   *

183

"Would Shakespeare's young lovers serve equally well in either his tragedies or his comedies? Support your opinion by citing specific characters and instances."

That is the entire exam. We look helplessly at each other, as though we are passengers aboard the *Titanic* and the lookouts have sighted icebergs. Then, several of the girls begin filling up their exam booklets. Mentally, I try casting Hamlet and Ophelia in *As You Like It*. Beside me, my little deaf blonde begins behaving like mad Ophelia. She is talking to herself and staring at me as though I must somehow know the answer. I shrug, and then realize that she is looking through me. I'm transparent.

Jenny often stares at me with this same absent gaze, as though I'm no longer important enough to be opaque. We have drifted even farther apart, Jenny and I, and for no good reason that I can see. I don't suspect a lover, nothing like that. It must just be the rat race and my being home every night. Maybe TDYs and honeymoon homecomings keep a marriage fresh; I don't know. I never tell her that I love her, although I do; I never tell her she's beautiful, even though I've seen her draw men's eyes. Guys spring to open doors for her; women admire her clothes, her swish. All I see of her at bedtime is that pillow over her head. If I awaken her, she comes up all claws like a grizzly out of hibernation.

Lost, I stare at my blank paper as though it were a fuel gauge reading "Empty" in midocean.

Through the plays I go—Rosalind and Orlando, Benedick and Beatrice, Ferdinand and Miranda, Antony and Cleopatra—scribbling as illegibly as my uncle, who is a doctor. Mrs. Caldwell wouldn't *believe* the syntax.

In the hall I wait for my little deaf blonde. I smoke and try to forget it. All that studying, only to blow the exam. Out she comes finally, stunned and soft as a sleepwalker.

"What did you decide?" she asks, already watching my lips. Like a child wearing her mother's clothes, she flounces down the corridor in her long skirt. A nice kid, probably some colonel's daughter, she keeps dropping things without realizing it. I trail along, scooping them up. She is totally disorganized, totally charming.

I tell her what I decided. She gasps and nearly knocks herself down with a slap to her forehead. Her pencils rain to the floor.

"Oh-h-h," she cries, "I *knew* it."

"Maybe I'm wrong."

"No, no, that's *right*. I see it now. I *began* that way. Damn! Excuse me." She sags, looks for a Kleenex. "My purse!" I hand it to her and, overcome, she squeezes my arm. We find a booth in the coffee shop.

"I really did begin that way," she tells me, eyes imploring.

"I didn't."

"But *you* changed your mind. Ooh! Have you ever seen a woman commit suicide?"

"Aw, he won't even grade them. He just wanted to make us think about Shakespeare's characterization. This exam was just another lesson. The best one, too . . ."

I stop and realize that I have hit upon the truth. There is something fortuitous about consoling others. Divine circuits in the brain close.

She is staring at me. Her hand rises to her lips. "*Yes*. How did you realize it?"

"Tell me, do you really think Shakespeare scholars would agree on an answer?"

"No," she says finally, her child's face still with awe. When her grin comes, it is really something. It is more than infectious; I laugh with pure joy. She squeezes my hand. "You *are* smart, aren't you?" Demurely, blushing, she withdraws her hand from sight.

"What are you taking next semester?" I ask, a little ruffled.

"Twentieth-century poetry? I'll have to check."

"American?"

She shakes her head. "What was Rilke? German? Austrian? Anyhow, European. What about you?"

"Whatever Dr. Johnson says."

"Isn't that a great name for an English professor? *He's* advising you? Gee, you rate. I've heard that he despises undergrads."

"Not me," I say. "Doctor Johnson's son was a pilot in Korea."

"Really? What's the son doing now?"

"Playing a harp," I tell her so softly that she can't hear me. If she were my daughter, I'd buy her a hearing aid.

Mrs. Caldwell is trimming our tiny office tree. Because it sits on the bookcase, she stands in a chair and shows off her pretty calves as she stretches. When she tries to attach the star, the colonel gives her a wolf whistle. Blushing, she hands me the star. We've all had a couple of belts of egg nog, and I mount the star crooked, drawing considerable criticism. Smitty says that he will photograph it so that Fat Stuff, who is on leave in Switzerland, can reflect it in my ER. Fat Stuff doesn't work during the holiday season, which is nice for everyone except the Swiss. He doesn't work the rest of the year either, but he is here.

Deliberately perhaps, Mrs. C. has paused under the mistletoe, so I kiss her. Smitty does, too. The colonel shies away.

"Olivia de Havilland," I decide. "You are a dead ringer for Olivia de Havilland." Her cheeks have color now. Her eyes lift, soar around.

"Well, of course. I *am* Olivia de Havilland," she announces, and strikes a pose.

In comes Connie, the sexy little toot from next door, Smokey's ideal woman—all body. Hugging her and spilling egg nog is a tall man wearing civvies and a Santa Claus mask. He steers her under the mistletoe, momentarily lifts his mask to kiss her, then turns to us.

"This little doll is reserved for good little boys. Line forms on the left."

He whacks her on the bottom, and she vibrates and coos, squeals and giggles.

"Jesus," Smitty, white-faced, breathes, and jostles all of us aside. He grasps her. The proprietary Santa Claus hangs on. Aggressively, Smitty steps between them. Santa emits a command bellow much like Scooter's rogue elephant.

"Oh, sweet Jesus!" Smitty grovels. "Excuse me, General."

"No sweat, son. Just get off my foot." He sees Mrs. Caldwell, gasps, holds both hands to his heart. "Who is *this* beauty?"

"Olivia de Havilland," I inform him.

His chin lifts. With satisfaction, he looks her up and down, and nods. "By God, Copley."

I kiss Connie. Her eyes are like glass. She hangs on as though she is drunk and perhaps a little afraid. I look again at her. No.

Gravely, the general busses Mrs. Caldwell, waltzes her around. I sense real affection. A courtly bow. Smilingly, she whispers something in his ear.

"Yes, ma'am," he concedes. "I sure do. Like it was yesterday. When was it?"

"Nineteen forty-eight."

"Before Eisenhower."

"Mr. Truman."

"Oh, boy. *Well*. You're never going to let me forget that, are you, Minnie?"

"Olivia," she corrects him.

Gradually, a smile settles over his face. He kisses her forehead. "You were something else, you know it?"

"Were?"

"*Are*."

"Thank you."

"It's true, Minnie."

Briefly, there are tears in her eyes. I turn away.

"Well," the general says quietly, releasing her hands and absently corralling Connie. "Merry Christmas."

As he leaves, he growls at us, "Merry Christmas to all; and, to all, ten years for drinking on government property."

I should try to finish this letter for the colonel's signature, but who can concentrate while Monk is singing "Adeste Fidelis"? West Point Glee Club, my ass—unless he's singing the harmony.

"Well," Smitty says. "You know how the Academy guys lie. Especially after they've become LCs."

Ten more verses. Okay, Monk, you *were* a member of West Point's Glee Club.

No matter what I do to this sentence, it comes out as though Pancho Villa wrote it under duress—in English. I crumple the page. Next door things seem to be getting out of hand. Is that a man or a woman screaming? Mrs. Caldwell grimaces but keeps typing.

"Hey, John," Smitty says from the doorway, and jerks his head. "C'mon. They got the real thing down in Ops, old buddy." He enters and holds his cup under my nose.

"Gin?" I say. "So what?"

He bends, cocks one eye sidewise at Mrs. Caldwell. "I'm talking about something else, my friend," he says. "They are locking up and switching off the lights." Lewdly grinning, rubbing his hands, he adds in a whisper, "But they ain't going home." He straightens to rumba around. "You get the picture?"

Blushing slightly, Mrs. Caldwell tries to maintain her typing speed.

"You better come on, old buddy. Adele and that other blonde sent me to get you. Connie told 'em you are just too cute for words, you know?"

"Maybe that's why I can't write. Nah, Smitty, I'm way behind on this. Thanks anyway."

"You're way behind on lots of things, my friend. Well, Merry Christmas, everybody. If my wife calls, tell her I was suddenly called down to the Command Post. Make up some emergency. The Mexicans have invaded. Anything."

Winking broadly, swirling his drink, he waves, beats on the wall and yells, "Let's hold it down in there. General White is in here inspecting." He leaves.

Monk bursts in. "General White?"

Monk was *not* a Rhodes Scholar. His making LC gives me hope. Puzzled, he asks, "Where's the colonel?"

"Escorting General White," I tell him. I jerk my thumb down the hall.

When we're alone, Mrs. Caldwell asks above the noise whether I'll have the letter ready to be typed before 1700.

"No. Maybe never."

"Well, I suggest that we abandon all attempts to salvage this afternoon." She rises, straightens her desk, hoods her machine. "I've meant to ask you this a hundred times: are you related to General Copley?"

"Not to my knowledge, but thanks anyway."

"Umm," she says as she opens the safe. "Any classified to go in here? No? Well, I'll bet you are, or were; he's dead now. His home was near Louisville, just across the river from Indiana."

"A good general? Could he spell?"

"He was a splendid officer, John."

She called me John. She never calls anyone by his first name. Her expression at this moment, a sort of smile, really does remind me of Olivia de Havilland. It starts grand music in my head.

As I unlock old Porsche, I still hear it. It will be my best Christmas present.

Which reminds me: I've *got* to do my Christmas shopping. Another robe for Jenny and . . .

In June, when the local schools release our hostage children, one-third of the military personnel in the area transfer. Smitty has his orders, his final E.R. He is jubilant. Eyes slitted, he shows me all the Xs along the right side of the report.

"By God," he murmurs, nodding, "I *told* you: a little patience, a little observance of the 'No Wake' signs . . ."

"A little brown-nosing."

". . . a *lot* of brown-nosing," he concedes, "but, look: I am shipping out clean and whole with sweet orders in my goodie bag. And you can do it, too, old friend."

"You are going to where—Westover?" I tease him.

"Where am I going? Why, ask anyone. Ask General White. My friend, I am going to God's green heaven, to His most sacred spot on this blighted earth. Good buddy, I am going to Columbus Air Force Base, Mississippi." He comes to attention and places his hand over his heart.

"My condolences."

His middle finger, shielded by my desk from Mrs. Caldwell, rises and quivers. "May our beloved Fat Stuff have your carpetbagging ass. Yankee, go home. Hey, have you heard where our beloved is going, my friend? He swung a real deal with Personnel."

"Where is our beloved going?"

"NATO Headquarters."

"That figures."

Flying has become peripheral, a nuisance.

"During your penetration, Major," the captain says, "you doped off. You would have flown us right into the ground." He leans back in his chair and looks at me.

"No, I wouldn't," I lie. "I was just a couple of hundred feet behind the altimeter."

"Behind *my warning,* sir."

I drop my gaze.

"Now then," he says finally, "what should I do about it? Well, I can play it one of two ways: I can flunk you and set you up for a recurrency check, *or* I can trust you not to fly when the weather is bad. After all, this wasn't an instrument check. This was just supposed to be a VFR Annual Proficiency Check. And, VFR, you're okay; but your gauges are danger-ous. They are the first things to go. Don't take this too personally; you're like most of the others over there flying a desk."

I nod.

"Can we work a deal, Major?"

"Yes."

"All right. Scout's honor. I'm going to sign you off and I'm going to trust you to cancel if the forecast is doubtful."

"I'm not to fly the mails?"

No smile. "That's right, sir."

We shake hands on it. It's a delicate arrangement, and one that I had better respect. Still, his pen scratches right through my flesh as he signs the form. By God, I think, a little respect, son. I was flying *missions* out of England when you were in the ninth grade.

But I don't say anything, of course. I drag on my cigarette and stare out the window at the flight line which seems almost alien to me now.

He completes the form, tucks his pen into his sleeve pocket, rises to shake hands. His flying suit is pressed, his boots are shined. His life is still under his own control. Then, formally, he steps back one pace and salutes.

I return it, hating him as I gather my battered helmet and mask, my knee board with its dead penlight batteries. But he's right, of course. A thick Form 5 doesn't impress a guy who knows you can't fly. Nor does it impress those old birds sitting out there with their red safety streamers twirling in the breeze.

Fat Stuff is delivering his farewell address to us, his loyal troops. His voice struggles manfully with his deep affection. He is Henry the Fifth at Agincourt. Apparently we have been through hell together. He wears a sad little smile. *No,* he tells our wives, *he* does not deserve the credit; *we* do. First time he's told the truth. But there's always something about farewells, as there is with memories, that dissolves the lumps and bumps. There is a tendency to forgive, and one must guard against it.

Ah, Christ, what an actor! His voice becomes husky, his eyes misty with manly love. He bows his head, lets his voice trail off.

Jenny elbows me and hisses, but I can't quit laughing. All I can do is swing away and pretend to blow my nose. Disgusted, Jenny again lifts her chin.

Fat Stuff stirs himself. Slowly he raises his wine glass. "*Auf Wiedersehen,*" he whispers. "*Prosit.*"

Rocking around in his chair, hoping perhaps that some hypocrite among us will begin "For He's a Jolly Good Fellow," the colonel frowns at us, then cues his wife. Together, they falter into a duet ("C'mon," he hisses at us). They conclude it after the first "deny." Quickly the colonel's wife rises to kiss Fat Stuff and Mrs. Fat Stuff, who looks like him wearing a wig. Dutifully, the colonel slaps his back, but makes his speech as brief as possible, and my wife applauds.

Well, there is no civilized way to avoid hypocrisy; we line up to shake hands. Poor NATO. What we should do is send him on exchange to the Russian Air Force—except that they might conclude that he is a typical

American and thereby smother any qualms they may have about atomizing us.

What is he asking Jenny? Can we drop by for a nightcap? *No,* I vow. Yes, she nods, "but it is really up to John."

"Wonderful!" he says, and drapes his arm around her bare shoulders. She simply walks out from under it.

"No kidding, I've really enjoyed working with you, Johnny," he assures me. "Have you seen the ER I wrote you?"

"No, sir."

"Um-m. Well, see it. And don't thank me; you earned it. You *are* coming over?"

"Well, I . . ."

"Tomorrow is Saturday, you know. No work."

"Our babysitter is awfully young, sir."

Our babysitter is, in fact, sixty-two and never misses the late show.

"Uh, *this* might decide you: the Camstons will be there. Betty is looking forward to seeing you again."

"Jenny," I call.

She has been supposedly engrossed in a conversation with Mrs. Fat Stuff, but she hasn't missed anything.

"Very well, sweet. We'll go."

Georgetown by night, gaslit and elegant, trees along the sidewalks, iron fences edging the restored town houses.

"Here," she says. We climb the steps.

"Look at this *door,*" Jenny whispers.

Inside, more gaslight flickering on antique patinas, on imperfect glass. There are Oriental rugs and wide-board floors. Every wall has a painting, every room a piece or two of sculpture. The furniture is Danish. Still, it is a gloomy place. There aren't any windows to speak of, and if there is central air conditioning, it can't cope with even this small crowd.

Betty and I stand in the elaborate kitchen. The swinging door flies open and Fat Stuff enters, pitches his ice into the sink, and, ponderously stooping, searches the lower cabinets.

"What are you two doing here in the kitchen? Umm? A little pantry petting? You find my party boring?" He straightens and holds to the light a bottle of Grand Marnier. "You aren't drinking. Have some brandy." His eyes are red, his stance wavering.

Betty, the fool, tips her head back and opens her mouth. "Okay," she says hollowly.

"Oh. Glasses. 'Scuse me." He bangs cabinet doors. "Goddamn maid hides everything. You like Courvoisier?"

In clinking snifters with us, Fat Stuff has to side-step to regain his balance. Giggling, he cracks (literally) his glass against mine. Perhaps he doesn't notice the crack. *Auf Wiedersehen?* Coolly, I watch.

"What? You haven't seen the house? Well, you must. Where were you, Johnny, when Eric was showing it to your charming wife? Ah, don't answer that. Come, I will show you."

"I've seen it, Clyde," Betty says.

"You have seen the wine cellar?"

"No, not the wine cellar."

"It is downstairs," Fat Stuff says.

Betty winks at me and taps her temple. The cellar light bulb flashes and burns out. We proceed by the illumination of my Zippo and his Ronson.

Supporting the moldering pine joists are brick partitions, scaling into rose powder. A foot above my head, shoes scrape and clop away. We hear no conversation, only the louder exclamations and laughter. I recognize the colonel's bellow of welcome to someone. Of the music above, we hear only the beat. It is strange as hell being down here with Fat Stuff's eyes glittering in our lighters' flames. He looks especially villainous, Betty particularly vulnerable. Old Zippo is still going because I refueled it this evening, but Fat Stuff's Ronson has sparked to extinction.

"Now, *these* racks," he says thickly, "contain the French reds—the clarets and Burgundies, the Beaujolaix and Rhones, and so forth. Where do you shop, John, for your wines? Harry's?"

I shrug. "In our shopping center."

He is perturbed. "Well, you are wasting your money. Never mind now. Over to the right are the French whites. To the left, the rosés." My lighter shows only dusty glass. What are we doing down here? "And beyond this partition, everything else—the Italian, the Portuguese, the Mosels and Rhines; no German reds, of course. Is this bottle leaking?"

We shall never know. My Zippo sputters and sparks. We move toward the stairs. Fat Stuff climbs upward. Without warning, Betty wheels me around, slips her hand behind my head and pulls me down to her lips.

Surprised—her initial reunion kiss had been that of a skittish young cousin—I am a little slow to respond. By the time I do, she has pulled away, laughing, and we hurry to overhaul our host whose bulk blocks the light.

"Will there be lipstick?" I whisper.

"Sure," she says.

Hurriedly, I scrub with my handkerchief while she laughs. "That will teach you to be more observant," she murmurs. "I never use lipstick." Her arm is about my waist, mine about her bare shoulders. She squeezes me, then pushes me away as Fat Stuff turns. He is winded.

"Now *this* is the master bedroom," he says. From the massive, canopied bed and all the heavy furniture, even I could have guessed that. Imagine sleeping under a canopy; I doubt that it is anything like sleeping in a lower bunk.

His wife calls up the stairs, "Clyde! Telephone."

We kiss again. Oh my God! Affection has been absent so long from my life that I can feel tears. And when she opens her eyes, tears glisten there, too. Her breath is sweet, her freckles charming. She blows a wisp of her hair back and smiles. "Hey," she says, and lays her head against my chest, "what's *with* you?"

I can't speak.

"Are you happy?"

"Now? Yes."

"The rest of the time?"

"I don't know. I guess so. How can you tell?"

"You can tell," she assures me, her gray-green eyes moving around my face. "Believe me, you can tell."

"Jenny is a fine woman," I say.

"And very beautiful."

"Very."

"You've got it made."

I remain silent.

Slowly, she searches my eyes. "What's wrong?"

"I don't know. Nothing. It's just life."

"She has heard all your combat stories."

I nod.

"Well, Clyde," Eric says, "I have shown Jennifer your wondrous museum, and now I expect recompense."

Jenny is very animated. She and Betty are hanging onto each other and laughing like former roommates. They present a lovely contrast in coloration and style—Jenny, tall and blond, full-figured; Betty, almost boyish, auburn hair cut short and shaped, cat's eyes, small but perfect breasts.

"You like my house, Jennifer?" asks Fat Stuff.

"You have some lovely pieces. I may steal that secretary."

"*Secretary?*"

"Desk."

"You want some brandy?"

"Yes, and Eric, too. Could we have it in glasses?"

"Second time tonight," Fat Stuff says and tries to snap his fingers. He can't do it. Looking at them with amusement, he tries again.

"Here, Clyde," Betty sighs, "*I'll* be barmaid, okay? Where do you keep your peasant blouses?"

"Than' you. You are a gen'man."

"A lady."

"Lady." He nods reasonably.

"Show Betty your nails," Jenny commands me. My hands are trembling, I notice. "Clutch job on the Porsche. I helped; I jacked up the engine."

"If you are going to make a career of working on sport cars," Betty says, "you gotta bite your nails, okay?"

I can't take my eyes off her.

Eric crosses his arms. "Betty, you are terrible."

In one of the dark bedrooms I find Jenny's purse and scarf.

"Gotcha!" Betty whispers, sliding her arms under mine and clasping them around my chest. Turning me, she lays her head against my chest, listens. "Erratic. Pulse irregular. Not so good." She unbuttons a button on my shirt and slides one hand in. "Let's play doctor."

"Doctor, I hurt *here*," I whisper.

"Yes? Well, undress please." Her chin rises.

"Betty . . ."

"What?"

"Nothing."

"Nothing, hell. What?"

"Good-bye, I guess, for six more years."

"Not good-bye." She shakes her head.

"No?" I lift her chin again. "You know a secret?"

Like a child, she nods.

"What?"

"What is your security clearance, Major?"

"Top Secret."

"That doesn't get it, buddy."

Across the black Potomac, the floodlit monuments sleep. The mall is deserted. In the suburban motels, exhausted tourists lie beneath air conditioners. I cannot remember a hotter August, hotter or more humid. The Pentagon is dark but, deep within the building, men drink coffee as usual and monitor the telephonic consoles, the teletypewriters. All over the world, their counterparts watch and wait. On both sides of the Iron Curtain.

Shirley Highway is deserted. I wind the Porsche out in third to burn off a little carbon. In the glow of the instrument lights, Jenny's face is cold. She stares straight ahead, says nothing.

I reach over and pat her leg. She pushes my hand away.

"I meant to tell you, Jen. You were beautiful tonight."

"How would *you* know?" she snaps without looking at me.

Well, I'm in no mood to fight. I switch on the radio. Ike and Mamie are at Camp David for the weekend. The Russians have launched a dog, the bastards. Kennedy is already beginning to campaign. He's in Indiana now; God help him if he asks my dad for his vote. Democrats, Socialists, Communists—they're all the same to Dad. "The Free-Lunch Crowd," he always snarls and goes into a silent rage.

Jenny switches off the radio just as Tormé comes on. Well, I'm in for it. She will sleep in the guest room tonight and, in the morning, she will throw the dishes on the table. Which reminds me, I'm starving.

193

Conceivably, that pizza place at Five Corners is still open.

"Could you eat some pizza?" I ask her.

Incredulously, her eyes widen. Without replying, she turns toward the window.

"Okay, okay. Sorry. Jesus."

Through gritted teeth, she says, "If you use the Lord's name in vain *one more time . . .*"

My orders are in. I can feel it in my bones, see it in Mrs. Caldwell's eyes. When I look askance at her, she begins typing.

"Where?" I finally ask her point-blank.

She smiles and looks away. "Why, Major Copley. I can't imagine what you mean."

"C'mon."

"I think I'd better let the colonel tell you."

When the colonel has had his first cup of coffee, he leans out of his office cubicle and jerks his head at me. Mac, Monk's replacement, grins.

"Yes, sir?"

"Sit down. Good news, John. Your orders are in. Guess where you're going."

Well, I know exactly how many bases the Air Force has, but there aren't that many fighter bases. On my dream sheet, I had listed fighters as my first preference, and the southeast—simply because Jenny and I have never been there—as my first area of preference.

"Myrtle Beach, South Carolina."

"Wrong. Guess again."

"Langley Air Force Base, Virginia."

"You're *very* warm."

I try to think of another fighter base in Virginia. There aren't any. South Carolina? "Shaw?" No, that's reccy.

"Think bigger, John."

"Bigger? Not another headquarters?"

He holds up both hands and laughs.

"I said *good* news. Think school."

"School?"

"Why, certainly. You are at that time of life, you know. In fact, you are overdue. You are field grade, middle management, and all that. You gotta get ready for the menopause."

"A school in Virginia."

"Right."

"I give up."

"Armed Forces Staff College," he announces with immense satisfaction. Mac, our resident West Pointer, leans in and kisses his fingertips. "Excuse me, Colonel. Hey, a winner, Johnny. *A real winner.* How did you swing it, man?"

I ignore him. "How long is this course?" I ask.

"Six months," Mac answers. "Which beats the hell out of eleven months at Command and Golf down at Maxwell. And this is a great school, John. It's a plum."

"Teaches you not to hate the Army and Navy," the colonel adds.

Mac, arms akimbo, watches me with disbelief. "What'sa matter for you, GI? Why you no speak? Is he still thinking fighters, Colonel?"

"Let it sink in, Mac," the colonel says.

"Holy—" Mac begins, then calms himself. Mrs. Caldwell now docks us fifty cents every time we use improper language; the coffee can on her desk is already half full. It goes to the Arlington Community Chest. "They give him a select school and he wants to go fly airplanes, for . . . Pete's sake." He leans out to peer at Mrs. Caldwell. "I didn't say it, Mrs. C."

Mac slumps into a chair, preparatory to giving me a high-pressure pitch. It's probably the same one he gave the cadets when he taught at the Academy: "Career Guidance 402" or "Professional Counseling 401," or whatever they call it. Mac's a nice old biddy. I'm sure he's a competent instructor. But he has never flown fighters. He thinks a B-47 is an airplane.

"Sit down, Mac," the colonel says with heavy irony. "Please have a seat. Now, then, what were you saying?"

"One thing, Colonel, and I'll shut up. John, baby, look: You're Regular and you gotta stay for at least twenty. Which means you need to make LC at the eighteen-year-mark, right? Okay, then, promotions and schools go together like bacon and eggs. One shoe falls and you wait to hear the other. The same selection board usually handles both."

"That's one thing, Mac," the colonel says.

"No, sir. That's background; he already knows all that. *This* is the one thing: Fill this block, John, or you're dead, baby. They will never seriously consider you again for anything but out."

"He's right, John."

"Bet your sweet ass I am," Mac nods. He winces and reaches in his pocket for a half-dollar. "Honor Code, Minnie. I'm coming."

I'm almost afraid to tell Jenny. We'll move in June, again in December. All our Goodwill furniture will go into storage; the rest, the pieces of lesser quality, we will discard. Five moves equal one fire. A furnished apartment and two more changes of school for Sam.

"Norfolk?" she asks. "Is that on the ocean?"

"Practically."

We look at a map. It is almost surrounded by water. We brighten. We shall rent a house on the beach, we shall finally buy a sailboat. No more weekend work, no more Pentagon. I mix us some killer martinis and, eventually, she leans against me. Yeah, Mac was right; West Pointers know. And I need to learn planning and management, joint operations and logistics. Or they say I do.

When the day comes and the moving van backs over the shrubbery, when the two men have taken away every familiar thing, Jenny and I roam the empty house scrubbing the woodwork, tiptoeing in old sneakers across fresh wax, reassuring our ancient schnauzer when she can't find her bed.

Another new beginning. They are always exciting. Jenny scolds the kids for tracking in dirt, pushes me away when I get amorous. We finish the last of the wine and whistle to the overmodulating old portable I bought in Japan.

The telephone is always the last thing to go. It's like the brain. Just as the Chesapeake and Potomac truck arrives, it rings. Reverberating through the empty rooms, the sound is startling and ominous. I lift the receiver. "Major Copley."

"Sergeant Fowler, Major. Thought I might catch you, but I was half hoping I wouldn't." It's the Air Force Command Post. Fowler was Pete's operations specialist in France. "Bad news."

I settle cross-legged into a seated position on the hardwood floor.

"Crash report. Fatal."

"*Who?*"

"Major W."

Major W. He is telling me something.

"*Whit!*"

"Yes, sir."

I can't talk. I can't think. I lower the phone a few inches. Tinnily, he adds, "In a T-Bird on takeoff from Tinker." Pause. "Goddamned shame," he says.

"Do they know what happened?"

"Not yet."

"Thanks, Al."

"Sorry. Hey, keep in touch, okay? God knows I'll be here. Or in Saint Elizabeth's."

I set the latch and ask the phone man to close the door when he leaves. The neighborhood kids are all standing around the wagon and the Porsche. Good wives are out to load us down with sandwiches and cookies.

"Bye, John," one of them sniffs. "Got a kiss for a drab old civilian housewife?"

"You betcha."

Jenny starts the wagon, I the Porsche. Everyone's waving and trying to smile. We roll, the signal for the neighborhood dogs to give chase. Sam's with me. He wipes his eyes with the heel of his hand and looks at me.

"Men don't cry, do they?"

"Nope." I pat his leg.

Southward along U.S. 1 we go. It is beginning to drizzle. Along the telephone wires, birds sit like commas. A gray day, a gray time. For three years I have dreamed of this departure. Back there somewhere, lost to me forever, I hope, is the Pen. I can just glimpse the Washington

Monument and corners of white Doric architecture. It is our Acropolis, this fever-stricken lowland. I am retreating toward Richmond, as Lee once did, down the west bank of the Potomac.

15

NORFOLK

NORFOLK IS AN old Navy town and makes no bones about it. Everyone here is service or ex-service. The young waitresses are Navy wives from Kansas or somewhere, the service station owners retired chiefs. Ship movements are common knowledge, destinations no real secret. For the most part, they are simply rotations, to the Med or Gitmo. But occasionally, overhauls or refittings break this routine. Along the wharf of Main Base, you can drive for a mile and see famous names on the towering gray bows and transoms. Flight decks loom almost over the tracks. Anyone can watch the cargo slings and hear the roll calls near the gangways.

"Yeah," the old chief nods, watching the meter. "Sure. I miss it. I'll admit it. When I see the *Roosevelt* putting out, it's like watching my goddamn house go by. I'm edgy for a week after I notice her getting up steam. When I'm home, which is *every fucking night* now, me and the old lady fight. We miss the old days and the honeymoons every six months."

He sunsquints at the meter, bumps another three cents' worth into my gas tank, then hangs up the nozzle, screws on the cap.

"You're gonna miss it some day, Major. What're you, a fly boy? Same thing. You're gonna miss it when all there is is memories. You and your old lady will stare at each other until you go out and get drunk."

He wheezes on his cigarette smoke, coughs as he counts out change. "Jesus, I'd like to get back to old Napoli one more time before somebody slips me back into that uniform for the burial."

We live on Willoughby Spit, out past the roller coaster and the rooming houses along Ocean View Avenue. Through our picture window we can watch the Navy steam silently out on Monday mornings and return on Friday afternoons, most of them, just as the Navy did at Pearl Harbor in 1941. What the hell, people don't change: when the weekend comes, you want to be home; on Mondays you want to go back to work. So there will be more Pearl Harbors, because we're human. During the week Norfolk is a town of girls. They sit around the laundromats, their hair in curlers, snapping gum. A few hold babies. A few who are no longer girls give me the eye.

My life is based on promises and, of these, a recent one concerns buying a sailboat. If a Sailfish is a sailboat—Jenny, who once spent a week sailing a lapstrake dinghy on Buzzards Bay with her Bennington roommate, insists that it isn't—I have kept my promise. I concede that a cockpit would be nice, especially during these last, raw days of April, but the 'Fish is easy to beach and carry behind the dunes. Besides, it handles like a fighter.

Each evening until dusk a couple of us are out beyond the jetties, spanking through the wavelets of Hampton Roads, tacking toward Fort Monroe to engage the *Monitor*.

"Aw, Dad, it's sunk," Sam explains impatiently while Becky loses the moment pondering the various meaning of the word "engage."

Today Becky and I are out here, heeling with the gusts, hiking out like acrobats, splatting through ripples, shivering. Aerodynamic lift sucks us along, causes our tiny sail to drum and quiver. Out farther, in the channel, is a destroyer putting in. A destroyer isn't a boat; I've learned *that* much at AFSC. It's a ship.

"Nah," says one of my Navy seminar mates, "it's a can, a tin can, and it's one miserable way to go to sea. I'd rather go over Niagara Falls in a barrel than serve in one again."

"Stand by to come about."

"What?" Becky asks, her nose crinkling in puzzlement. I love it when reflected light plays under her chin.

"Left turn. Now, pay attention. You have got to learn to sail, too." Oh, boy, we're in irons. I fan the rudder.

"What are you doing, Daddy?"

Her emphasis, her amused eyes are Jenny's. Her hair is beginning to sun-steak. By August she will be cotton-topped and brown-shouldered. When, finally, I roll out on the new heading, she sighs in exasperation, exactly as her mother does, and lifts her right knee to form a shapely leg. I am hopelessly in love with her, this child who was born a woman.

"You like sailing?" she asks, frowning at me. Her nose is probably going to peel.

"Sure. Don't you?"

"No." She hugs herself, huddles within her orange life jacket. Her eyes are changing with the water from green to blue. "I'm freezing. Let's go in."

"Oh, nonsense."

"Let's go *in*, Daddy. This isn't fun."

"What about the destroyer? Don't you want to catch it? No? C'mon. Oh, all right, jibe ho."

"What?"

"Duck."

As the stern swings through the wind, we duck and grimace at each other. The wavering boom, finally committed, jars us. I'll never learn how to handle a mainsheet. Almost instantly, the slap, slap, slap of the bow wave changes to a rustle, then a hiss. We are planing. There is a new tautness, the strange drumming of hydrodynamics.

Silently, exultantly, she lifts her eyes to mine. She points to our miniature rooster tail. "Look!"

"Okay, raise the centerboard. Higher. Now lean back against my knees."

Reclining, she cocks her head to watch Blue Two, our faithful wingman. Blue Two may be a herring gull. Motionless and immaculate, he somehow rides this tailwind at our speed without stalling. It's a good thing he's never studied aerodynamics. But he is not much interested in anything except food. Ever since Becky threw him a piece of her peanut butter sandwich, he has kept one expressionless eye on her.

"Look how his legs fold straight back." She points and squints.

"Like a P-40."

"P-40? You are teasing me. There's no such thing."

"Well, you're right."

Ahead, in the Winslow Homer light, are the cottages, almost touching. Ours, the least paint-covered, is almost unprotected since the Ash Wednesday storm washed the dunes away. There were telephone poles in the surf. We had watched them heave and retreat.

"You know something?" I say. "You have salt in your earluhs."

"Not *earluhs*, Daddy. *Ears*. That's baby-talk."

"How old are you? Four?"

She sighs. She's not going to rise to it. Eventually, her eyes lift to mine. She grins and pulls my head down to look in my ear. Jenny's arch smile of satisfaction. Slyly, she goes dead-pan.

"You know what you have in *your* ears, Daddy?"

While I pretend to ponder, she giggles in anticipation.

"What?" I ask finally.

"Dead fish." She laughs behind her hands.

We beach the boat and I drag it (her?) above the high-water mark. Overhead, our wingman makes one last reconnaissance pass, then heads south along the waterline and becomes lost in a crowd.

Our cottage lies exposed behind the eroding dunes. Its sills are rotting, its porch railing less reliable each day. The windows are cloudy with salt. Becky stoops to pick up a shell for me to name. She is already giggling.

"It's a sea shell," I tell her confidently.

"Don't tease, Daddy."

"All right. A *Norfolk* sea shell."

"No," she says. She is delighted.

"Sure it is. Ask Sam." Sam has a book; he's our shell-and-tidal-pool authority.

Jenny is cooking supper. "Taste," she says, holding a bite of something under my nose. I notice that I have to step back to see it clearly. Maybe I need glasses.

"Just taste," Jenny says impatiently.

It's delicious but, as always, I make a face. "I prefer the way Mother makes it."

"Hey!" she says. "Your mother never made this in her life. She's a *terrible* cook."

It's true. That's one reason I left home.

"How'd it go?" she asks without interest. "No, first, fix us a bunch of martinis; we're going to need them."

I look askance as I grope in the cabinet.

"Never mind. Just fix the drinks."

"We are overdrawn?" No, she has always carefully managed our money. I never know our bank balance—or care to know—unless the Porsche needs something.

"The *Porsche!*" I exclaim.

She nods, surprised. Laying down her big spoon, she wipes her hands. "I dinged it—the left front fender and door. The bumper, too."

I stare at her in disbelief. She hugs me.

"Really, John. I should be jealous of that little turtle. The kids and I could be lying around with bubonic plague, and you'd accept it with equanimity."

I inspect the damage. It's not too bad. A new bumper and headlight, pound out the fender. The door damage is superficial. Two hundred bucks. If I add a hundred, I can get the whole car repainted.

To make sure that I don't kill myself, she comes to the door. So I put on an act. On my knees, I inspect the underside.

"Oh, no-o," I groan, and close my eyes.

"What is it?" She comes outside. "What's wrong underneath?"

"*Look* at it!!"

Concerned, she stoops, kneels finally and, holding her hair with one hand, peers. I leave her there, quietly close the screen door, and begin mixing the drinks. When she straightens, talking, I'm at the kitchen window drinking.

"Bastard!" she says silently. She comes in, accepts her drink. "John, I *am* sorry about the accident. This guy was turning left, and I thought he would wait . . ."

Sam bangs in, sails his fielder's glove. "What happened to the Porsche?"

I grasp him by the shoulders, nudge his chin up. He's got my freckles and homely snub nose. "I don't know, Sam. I was going to ask you. It looks as though a baseball may have hit it." I sip my drink. "Where were you guys playing?"

"Baseball? Aw, Dad, come on."

"Out of the kitchen, you two," Jenny says. "Hurry and shower."

I set down my martini, rotate Sam, and squeeze the breath out of him. "I've seen you sling a bat."

"Dad! Don't tickle, okay? Please . . . Dad! . . . No-o-o!"

"John!" Jenny says. "Quit it! Stop it this instant. You'll make him stutter."

Releasing him, I grab her. "What?" I am amused. "Who told you that?"

"It's true." She tries to push me away. "Get away, you fool. Am I forgiven?"

"Ancient custom say . . ." I intone Orientally.

She mutters and bends one of my fingers back.

"Ancient custom," I continue, wincing, "say husband must cut off reft front rimb of wife and—"

"Left hand?"

"Whatever sticks out farthest." I nod at her breast.

"Ha! I've got a picture of *that*."

"No." I change my mind. "Death by tickring."

"John, I'm *not* ticklish. Never have been. Dad gave up years ago. You are—John!—wasting your time, and dinner is burn . . ." She collapses in howls, weakly trying to fend me off.

"Daddy!" Becky yells. "Stop! You'll make her stutter."

Sam is pulling on my bathing trunks and the treacherous schnauzer has my ankle. Ah, God. Life is sweet.

Armed Forces Staff College *is* a good school, I think. I'll bet it's a lot better than most civilian colleges. Strangely, there are no exams and no grades. You just go there like a big sponge and, because you're interested and because you don't want to appear an amateur among professionals, you work your can off. College kids wouldn't believe that, but it's true. College, like youth, is wasted on the young.

Every weekday morning the entire student body and faculty assemble in the auditorium to hear two or three bone-dry lectures by important people, both civilian and military—once the Secretary of State himself *and* the chairman of the Joint Chiefs of Staff. Imagine such brass turning out for two hundred little field-graders. I guess they welcome every opportunity to get out of Washington.

Even the deputy secretaries and three-star generals must be important because they also *read* their scripts. They can't deviate from national or Defense policy by one word. If a guy speaks from notes, naturally he's more interesting; but he's no one, really.

What's good about the real wheels though is that, during the question-and-answer period, local dignitaries, reporters, and all foreign students are ushered away somewhere to have coffee or watch a military demonstration. Then anything goes, so long as we preface our question with "Sir." They give you a quick, flat answer, then point to someone else. *That's* the education.

In the afternoons we go to our seminar rooms and discuss what we heard or perhaps work on a planning problem. Most of the problems deal with contingency situations. One situation concerns an imaginary peninsula that looks exactly like Southeast Asia, but the French surrendered there in 1954, so it's pretty academic.

With each new situation, we change staff roles. At the moment, I'm J-4, which is ridiculous. I've never learned a thing about logistics and don't care to, but I don't say that, of course. You've got to have logisticians, I know. It's true what they say: most statues of generals show the mossy old hero astride a noble horse like the Green Knight, but to have cast him riding on the back of his logistician would have been more honest.

Anyhow, I am up here at the lectern trying to fake it through this logistics annex to an amphibious operation and trying to avoid eye contact with Duffy. Duffy is an old Marine grunt with a Silver Star, and he has to keep wiping off his shark's grin. Finally, both he and our Army instructor have to excuse themselves and go out into the hall.

Ah, Christ, it's funny. Even the SAC guys sometimes laugh at the right times, as when the chaplain in our seminar briefed the Operations portion of the plan. "You are going to land *fully loaded* KC-135s on a PSP strip?" they ask incredulously.

"No," the chaplain smiles, *"I'm* not, *you* are. I'm just a Headquarters wienie. I just make policy."

"Then Christ help us."

"Exactly," he nods.

The whole idea, of course, is to teach us to respect the other services' problems. It's amazing how close we twelve guys in the seminar have become. My closest friend here is not Air Force at all; he's a destroyer man and a sports car nut. During World War III, we worked as a joint Operations team—Iceland won, if there can be such a thing as winning that one—and, as in real life during crises, we worked around the clock. Stubble, coffee and cigarettes, maybe an hour's nap on a cot. But there's no way to simulate horror.

Jenny took that week hard because her folks were here, and I hardly saw them. I was too busy deploying a ravaged tactical air force in some final, pointless spasm and was too seedy-looking and punchy to behave civilly. I was like our old football coach.

One more month, I tell her now. Then back to fighters. It's time. Sea duty alternated with shore duty, as the Navy says. But when the orders come, I don't know how to frame my shout; I'm that ambivalent. In truth, I had been warned that I might draw an assignment with a joint staff, but they didn't say that it might happen *immediately*. But what a staff! And what a *location!*

Duffy scans my orders, lifts one red eye at me. "Oh, *yeah.* Oh, *tough duty,* man. Who do you know? Don't tell me you didn't set this up." He breaks my hand, slaps my back. "Fuckin' fly-boys get all the breaks. Well, two months there and you'll be even more worthless. Polynesian Paralysis."

Placing a copy of the orders where Jenny can't miss it, I take my drink out onto the sun deck where a steady, twenty-five-knot wind wets the chairs and railings with salt. Like a pale Japanese kite, Blue Two or somebody watches me with one black eye. I hold up a cracker for him, but he won't take it. I hurl it straight up. The wind takes it, and him, away.

I hear the screen door close, but I keep looking at the waves. Her arms slide around me. "You realize what this means," she says into my ear. "We can't afford it."

Sometimes she could pass for thirty. The wind blows her hair around her face. She lifts one hand to free it, sips her drink without letting her eyes slide off mine. We kiss, the first real kiss in weeks.

"I'll need a whole new wardrobe, Ace—bikinis, muumuus, the works."

"No way. We have to pay shipment on the Porsche. And the *Deutscheshund.*"

"We can afford it."

"How?"

"Give up booze."

"Be practical."

She laughs, squeezes me. The dampness has flattened her hair, rumpled my uniform trousers. She rubs her damp face against my bristle, then remembers the roast. Wildly she spins away. "Sam! Becky!" she calls.

Well, I think. Inside me, lines are shifting into accommodation. My outraged half weakens, succumbs. Everything happens for the best, my haggard mother insists. Hawaii! No sane person refuses a tour in Hawaii. It is a lieutenant's dream realized.

I take the orders with me to the table. Sam says the blessing. We have gotten beyond the "God is Great, God is Good" stage. Jenny has taught him a new one. With it, the words on my orders mingle: "J-3, Staff CINCPAC, Camp Smith, Hawaii. Amen."

In her sleep Jenny murmurs something. Her id is putting her through some semaphore drill. Maybe we've been on the water too long. Sometimes I tease her by asking, "Why?" She laughs and jerks her head away. In the dim glow of the night light, I watch her. She swallows. Where is she?

For that matter, where am I? For all its glamour, I'm not sure about this Hawaiian assignment. Oh, sure, Mac, the colonel and all my seminar mates would jump at it. But I have the feeling that some slick salesman has sold me another Jaguar.

Everything happens for the best. Maybe so. Yesterday we got a Christmas card from Scooter. He's one of the few still in the fighter business. F-100s out of Myrtle Beach. The road not taken, as old Frost wrote.

Scooter had datelined his card Sarasota Springs, Florida. "What does he mean?" Jenny asked. "It's postmarked Myrtle Beach."

"The circus. Winter quarters."

"He's *still* an elephant? Is this Freudian or something?"

"It's something." I shrug.

"Hey, gang, forget it," Scooter had scribbled. "It just ain't the same. These birds are a mess. They fly like they're carrying two elephants. If you look at them wrong, they go J-Cing like broncos all over the sky. To do anything, you need afterburner, and there goes your petrol. Which reminds me, last week we had a—get this—*night, midocean* rendezvous with this gas-passer, and I broke off my dong. *Wild,* man. It was like a boar fight. Not a urologist in sight, and Lages one-plus-thirty away. I never saw a runway look so good. I have, in fact, renounced my citizenship and become a Portugoose. They are still looking for me, I think. Maybe not, the bastards. Well, you get the picture: *bleak,* man, unless you like Turkey and I don't. Turkish whores *need* veils, believe me. I guess you already know about the Korean ones. We were there last Christmas. Couldn't find a tree, must less vines, anywhere. Our divorce rate is higher than SAC's. We're gone all the time. Eight months last year."

SAC? He used that dirty word. I don't let myself think about *that.* There are guys, believe it or not, who like a handful of throttles. More power to them, as the old pun goes.

Sam cries out in his sleep, but it is a joyful cry. Jenny raises her head to listen, sinks back again. She smiles, pats my hand, drifts away in contentment. Her face goes almost slack. But, dimly, I can still make out the smile parentheses. I guess Jenny and Sam are already there with the green-white, spilling combers and the perfect beaches. We'll have to buy snorkel masks. When I think about it, the swaying reefs pull me down to sleep.

CINCPAC is a man as well as a Unified Command. He is a tanned little naval aviator whose serial number is the lowest on active duty. By his own desire rather than that of the President or Secretary of Defense, he happens to be CINCPAC rather than Chief of Naval Operations. Sixty, he has only two more years until mandatory retirement, and he has no intention of spending them in the Pentagon. Hawaii is his chosen home—past, present and future.

The Pacific Command is the largest of the Unified Commands, both in geography and in military resources. It extends from California to the Indian Ocean. Three four-star officers report directly to the admiral who commands the bridge at Camp Smith. Kings and prime ministers seek his favor; ambassadors are careful to keep him informed. This man will be my new boss.

While we drive to California, paying duty visits to our parents in Indiana, who, sadly, keep asking why we can't get stationed at Chanute Field—my father's World War I helmet hangs as a planter on the porch—I think of this admiral. I remember seeing him at Norfolk, splendid in blues, flashing light with his gold forearms as he paced the stage and dragged his microphone cord along. Behind him, as a stage-wide backdrop, was a chart of the Pacific. Without looking at this chart, without releasing us from his hypnotic eye contact, he would stroll over and point to, say, Indonesia and tell us about this man Sukarno. He knows Sukarno well, was in Djakarta only last month.

Although the admiral's eyes are dangerous-looking—I suspect that he has used them to good effect on wavering personalities along the littoral of Asia—he is, I sense, the most stable of men. He does not bluff. He would have locked forearms with Caesar. Caesar knew, as the admiral knows, that presence is everything. A weak man must frequently resort to force; a strong man need never raise his voice. We listened in an absolute hush for each nuance. He is tough, I realized, city-tough. And yet he is a product of Iowa, or somewhere else in the Corn Belt.

"Why the Navy?" he had asked us, shrugging. "I don't know, except that I had already seen the farms. The oceans I'd just heard about."

"Did you notice his eyes?" Duffy had asked me later. "He's been in the Orient too goddamn long."

Quiet as a Pullman (and with approximately the same weight and maneuverability) our station wagon traverses the bleakness that is Oklahoma. Jenny is asleep. The old schnauzer, farther than ever from Germany, helps me watch the road. Occasionally we exchange glances, this old *Frau* and I. She trusts my driving, but today rides shotgun against new smells which raise her muzzle.

"It's mineral," Sam says to Becky and me.

"A hamburger!" Becky decides.

"A *hamburger* isn't mineral, is it, Dad?"

"Some may be."

I see the admiral sitting formally but at ease with the emperor of Japan, beside the young king and queen of Thailand. I hear him fielding the questions at Norfolk.

"Yes, sir?" He points to an Army LC in the rear. The LC accepts the proffered microphone. I *am* deaf. Duffy has to fill me in. "Dumb shit," he adds.

"No," the admiral replies flatly.

The LC blushes, finally realizing the shallowness of his question.

"In Teddy Roosevelt's day maybe," the admiral adds to soften his riposte.

Twenty hands rise. Calmly, he fields them all, never waffling, never arrogant, but always quietly in control. The rebels test him, back away astonished. He is smart. He doesn't stoop to pull rank. Instead, Socratically, he poses a second question. Finally there are no more challengers, and we have sunk within ourselves to consider it all.

He grins, unclips his mike, points to the map. "It's too big, right? Frankly, it's over my head. But, it's not over *our* heads, gentlemen. If I didn't need you, I wouldn't be here. *Would I?*"

Nodding, smiling, tan and fit, his hand held high like some beloved retiring champion's, he had moved up the aisle as easily and confidently as Caesar. Our lanky two-star commandant had had to hurry to keep pace.

The final dance. Everyone digs out his dress uniform. Shoulder-boards, ribboned medals, the tiny chain across the navel. A last look in the mirror. Haircut! In the barbershop, the old black looks up as he snaps his shoe-shine cloth. "Law, Cap'n, you is dressed up like a line-tamuh." Big grin.

16

HAWAII

OUTSIDE, THE PALMS rustle and lean a few degrees in the freshening Trades. Here, the season always seems summer until one learns the subtle distinctions. The admiral's aide-de-camp looks through the port-hole in the door, nods. I walk in and salute, wincing while I still hold that position. Naval officers never salute when uncovered. So the admiral can't return it. But, out of courtesy and compassion, he does anyway. That, I realize later, is one of the ways you can tell who is who. The phonies, insecure, demand rigid protocol. This guy simply smiles and gets down to serious assessment. The admiral, CINCPAC, has served more than forty years. He has seen us come and go, us semipros, us gold leaves who may chuck it at twenty and become brokers of one sort or another.

He laughs, then completes his initial gesture, that of shaking my hand. Crisp in suntans, his shirt-collar tabs flashing linear constellations, he nods toward a chair. At close range, he resembles my old algebra teacher.

Informal in scuffed, brown flying boots, he leans back with his easy smile. Am I still living on the beach? Does my family like Waikiki? How long is the housing list at Hickam? A sympathetic wince.

"Fighter pilot?"

"I used to be, sir."

"Didn't we all? Do you smoke? Sure? And what are you now?" His eyes lose a little of their humor. He looks at his cigarette with distaste, puts it out. Somewhere a naval chronometer rings two bells.

"My orders state that I'm an Operations briefing officer. Whatever that is."

"You are concerned?"

"Yes, sir."

"Why?"

"I've never briefed."

"Statistically, it's less dangerous than flying, Major Copley."

"And, well, I saw you at Norfolk, sir. At Armed Forces Staff College."

He grins. "So?"

"Well, how can I tell *you* anything new about the Pacific?"

"Lots of people do. Every day. Hey, I'll tell you a secret: I am not omniscient." A grin begins in his eyes and spreads. He rises and walks to a large window. "Come here, Major Copley. I'm going to do my impersonation of Lionel Barrymore."

Together, we look down on Pearl Harbor and Hickam Air Force Base. From Aiea Heights one can view almost the entire southern shore of Oahu from Diamond Head to Barber's Point Naval Air Station. It is pretty heady stuff for an old Mobile Controller.

"Busy, huh?" he asks. At Pearl, the largest crane, the one with the tapa print, moves almost imperceptibly along its tracks. In the channel, putting out, is the carrier *Constellation*. At Hickam a flight of F-100s is on the roll.

The admiral nods toward a destroyer in drydock. "New five-inch mount," he says.

"And," he adds, "there are Subic and Sasebo, and all the others. The airfields on Oki and in Japan. Korea. Seventh Fleet. Second Fleet. The two Marine divisions, the two numbered air forces. Lots going on."

"Yes, sir."

"Around the clock. Reports pour in all night, all weekend. The Russians are snooping around Guam."

I nod.

"Do you think I stay up all night reading the traffic?"

"No, sir."

"That's right. But *you* will. You or the other staff duty officers. I'm going to have to depend on you. When I come aboard in the morning, you'll fill me in. That's all. That's reasonable enough, isn't it? When I was your age, I stood watches. Now I'm an old man who needs his sleep."

He pats my shoulder and returns to his desk, leaning against it, folding his arms and watching me. His ankles are crossed, his scuffed flying boots a little arrogant on this, once Nimitz's prestigious bridge. Then, rocking forward and half-circling his desk, tugging up his belt, moving with the balance of a judo instructor, he resumes his original position. He is only, what, five-seven? Apparently, height is important only when playing basketball or watching parades.

"Now, then, don't you think that, out of all those messages and all those phone calls you'll receive, there'll be *something* that I ought to know? That the staff ought to know?"

I have counted seventy-three officers here in the War Room. Everyone is wearing suntans with short-sleeved, open-collared shirts. Only the colors of the webbed belts and shoes—at close range the sizes of the insignia—distinguish one service from another. And the flag rank! There are three four-star officers alone. Stars have, in fact, overflowed the horseshoe table into the first row of theater seats.

There are no women here and few anywhere in the building. Women do not run the Pacific. This headquarters is as inviolate as a warship, as a men's club in London. Even the typists are usually male, yeomen or sergeants, and many, like my Marine Gunny, a decorated veteran of the retreat from Chosen and a former Camp Pendleton DI, cheerfully type with two fingers. Hawaii is good duty.

Sitting at the horseshoe table covered with wardroom-green felt are the three subordinate commanders. Clearly, they do not much like it up here at Camp Smith. They have become acronyms. Sighing, CINC-PACAF slides a silver carafe of coffee to CINCPACFLT. CINCARPAC sits in silence and looks at his nails. They don't seem to know each other well, these four-stars. I suppose that they are firm disciples of service parochialism who will always regard the other branches with amused tolerance. Professional but sympathetic enemies, they probably see each other on New Year's Day in reception lines, at joint conferences here at Camp Smith, or back in Washington, perhaps briefly at the Cannon Club or at some big Honolulu social function.

Having proved that he is not bucking for chairman of the Joint Chiefs, the admiral can work as hard as he likes without incurring the enmity of his military contemporaries (or so I've heard) provided that he doesn't expect the same enthusiasm from them. But, of course, he does, and especially of his four-stars.

"The pay is excellent," he once reportedly said. "Earn it."

Apparently without hobbies himself and married to a lady who must either be equally dedicated or finally reconciled, the admiral has little patience with the "yacht club crowd" or the "polo players." Golf? Well, it is silly, but he gives it an afternoon a week with a civilian buddy. Even then, his mind isn't on it. It bores him. He is almost too easy to reach on the radio attached to his golf cart. The man can't forget Pearl Harbor. When he golfs—it's always Wednesday or Saturday—he simply works later in his quarters.

The Smile. It is notorious. Only strangers are taken in. When it first appears and grows, it is like a spring being compressed, a trap being cocked. A few congressmen, and more than a few correspondents, have seen the trap close. Its mechanism is simple: he listens for contradictions, nodding and smiling, then the smile fades and you are left with the hard eyes. A few senators have curtailed their public itineraries without comment.

It is no wonder, then, that these three old veterans are girding themselves with transparent nonchalance for still another plunge into the breach. "How many planes, how many deep-draft ships, how many battalions do you have here?" the admiral may ask off-handedly, pointing at a map. He knows the answers, of course, and they know he knows the answers. With dignity, CINCPACAF turns to a smart young brigadier in the first row. "How many?" The brigadier provides the answer. CINCPACAF repeats it.

But, thereafter, the admiral puts his questions directly to the brigadier, who glances uncomfortably at his sullen boss before replying.

The Smile. "Five-fifty? Are you sure?"

"Yes, Admiral."

"Thank you, General." The smile becomes genuine. The young brigadier's eyes, released finally, do not again meet his boss's. He is marked, this exceptional officer. I cannot begin to gauge his present worth.

Now, months after that embarrassment, a little shaky, CINCPACAF stirs his coffee and blows cigarette ashes out of his lap as he listens to CINCARPAC. The trim Army general is telling him something. Clearly, from the sudden close attention that the Air Force general pays him, it is an important conversation. Perhaps it is something that I, as the Operations briefing officer, should be aware of. This will be my first briefing, God help me, and, if I can believe the horror stories involving indiscreet or ignorant briefers, perhaps my last. I listen while I stand at the podium and pretend to review my notes.

Suddenly the Army general stands, clasps his hands in front of him, arranges his stance, looks at one of my chart boards, then back at his feet. Gracefully now, he draws back an imaginary driver and swings. Both generals watch the chart.

"Right in the fucking water." The Army general nods, then, belatedly, cringes and looks around to see if any females are present.

Laughing, coughing smoke, and wiping his eyes with the heel of one hand, the Air Force general nods. "Yeah, yeah."

"Gentlemen!" someone calls from the doorway.

Guiltily, smirking like children out of their classroom seats, senior officers collide as they hurry to their places. Slowly CINCPACAF stubs out his cigarette and stands. A hush settles. We can hear people in the corridor.

The admiral's aide and his chief of staff step inside. I half expect them to raise heralds' trumpets. But, quickly, two other men wearing business suits enter uncertainly under the admiral's close escort.

"Good morning, gentlemen," the admiral calls. "At ease."

Today, dark from his customary Sunday afternoon visit to Keehi Lagoon, where he relaxes in his beach chair and drafts messages, the admiral looks even more Oriental. He is wearing his naval aviator's jacket, his way of warning that the air-conditioning thermostat is set too low. J-3, a Marine brigadier, glowers, and a major and a sergeant race to check it.

One of the civilians reminds me of that British character actor who usually plays an ambassador. The admiral introduces him. My God, he *is* an ambassador. I have, in fact, read many of the cables he has sent to State. A career diplomat and not another of Kennedy's political appointees, shaking hands like a cautiously optimistic banker, he sits and looks at the row of clocks along the front of the room. He resets his watch to Hawaiian time, crosses his legs. The other guy must be his pet spook— his CIA adviser or USAID chief. He nods, smiles wanly, and blends back into the scenery.

Now, like some benevolent beacon, the admiral slowly revolves his chair through 360 degrees. His staff smiles tentatively. Generally, they are as motionless as birds when a hawk is present.

"Glad you could make it, Smitty," he calls to a feisty little LC up in the last row, the court jester.

"Some of my guys like to sleep in on Monday mornings," the admiral explains loudly to his guests. "Too much Waikiki over the weekend."

There's the expected howl from the jester. He's a daring little bastard "who may get eaten some day," according to Bob, my immediate boss.

"What?" the admiral cups one hand to his ear.

"Admiral," the jester whines, "I was up half the night working."

"Yeah? Who was she, another schoolteacher from the Mainland?"

There is dutiful laughter and more chatter from the jester, but the moment has passed. Completing his rotation, the admiral sips his coffee, allows his smile to fade, settles himself and lifts his eyes to mine. My vision becomes tunnel vision. We are alone, he and I. It is a little like being near an overwhelmingly powerful radio station: all other signals are drowned out. I expect to see St. Elmo's fire. The very hair on my arms rises. Then he softens his death-ray with a smile of encouragement. He nods. I'm on.

"Good morning, sir," a strange voice quavers. "I am Major Copley"—I should have put that as a question—"the Operations briefing officer. During the past sixteen hours, there has been little activity reported from WESTPAC and, elsewhere, only routine deployments and rotations . . ."

"In other words," the admiral interrupts, "Operations has nothing to report." He shrugs. "Fine. Thank you, Major Copley. Go get some sleep."

I knew it. I told Bob and Colonel Nelton that's what he'd say. The admiral is a sensible man. He has no time for dog-and-pony shows.

Happily, I gather my briefing cards and head for the SDO booth.

"Hold it," the admiral calls. "Did those F-100s ever get to Japan?"

"No, sir. They're at Anderson."

"Anderson? I thought they were at Anderson yesterday." He leans forward in his chair so he can look past the ambassador at CINCPACAF. "Hey, Tommy, what's with your guys? They left Myrtle Beach six months ago."

The commander of Pacific Air Forces winks at me. "Tell him, Major."

"Three days ago, sir."

"Aw, don't give me that. My God, Tommy, I could have steamed a task force around the Horn quicker than these guys can. . . . What are they doing, taxiing?"

I have heard that CINCPACAF has almost reached mandatory retirement age. Even now, I'll bet, they are planning his parade and fly-by down at Hickam. He grins in the general laughter, but then calmly looks at his operational, if not administrative or logistical, boss. "Admiral, the Navy needs more than three days just to get up steam."

"What?" explodes CINCPACFLT, who tries to appear properly outraged. "What was that, General?"

"'S a fact," CINCPACAF nods. "Then they gotta steam around in circles for a while and run all their flags up and down." He drops a straightened paper clip on the green felt and leans back, rocking with satisfaction.

The ambassador smiles his banker's half smile but seems to find this horseplay juvenile. For an instant, his eyes meet mine, and I am not sure what I see there.

"Okay, gentlemen, *okay*," the admiral's voice rises good-humoredly, "let's belay all this Billy Mitchell stuff. The ambassador will doubt that this is a Unified Command. Let's just say that this squadron seems to be stationed at Anderson, and go on."

Rocking forward, CINCPACAF glares over his spectacles at the admiral who, still smiling, nods at me. "Thank you, Major."

Behind the glass of the booth Bob toasts me with his coffee cup, gives me a thumbs-up. His shirt is slack in the waist but tight across his chest where the Master Parachutist's badge rests. He is off jump status now, knocked off that status and therefore out of serious command consideration by a recent heart attack. Bob is the sort who considers a heart attack a temporary setback, to be forgotten as the lapse of an improperly directed mind. Now that he has been tricked once by an undisciplined auricle or ventricle, it won't happen again. The cardiologists at Tripler have suggested that he strengthen his heart by jogging around the base. Without seeming to notice his inverted wedge physique, his doctor had asked if he had been exercising regularly before the cardiac arrest.

"No," Bob had reportedly answered, shaking his eagle's head. "You see, I was with the Hundred and First Airborne, and all we did was shine our jump boots and go down to Little Rock and Ole Miss."

"Umm," the frail doctor had nodded.

As I enter the booth, I see Colonel Nelton leave. From the flush of his face, I gather that he is displeased.

"Way to go, kid," Bob says.

I jerk my head toward Colonel Nelton's office. "He wasn't exactly thrilled."

"Sure he was. You should have seen his face when you said that nothing happened last night."

"Did I miss something in the traffic?"

"Not a thing."

I look at him awhile. "C'mon."

"Where we going?"

"Critique me."

He sets his cup on the desk. "Oh, very well. You want the Leavenworth parade-rest-and-pointer drill or the SAC thirty-five-millimeter-color-slide routine?"

"It's your neck as well as mine."

"Nervous Nellie? He's no threat."

"He writes your effectiveness report."

"Nah. He's supposed to, but he can't write. He's too nervous. Every time he begins to relax, I yell 'LeMay' and around the walls he goes again. He can't write."

"But he can 'X' the wrong boxes."

"Relax. The chief writes my ER, don't you, Chief?"

"Aye, aye, sir," the big CPO at the typewriter says without looking up.

Bob gets this sick look on his face. " 'Aye, aye, sir'? Aw, come on, Chief." He walks over to the chief and shows him his collar insignia. "Look. A big bottlecap, see? We Army o-5s wear big bottlecaps. Say, 'Yes, sir,' or, alternatively, 'Drop dead, sir,' but, please, no more babytalk."

"Drop dead, sir," the chief intones, smiling at his typewriter.

Bob nods with satisfaction. "See, John? It's not true that the Navy is too dumb to learn. They just haven't had the advantages. All they need is a little leadership. Now, what were you saying, Major?"

"Colonel Nelton."

"Right. Well, he's *my* problem. *You* please the Admiral, and . . . it never hurts to be nice to old Tommy if one wears the blue. To tell you the truth, when I was the raw meat they pitched to those old lions out there, I didn't give *any* four-star a lot of lip."

"Except the admiral," the chief says as he types.

"*Me*? When did I sass the admiral?"

"You'd kid him."

"No, sir."

"That time you said it had been a quiet night in the Pacific, and then you had the projectionist flash that picture of the *Arizona* sinking?"

"Yeah," Bob grins and turns his cup. "He enjoyed that." He swings to me. "Okay. Critique. Call him 'Admiral' instead of 'sir.' End of message. New message follows: 'Yankee, go home.' "

* * *

Round Two. This time I have a rostrum full of briefing cards. A lot happened over the weekend.

"Well," Bob shrugs, "that's show biz, kid."

"Except that the admiral has already read most of the weekend traffic. We had a courier run down to Makalapa at twenty-one hundred last evening."

"So? Has the *staff* read the traffic?" He leans against the console. "Let's face it. Officially, you're briefing the admiral. Actually . . ."

Cross as a bear awakened from hibernation, the admiral snaps at everyone, including his motherly three-star chief of staff. His expression reminds me of Edward G. Robinson's when Pat O'Brien would tell him over the bull-horn to come out with his hands up.

"Yeah?" He sails the JCS message down the table to J-6. "So what?" There are no visitors today, so his geniality is absent, too.

Fiercely, he nods to me, and I'm off like that bunny at the greyhound track. When his eyes become incredulous, I gibber even faster. I am going like a tobacco auctioneer, practically dueling the charts with my pointer, jerking around and pushing buttons like Charlie Chaplin at his lathe.

"By zero nine hundred Zulu," I say, "four naval vessels had arrived at the A-4 crash coordinates and—"

"Hold it. Christ, hold it!" the admiral interrupts. "Major, is the building on fire?"

"Not to my knowledge, sir—I mean, Admiral."

He vibrates his head sideways as though to clear it. "Then *slow down*, goddammit."

"Yes, Admiral. By zero nine hundred Zulu, four naval vessels . . ."

"Hold it," he interrupts again. Wearily, he looks around, summoning his patience.

"Major Copley," he says. "Naval ships are *never* called vessels. Never. A chamber pot is a vessel. A ship is a goddamned ship."

His showboating sends a little wave of anger through me. I nod. "By zero nine hundred Zulu four goddamned naval ships . . ."

There is an explosion of laughter. The Marine brigadier who is J-3, my big boss, leans forward and puts his face on his arms. All over the room men are leaning on each other. All this I catch peripherally; my eyes are still locked with the admiral's. For a long second his pupils search mine, then he throws his pencil down and leans back laughing. I am harmless. Socking his forehead with the heel of one hand, he, too, collapses on the table. My eyes shift from him to the SDO booth where Colonel Nelton, beet-red, and Bob stand. Bob is beating the chief on the back.

"Okay," the admiral says when he can be heard again. "I deserved that, Major. Can we compromise and simply call a ship a ship?"

I am calm now. The tension is gone. I have crossed some magic little line. Slowly and with a little authority, I brief him as I might brief some general I was checking out in the F-86. I have studied this traffic, so I really don't need the cards except to remind me of the next subject. I finish and lay my pointer aside.

"Questions, Admiral?"

He considers, then raises his eyes to mine. "No. Thank you. Good briefing."

Colonel Nelton has had Bob nodding and nodding, but the instant I enter the booth, he leaves.

"Sorry," I tell Bob.

"Why, for God's sake? You done great. We can't have these admirals thinking they run this man's Army."

"Colonel Nelton shares your opinion?"

"Well, roughly. But you know Nervous Nellie. Old Dry-Run Nellie, we called him at SAC, LeMay and I."

"Good morning, Colonel Nelton," the chief says.

"Screw you, Chief. Naw, if I ever decide to kill Nellie, I'll just tell him the admiral wants *him* to brief. He's scared green of the Old Man."

"But you aren't?"

"Shit, no. Who, *me*?" Fiercely, he draws himself up. "Me? An old Screaming Eagle from the Hundred and First? Man, we *eat* admirals." Blowing smoke up at the ceiling, he sits on a table and clacks his wobbly Zippo. Alternately glowering and laughing at his self-parody, he leans his hawk face confidentially toward me. The fluorescent light shows his tanned scalp through his crew cut. "And you know why?" he asks, drawing himself up. "Because we are *stupid*, that's why. We've been bounced off too many fuselages and horizontal stabilizers. Right, Cal?"

"Absolutely," Cal answers. A pudgy lieutenant commander wearing golden dolphins, Cal skims the clipboard of yellow Top Secret messages. He is the SDO on watch.

"Now Cal here isn't stupid," Bob continues, "he's legally insane. Which is okay, even desirable, if you're a sub-mariner. Now you may not believe this, but Cal once called a chart a map so they strapped a Momsen lung on him and fired his ass right out a torpedo tube."

On a phone now, Cal holds his middle finger before Bob's eyes.

"Yeah, the Navy is all screwed up about boats," Bob says. "If you can carry it on a ship, it's a boat. Unless it's a U-Boat. Now, Cal here commanded *Unterseeboot* Z-21, but it never left the davits."

Skipping back from Cal's thrown paper cup, Bob pirouettes back to me. "Now, then, what else would you like to do this morning, get some sleep?"

A week later the chief and I have the midwatch together. We relieve Cal and an Air Force master sergeant.

"I hear Bob's not feeling well," Cal says. "Of course, the nut won't quit smoking or drinking."

"Goddamned shame," the chief says. "The pricks keep going."

"Meaning me?" Cal asks, raising one eyebrow.

"If the jock fits, wear it," the chief says, opening a message tube while he runs his tongue around his jaw. "Sir," he adds, grinning at me.

"I'm gonna flog your ass for disrespect, *Seaman*," Cal promises.

"First time tonight," the chief observes.

Fall. Nothing changes much. Flowers bloom year-round; the grass remains lush. In November, rain clouds drift over the mountain rain forests to hide Mount Tantalus and the Pali. On Oahu, the annual rainfall contours during any given year vary from ten inches along the coast to a hundred and eighty inches on Mount Tantalus. I've never seen such a place. On Maui and the Big Island, the mountains become desert above sixty-five hundred feet. Every August, there's a drought, every winter whole villages beyond the Pali wash down toward Kaneohe Bay.

Becky is in kindergarten and is a big deal with her blond hair. Sam too stands out from his dusky classmates in their fifth-grade picture. They love it here, are radiating heat from stored sunlight when we sit down to dinner. Both are already fluent in pidgin. We can't understand them and are concerned. "Speak *English* to us," we tell them. Jenny asks me where we are now on the Hickam housing list.

Our neighborhood is predominantly Japanese. Everything is clean, the people friendly and disciplined. Our houses are of single-wall construction, meaning that just three-quarters of an inch of lumber separates us from outdoors. There are only two such boards and ten feet of perfect lawn between our bedroom and the Yamaguchis'. When someone sneezes, words of consolation are murmured from other houses. Luckily, we don't understand Japanese, or we'd know our neighbors *too* well. As it is, we get along fine. Mitsui and I examine his avocado trees while our children, his dressed in his old GI gear, run through the shrubbery firing and yelling, "Kill the dirty Japs!"

Sam instructs them in the method of ramming home wadding and shot using his toy Civil War rifle and cannon purchased at Gettysburg. Mitsui's boy wears a Confederate hat.

"Hey, man," Calito, a Filipino eight-year-old, says in awe, "Neat-kine canyon!"

Spring simply marks the end of the rainy season and the return of the Trades. There is no unlocking of the earth. Nothing has quit growing. During each season there is just a hint of the real thing—except in summer when, with the *kona* winds, there is a familiar Washington, D.C., August, complete with humidity, sightseeing buses, boats and traffic jams. The United and Pan Am jetliners continue bringing in old folks cautiously dipping into their savings. They are everywhere, thumbing through their coupon books, gawking at the radio station in the banyan tree, clapping for Don Ho, watching some naked savage leap around in a fire dance before he drives away in an old Chevy.

We ess past the Dole factory, past the Matson piers and the Aloha

Tower, toward the new high-rise hotels. Along the Kam Highway there are stalled pineapple trucks looming around us, asphyxiating us. In Waikiki, at traffic lights, Oriental girls with black-black, waist-length hair and slit skirts (or short *muus*) switch past the Porsche's front bumper. One turns her commanding eyes on me.

"Easy, old man," Jenny warns me. Her eyes engage the girl's.

Surfing. The little waves, I mean, Waikiki and Barber's Point—once, at Makaha, when the waves were no more than six feet. Never the big stuff. I can't control the board. Nor can Sam, although he's much better. Makaha scares me. I can't understand those suicidal types who dare the North Shore, especially in October when distant storms reinforce the wave rhythms. Frantic, squatting on their cantilevered boards, they dart in the shadow of the terrible curl, disappearing in its collapse. From the spume a board rises airily against the sky, falls back and, like a horse, comes in alone, to be caught by lunatics paddling out.

On Sunset Beach, below the great dunes, we lie in the sand and watch our schnauzer—liberated from four months in quarantine—chase gulls. By midafternoon the kids' lips are white with exhaustion. We gather up the folding chairs, bury the coals, and go back over the mountains, following Fuchida's low-level route. My God, I think. The whole panorama has opened up before us. Against the horizon I can almost see the dive-bombers rolling over, see the skimming torpedo planes and the black smoke.

Autumn. Monkey pods fall from the big trees along the boulevards of Hickam, are squashed underfoot on the shady sidewalks. There is no foliage change, no morning of sudden briskness. Perhaps the surf is a little higher. Up on Aiea Heights, the white flagship of CINCPAC and Fleet Marine Force, Pacific, steams on in relative motion beneath low cumulus, the garrison flag popping before the porte cochere. Every morning, precisely at 0720, the old black Imperial begins climbing from Admiral's Row in Makalapa up the long red hill covered with fragile pastel houses to Camp Smith. It is a cool, inviting base. Everything is polished. There are neat Marine signs of red and gold. At the gate, a Marine sentry whispers to a new assignee.

"Here he comes." The word is passed.

Silently, the polished Chrysler, driven by a CPO trained in judo, curves through the gate. Four white stars on the fender pennants flutter. In unison, the sentries salute. Smiling, the admiral returns it. This morning he is wearing blues, for some reason. The car glides past the flower beds. There is not an unswept pebble to jar it. It is a legend, this old Imperial. Like the admiral's obsolete prop transport, it is evidence of parsimony, but, like some of the old hotels, it sets the style on Oahu. None of the subordinate commanders dares afford newer forms of transportation. They even hesitate to renovate their headquarters or

have the flashy new communications consoles installed in their command posts. Old Zeus up here would hear about them.

"If I had a jet, I'd be there before I had finished my homework," the
admiral explains. And, of course, if he had a new limousine, visiting
senators might take his budget less seriously.

Simplify, simplify, another tough little guy wrote more than a century
ago. Thoreau hated the military, of course, but he might have come to
admire the admiral. I doubt that the admiral reads Thoreau.

Christmas morning. There is no briefing; the admiral won't be in. I'm
SDO and I'm yawning at the telephonic console. At 0700, the console
buzzes. It is the admiral's hot line.

"Where's my traffic?" he asks.

"I . . . Admiral, it's Christmas morning. I thought I'd let you sleep in."

"You did, huh? Major, I am well aware that it is Christmas, but I was
not aware that the military has been relieved of its responsibilities for the
day. If so, why are *you* on duty? Get it down here."

"Yes, Admiral."

"Say, 'Aye, aye, Admiral,' " my Air Force master sergeant whispers.

We live at Hickam now, back in the Air Force womb. The walls of our
quarters are eight inches thick. U-shaped, the building houses ten
families in relative privacy. "Ten-ements," the occupants call them, but
the rooms look permanent. You couldn't run through *these* walls. And
there are screened lanais along the alley where we can sit with evening
cocktails and listen to the C-124s running up.

Flying. I've almost forgotten about it. It is no longer important. Even
when I'm airborne, I am thinking of things left undone on the hill.
Thank God the Air Force never buys a new trainer. The T-Bird and I
have this understanding: if I fly her around like the old lady that she is,
never trying anything fancy, she won't kill me. I'm making a career of
this old bird. Some other Headquarters wienie and I run down to the
Big Island and back, pausing at Maui for an ADF letdown or scaring
ourselves in the acrobatic—aerobatic, they call it now—area with simple
loops and Immelmanns. In a way, they too are boring—and tiring. We
wear no G-suits to catch our sagging bellies, to keep blood from pooling
in our legs.

It's eerie circling inside the extinct volcanoes. Better yet, sometimes
the whales are running, herds of them between Maui and Molokai. We
buzz them to watch them spank the water and sound. Their grand flukes
seem to wave in slow motion. Down they go, lost in the channels,
discussing us, I suppose, as they flare out near the bottom.

Night. Scary out here beyond gliding distance of those bright orbs of
land. At the rims of their controllers' scopes, Air Guard F-102s leap like
trout for our tinfoil. They are, more often than not, piloted by
Japanese-Americans. Crazy. The intercept completed, they ease along-

side—My God, I *am* Navy—and we consider each other while, below, some fishing boat, simply lit, slides behind.

Viet Nam. Is it one word or two in English? We see the name more often now in the message traffic. Our embassies in Saigon and Bangkok are becoming alarmed. Villages are being overrun, province chiefs kidnapped, schoolteachers murdered. The admiral's face darkens. Is there nothing that we, with our global responsibilities, can do about this? He orders a few plans dusted off. J-5 works late, suggests more simple variations. Suggestions bubble up toward Washington. Kennedy is receptive. He is the Father of the Green Berets, he and Maxwell Taylor, whose book concerning the necessity for a flexible response and whose personal charm appeal to the New Frontier. Kennedy, in an unprecedented move, has even brought Taylor out of retirement to become chairman of the Joint Chiefs. I can't make up my mind about this President. His charisma doesn't seem to compensate for his apparent arrogance. And I never did understand the logic behind his stance on the Cuban Missile thing last fall. Why get so upset over Russian land-based IRBMs and yet ignore their missile submarines? But Kennedy makes sense, I think, in sending advisers to teach the South Vietnamese villagers how to protect themselves. Further, the UN being toothless, *someone* should remind the Pathet Lao and Viet Cong of the Geneva Accords of 1954. Along their infiltration routes, the Seventeenth Parallel has become just another checkpoint.

Testily, the admiral hovers over J-5's messages, his black grease-pencil deleting whole lines, often whole paragraphs, once several pages, and substituting perhaps a single sentence that says it all. Direct, precise language flows out in his firm handwriting. In the margins, or attached, may be other colors of grease-pencil—red signifying the chief of staff, brown Plans and Operations; but the black is always the most eloquent. *Neat-kine* system.

All through the headquarters, the tempo is accelerating. Key staff members often return to their desks after dinner. A few work until midnight. Kennedy himself is coming out. Where are we going to put his rocker?

"The mountain is coming to Mohammed," Bob says with satisfaction. "About time."

"To see the admiral?"

"No, sir. *Me*. He wants the straight word from an Irishman."

"You'll brief Ops then. Thank God."

"You betcha. I'll brief him in the mother tongue, and he will believe everything I say."

"Because? You're Ha-vud?"

"Because I drove the blankin' snakes out of these islands, and he knows it."

It is Wednesday afternoon, and the admiral is winding up his quick nine holes. CINCUSARPAC has him down four strokes. Twice, using his VHF walkie-talkie, the admiral has had me connect him with J-3 in Washington. As SDO, I monitor with one ear, in case the circuit fails, and listen to the chief's sea story with the other ear. The two admirals are tiptoeing around the TS message received at noon from MACV in Saigon.

"Who's on first?" the admiral asks his old friend.

"God knows." J-3 sighs. "They're playing soldier across the river. I suppose they'll fill us in some day." State? No. The White House Situation Room. There have been increasing encroachments. The Kennedys like playing soldier.

"Keep me posted," the admiral concludes.

"Right. Love to my girl."

Saturday afternoon. At the horseshoe table, a brigadier seated on either side of him, sits the admiral. He was up half the night. When the Whiz Kids work on Saturday mornings in the Pentagon, everyone works—regardless of time zone differences.

The admiral lays the yellow message on the green felt and pinches the upper bridge of his nose. He looks his age now.

"And what have you done about this?" he asks J-4 and J-6, his logistician and communicator respectively. "Anything?"

"Admiral," the J-4 brigadier says, "those PRCs were on our shopping list and the Joint Staff has that list. Your chop was on the message."

"Um-m. But you've jogged them a little, surely? Reminded them of their new priority now that the villages are being frequently overrun?"

J-4's lips are compressed. "No, Admiral."

"How about you, General?" Eyes still closed, his fingers on his eyelids, the admiral rotates his chair a few degrees toward J-6, an Air Force nonrated brigadier of proven competence. The formality of the address is not lost on him. "J-6 staffing this as a matter of urgency?"

"I assume so, Admiral."

There are only the three of them in the War Room. Unaccountably, one of the table mikes is hot. I should walk out there and switch it off.

"You *assume* so. I see. In other words, if the VC hit a village tonight and a few score villagers get wiped out, we can tell MACV we *assume* his radios are on the way?"

Silence.

"I, ah, of course, remember our shopping list," the admiral continues. "The date-time group was 03/2102 Zulu, October, wasn't it? And here it is December, and no one has jogged anybody."

Suddenly, like a Claymore mine springing up and exploding, the admiral jumps to his feet and his voice rises in terrible crescendo, becomes almost incandescent.

"Get off your goddamned asses and get on the horn! I want an answer—how

219

many, where and when—before you go home tonight, is that clear? If you need more horsepower, you want ass kicked, just say so. By God, I can kick ass, and if you don't believe me, bend over. Dismissed!"

White-faced, they reel back as though hit by a whole gale.

The chief's eyes roll around. Fondly, he watches the admiral hitch up his trousers. "Best I've heard since I was on a sea-and-anchor detail."

"I'm lucky to be alive," I say.

"The 'goddamned ships' incident?" the chief asks. "Nah. He doesn't eat majors, he eats stars. Maybe as an hors d'oeuvre, even then not Beaufort Scale ten. Maybe eight."

Fifteen minutes later, the admiral lifts his office hot line. My console buzzes.

"Yes, Admiral?" I quaver.

"Get me the NMCC in Washington," he says cheerfully.

A Chagall Christmas card, tasteful and expensive, from the Camstons: They are coming *here,* Betty writes. Eric is being assigned to PACAF. "How is the housing at Hickam?" (For full colonels—Eric wears eagles now—the housing is just a couple of notches below Beverly Hills.) "Do the beach boys serenade you with ukuleles?" (Perhaps in Betty's case they will, or maybe *I* can learn to play the uke.)

Suddenly, Oahu becomes the romantic place suggested by the lovely hula hands. Dog-walking at night, I look at the stars, at the moon clearing the Pali. I hum "Moon River" and "Beyond the Reef." Along with Brubeck and Getz—more serious musicians—Henry Mancini plays a part in our lives.

"What's with you?" Jenny asks. Her eyes drift over my face. "I haven't seen you like this since eighth grade."

"What happened in the eighth grade? Charles Lamb?"

"Shirley McGraw."

I laugh. I haven't heard her name in a quarter-century. Well, it's true. She *was* something in those days, a little early in reaching puberty, full-breasted by the time she was fourteen. The teacher had no attention steps that could distract us boys from those breasts.

"Yeah. But she went to fat, I hear."

Jenny smirks.

"*You're* the doll," I tell her, and I mean it. "You've got it all." I hug her, but she is cautious.

"So why this tap-dancing routine?"

Eric will be Special Projects Officer. I gather that it's a horse-holder/protocol assignment. Set up luaus for fact-finding congressmen, schedule the VIP quarters, involve their wives with our Wives Club sharpies who will take them shopping, take them to the Bishop's Museum, to the *Arizona* memorial, see them off with orchid leis. Eric was born for the job.

*　　*　　*

Jesus, look at all the wheels in the War Room. Another "Palm Tree Conference," as the press dubs these boondoggles. From the SDO booth, we can see Secretary McNamara, the Bundy brothers, Sullivan, General Wheeler, many others. Who's watching the store back in Washington?

There isn't room for the subordinate commanders at the horseshoe table. Even the admiral is down at one end. He seems sullen, distracted by this three-ring circus that has come aboard. Clearly, McNamara is the ringmaster. His suit coat hangs on the back of the admiral's central chair, his long legs are propped up on the sacred green felt. The chief at the typewriter is incensed. "*He's* a genius? Who says so—*him*? Because he can speedread?"

The logisticians have the floor. They buzz for new slides. Colored rows of data glow on the slanting screens above the battery of clocks.

His hair glued back, his spectacles flashing, McNamara keeps interrupting. He leans back in his chair, his fingertips pressed together. "May I have last fiscal year's slides again, please?"

"I'd like to ask him why the doors on my Ford won't close," the chief says.

Finally, the admiral gets to make a point. General Wheeler's hand flies to his chin. He looks at the admiral, is obviously interested. Secretary McNamara didn't hear it; he is lost in his figures. There is no sign of Kennedy. He is, I hear, a guest at the admiral's quarters at Makalapa. I suspect that the admiral had to move out.

The press will decide that momentous decisions are being made. Every bar in Waikiki is probably full of reporters. Outside the gate there are a few photographers. Typical.

Two evenings a week I attend classes down at the university. My Shakespeare prof is Chinese-American, born here and educated at Berkeley and Yale. He is excellent, I think. After a while, you don't smile at the incongruity of an Oriental Prospero. The old magician has just freed Ariel: "Now my charms are all o'erthrown. . . ."

Here, he pauses and raises his gentle eyes to survey the class. There are tears welling in them. He is overcome with emotion. Suddenly, it hits me who is really speaking and what Ariel represents. The prof removes his glasses, inhales to regain control, replaces them. When he finishes, he tries to smile, to add something, but cannot. He just stands there with those tears streaming down his face. All the girls finally start crying, too. It is the end of the course. Nodding in farewell, such a gentleman, he leaves the room. Shakespeare lives.

Betty! I see her coming down the gangway, and the music begins. I can't hide my joy. We fly to each other, rock back and forth. Her eyes glisten. I arrange the lei around her, kiss her on the mouth.

"What *about* these two?" Eric asks Jenny. He laughs uneasily.

"What, indeed?"

That evening, in our quarters, Eric notices the old schnauzer. He has little choice. Grinning and panting, she leans against his shins, sits to offer a paw.

"Aw-w, look at her," Betty croons. "Eric, she's trying to shake hands."

Distastefully, he stoops to shake, backs away quickly. "Same old dog? Amazing." He has no use for animals. "So, how have you been?"

While Jenny puts the kids through their paces, Bob and his wife arrive. She has bought him a new Spitfire out of her earnings. They drove over from Fort Shafter in it, top down, radio playing.

"Spitfire? That's the little Triumph roadster, isn't it?" Betty asks Bob. She is wearing a brand-new, low-cut muumuu. Entering our doorway, she had turned to show it off. "Five hours on the island, and I have already gone native."

Bob leans against her. "No, ma'am. That's a propeller-driven RAF fighter, by God."

"Hey," Betty says, hugging him and looking over her shoulder at me. "Where'd you get this guy, John?"

"I go with his job," Bob explains.

She puts her hand over her mouth. "You're his boss? You're a big deal?"

"Absolutely." He strikes a stern Tecumseh pose.

"Oh," Betty laughs. "I *love* this guy."

"*All* guys," Jenny says. She accepts one of Eric's cigarettes.

Betty looks at her, amused. "Almost," she nods.

"Martinis?" I ask quickly.

"Not for me." Eric holds up both hands. "Scotch? Scotch and water."

"Martinis," the rest agree. "Down in flames."

"Supervise, Robert," Bob's wife warns. "I remember last time, or rather, I *don't* remember last time."

I swirl vermouth in a glass, pitch it into the sink, add ice and ninety-four-proof gin. Bob tastes it, makes a face. "That's hers. Okay, hold the vermouth on mine."

We are reeling around in the kids' bedroom. I don't know how we got up here. The music rises to us. Jesus, I'm feeling no pain, but I'm feeling nearly everything else. As I suspected, she is wearing no brassiere. Except for Jenny's, these are the first pair of breasts I have ever felt. Since infancy, at least. Her nipples have peaked. She hangs onto me.

"Are you sure they're asleep?" She nods at the kids.

"Look at them."

I kiss her lips, her shoulder, the nape of her neck where the short hair curls. She has become limp. She moans. I have doubts about my degree of control.

"What are you *doing*?" she asks. "There's no room in here. They'll wake up."

"No," I say, and slide one hand forward past her hip.

A hand touches mine. Hers, I realize, are around my neck. I freeze.

"Dad!" Sam's face is upturned, his mouth contorted, his eyes brimming with tears.

Betty shrieks and flees.

Melting, almost falling in my shame, I stand there and try to collect myself.

"*Da-ad!* I thought it was supposed to be you and Mom."

I stoop and pick him up. He is almost too heavy to hold now so, lowering him again, I squat and hug him.

"It is, Sam. I goofed." Finally, I force myself to meet his eyes. "I'm sorry."

"You like *her?*"

I nod. "I must."

"She isn't as pretty as Mom." He is definite about this. I use my handkerchief to wipe his eyes. "Blow."

"She is funny?"

"That's it."

Kennedy has been *shot.* I can't believe it. Some kook in Dallas. A planeload of Washington wheels is en route to Japan; the admiral raises them via Navy Single-Sideband. They are returning to refuel before heading straight home.

This is big, very big. We are not sure what comes next. I find myself reviewing Emergency Procedures. Only the President, in time of peace, can authorize the expenditure of nuclear weapons. In penance for the episode with Betty, I haven't had a drink for two months, so I'm as cool as a snake. Everyone else seems nervous. Discontinuity is what spooks soldiers. Oswald kills a cop in a theater. He is arrested. Johnson has been sworn in? No, not yet, but Kennedy's party has retreated to Air Force One.

"Okay," NMCC tells us. "It's done. Business as usual." The duty officer authenticates with code. We know his voice, of course; still, we would insist on this formality, this reassuring ritual.

April. The rains have ended. I am wearing blues for the first time in eighteen months; Jenny is formal with a hat and white gloves. The entire staff is assembled here on the hangar deck of *Ranger,* wisely when one recalls how many such ceremonies have been routed by spring showers. Too bad, though, that it couldn't be topside where he can survey it all for the last time while it is still his. We officers are in ranks along one bulkhead, our wives more or less in formation fifty yards away. There is the standard deafening band. The governor is here. Overhead are flags and bunting. It is supposed to be a joyful occasion.

When the admiral and his wife appear, we cheer, then hit attention.

From him, a little wave of appreciation. Calmly, he reads his own orders. It's just as well. No one else here could have gotten through them without becoming, at the least, husky-voiced.

"By direction of the President," he begins, holding the orders steadily, in the prescribed scroll fashion, his voice as deep and controlled as ever. Forty-something years in the Navy, and not a hint of emotion. She is less calm, but an old pro, too. This is the way it's done, their manner instructs us. The huge open elevator ascends to become part of the flight deck. "Anchors Away" reverberates around Pearl Harbor. A last glimpse of him saluting, still grinning and waving. She blows kisses before retreating behind her handkerchief. Zeus and Minerva are gone.

Two weeks later, in a simple ceremony at Fort Shafter, Bob and his wife also retire. CINCUSARPAC hangs a Joint Service Commendation Medal on Bob, shakes his hand, hugs her, presents them with leather-bound certificates of appreciation from Chief of Staff, Army. A last, solemn exchange of salutes, flashbulbs, punch and cake. All their friends crowd around. Standard. A little glimpse of the future, God willing.

Jenny and Bob jump into the Porsche, Bob's wife and I into the Spitfire. Out the gate we roar, the women driving and racing each other, Bob and I, white-faced, hanging onto the grab-handles. Somehow, we make it down to the Surfrider without being stopped. In the Harp Bar, the harpist is playing "Moon River." He's in love with Jenny, knows all her favorites. She watches his hands move over the strings and sighs as though he is stroking her. He laughs. Old pro.

But the music, most of Mancini's music, reminds me of Betty. It may not be serious, but it is fun, evocative.

Life comes in bursts of a kind, of joy or sorrow, so beware when perfect days come in an endless string. My sister writes that it might not be a bad idea to inquire about emergency leaves—you know, in general. When I phone her, I learn what I'm not supposed to know: Dad has cancer. Metastasis is part of his history. He had tried to keep it a secret from us all. Guts ball. He sees the specialist again Monday. Will money become a problem? A foolish question.

While I am trying to digest this, Jenny says that our old schnauzer can't get to her feet, that she won't eat. I whistle and call her. She pulls herself toward me but gives up. Jenny begins crying. I lift our old friend into the Porsche, drive toward Honolulu. She pants and grins, tries to stand and peer through the windshield as she did before we left Bitburg.

A friend by now, the Japanese veterinarian comes out to the car to examine her. He was educated at Cornell and is excellent enough to publish in the veterinary journals. Well, she is dying, he says matter-of-factly.

"She is in pain?"

He is already preparing the hypodermic. He knows me. "Yes," he finally answers. I hug her and try to keep my mind blank. Then I wrap her in her blanket. Otherwise, she will be too limp to manage. Her head lolls into view. Ah, God, her eyes are open.

Up into the rain forest beyond Camp Smith we go. Her blue coffin is stenciled with Air Force parts numbers—the finest crate in Hangar One's tool crib. Luckily, the old, drunken sergeant who works there remembered me from Hamilton. I pant as I dig. No sleep last night, and I go on duty again at midnight. Before I nail down the lid, I feel her again. It's crazy, I know. I arrange her blanket, nail, then shovel in the dirt. Below, Camp Smith, Pearl, the whole panorama. She lies half a world away from home, but it's a better lot than any in the Punchbowl. Up here, there is, at least, a Germanic mist half the time.

It is 2 August 1964, and one of our destroyers, USS *Maddox*, is steaming northward in the Gulf of Tonkin approximately twenty-eight nautical miles offshore. North Vietnam claims that their territorial waters extend twelve miles out, so the skipper of *Maddox* is careful to observe this limit. It is a routine reconnaissance patrol in international waters, one of a series conducted over the years. I am on duty in the Command Center. The console buzzes. It is Washington.

"Secretary McNamara is calling CINCPAC," the NMCC duty officer says.

It is 0400 Hawaiian time. The new admiral awakens instantly. I connect them. Washington has received a FLASH message from the *Maddox*. She has three radar contacts closing at high speed; they are believed to be PT boats. She has opened fire with warning rounds and, unless directed otherwise, will fire for effect.

Now our copy of the message arrives, followed within a minute by another. The *Maddox* has engaged the contacts with her batteries, and one contact has disappeared. Sonar has picked up torpedo signatures. One PT boat has been visually sighted astern of *Maddox* firing a machine gun. At first light an air patrol sights two damaged PT boats limping toward estuaries, a third dead in the water.

Well, that's it, I think. Here we go again.

17

THAILAND

FORT APACHE, I called it—silently at first, then openly—and the name stuck. Thai carpenters had looked at sketches drawn in the dirt with sticks, gone into a huddle, and come out nodding and bowing. Working with their strange Oriental tools—their handsaws cut on the pulling stroke and have a machete handle—they had quickly thrown it together using clear, virgin teak, a building at a time. Lord knows they had never seen a cavalry post, but that's the way it came out—an elegant cavalry post.

Wing Operations dominates the quadrangle, and the squadron buildings square the perimeter. There is, then, a sort of gravel parade ground edged by tropical plants. Banana trees. Flower beds tended by a dedicated young Thai named Tsutin. In other words, it is a blend of John Wayne Traditional and one of Somerset Maugham's rubber plantations.

Each of the squadron Ops buildings has a token plot of grass and a tiny flower bed with the squadron's numerals inlaid with painted rocks. Parked around the perimeter are leased Datsun pickup trucks, chosen to match the squadron colors. If this were a Hollywood set, they'd have to become horses with U.S. saddle blankets. And we'd have to have a bugler. Old Scooter.

Despite my age and lack of proficiency as a pilot, despite my son's grave eyes, despite Jenny's tears, I have come here as Agamemnon (or maybe Charlie Chaplin) to lead a squadron. Through the checkout period in the F-105 at Nellis ("Colonel"—yes, I am a lieutenant colonel now, proof of the existence of our railroad-seniority promotion system —"you really oughta try to build up your proficiency before you go over there"); through Jungle Survival School at Clark, where our young noncom instructor had his reluctant Negrito assistant slit a pet monkey's throat, then cook him; through my periods of drunken introspection, I had seen myself leading the guys up North and doing whatever has to be done.

Now I stand in Colonel Hopwell's air-conditioned office and see them striding across the gravel quadrangle and through the gateway in our security fence. Jaunty in their olive coveralls and Aussie bush hats, they could be their great-grandfathers, some of them, especially those wearing yellow scarves and big mustaches. One pauses to talk with a slim man sitting in a blue jeep. They laugh, and the jeep swings into a parking place. Below the windshield, painted on a white board, is the title: DIRECTOR OF OPERATIONS. Colonel Hopwell, then. My new boss.

He enters, shakes hands without meeting my eyes, scans my name tag and untarnished insignia, cocks his head. Like a drunk, he seems to have to plan his movements and execute them with elaborate casualness.

"You come in on the courier?"

"Yes, sir."

He sighs. "Okay, let's go. Get your bag."

In silence we drive to the BOQ. The road is paved. On either side, freshly seeded grass struggles against erosion to become turf. The airmen's barracks, the chapel and Wing Headquarters are also new.

"Give him a room," he tells the BOQ sergeant, then searches the ceiling as though he's trying to recall some line of poetry. I complete the billeting card. "That was Major Norton's bed," the sergeant tells me without further explanation.

"Let's go, let's go," Colonel Hopwell says. "Throw your bag in your room." I comply.

"Okay, let's go."

We drive to the club, a rough packing-crate building reminiscent of Korea. Dark stain covers most of the stenciling. Unpopulated, it must be as dark as a tent but now, at 1700, the building is almost full. I don't recognize anyone. Over the bar hangs a bell and a warning about entering while covered.

Colonel Hopwell eases onto a bar stool, looks at himself in the wavy mirror, and with the immense dignity of a patriarchal baboon, arranges the three remaining strands of his hair across his head. He is gaunt, his eyes feverish.

"Whatya drinking, Comptron?"

"Copley, sir. Beer, thank you."

"Copley?"

"Yes, sir."

Suspiciously he examines my name tag. "I've never known a Copley. That's a funny name. Well, whatya been doing for a living, Copley?"

"CINCPAC Staff, sir."

"CINCPAC?"

"Yes, sir."

"Where's that?"

"Hawaii."

He smiles and rubs his nose. "No kiddin'? Navy, huh? You were on exchange duty?"

"No, sir. It was a joint assignment."

"Yeah?" He laughs. "I'll bet. Okay, what before that?"

"The Pentagon."

His eyes close, his head flops back. He shakes with silent laughter and slowly rotates his bar stool through a complete revolution. "Yeah, I *knew* it. You're a type, you know it? The whole world is made of paper, right? The Chinks are correct: our military *is* a paper tiger. Well, okay. How long since you been in a cockpit?"

"Two months, sir. At Nellis I got about fifty hours in the '105 and—"

"Aw, c'mon. I mean how long since you been *assigned* to an operational fighter squadron?"

"Eight years."

"Eight? *Eight?* Jesus Christ, man, what are you doing *here?*"

"I volunteered."

"Aw-w, ain't that sweet? What'd you fly in Korea?"

"'Eighty-sixes."

Howling, he rears back and beats the bar. One of the Thai girls tending bar comes running.

227

Annoyed by her misunderstanding, he says, "Naw, naw, *Jo-san* . . . oh, yeah—hey, bring this *F-86* pilot another beer." Sighing, he looks at his watch as though he expects the building to explode at a certain time. "Well, well, so you flew the Saberjets? That's just great. A fucking MIG-killer. Just what we need. Ah, Christ. Well, I don't know what to say. I just don't know what to say. We don't have many MIGs here. If you think Korea was the wrong war, wait'll you see *this* mess. Kennedy and Johnson, the fucking liberals, the do-gooders. They make good speeches. The MIGs get airborne when they're in the mood—but, mostly, it's bridges and roads and flak. People. In other words, fighter-bombers. Not much sport for a guy like you."

I don't say a word. He waits, but I outwait him.

"Yeah," he continues, "we'd see you heroes up there while we were down there doing the dirty work. Remember those bridges at Sinanju?"

"Yes, sir."

"Me. *I* led those strikes. And do you remember the power plant up at Mizu?"

I look at him in disbelief.

"*Me.* Old Watashi. Yessir. I led that one, too."

Naw, he didn't, I decide.

"When I got back to the ZI, my son asked me how many MIGs I got." He watches for some reaction while he crumples his beer can. I wonder if he crumples beer bottles, too. He rubs his hands up and down his thighs, then, unaccountably, yawns. He looks at me in the mirror. In it, we appear to be misshapen, not quite human. In it, I see him duck his head then swing his stool toward me. "I suppose you expect me to give you a squadron."

Not now. "No, sir."

"Good thing."

He laughs, straightens to rub his neck. "Let's face it, Compton, you aren't in demand, you know? There aren't many plums, and what few there are, I save for guys I trust, guys who came up the hard way—in the cockpit. Now, if you'd come in last month, I might have had to consider you. Did you know Don Emmons? Naw, you wouldn't. He was a real jock. You? You're classic—the Headquarters wienie who suddenly gets sucked into the pipeline. Anyone who avoids the cockpit for eight years . . ."

"I volunteered, sir."

He smirks. "You did, huh? When? After you were at Jungle Survival? Let's face it, Compton, you *love* headquarters. Nobody draws two in a row." He pivots on his stool so that his back is to me. A couple of jocks wave to him. He yells something at them, laughs. Slowly, he completes a circle.

"Well," he says, "I just don't know what to say. What'd you fly during the war?"

"Fifty-ones."

"Fifty-ones? Spamcans? Christ Almighty, I *knew* it. And you've come over here to dive-bomb?" Again, he looks at my name tag. "Aw, shit, Copley. Really? After being a big deal in the Pentagon, and CINCPAC? What'd you do, run around in a sailor suit?" He is right up in my face now, his crazy, blue eyes searching mine. "Hey, let me give it to you straight. I love them, see? Love them like sons. And I'm not going to have any Headquarters wienie getting them killed." He holds up two fingers for more beers. "Okay. All right. I've got a job for you. In a month, my TOC guy goes home, and it's a big job, see? Jesus, it's *big*. Frankly, I doubt that you in your little sailor suit can handle it. You'll be Chief of Tactical Operations. Yeah, don't gimme that look or I'll ship your ass to Saigon or somewhere. I know you want a squadron. . . . Look, I am not going to bump some guy who's been flying this bird for years—*years*, man; old Klondike there has fifteen hundred hours in the '105—just to put some new LC who's never dropped a real bomb in his life over them. Does that make sense?"

The dream fades. Secretly, I'm relieved—and ashamed.

"So you're TOC. Okay? You run it like Henry does, and we'll get along fine."

For a month I understudy Henry and, when he leaves, I run the shop exactly as he did—rather, I let it run itself and just pitch in as another Indian. Predictably, Colonel Hopwell and I get along fine. After another week or so, I ask if I can start flying missions.

"Sure. I thought you'd never ask. But no big stuff, see? Just trundle over to Package One or Two, and back. You're not going way up North. The Old Man doesn't, I don't, and you don't. Why? Simple. If any one of us goes in, everything stops until somebody trains our replacements. You've been here a month, and you're still learning. We provide the continuity. We're not like the jocks. In five or six months they finish their tours and go home. We're here for a year. No glory this time, Copley. No medals. We just pace ourselves. A couple of missions a week add up to a hundred in twelve months. The jocks never stay more than seven. It's fair. Think about it."

But *we* finally go home, I realize, and some of them don't.

I return to my room and lie on my bunk. Twelve months instead of seven. I write Jenny that she can forget about my being home for Christmas . . . unless, miraculously, the war ends.

I attach myself to one of the squadrons, and the squadron commander thinks he's had it. "No," I tell him, "relax; I'm just another attached wienie."

Twice a week, when TOC has squared away the next day's missions and assigned them by squadron, when everything seems under control, I pick up the phone and ask the squadron Ops officer if he has a slot. He always does. He makes room for me on the schedule.

My third mission has them all whispering and looking at me. God knows I'm scared, unsure of this big, complex machine and unsure of myself. I haven't seen flak in fourteen years, not since Sinanju when we had spiraled down after that MIG which was trying to get an F-84.

Gear up, and the distracting, beeping horn blows until the wheel-well doors close. Flaps up. The big fighter settles back in afterburner, mushing along with its ordnance. I'm carrying the weight of a P-51 under my short, swept wings. Just ahead, my leader disappears into scud. My instrument panel glows brightly against the gray clouds and drizzle.

A vibration. *My God.* It's increasing with airspeed. A loose access panel? No, now the whole plane is shaking. It's the engine! The bearings are seizing. Get out! No, a cool part of my mind says, make sure. Quickly, I scan the engine instruments: they're in the green. Does this rule out bearing failure? No, I don't think so. Foreign object damage? My problem—my diagnostic problem—is that I don't really know this complex machine. Others do.

"Two has a vibration," I call. The scud is beginning to smoke past; I trim nose-down.

"Two who?"

"*Redwood* Two," I say quickly. A lieutenant's bungle.

"Does it vary with rpm?"

"Stand by." I have five hundred feet now, enough altitude to experiment with power settings. Ahead lies a field of rice. I don't see any workers. I search for the jettison button, but I can't make myself push it. It would be like dropping a Cadillac, and I'm a taxpayer. And, Jesus, if they explode on impact, they dig craters four lanes wide and rain steel for a mile. I ease back on the throttle, but remain in afterburner. The shaking continues.

"Negative," I call, and sit here like some test dummy in a lab crash vehicle.

"Didya rock the bombs on their shackles?"

"Affirmative."

"If you can, come outa 'burner."

I snap the throttle grip inboard, she sags and—hey!—smooths right out. "That was it. She's like glass now."

"Good," my leader says dryly. "Meet you on top."

Like divers we ascend, each alone, toward light. He's probably laughing. "First time you ever had a rough 'burner?" he'll ask when we land. "Well, it won't be the last." Five years in the bird, fifteen hundred hours. Everyone will snicker. There is no way I could have led a squadron.

By combat standards, we live like nobility. The base is plush. Here, lieutenants live better than our colonels did in Korea. I doubt that anyone here knows how to light a Coleman lantern. There are no Lister bags. Two officers to a room, four rooms and a center latrine to a hooch. Air conditioning, privately owned stereo recorders and speakers. Cat

Man would roll his eyes. The Marine jocks fly their A-4s over from Danang on booze runs. Each returns with two baggage pods full. They come here on R&R and, as always, I can't resist their tough humor.

"You get overseas credit for *this*? A seventy-foot-long bar, for Christ's sake? Thai waitresses to rub your poor backs? What's that they're digging? A swimming pool? Where are we—Beverly Hills? Who's your tennis pro?" (They refer to our new club, still under construction.)

Yeah, certainly, they knew Mike. They know Spence. "Oh, he's big now, *big*."

"Fat?" I can't believe it.

"Naw. Here!" They point to their rank. "He's got a *star*, man. He's got a brigade."

"Spence? I don't believe it."

"So fuck you, Jack."

"John," I correct them.

"John." They shrug. I love them.

But it wasn't always this plush. Once when that first heroic squadron came down with Robbie from Okinawa, it was like Jamestown. Really. The bugs almost won. Bugs and rain and mud. Tents at first, of course. Then primitive screened hooches with corrugated metal roofs. No air half the time, much less air-conditioning. Mosquito bars and snakes. *Cobras.*

So new hooches were built, farther away from the noise of the flight line, and these were expensively air-conditioned. Theoretically, we are a day outfit, but we are up half the night. Often the first briefing is at 0215, with first takeoff at 0445. Then no one can sleep. For five minutes everything trembles and bangs and blats. This bird has what they call a "hard" light. What they mean is an explosion. So every fifteen seconds there's another explosion, sustained and additive, until there are eight moving sources, all blatting past the hooch area like some rolling cannonade. Later, when the guys return, they fall into their sacks and curse the noise of the afternoon takeoffs. If I have briefed the early missions, or flown them, I, too, crawl out of the pickup and lie down in my dark cave of a room. Sometimes I can squeeze in a quick nap before tomorrow's frag orders come in. The housegirl may enter and put my laundry away, but I won't hear her.

Each morning these girls rush through their chores and then, at about noon, sit on our screen porch and eat rice, fish and something that may be eels. Good, they smile. For some reason, perhaps because their *mama-san* rarely approaches our hooch, they congregate out there beneath the *Playboy* centerfolds, and giggle. Most seem to be in their late teens. From her centrally located hooch, *Mama-san* is watching to insure respectability. One word from her to the Civilian Personnel Office, and a girl will lose her pass and therefore her job. So I doubt that there's much shacking up. For one thing, Buddhists seem fairly puritanical; for another, some of us have daughters, so we regard these girls with fatherly affection. No, agreed, not the lieutenants; very little is sacred to a lieutenant. Six weeks between R&Rs in Bangkok or Hong Kong is a long time when you're twenty-four and full of sap.

Some of these girls are pretty, a few beautiful. Light skins and dark eyes set in Western sockets. There's just a trace of almond. They flip through our magazines, erotic and otherwise, apparently more interested in how our starlets wear their hair than how they wear their bikinis. Most of them whisper, "Ah," and tap the page. Then one will pull her hair up that way, pose, giggle, and let it fall again.

"What you call this?" Tanya asks me, holding the magazine toward me.

"Beehive," I say, and continue shaving.

"Um-m. Nice. Bee-hife," she explains to the others.

"What is this?" she asks, touching her own hair and turning.

"Ponytail. With bangs."

"Is good?" she asks me with no trace of coquettishness.

"For you, it's perfect."

"Perfect? Is 'perfect' good?"

"Yes. The best. Number one."

"Ah!" she smiles. "Number one," she tells them smugly.

I can see that I'm becoming the Bert Parks of Southeast Asia, that other girls are working up their nerve, so I gather my shaving kit and hurry back to my room. The guys at Clark wouldn't believe these girls. We leave large sums of money around. They dust around it, perhaps stack it neatly, but never steal it. No one even bothers to count it now. We trust them, and they us. If you give one of them a dollar, she tucks her hands prayerfully beneath her chin before taking it. Within a day or two, you find a bowl of fresh fruit in the refrigerator, or a bunch of bananas on your dresser.

"No, no, Tanya," I protest, and pull another dollar out of my drawer. "For you. *You.*"

Transistor radios are always their first purchases. Listening to what I had first assumed was a blend of several stations, all broadcasting different music, the girls sit on the back stoop of our latrine washing and ironing our clothes. Occasionally, one will gracefully imitate a temple dancer for a few steps, then hide her face.

If you gave small children wooden blocks, cymbals and vibes and told them to play circus music and simultaneously signaled some muezzin to chant the hours of prayers, you'd approximate Thai music. But Western culture, I note, is making inroads. Between songs, there is the noise of a trash truck dumping tin cans, superimposed over the frantic runs of some tone-deaf lunatic playing the xylophone. Then an unctuous voice, apparently giddy with delight, tells of some indispensable product. I know it's a commercial because the same word is repeated about fifty times. Then bedlam with the dumpster again. We stand there, weaving from lack of sleep, pissing into the urinals, while all this is going on just outside the screen door. Sometimes, without warning, the girls walk right in on us as children would, and we zip right up through foreskin.

"Tanya," I tell her one day, "your radio is broken."

"Broken, sahr?" Tanya is one of the beauties.

"*Kaput. Fini.*"

"Oh, *fini?* No sahr, not *fini.* Listen." She sways.

"Number-ten music, Tanya."

She gets it now. They like humor. "No. No, sahr, number *one!*" With a big grin, her chin up, she shakes back her glistening hair. She has the whitest teeth.

Once, a few days later, while I lie on my bunk and listen to a tape of Sarah Vaughan, Tanya silently enters, puts away my socks, and stands there listening. I indicate a chair, but she shakes her head and pads to the door. In the doorway, she turns, an imp in her eyes. She swallows, working up her nerve.

"Sahr?"

I look at her, beginning to smile myself. I know what's coming.

Big grin. She claps her slim hand over her mouth.

"What, Tanya?"

"Number ten!" she says and quickly closes the door.

Three months have passed, and I've logged only seventeen missions, all except one over in the moonscape panhandle of North Vietnam ("Vit-*naam*," President Johnson says; no wonder the North Vietnamese hate him). Calmly we fly over there and try to crater a road or fluff up that abstraction called the Ban Katoi Ford. The only rail line is already a string of metallic Morse dots and dashes, and most of the bridges are down, too, or seem to be. Intelligence tells us to look for bridges just beneath the surface of the rivers and camouflaged, swinging bridges which, during the day, lie neatly in slots along the riverbanks. At night old Route One down there must look like Sepulveda Boulevard, with endless convoys of slitted headlights making sine waves along the crater rims. When the bridges get to sagging with bumper-to-bumper traffic, Intelligence says, they transship the supplies from trucks to boats to trucks. How the liberals at Berkeley can maintain that Main Force units aren't invading South Vietnam beats the hell out of me.

By daylight, however, the land seems deserted. Nothing, absolutely nothing, moves down there. There are just a few farm villages, deserted apparently, but if you look closely you can see tire tracks leading to the walls of the farmhouses. In one remarkable night, low-level photo, you see, by flarelight, a truck entering a fake house while broom-wielders erase its tracks. Nevertheless, they aren't targeted, these garages. What am I suggesting? I don't know, except that we aren't permitted to expend ordnance wherever we please. Oh, I'm sure that some guys do and say that it was a rack malfunction, or simply lie about it. No one can disprove it. In any case, these North Vietnamese are like ants. I'm beginning to wonder if we can stop them. While we sleep, the stuff keeps flowing south. Now, if this were summer in the Land of the Midnight Sun . . .

So, without conviction until we see a few secondary explosions, we bomb patches of woods along the supply routes. Agreed, these are the logical places for truck parks—when daylight comes, they have to hide somewhere—but it's not very satisfying to bomb so blindly. Sometimes we must be simply converting trees into toothpicks.

"Oh, no," our bespectacled Intelligence lieutenants say. "You are doing a lot of damage. Look through this stereoptican lens. See those tire marks?"

Anyhow, we bomb them day after day, rarely seeing flak and then usually only thirty-seven-millimeter stuff—harmless-looking gray or white dandelion puffs. I'm always surprised when someone picks up battle damage, and I was stunned one sunny August morning when my leader torched and went straight in. An old head, too, who had been way up North several times.

The other day I saw a map in Intelligence that shows a dot wherever a friendly aircraft has crashed. Most of the dots are down in the panhandle, but that's where the preponderance of sorties are flown. Statistically, the armed reconnaissance "packages" farther north are much more dangerous, especially what are termed Packages IV and VI (inevitably "Six-Pack"). Pack V, too, along the Red River. The northwestern rail line leading into Hanoi from Communist China lies in the valley of the Red. Like the northeastern rail line, it is really bad news. Eighty-five-millimeter emplacements all the way down to where the lines "Y" in the Delta. Near the big marshaling yards on the outskirts of Hanoi, there are even one-hundred-millimeter guns. Just looking at their order of battle gives everyone a chill. Sometimes I try to recall how many big guns there were in Hamburg and Berlin, but I can't remember. It was too long ago. All I remember is that they could put up a black, metallic overcast within a few minutes. But so can these guys, according to the kids that have been up to VI. And the Germans didn't have SAMs.

"World War Two was *nothing*," a lieutenant almost spat at me. He must have been a baby at that time. I can't say yet. Obviously, however, you can't go by the panhandle.

Typically, I have my briefing slides ready when, at about 0200, I hear the first boots on the porch outside Intelligence. Sullenly, they enter. They may nod their tired faces at me; they may not. Their bush hats are now part of the uniform, and they probably sleep in them. For a while, there's not much banter. From labeled pigeonholes along the wall, they extract maps and begin ripping off unneeded sections to reduce them to strip maps. The floor becomes littered with pastel colors. Then, squinting, they copy data from the back-lighted Plexiglas scheduling boards. By fives, the men group. The fifth guy is the spare. God willing, he won't have to take off. On the other hand, he may miss an easy counter. There are a lot of diversions to Pack I.

"*Nineteen* thousand?" One of them turns to me. "Jesus, Colonel, we can't refuel at nineteen with this load."

"I know it, Andy," I tell him. "Seventh Air Force is working on it. They've got an extra problem with the '104s."

"Aw, shit. Leave those worthless little toys at home." He scowls and bends over his card again, copying the information. "Goddamned grunts down at Seventh ought to have their fuckin' heads examined." His felt-tipped pen goes dry and, muttering, he throws it into a wastebasket.

"Whatsa matter, Andy?" a captain asks without pausing in his copying. "You don't like grunts? Hell, man, I *like* 'em. And I *like* refueling while I'm standing on my tail, like a fucking cobra."

"Screw you, lifer."

"Yeah, Andy," another drawls while writing. "A grunt is man's best friend." He straightens and looks around. "Which reminds me, where's Roscoe this morning?"

"He'll be along," a third says. "He rides down with the blue-tailed queers."

"What're we?" a fourth asks in falsetto, "the red-tailed queers?"

"Speak for yourself, Red Ass."

Finally they settle down and begin drawing course lines on their maps. By now other groups are filing in, grouching and insulting. The room fills.

"What is this?" Andy asks. "Finocchio's?"

"Fuck you, Jack."

"Andy."

"Andy" (agreeably).

Roscoe has arrived. A medium-sized, long-haired, red mongrel, possibly a mixture of collie and *poi* dog, he glowers at everyone, then pads over to the water cooler and stands there. It's the old-fashioned kind with the inverted bottle, and conical paper cups.

"Lieutenant," a southern major sighs, "kindly remember the primary reason you're here. Please step over there and give that poor animal some water."

"Yeah, Lieutenant—*Officer Blackwell*—Roscoe is thirsty."

"Goddamned mongrel has been on R and R in town chasing Thai bitches."

"Who? *Me?*"

"Roscoe."

"Whatsa matter, Roscoe?" The lieutenant stoops to the cooler and fills a paper cup. "Are you dehydrated? Well, okay. Here you go. Hey, you better watch that Six-Pack dog, Roscoe. He's hanging around the ordnance area, and that big sonofabitch is gunning for you. Goddamned *wolf*, that guy."

A sergeant from the command post enters. Everything stops. He reaches for a tissue. Poker faced, he erases something.

"Go alternate? Go Pack Twos, Sarg?" someone asks.

He corrects the refueling altitude to seventeen thousand and leaves.

"There you go, Andy. See? Grunts are almost human. Now you don't have to do your porpoise act."

Roscoe has disappeared. I know where he is—in the briefing room sleeping in the Old Man's plush chair.

Briefing time comes, and still no word from Seventh. Seventh is desperate, as usual. The pressure to get this target begins in Washington. The new admiral at CINCPAC, the new general at Hickam—everyone is waiting. For a week, weather has protectively smothered the delta south of Hanoi. Meanwhile, everyone has been diverted to the panhandle to log easy "counters"—missions that count toward one hundred. But now the long-range forecast indicates a break. There might be enough surface heating to burn off that stratus over the Delta.

Nervously kidding each other, they file into the adjacent room and slouch in chairs as near the door as possible. It is important to be first in the breakfast line at the club if you want to catch a nap afterward. I switch on the rostrum light and call the roll: "Mercury. Lightning. Vulture. Killer." No one uses the old color system now because either it requires prefixes when several squadrons are involved, or you have to use the colors queers wear. Pink.

Weather. The sergeant has been in Thailand ten months, in the Air Force twenty years. He has finally discarded his Stateside climatology and learned the local one. Now he knows better than to expect a cold front to clear out stratus. The jocks write on their knee-board cards the altimeter settings and bombing winds.

Intelligence. Spectacles and a timid monotone. He has an Intelligence sergeant project dim, obsolete photos onto the screen. Hesitantly, he reads the special instructions provided by Seventh. Seventh's naiveté is pathetic. The jocks laugh in his face, then look at each other, shake their heads.

"Heavy thirty-seven, fifty-seven and eighty-five-millimeter antiaircraft fire can be expected," he is saying. God, yes. Hanoi lies just to the north. They close their eyes, cross their legs, and lie rigidly with their necks on the chair backs. *There ain't no way, Babe. To live through this war* is the rest of it. That's what those closed eyes mean, and that's why they hate the grunts who will survive. Now all they can hope for is for that good old monsoon weather to hang in there. But not over *all* of North Vietnam, please God. Leave the panhandle open. Mugia Pass counts as much as Hanoi toward one hundred. Let someone else end it.

Operations briefs last. I have the refueling slide flashed on the screen.

They open their eyes and begin copying. Now they can see the whole picture in tabular data: the cells of tankers, which flights will precede them, which will follow, times on target, rescue orbit coordinates. It's a big effort. Maintenance is still trying to come through with enough aircraft so that each flight will have a spare. In the other room, tail numbers are being changed. Out on the flight line, the darkly camouflaged birds, their tan rippling through green, lie in dazzling, stainless-steel bays. All night, loading crews have been maneuvering the olive bombs through floodlights. It's all the same to the birds—Hanoi or Laos. They alone are fearless, these slim birds.

I pause in midsentence. They are all looking at the door. The command post sergeant stands there.

"Go primary," he says.

Go primary. Like ether, the words settle into them, taking them down. The lines on the maps become real; they are *really going to Hanoi,* or very near it. Few of them, not even the old-timers, have been there. Now is when old Henry the Fifth would be pumping them up about Saint Crispian's Day: "The fewer men, the greater share of honor, / God's will! I pray thee wish not one man more." And because he was saying, *we* few, *we* happy few, *we* band of brothers, they tolerated that crap. I can't say "we."

What *can* I say, I who am not going? The less the better. I give them a time hack. "Okay, watch the weather. If it stinks, turn back. That target doesn't have legs; it'll be there next week."

I want to add something, a benediction perhaps. From the stage I look down at the rows of dead faces, but there is no way to soften those two words still echoing. So I only say, "Dismissed, gentlemen," gather up my notes, and switch off the little light. On the wall behind me is a neatly lettered sign someone placed there a long time ago. I think I know who it was, and he is a POW now:

> *The mission of the United States Air Force*
> *is to fly and fight.*
> *Don't you ever forget it.*

Yawning repeatedly and openly, Roscoe jumps down and stretches. He has to hurry if he wants to catch a ride to the club. Outside, the Datsuns are darting back and gunning away. Their headlights sweep across each other. On wooden side benches in the rear, pilots shield their eyes. Within a few minutes, the parking lot contains only the DO's jeep. Colonel Hopwell loans it to the early briefer. I light a cigarette and stand by it a minute, listening to the rustling of the banana fronds in the "U" of the building. What they need, of course, is an overall mission leader, a famous pilot wearing eagles or at least silver leaves. But *I'm* not the guy. I can barely get myself up and down in one piece. They need someone who was born and raised in the fighter-bomber business, someone who has fought to stay in the cockpit, to stay proficient.

From the building comes the timid lieutenant who briefed Intelligence.

"Ride, sir?"

"Sure. Hop in."

Off we go, we two miserable grunts. We are *not* members of that band of brothers. We are not really in the mission-flying business. We are more like that Duke of Exeter, who seems to have been in the longevity business. Sometimes I think that longevity in a fighter pilot is no more desirable than it is in a piece of cordwood.

Within two hours the first birds will lift off into the paling east and their silhouettes will curve northward toward their tankers.

Some general is always dreaming up a surprise attack. Absolute radio silence. Light signals from the Aldis lamps in the tower. Low-level ingress, arriving over the target like a pack of silent wolves at first light. I skim the message and, wordlessly, lay it before Colonel Hopwell. His eyes rise to mine. Angrily he snatches it and props up his feet again. His lips frame the words as his eyes move from left to right, then back. Becky, I realize, reads much faster.

"Aw, Jesus!" he says, laughing and shaking his head. "He's reinventing the fucking wheel. Where was *he* last February?"

Yes, it has been tried before—disastrously. They lost three out of twelve, worse than yesterday when Andy and Moe checked into the Hanoi Hilton as POWs. And it had been professionally executed. What the generals don't realize is that this war isn't like the others. Everyone up there who can hold a rifle is contributing to the barrage of small-arms stuff. Everyone else provides early warning. So all those Aldis signals, all those tanker boom-waggling signals, all that skimming below the radar lobes, all that tapping of helmets and holding up fingers to indicate UHF channel changes, was in vain. The enemy was waiting, as usual, and caught them in the pop-up to dive-bombing altitude. I guess they knew when the first tanker took off. From hilltop to hilltop the message was flashed, and as primitively as the Apaches did when some cavalry general wrote the first version of this message.

But management is what is taught in the senior schools today—not strategy, not tactics, as they were in the days of Claire Chennault and Possum Hansell, Ken Walker, and Harold George. Larry Kuter's name is still big at Maxwell, but Maxwell hasn't known the score for twenty years. (That's not fair; how would I know?)

Well, no big deal. What we have here are a few theoretical straws from the new broom. He is new, this general, and he doesn't see why this war is any different from the days when his A-20s skimmed across the canals and salt marshes of Holland. He has to be convinced, shown by statistics.

Smiling his wry smile, Colonel Hopwell returns the crumpled message to me. I unfold the ball, smooth it.

238

"*You* handle it," he says. "It's my day to fly." He claps my shoulder, chucks my chin up, squares my shoulders, turns me and pushes me back into TOC, laughing as he goes out.

I pick up the phone. Two survivors of that February debacle are still around. I ask them to come in. When they do, I hand them the message, and they read it together while I watch their faces.

"Fuck *that*," one says almost immediately.

"Well, okay, Colonel," the young major says when they've returned it. "I'll go, all right? But under one condition: I want an F-Model and I want this general in the back seat."

"In other words, you think we should kill this concept?" I ask.

"Goddamn right," they fiercely agree, nodding at each other.

"Very well. Let's kill it. I'm going to need facts: dates, losses, all the details."

They talk, and I write it. It turns out to be a long message and more scholarly and dispassionate than all those term papers I wrote for the profs. It has more authority.

A pretty good general, I guess, because we don't hear another word about low-level. I meet him later when he visits the base, and he looks us all in the eye without mentioning it.

Tim is sexy. There's a softness about her, especially at breakfast. She walks into the dining room and you just have to watch her. Other waitresses match her in the important measurements, I suppose, but she's the only one you mentally undress. She swings her bright face and bosom toward you, and you hesitate to ask her for anything trivial. She places a platter of eggs before one of her favorites, and he leans his head against her arm. Clasping his head to her breast, she smiles at us. Even her fingers are sexy. With them she strokes his hair, then pinches the skin on the back of his hand. You expect her to swing away and begin stripping. She's an animal.

And yet, if she has slept with any of the guys, it has been a quiet thing. Her parents are wealthy. They own a restaurant in town. A first date with Tim, they say, is not what you'd imagine. You have to meet her parents and have her home by eleven. They would like an American son-in-law, but want no American bastards.

What would it be like to take her home? To the States, I mean? Some have pondered this seriously. Would her bright smile compensate for her dark skin? Not that she's very dark. Some of us, tanned now, are darker. Nor would anyone suspect Negro blood. Those eyes tell you she's Asian. Her hair, heavy and black, is almost straight. She's a poster, but not of Thailand. Bali, perhaps. The opposite pole of Scandinavian fairness, but no less attractive. Less noble, less wholesome perhaps, but no less beautiful. She could hold her own with the best, you decide. Until her ripeness, in middle age, became fat. Then what? I've seen her mother—a fat, almond-eyed Mexican. Rice is like cornmeal. And Tim has no willpower. She will never diet. So there will be another decade of beauty, then a coarsening. Her belly will swell. That perfect hipline will disappear. The breasts will be overcome. Those brown eyes will still smile, she will still know the earth's secrets, but the magic will be gone. Now, though, *watch her move*—dusky, sensuous, alternately pouting and smiling, sure of her beauty, waiting for someone. Thinking of her at night, I writhe, look at my watch, calculate the hours of sleep I'd get if I were already asleep.

Well, it's worth it, to rise tired, hopeless, frightened, and find her fresh, with so little sleep, moving toward you. You remember her as you taxi out. You wonder if she'd notice if you weren't there the next morning.

No, she wouldn't. You may as well accept that. Tim is Life, Charles would probably say. She has her job, and you have yours.

I just heard that they captured Butch. He must have been nearly through with his missions, with his *third* war. That shakes me. I guess it shook a lot of guys, especially the old tigers. Experience, confidence, personal discipline—he had them. Taken together, these assets used to guarantee honorable survival, and Butch, in particular, wise as an old bass, was the last name I expected to see scrubbed off the boards. Now they'll have to lean on the Golden Beebee theory, or they'll have trouble climbing those ladders tomorrow. Losing a guy like Butch hurts morale worse than losing three wingmen. The old tigers suddenly feel vulnerable and the young ones have lost a father image, a squadron commander.

Radio Hanoi just announced his name. Apparently, there was a little parade in Hanoi last night, with Butch and two others marching, hands bound, ropes around their necks. Yelling crowds and French correspondents. I wonder though if, seeing Butch, they feel more afraid than triumphant. I can see him striding along, scowling in apparent boredom, dirty but hiding his exhaustion and despair. If he bothered to look at them, they saw contempt in his eyes.

There aren't many Butches in the Air Force. A handful. He could have been a frontier marshal. He has that same authority. Without saying a word, he dominates others. If you are senior to him, you want his respect and backing. If you are junior, you'd better do your job right. He has only one or two close friends—other old tigers. With everyone else, he is aloof, formal, brusque. He is never at a loss over how to handle a situation. He knows the regs and he knows men. He maintains an angry exterior. When he answers a phone, the caller hesitates. He has hands that can slap you around, a voice that can intimidate you.

"Okay, *I'll* handle it," he'd say. And he would. He'd stride across that parking lot and into Wing Ops like the sheriff entering a saloon. When he walked into a room, everything stopped while his eyes searched for whoever needed straightening out. Pale eyes like a huskie's in a tanned, hard face with good planes, a jaw rippling with muscle, and straight, parted hair.

But he was usually right in his indignation. Someone had goofed. The schedule was unfair, or the ordnance was wrong. Sometimes, though, nothing was wrong. Nor was he mad. Gradually, everyone realized that he always wears that expression, always strides that decisively, and always scans a room imperiously. Those curt angry phrases are just Butch.

Well, they've got him, and I imagine that their interrogators, professionally tough guys though they are, have already run out of ideas. They'll waver before those eyes. They'll lose that battle.

18

THAILAND

JENNY, NOW LIVING in our old hometown in Indiana, is X-ing off the days on her calendar. Her letters are warm and sustaining, often begun at three in the morning. Sometimes Sam encloses a spidery note: "Honor roll? Are you kidding? Mom says you never made it either. Send me a Communist bayonet or machine gun when you have time. Thanks. Love, Sam. P.S. I'll be glad when you return so I won't have to wash the car. (Ha, ha.) P.P.S. Thanks for the bush hat." Jenny's hand is heavy in the correction of spelling.

Becky writes on such perfumed stationery ("This was *her* choice," Jenny explains) that, by smell alone, I could find her letters. She is all woman. One month her handwriting slants from left to right; the next, from right to left. She is ten—and obviously experimenting. Sometimes she encloses a drawing. Not bad, really. ("Well, you're right," Jenny writes. "Her art teacher says we should *do* something and not let it go to waste.") One sketch is of Fang, our new mongrel, whom I haven't met yet. I judge that he is a wolf, so it's just as well.

"Oh," Jenny says, "I've told him about *you*. You are two of a kind: you both like to hang out the window and go fast. He's the best yet. You won't beat him at tug-of-war. But don't just open the door and walk in. I don't need a paraplegic."

Meanwhile, at Fort Apache, I'm putting in an eighteen-hour day, seven days a week. I've lost fifteen pounds, which is good, but I've caught every cold that comes through the front gate. What lies beyond the gate? A dusty village, they say. I wouldn't know. When, finally, I do get airborne, I'm too busy trying to find the landing gear handle to look down. A big job, TOC, Colonel Hopwell had said that first evening five months ago. Yes, and a monster when you've seen three of your five assistants rotate before their replacements arrive. The new Wing Commander tells me I look like "a fucking ghost," which must be white indeed, and suggests that I take time off and run down to Bangkok or Singapore or somewhere. *He* does, he says.

"He did, huh?" Colonel Hopwell asks. "Well, I just don't know what to say, John. Who'd break the frags, who'd brief the flights? Tell you what: we've got jocks coming in all the time, right? Grab somebody. I mean it. You're about to fall down, man. Train a guy who can double for you, *then* take an R and R."

A reasonable theory, but as unworkable as most theories. In they come, mustaches already started, rubbing their hands. "Which squadron, sir?" they ask. "Klondike wrote me to tell you his squadron. You see, we flew '105s together for three years in Germany."

"I see."

I'm the wrong man for this job. It requires a hard-ass. Here I am, offering them something precious—survival, no less—but, instinctively, they back away. It's the "year" part. You'd think a year is forever, that this extra six months makes a big difference. When you're thirty, it does. You're still a dumb kid. Nothing scares you then. Now, I'm forty-three, and *everything* scares me. Life itself scares me.

Anyhow, I don't force them into it, don't make eunuchs of them, because I remember being thirty and because, God knows, we also need experienced flight leaders. Yesterday we lost *two*—one over Laos, for chrissake. So I keep scanning the Inbound lists furnished by Personnel until one evening this name flies up at me. *Scooter!*

Hell, I thought he'd finally gotten out and gone with the airlines. No, he's too old; he's what—thirty-three, thirty-four? He's going to the other wing. *No, he isn't,* I decide, and call an old buddy in Personnel at Clark.

Two weeks later I hear his voice on the porch, and the door flies open.

"Hey, hey, sports fans!" he calls. "At ease. Smoke if you got them."

He seems unchanged. A little heavier, perhaps. Aw, Jesus, he's doing his Pope routine, making little Signs of the Cross, and sprinkling imaginary holy water on everyone. I haven't laughed in months, I realize, so letting go like this, I'm a little hysterical. The Command Post duty officer is staring at me. Scooter holds out his ring for me to kiss—no, it's a wedding band he's showing me—but, unashamedly, I embrace him while he kisses my forehead. Nine years.

"You have a part for me, yes?" he asks. "A leading role?"

"Umm."

"I am not simply to be another young understudy?"

"Oh, no," I assure him. "You will remain in the President's Cabinet, of course."

"Good."

"However . . ."

"Oh-oh."

"However, wheel or not, we need a troubleshooter—the trouble being Communists who won't stay home."

"I see. They wear black pajamas?"

I nod.

"Well, that's reason enough. I remain the Secretary, as I understand it—but of what?"

I shrug. "State? Defense? Commerce?"

"Umm," he repeats after each possibility. "Well," he decides, "for now, just Secretary." Graciously, he shakes hands with the guys. "Relax, relax. Ah'm just folks. But don't relax too much, heah? Because Ah'm also the Secretary."

Returning to me, he elevates his chin. "Your ad mentioned that you need someone attractive, personable, and capable of light typing?"

"A WAF was what I had in mind."

"You seen these WAFs? You queer or something?"

I nod at his wedding band. "You're not, I see."

"Who? *Helmut?*" he asks mincingly. Then, proudly, he flips his wallet open to her picture.

Serious eyes, heavy hair, a face I know. "Anne," I say.

He cocks his head, half frowns, half smiles. "Yeah. How'd you know?"

"At George. She was Brad's fiancée."

He looks at me and, gradually, becomes serious. "I . . ."

"I understand. She is a doll, Scoot."

"She's something else, you know? She's great. My old toot. I love her. She understands that I'm crazy. Already I miss her."

"Kids?"

He holds up two fingers. "Two girls. Vee for victory, man. Two dolls."

"Girls are better," I say, looking at their pictures.

"Who are you telling?"

"You are a lucky old elephant. Scarfed that beauty right up, didn't you?"

Grinning, he raises his limp arm but does not trumpet. "Now, then, to trivia. Is the war still on?"

The Command Post guys look at me, drift away. "It's rough, Scoot."

"Yeah. I heard."

"We've lost a bunch. A whole bunch."

He nods.

"It's especially tough if you're a squadron jock." I've got to play this just so.

"But not for you wing wienies?"

I explain it to him, and I have trouble maintaining eye contact.

"How is it for us Secretaries?"

"Oh, *well*. Stateside. You won't know there's a war on. You just lie around in a toga eating grapes."

"Un-huh," he says, "well, I've promised my doll I'll be home in six months, so no way, John-baby." He's weighing it though. "Just lie here eating grapes, huh?"

I nod.

"You have a pension plan?"

"The best: *we live to collect ours.*"

"Is this an order, Colonel?"

I shrug. Everyone else is busy again. "If you like," I say. "Otherwise, disregard."

His half smile fades. "Okay, let's forget your kind offer. I'll pay regular admission and take my chances. But thanks, kid. I love you, but your eyes are too red, okay?"

I nod. I knew what he'd say.

"Amigo?"

"Amigo."

"Nah. You hate me, don't you? I'm letting you down. You're hurting, man. You've got piles."

"I'm hurting, all right. At the moment I'm three people, all with piles."

"Get somebody else. Some old guy like yourself."

I nod. He watches my face, and for some reason I am having trouble controlling it. "Hey, man," he says softly, touching my arm.

He walks over to the window and jingles coins in his pocket while he surveys the ramp. "Oh, shit," he says finally, "I'd become a brigadier overnight?"

My heart leaps. *"Absolutely."*

"A brigadier is higher than a major?"

"Some think so."

"You ought to sell used cars, you know? Okay, I'm hired?"

"Let me see your legs."

He raises his trousers and leans seductively against the wall a moment before going into a frozen-smile tap routine, turning slowly and humming. The two sergeants stare at him.

"You'll do, kid," I tell him. "Rehearsal is at zero-three-hundred."

If nothing else remains, if the visual record blurs with time, the sounds will always bring it back. During periods of light sleep, years from now, the sudden escape of steam from some power plant will become the rush of a cartridge start. Automatically, I will roll to my alarm clock, stare at the floating luminescence, and guiltily check the button. Because fatigue muffles sound, I always set two. Now, the button is up on both. Oh, I'm not briefing; Scooter is. His bed is empty. Ah, God, such luxury. I lie here enjoying it, but listening out of habit to that frantic, endless hissing of air which spins the big engines up to that exact note—F-sharp, Scoot says—of idle rpm. They sing and drum in resonance with each other, howl a little as they surge out onto the taxiway. I slide under my pillow and try to sleep.

Boom! The first afterburner of the day, cracking and searing, begins racing through the night, spreading its shuddering sonic envelope across the base and the numb, peripheral villages. The pillow doesn't stop it. All the furniture is trembling. *Boom!* goes the second. All over the base men twist in their sleep. Through the thin wall, I can hear Doc's bed creak. *Boom!* In a martial matins, they crackle and thunder by. *Bang!* goes the fourth.

A short interval of barely audible singing, then another mild crescendo of drumming. *Bang!* The second flight leader rolls. I hear their voices because I know the schedule. I see their eyes above their masks. They nod in the old signal. They roll, they lift, attain some identity I cannot name. But they never meld into one face.

Throughout these laden, dubious ascensions, I lie there, sometimes lifting the pillow to listen better. There should be four flights. They are going up to Package V. I've been there twice and most of Five is not really more dangerous than, say, Package II until you get along the boundary with Pack VI, along the Red River. Once the sixteenth afterburner has faded, I can relax and sleep.

One morning last month the booming litany was interrupted when one of the leaders, apparently lifting off at less than the recommended 190 knots, suddenly penetrated some graphed envelope in the performance charts, and fell back onto the runway. By then, the landing gear had almost completely retracted, so the bird was sliding along on its external stores. The fuel tanks ruptured, of course, and friction ignited the twin streams of JP-4. Soon thereafter, the belly was sliding on spherical frag bombs. Somewhere beyond the perimeter road the whole burning mess blew up. Number two, committed, kept blatting right through the explosion. Three and four aborted. By then, of course, I was out of bed, buttoning frantically while I listened. For a full minute, there seemed to be no acknowledgment of the crash; then, thinly, a few sirens. Who? Who was leading the third flight? Sugarman, an old head, one of the handful who had seen action during the big one. He'd flown P-38s at the very end when he was nineteen or something, and he remembered how powerful engines could make you a hero by permitting premature gear retraction. You could lift the handle *on the roll,* and nothing would happen—until the oleo-scissors microswitches closed as the wing absorbed the weight of the bird. Then, *slurp,* the landing gear retracted while the bird remained at exactly the same altitude. Most of the time it worked, and the kids were impressed. Airshow stuff.

Well, who knows? We know where he touched down again. Really, that's all. But even that raw concrete was inside the computed takeoff roll. So maybe it's fair to say, "Who needs it?" Times are tough enough now without heroics—short takeoffs and tight landing patterns. Kid stuff. And it's sad because he was almost my age, and I thought he'd outgrown all that. He was experienced; he had led big missions.

It was a messy, dangerous job to gather up all the bomblets and detonate them. In the process, a new, unlikely hero emerged. A *grunt,* for chrissake, a cheerful, fat, bald guy, the commander of the EOD team who personally collected all those armed bomblets. *Armed.* They had spun enough to become armed. Everyone who, from a safe distance, watched him ease around like some big genie minesweeper loves him. Let's face it: *leadership involves exposure.* And on that thought (but, guiltily) I hear the sixteenth 'burner fade and, perhaps hours later, dream of Olivier as Henry the Fifth, twisting in his saddle, his horse rearing in an excess of spirit. He points with his sword, raises it, yelling, and sweeps it down. From horizon to horizon his cavalry accelerates while, above, the sky is darkened and haunted by the terrible drone of arrows.

We drive a quarter mile between herringbone rows of revetments, pausing occasionally to drop off a pilot. I swing down out of the milk truck. It's still dark and the bird is a heavy silhouette. The long needle of the nose is above me. A sergeant hurries out of the shadows to take my helmet and goodie-bag, choked with maps.

"Morning, Chief."

"Morning, sir. Want your chute in the cockpit?"

"No, thanks. Never wear one."

He grins, takes the parachute. Yesterday was a bad day. There are several empty bays. He climbs the ladder.

I skim the pages of the form and then begin the walk-around inspection. It's pointless, and I behave accordingly. The bird has been checked and signed off by professionals. Unless she were lying on one wingtip, a pilot wouldn't notice. The crew chief follows, collecting the streamered landing-gear pins, and watches my flashlight play over the undersurface of the wings. Back in 1960 a pilot found something wrong, so we still have to perform the walk-around. The faster I walk, the less insult to the crew chief. I don't really look at the bird until I get near the tail and then I look forward along her flank, simply because I enjoy that view of her. From there she seems to go on forever. The fuselage narrows, distends slightly, then tapers in a pure mathematical curve to the needle nose of the pilot boom. Short wings slope up to her shoulders. Her landing gear struts are too far away from her weight. How *big* she is! We move like children beneath her. I can't believe that I will lift this static shape into the night, control her vast weight, aim her precisely—and I am right. Instead, I always feel like a tourist swaying in awe on an elephant howdah.

I walk around the low horizontal slab of the tail, peer up at the rudder, shine my light into the great tailpipe. The speed-brake petals droop. Within the tunnel lie rotary blades and the annular screen of the afterburner. In half an hour this tunnel will be a white column of fire and sonic, blue triangles of heat. Fuel will be pumped at fire hose rates from that screen. Now, though, she lies as quietly as a yacht, cold to my touch. I pause, remember the small exhausts of just a decade ago. You could sit upright in this one. Around the other side, stoop to rock the bombs in their shackles, and I am back at the foot of the ladder. My hesitations here have grown longer since spring, I realize, but I finally begin climbing, murmuring my childish prayer. I don't know why.

I settle myself in the cockpit and shine my light around. She's cold and dead. The sergeant appears beside me, helps me with the straps, shines his light where I should be looking. I bounce around in my seat, pulling straps tighter, don the cold helmet, and plug in the radio cord and oxygen hose. Something in my survival vest—the .38 I guess—is breaking one of my ribs. My light plays around the cockpit, over the meaningless switches, dials, levers. Somehow I'm to breathe life into this dead beast. It's done with hand-signals and a couple of key buttons. The chief has started the external power unit, and I give him a signal with the flashlight. Soft lights glow in the cockpit. It seems more possible now. I talk with him on interphone, run through my checks without using the checklist.

"Ready, sir."

It's time. My watch confirms it. I push the start button. There is the smell of cordite and a rushing of air. The needles on the instrument panel surge, and the engine begins climbing through its octaves. Throttle to idle position, and the singing pierces my helmet. The tachometer stabilizes, the engine drums in resonance with others on the flight line. The base is coming to life. Behind me fuel pours into the fire. I'm conscious of the waste and hurry through my checks. My wingtip lights flash against the metal bay walls. The radio brings voices. Flights are already checking in, taxiing. Someone has aborted and a spare takes his place. I no longer know who is flying where. I haven't checked all my systems; there are *pages* of checklist remaining. But already I know that the important things are right. Quick token checks. The sudden red brilliance of the gunsight blinds me. Navigation lights drift by my bay. I see the dark shapes pass, anonymous in the general confusion, mottled bulks freighted with bombs, masked faces I know. Their helmets turn toward me blindly.

That's enough, I decide. We're next and we'll go. A strong engine, a good sight, controls. The rest is gravy.

I advance the throttle and surge out of the bay in a blast of power. The chief waves and I nod. The long, delicate nose turns into the stream of blinking lights, and I feel her weight jouncing over the cracks. The flat spots of the nylon tires heave me along in little surges. The taxi light swings, the nose follows.

Abeam now, as we coast along the blue taxiway lights, shapes rush out of the darkness at fifteen-second intervals, lights blinking evenly. They rotate and stand on tails of fire, rising, blatting, momentarily dominating the airfield with power, fading, dwindling, become bright moons curving northward, disappearing. If you look closely, though, you can still see the flashing navigation lights.

Orange tubes of plastic, the armorers' wands, guide us into position near the end of the runway. I apply the brakes gently to stop, rocking, and place my hands in sight on the windshield coaming. The wands disappear, and men with flashlights race toward my ordnance. Safety pins are being pulled from my fuses. I tighten my mask and relax in the beat of the engines.

Whatever my fears, it's too late now. Unless they find something wrong, I'm going. The tankers passed overhead half an hour ago.

Scooter returns from his first mission and solemnly states that he has destroyed all of North Vietnam. Does the President have any other piddling chores for him? Then, one day, I see his name scheduled for a Package VI. I don't say anything, and neither colonel notices. When Scooter returns that afternoon, all smiles, he sits at his desk and starts working up tomorrow's frags. A few of the jocks wander in and lean over, whispering to him. He looks sidewise at me and, out of the corner of my eye, I see him put his finger on his lips and grin. They beat him on the back and wander through TOC into the Command Post.

My mind freezes at the thought. Without a single day off, I have worked here five months, managing to keep going with only three hours of sleep out of every twenty-four. I need a rest. But something in Scooter's composure rankles me. Jesus, I was flying missions when he was in the seventh grade; I don't have to prove anything to him.

That night I talk with Fred, who commands the 72nd. He shrugs, erases a name, and writes mine in the number-two slot. I don't sleep a wink.

In the morning Scooter briefs us. He gives me this relieved little grin. But we go to our alternate in Package IV, and even that target is socked in, so we expend our ordnance on a road junction and come home.

"That's too far north, John," Colonel Hopwell says later. "Knock off that crap. I go home in two months, and somebody's got to run Ops."

A week later, Fred says he needs a Package VI slot filled if I can slip away. I do, but my radio won't channelize, and the spare takes off in my place. He doesn't come back.

In the Command Post, Father Barker is standing. The pilot who's down is Catholic, he tells me. Father Barker, a Franciscan, lean, balding, so quiet that I have to lean my head close to hear him, is new and unsure of his responsibilities. What should he do? Hang around the Command Post? No, I tell him, there's nothing you can do. Pray? Yes, pray. We never think of that, and it might help. Why I think that, I don't know. Up there in Six there are Catholics, too. Gasoline and oil are stored in drums around their churches. The incongruity of the chaplain's role must eat at him sometimes. Where does spiritual guidance end? Teilhard de Chardin wrote that he would have been correct to man a machine gun during World War I. We are all screwed up.

Out in the arming area before a big mission, you will always see the Protestant chaplain. When the birds taxi up in echelon to the armorers, he walks in front of the sensitive Sidewinders while they are being armed and gives the pilots a thumbs-up, a big grin. His thumb and forefinger become a circle. With his other hand, he points to the bombs. He nods happily. Some days be leaps around holding his fingers in a vee. They say that, unlike Churchill, the schoolchildren in the States use this for a peace sign. It's Indian or something. Maybe the signs simply change with the wars.

"Should *I* be out there in the arming area?" Father Barker asks me. "Tell me truthfully."

"Even though I'm not a Catholic?"

He blushes and laughs, sips his drink.

"I don't know," I concede. "Probably not. If I were you . . ."

"Yes?"

"I wouldn't be out there. It's a dirty business."

He looks at me. I order us a couple more. I shouldn't have said that. Vee-for-Victory, Father.

"What," he finally asks, "do *you* think of this war? Do you understand it?"

"Sometimes."

"And the rest of the time?"

"I go anyhow."

"You're a professional."

"I try to be."

"Whatever they say."

"That's right."

Colonel Hopwell is on R & R in Bangkok. Before he left, he told me there's a new LC coming in to take over TOC. I'm to become assistant DO. He shakes my hand, so I guess it's a promotion. While he's gone, I am the acting DO.

"You, my friend, are the big nigger." He laughs.

Meanwhile, Scooter is settling in nicely. He could run TOC if he had to. A good briefer, he always has some crazy attention step that eases tension. "Today, men," he'll say solemnly, "our target is Saigon."

He is trying to break in this newly assigned major, a grizzled old goony-bird driver whose attention rarely wavers from his bowling scores. "I've got a whole caseful of trophies," he tells us, "and my wife's got a mantel full of 'em. Bowling takes lots of concentration and coordination."

When the phone rings, this meathead steps into a wastebasket, then fumbles the phone. Deftly, Scooter catches it and murmurs into the instrument, "Yes, Mr. President." Later, hanging up, he says, "Major, you do good work."

"That was *President Johnson?*"

"Yes," Scooter replies. "Why?"

Jesus, the old guy's mouth is hanging open. He begins looking all around. "That was the President," he informs me.

"Yeah? What's old Lyn want now, Scoot?"

"The name," Scooter says while he modifies a briefing slide, "of a good bowling ball manufacturer."

The major's eyes illuminate. We can hear some lobe straining. He lights his cigar while he considers the likelihood, then turns away angrily, upsetting the wastebasket again. Scooter says that old Einstein here is undergoing executive training, that the Air Force is grooming him to become Chief of Staff.

Fred's squadron is really hurting for replacements. They are still somewhere in the pipeline. Not having flown for two weeks, I secretly sign on for a Pack V, hoping that weather will divert us farther south. Instead, we are told at 2200 the night before that we'll be going after the northwest rail line, just inside Pack VI.

It is 0530, and we are already past the Mekong and over men who would drag us by our heels through the jungle, stake us out at night. Under FAC control, I've already killed many of them. Napalm right through their bivouac areas, once a whole battalion. I don't think about it, or I'd go crazy.

Golden in the sunrise, our tankers orbit in a loose staircase. Fred homes in on ours, sharply dips his wing to send us sliding into echelon right. Our airspeed tapes ease vertically to the correct refueling airspeed without our having to change power settings. Beautiful planning. He closes, and the boomer stabs him. I open my receptacle door, go to one hundred percent oxygen, and extend my leading-edge flaps. Two minutes later he's beginning to vent fuel. He's full. Disengaging, he slides farther left. I'm next. The flutter of wake and exhaust lies just above. Almost imperceptibly, I'm shaking like a towed ship's dory. The boomer is an old pro; he's going to let me put it in. They say that one '105 has a woman's legs and belly painted around the receptacle.

I feel the latches close. I'm locked in like some happy dog, and we bounce together with the gusts. My fuel needles are rising. Near the arch of my windshield is the face of the boomer. He winks and, without warning, is supplanted by a *Playboy* centerfold. Breasts and long legs. I nod with false enthusiasm, bouncing up and down to simulate laughter. Actually, I'm like old Sir Gawain when Bercilak's Lady came around. Fear of the Green Knight, of the hangman, keeps the mind concentrated, as Dr. Johnson knew.

"Single-pump, Four-Two," I call. I'm almost full.

"Single-pump," he replies.

Ten more seconds and, as I hang there nursing and adding backtrim, suddenly my windshield blurs with fuel. Blindly, I throttle back to disengage, but he has already telescopically retracted his nozzle. I settle, ease under Fred's exhaust, and rise again. Eventually, Three and Four will complete Echelon Left.

We are deeply into Laos now, just east of the Plaine des Jarres. I remember briefing the admiral about the comic-opera war being fought there. No Westerner could ever figure it out. It seems sometimes that these guys who are actually related, these princes, are playing us for suckers. Their old man spends half the time in Paris living it up.

It seems quiet down there, but the jungle canopy hides a lot. There are two surfaces. If you eject, you may snag your chute in the top of some tree. *Hang there,* they told us at Clark. Wait until daylight. You may have eighty feet to go. Well, everything's relative. I grew up climbing trees on our farm, so that's not what is tightening my scrotum.

What I hear are the first calls of the Weasel, the flight configured to hunt and kill SAMs, surface-to-air missile sites. It's like listening to astronauts: the crackling voices are remote, disciplined, charged with excitement. They must be near the Red, rushing across the jungled hills, monitoring the chirps and squeals of their electronic warning equipment. These Six-Packs remind me of some wild, twentieth-century classical music—Hindemith or Stravinsky—often dissonant, rarely melodic, invariably disturbing. No, an *opera* by some modern composer, an opera because there are always voices, mostly a cappella. When everything is going well, there are the clear calls and even responses, often triumphant. More often, the calls become cries, the chorus dissonant, the accompaniment blocking out half the voices, and finally the egress described in tragic diminuendo.

What must it be like to eject over the target? Nothing in our training can prepare us for *that.* It must be like descending into an active volcano. You'd hang there in your chute harness, already thirsty from all the adrenaline being pumped, frightened out of your mind. And maybe you'd think, Jesus, four hours ago I was in the club watching Tim and feeding scraps to Roscoe.

We have let down to five thousand, just above the range of all those grandmothers and kids with rifles. Not that I blame them. God knows our bombing isn't always textbook stuff. The winds aren't as forecast, or there are SAMs or MIGs to distract us. Our winces on these occasions hardly suffice as apologies, much less as indemnities, to those on the ground.

One thing is certain: if one lives through capture, he will face a very stern interrogator. You are a criminal, he will say, and you may be—in his eyes. There would be no professional understanding. You are a mad dog, he would say; you have deliberately killed innocents. *Deliberately,* he would say, and torture you.

Below, the green hills rise to meet us. A peaceful Sunday morning.

The radio is silent. Down on my right console, my Doppler continuously displays our latitude and longitude. On my instrument panel a needle indicates that the turning point lies straight ahead, but already Fred has begun his turn. Yes, now the needle wavers and swings. Suddenly, directly beneath us, deeply cut in the green valley, is the Black River. We cross it, and I scan the eastern horizon where our target must lie. Except for a few electronic chirps from my radar-warning scope, all is quiet. But I have become as restless as a blind man who smells smoke.

"Green 'em up, Panther," Fred says.

I remember my first missions when I had to follow the checklist as I armed my ordnance. Now, my fingers know the sequence. The tiny green lights glow. Solenoids have closed to grasp arming wires. The gun is ready.

Fred is banking again, taking us around in a giant half circle. We are going to come in the back door so that if anyone is hit, he'll already be headed home. Gradually, we have accelerated to 540 knots. The little scope by my gunsight flickers with thistle patterns; gun-laying radar is tracking us. Muzzles are rising, computers are talking to them. Men are monitoring, technicians like ourselves, probably sipping tea or vodka. Possibly they are more civilized than we.

"Panther Three has a two-ringer at ten o'clock."

"Okay, watch him," Fred replies.

Things are happening too fast for me. I can't recognize anything below. I feel as though I'm in the cab of a runaway locomotive. There's a small lake. Son Tay? If so, Hanoi lies only thirty miles to the east. Ahead, in misty confluence, lies the Red; and there's the horseshoe with Viet Tri on its northern rim. The Delta is half covered with fog; but, to the east, glinting in the rising sun, as mysterious and unapproachable as the Magellanic Clouds, lie Hanoi and, farther yet, Haiphong.

My radar-warning scope is frantically displaying patterns, including a pencil line of light—two actually, forking and extending. One of their SAM sites—Lead Eleven, as I recall—and we are well within his range. He might do it. He knows we aren't a Weasel flight. Suddenly, my earphones fill with the rattlesnake clicking of high-pulse-rate frequency. I know he will launch. At eight o'clock points of orange-white light ease around above smoke.

"We have a launch, Panther," Fred says. "Let's take it down. Here they come, from seven-thirty. Steeper! *Right on down!*" I am terrified. We descend behind a hill. Within seconds, the missiles flash over us, a hundred feet higher. One explodes, the others curve down, hypersonic, menacing, but too far ahead.

"Panther's in the pop," Fred almost sings.

And up we go, our afterburners lit, our instrument tapes sliding vertically. I have decided to ignore my little radar detection scope. Sometimes it's better not to know. Ten thousand. I feel completely naked. Above, flak bursts form a ceiling. Steel shards hang in suspension. Through them we climb and then half-roll so we can look down. Where's the target? There is Viet Tri, pulsing with muzzle flashes, but where is the rail line? Inverted, Fred banks farther westward, then plummets. I follow, approximating his dive angle. Okay, there's the rail line, but where's the bridge? *There!* There it is. Hurriedly, I raise my pipper a little, and pickle.

Strings of colored lights rise, hesitate, flash past. The air must be saturated. We jink right, then left. Dirty puffs are walking up toward Fred. I warn him. Just in time, he jinks away. Leveling, we continue to writhe across the river, then settle behind a sheltering ridge. Something resembling a camouflaged telephone pole races past. *Jesus.*

As quickly as the action developed, it ends. We are back over the green foothills, effortlessly climbing the darker mountains. We are still maintaining 700 knots when Fred comes out of 'burner. Time remains compressed, but I am adjusting. I notice Three and Four closing on us. I check the sky behind them. Pillars of earth poise motionless near the bridge. Hornet Flight. I can't tell whether the bridge is down.

A flame. Something is burning in the sky, falling.

"Get out, Hornet Three! Get out!"

Ah, Christ, Fred is curving back toward the target. Jesus, *we are going back to Viet Tri.* Then I hear a beeper on Guard Channel.

"He's ejected," someone calls. "Hornet Three has a good chute, Leader."

"I don't have him."

"He's right over town."

Fred completes the circle. Thank God—shamelessly I repeat it—we are going home. There's no point in setting up a RESCAP. At best our jock will be captured immediately. Magruder was Hornet Three. A tough little guy who could do fair imitations of Bogart. Air Academy, Class of '63.

Debriefing. We are drinking beer and trying to settle down. I am exhausted, yet elated, one of the jocks again. Fred is the only one making sense. Calmly, he answers the Intelligence lieutenant's questions, taps the map with his pencil.

"Was the target area overcast?"

"Absolutely," Fred nods. "Four-eighths stratus and four-eighths cordite."

The lieutenant writes it down before he gets it. He blushes. "Lead Eleven, you say? How many launchers did you see, Major?"

Fred laughs, closes his eyes. The lieutenant is a wienie; he doesn't understand.

"And where did your bombs impact, Colonel?"

I've drifted away. "What?"

"Your bombs, sir. Where did they impact?"

"God knows."

He can't imagine it. *I don't know?* Number Three says they hit a little to

253

the south, right on a highway. I shrug. Could be. The lieutenant slides the photo over to him.

"Here," Number Three taps.

"He cratered *that* road?"

"I'd say so."

"Oh, boy! Seventh will have a hemorrhage. That's *tomorrow's* target, that road."

We howl, cough, upset our beers. Fred can't get his breath. Weakly, he pats my shoulder. The lieutenant smiles thinly. The general, he says, won't think it's funny. He's right, too; this lieutenant, I mean.

"Don't report it until tomorrow night," Fred says. "Hey, that's great. We can sleep in."

The summer drags on. There's fog over the delta every morning but, by afternoon, only haze. The two F-105 wings alternate going up to Pack VI. Rarely does everyone return. We lose a bird every other day. Morale falls. One flight has three separate salvos of missiles fired at them. They finally have to turn back because they lack the fuel, after all that maneuvering in afterburner, to continue. Fred loses his Operations officer who had been earmarked to inherit the squadron. Colonel Hopwell loses a wingman in Package II up near Vinh. We set up a RESCAP, and the Jolly Green choppers pick him up.

I slip away on another Pack VI, but we ingress so far north of Hanoi that it is no worse than a Pack IV. Colonel Hopwell chews my ass, of course, but I've begun to like him. He'd go to Six if the Old Man weren't watching like a hawk; and it's eating at him. He's a mess. Forty-seven and he looks even older. His nerves are shot; sometimes he gets to talking about losses, and I realize that he's talking about Korea, or World War II. I'm beginning to wonder if he can hold out another month. He talks so much, repeats himself. The same old stories over and over. He's going to be a grandfather, he tells me without smiling at all. One afternoon he goes up to Pack IV and a new SAM site nearly gets him. He comes back, white as a snowman, goes into his office and closes the door. I hear him throwing up into the wastebasket.

The more frightened he gets, the more he curses Seventh. Twice he does it on the scrambler phone. Everyone in the building can hear him. "He's got some senior colonel on the line," the captain behind the console whispers to me.

"My guys aren't *supermen*, y'know," he's saying. "They're just guys. They auger in like anyone else when they're hit. Maybe that hasn't *occurred* to you, Colonel. Every time you have a tough one, you pick us, right? What's that? We do good work? You bet your sweet ass we do. But we lose 'em, see? We're down to thirteen guys in one squadron. Thirteen! Out of twenty-six. And where do you have us going tomorrow? Back to the same fucking POL dump. They've got two fifty-five-gallon drums of fuel up there guarded by five hundred heavy guns. Don't you read the mission reports? There's no POL there, don't you understand? They've moved it downtown and put it around the churches and embassies. What's that? You can't hear me?"

He hands the captain the phone and snaps his fingers. "Get him on the hot line. This Donald Duck thing isn't worth a shit. Hello, you read me? . . . Yeah . . . Yeah . . . Oh, hell yes! We're going. Right. We'll launch 'em. Our briefers are numb, too" (he looks at me). "Yeah, they can circle a target with crayon anywhere on the map and not fall down. They used to fall down, y'know. And, say, that route you picked is a beaut, a real dandy. Who picked it, Ho Chi Minh? It doesn't miss a single flak site. Yeah. When the guys see it on the map, they ask whether Seventh is a friendly or an enemy headquarters. Yeah, yeah, buddy. But *we're* supposed to keep a straight face, see? *That's* what's hard. We tell 'em that your EOB experts have calculated all the risks, and this is the best route. You know what they say? 'Colonel, you gotta be shittin' us.' That's what they say. And let me tell you something: *they're* the fucking experts. They've *been* there. Don't you ever forget that!"

The colonel swings his back to us, and I make cord-jerking motions to the captain; but Hopwell swings back again, so the cord stays put.

"Battle Analysis?" he asks incredulously, then laughs like a bastard. "Oh, that's great. That's shit-hot, as the guys say. What are they using, 1918 maps? Well, look . . . No, I'm telling *you*, see? You listen to *me*. I'm telling you that your wienies wouldn't know a flak site if they saw one. They're wearing Coke-bottle glasses, and they've been to some goddamn school in Colorado or somewhere, so they're experts, right? And the rest of you flew balloons or something during the Civil War, and that makes *you* experts? . . . This goddamn phone's dead," he says, looking at it.

When he'd gone, the captain explained that he hadn't disconnected the two colonels. Seventh had hung up.

The dark command post becomes quiet. Flights check in, taxi and take off. The captain and the sergeant move familiarly around each other, deft as short-order cooks in avoiding collisions. One changes with a crayon the tail numbers on the backlighted Plexiglas; the other maintains liaison with Ordnance and Maintenance. Discipline and momentum launch the mission. I know that by the runway, a gaunt man sits in a blue jeep and watches each bird rotate and lift off. He has killed himself. Surely the realization has pierced him by now. He mutters to himself; his eyes, cornflower blue, jitter. The thunder fades. I point to the switchboard and twirl my finger. The sergeant nods and rings Seventh.

"Relax, it's just me," I tell the Seventh duty officer. "Who was the deaf colonel on your end of the line?"

"Colonel Allen, sir. Wrong guy, incidentally; he's new. Brigadier selectee."

"Allen. Chuck Allen?"

"Beats me. I call him Colonel Allen. Stand by. Right. The roster says Charles. Charles E."

"Tall and slim? West Point?"

"Rog on the dimensions. Stand by." He questions someone. "Right. Hudson High. Sharp as hell. Here he comes again with about twenty feet of teletype paper. Want to speak with him?"

"Unless he's putting out a fire."

"Well, he always is. Stand by. He's right here."

"John?" a familiar voice says.

"Hi, boss."

"Where are you? Hawaii?"

"Well, I was. Until this war came along."

"Right. I know what you mean. I was snoozing in the Old Soldier's Home with my teeth out when somebody came in blowing a bugle."

"Old fire horse."

"Old jackass is more like it. How are Jenny and the kids? Back home in Indiana?"

"Yes, sir. As the song goes. How's Kate?"

"Furious, meaning normal. She's a chauffeur now. Trundles the girls around the beltway to riding lessons. Wants to retire and leave Washington. Unpack finally. You leading all the big ones?"

"No, I just brief them. I lead the big ones to Package One."

"I'll bet."

"Seriously, I'm just a wing wienie, so I'm not really in the mission business. Mister Magoo, the jocks call me. I'm here for a year."

"You're in the longevity business?" he asks, laughing.

"Absolutely."

"Well, I see that I'll never get the truth out of you sober. Now, then, is this purely a social call, or do you want to chew me out, too?"

"Gee, I don't know. I've never chewed on a brigadier."

"Oh, that. Well, no halo for a few more months, so lead off."

"Congratulations."

"Well, thank you, but no big deal. I was overage in grade, et cetera. Same old one-celled brain. But our bank was impressed."

Silence. He is courteously waiting.

"About Colonel Hopwell, sir . . ."

"Um-m. Tough, loud guy? Fairly opinionated?"

"Somewhat. Uh, well, he's *not* a bad guy. Sort of a skinny, exhausted Colonel Nasser. Colonel Bronton, I mean. Exhausted and scared. On the ragged edge, both physically and emotionally."

"What they used to call combat fatigue, before the term became professionally unacceptable?"

"Well, I can't diagnose anything except mumps, but let's say that he's been here too long."

"Agreed."

"So no hard feelings? You understood? Gee, that's great. I'm sure he'll call back to apologize. . . ."

"I see. He's going to apologize for having combat fatigue? No, Johnny,

256

you know better than that. It's not a matter for either vindictiveness or forgiveness. I trust that you understand me better than that. It's just that, whatever you may have heard to the contrary, Seventh Air Force lies roughly within the wiring diagram, and it says here that we are the ones who get to yell, not you blue-collar types. *Droit de seigneur* or maybe *noblesse oblige.* Something like that. RHIP? Anyhow, we can't do business Hopwell's way."

"I understand, but he leaves in two months, sir."

"Even for two months. Even for two minutes. No, sorry about that, but we are used to having our way, you know. Bad form otherwise in that the troops get restless."

"Curtailment, then what . . . retirement?"

"Curtailment, yes. By about two months, I would guess. If Colonels' Assignments has ever gotten their computers on line. They are probably already searching for someone I can beat. Or at least out-yell. How loud can you yell? Okay, you'll do, I expect, until the slavers catch up. I know for a fact that I can beat you at anything except drinking."

"That, too, probably."

"We'll see."

"How was TAC Headquarters, sir?"

"Typical. Imaginary crises, real heart attacks."

"Did you get down to Seymour-Johnson to see Charles?"

"Every time I could break away. In fact, thanks to his kind sponsorship, I accumulated two hundred hours in the '105."

"Really? We are close. How's Charlie making out as a flight commander? Except for Christmas cards, I never hear from any of those clowns."

"Not so good. Hurt his back in an ejection. One of those explosions due to fuel fumes in the bomb bay, they think. He has been grounded pending further medical evaluation. Meanwhile, he made major and got tapped for Armed Forces Staff College. From there, he's going to the Pentagon and work in JCS Plans, I hear. Now, please shut up so I can make my pitch. Next week, God willing, I am going to take a few days of R and R and I thought I would offer my combat-ready body to some lucky Ops officer as cannon fodder. One of my old Langley buddies is DO of the other '105 wing, but now there is you."

"No way. Forget it."

"Am I going to have trouble with you, too, Lieutenant Colonel?"

"Better trouble with you than with Kate."

"Don't they teach anything about basic tactfulness at Armed Forces Staff College?"

"No, sir. Colonel Hopwell really got to you, didn't he?"

"Well, your amiable DO *was* correct about one thing: the last time I heard a shot fired in anger was at Richmond when my balloon drifted over the Confederate lines."

"So you want to rest and relax over North Vietnam. I see. Kate is right, you know. You are no one to assess Colonel Hopwell's behavior, sir. Frankly, I doubt that you are even current in the bird."

"Currency, currency, that's all I hear. John, please don't make me lie. Okay, tell you what: I know you've got one two-place bird that isn't Weasel-configured; so, to keep us legal, how about setting me up in that with some ludicrously loose instructor pilot for a quick recurrency check? Oh, and, say, load it with some old muddy bombs you'd be ashamed to expend farther north than, say, Package Two. That way I can trundle over to the panhandle and get a counter."

"Colonel, you're too much. Kate's right. Well, we'll see, but the Old Man may overrule me, or the bird may be out of commission. No promises."

"Thanks, John. Honestly, I couldn't have afforded Hong Kong *and* the riding lessons."

"Will Colonel Hopwell be retired, sir?"

"I doubt it. Not unless he puts in his papers. My guess is that they'll promote him to general so they can capitalize on his irascibility. That's how I made it."

"Before you hang up on me, sir, guess who's here? Scooter! No, sir. No camels, but he still has his trumpet. He runs TOC. Absolutely. I'll tell him. We'll be waiting. See you on the Scatback Courier Tuesday."

First light. Below lies the Fishmouth, North Vietnam's westernmost protrusion into Laos. The land, jungled and mountainous, inhabited only by hill tribes, lies in chiaroscuro. My radar detection scope shows only sporadic and faint blips and chirps. Orbiting at ten thousand feet, we are perfectly safe. There are no known SAM sites in this portion of Package III.

As the land gains color and terrain definition, I can make out the major valley cut by the Song Ca River which drains the easternmost portion of the Plaine des Jarres into the estuaries near Vinh, one hundred nautical miles to the southeast. Paralleling the Song Ca in the same valley is Route Seven, a main supply route when the Pathet Lao make their big annual push to regain control of the Plaine des Jarres from the Royal Laotian Army, but ordinarily fairly inactive.

"Chevy Leader, Jaguar," I call. A minute later, I repeat the call. Silence. His survival kit radio may be dead by now. "Let's troll, Jag Two," I tell my wingman. We descend.

Yesterday afternoon, unforecast, the stratus overhanging the Fishmouth burned off and a flight returning from Package V sighted a convoy of approximately fifty trucks heading northwest. Seventh diverted Chevy Flight, led by Colonel Allen on his fifth mission, from Pack I to engage the convoy. When I heard of this diversion, I wasn't concerned because I assumed that Chevy still carried their external ordnance. Using bombs, one can crater the road at both ends of the convoy and then, at one's leisure, string trains of bombs in between. So long as the attacking flight stays above the small-arms fire, there's little danger in a remote section of enemy territory. But Chevy had already expended their external ordnance, and Colonel Allen had led repeated strafing attacks with his Gatling gun until, without warning, two thirty-seven-millimeter sites, apparently especially set up to protect the convoy, had opened fire. Instantly, his bird had become a torch. He had ejected below five hundred feet and at a dangerously high speed, but his chute had deployed and, later, members of his flight heard him on Guard. They had established a RESCAP and Rescue birds took absurd risks until dark, but armed enemy patrols were too close for the colonel to expose himself. He had had to sign off for the night and evade.

"Try your luck, Jag Two."

No response, but that could mean anything. We descend to one thousand feet and race along over the battered convoy. A few trucks appear to have suffered only slight damage, but most are black skeletons with tires still smoking. No muzzle flashes from the hills. We search in vain for survival flare smoke. It is too early to expect mirror flashes.

As we ascend again, we hear them coming, the heroic little procession of Rescue birds. There are two Jolly Green Giant helicopters, and each is escorted by two propeller-driven A1E Sandies, heavily armed. They work as two trios, and the Rescue mission commander flies the leading Sandy.

"Negative contact. Negative hostile action noted," I report.

"Ah, rog, Jaguar," Sandy Leader acknowledges. "Maintain your present altitude, please."

The two low Sandies make slow trolling passes along the hillsides. There is almost an insolence in their courage, in their calm transmissions to each other.

"Okay," Sandy Two calls. "We're beginning to pick up some light stuff from your nine o'clock, Sandy Lead."

Chandelling in absurdly tight turns, they turn back and each lays a fraction of his ordnance along a ridge. The flashes are startling in the blue-gray light. Again, they troll the valley and begin trying to raise Colonel Allen. When, finally, I hear his voice, guarded, almost a whisper, barely audible above the engine roar of the Sandies, I shout with relief and joy. We are beginning to realize that he dare not transmit until the covering noise is almost directly overhead. We need to distract the troops who must be searching in his immediate vicinity, and quickly. But how?

The Sandies continue their search pattern until they are about a mile east of the coordinates which I would suggest and then call in the low Jolly Green. Contour-flying, its seventy-foot rotor flailing the jungle canopy with downwash, the chopper hurries forward like some great insect wading across a scummy pond. Once within the circle formed by the two Sandies, the big machine rears into a hover and lowers its jungle penetrator.

"No, no, you idiots!" I think. "You were directly over him a minute ago." While I'm almost crying with rage, it occurs to me that maybe these Rescue guys are creating the diversion I had been casting about for.

"Okay, high birds," Sandy Leader says. "Suggest you ingress along the lane we've swept."

Camouflaged almost into invisibility from our altitude, the second pair of Sandies and the high Jolly Green are suddenly over the correct coordinates. "Can you pop an orange one for us now, Chevy Leader?" God, it's such a pleasure to watch pros operate.

"I've got to risk it," the colonel replies. "I think they've moved out. I hear them shouting from the east. Here goes the flare."

Within a few seconds, a smudge of orange spots the green. "Okay, Chevy," the chopper pilot says. "We have you. Look for the penetrator."

The jungle penetrator is a cable-hoisted device which, like a metal flower bud, opens petals to form seats for two. By God, I think, they are going to get him out. I am weak with exultation and relief, with exhaustion. What a story *he's* going to be able to tell when he gets back to Seventh!

Colonel Allen reports that he is seated on the penetrator and is ready to be hoisted. A note of triumph is evident in his controlled transmission. Suddenly, almost insignificant in the stupefying noise created by the turbines and blades, I hear the *pat-pat-pat* of an automatic weapon on his radio, and then, abruptly, all the noise ceases. The Jolly Green lowers its nose and, essing, retreats into the hills. Bird-dogging ahead of it are the high Sandies. The other Rescue birds are departing the area, too.

"Did you pick him up?" I ask the Rescue commander.

"Negative, Jaguar. You are released. Sorry."

All the way back into Thailand, I curse myself. I see him lying there, abandoned to those barbarians. I pray that he is dead. If not, he has worse to face before dying. God, if I had a few of those nukes now, right now while I'm mad enough . . . No, he would be the first to disown a lunatic.

"Uh, *how,* Colonel," Fred asks me as he carefully stirs the olive around in his martini, "do three company-grade wingmen stop a full colonel flight leader from making multiple passes with the gun?" Then he thumps the olive at a lieutenant, who, mouth open, darts sideways trying to catch it. "Shoot him down?"

Fred commands the squadron that I had attached Colonel Allen to and is beginning to look at me as I used to look at Colonel Hopwell. For fifteen minutes, I have been raving about the stupidity of multiple passes in a small-arms environment.

"I understand that it was a thirty-seven, not small arms, that got him," he adds, looking me in the eye. Gradually, we both begin smiling. He claps me on the shoulder. "Look, Colonel . . . look, *John* . . . your buddy Allen was a tiger, right? You see him—saw him—as a future chief of staff, but I saw him as a real combat leader. He was what we have been needing around here all along. Maybe the two go together. Maybe . . ."

"And maybe he just got carried away." I set my glass down much too hard. "Showing us how, and all."

"That's bullshit, and tomorrow you'll be the first to admit it."

"Yes," I concede and, forgetting dinner, return to the hooch.

"Dear Kate," my letter begins. That's as far as I, numb with gin, have gotten. Such letters are officially discouraged for fear of confusing the next-of-kin with contradictory details. Sometimes the very tense of a verb proves later to be wrong. So I must be careful. My letter will be preserved. "Dear Kate . . . You once said that he is a real George Washington. You were more right than you know . . ."

Before sleep takes me, I remember my phone conversation with the lieutenant colonel who had been Sandy Leader, a former classmate at Norfolk, as it turned out, one of those big-bottomed MATS pilots I used to knock. "Well," he had said, "when you have been through fifty or sixty of these operations, you get so you know what to expect. There wasn't any point in letting the para-rescueman ride that bloody penetrator down and get his ass shot off, too. Besides, he saw the bursts catch him. Knocked him right off the seat and set the cable swinging like crazy. Otherwise, we'd have stuck around. Okay?"

Then—perhaps I am dreaming now—I see him, a silhouette, poncho-clad, stooping with his clipboard in the German drizzle of December, while his flashlight plays over the glittering weapon with its blood-red streamers. Wraithlike, he rises from a crouch and stares at me.

19

BANGKOK

OUT OF THE black rain they come, leaving rooster tails, the leader's landing light skimming the puddles. It is a scene embodying the medieval symbolism of the four elements: earth, air, fire and water. Now the blue-white beam tilts upward as though indicating the new path and, obediently, the two silhouettes rise. Like slim, black swans during the first powerful wingbeats, they lift, shedding water, carrying their fire with them. Centered in their white-hot exhausts are even brighter, blue-orange diamonds of supersonic gases. Suddenly, the leader's landing light snaps forward and disappears. There remain only the navigation lights and heavy silhouettes working to become synchronized. Within two seconds, they are gone in the scud, as pitiless as sharks. Their thunder fades. Cold drops of rain hit my face. I open my eyes to bright sunlight.

Standing over me is a young man in bathing trunks, dripping and looking concerned. His face seems familiar, and I think I see semirecognition in his eyes.

"You alive now?" he asks. "I thought I'd better wake you while you're just medium-rare."

I lift my head to look down at my pink body, press my hand against my chest and leave its white imprint there. How long did I sleep?

"Yeah, thanks," I tell him, sun-squinting at him. Smiling, he dives in again and languidly strokes across the pool to emerge and stand between two attractive girls lying in deck chairs. He holds his dripping arms over their bellies. They push him away and close their eyes again, their irritation fading. Like bored, indolent goddesses, they drowse, string-bikinied, concave-stomached, confident. Drugged by the sun, they lapse into smoothfaced serenity.

It is an effort to force my gaze away from them. I roll onto my stomach, find my watch, and learn that I had slept an hour. With my chin cupped in my hands, I try to force myself not to stare at them. Does one resemble Betty, the short-haired one with the pug nose? I invent excuses to look.

In a Christmas card from California, Betty had, according to Jenny, explained that, again, her mother's failing health had caused her to return to California. We wouldn't recognize Southern California now, she had added. "Something has to be done about the smog; it burns your eyes. A freeway practically runs through Mother's living room, and the poor thing remembers when it was all citrus groves and sunshine."

No mention of Eric. Her love to me.

Splat! A sheet of green-white water fans from the pool and sends the goddesses shrieking out onto the lawn. His watch flashing, a man happily backstrokes in retreat. His hair is gray. Okay, I get it now.

Running footsteps, and I look up to see, poised memorably against the sun, the short-haired stew, half naked, arching almost over me into the pool. Meanwhile, the other girl searches in a frenzy for something to throw.

"You . . . !" she begins, teeth clenched, and her lips complete the word "bastard." Wildly, she hurls a thong sandal at him and nearly hits the old lizards playing bridge.

"What?" the gray-haired swimmer asks, cupping one hand to his ear. "Say again, Kitty."

The old satyr laughs and leans back against the tiles before he senses the underwater approach of that lovely, human torpedo. A trail of bubbles gives her away.

"Argh!" he shouts, and launches himself along a diagonal escape route. Surfacing, slick-haired, as determined as Diana, the girl who reminds me of Betty strokes to cut him off. Biting her lip, an imp in her eye, she closes with an easy watchful breaststroke.

"First Officer! Help! Careful, that's my—ouch!—throttle hand. *First Officer!*"

Behind him, the other stew stealthily approaches with a cardboard ice bucket. Grimacing, grappling, the captain hurriedly promises lavish amends. "Wine, a big steak, rubies, anything!"

"Anything?" She pauses to consider the possibilities; her eyebrows rise. She nods, releases his finger, and retreats in time to avoid the ice water. Open-mouthed, gasping, he bleats for revenge as the girls flee to the First Officer, who protests, "Oh, no, not me. I'm getting crew rest, and you know how important—"

"Please!" they croon, and stroke him. I almost moan aloud. The cab driver was right: this is the place to stay, the newest and best in Bangkok.

"Yes," he had nodded with his conspirator's smile. "Pan Am. *Compris?* Pretty American fly-girls for you, sahr."

Too exhausted to lift my head, I had tipped him and followed the doorman and my old, original B-4 bag through the doors. And, without warning, something had penetrated my stupor. I am trying to relive it. The architecture! Two stories of teak and glass had literally forced my eyes up to the lofted ceiling, then allowed them to fall along the chains to the soft lights. From them, I had only to drop my gaze and I was looking at the most beautiful Asian I had ever seen. Coiffed, sloe black eyes that calmly assessed me, she rotated the guest register and handed me a pen. I had forgotten to ask about the rates.

Now, by daylight, restored by ten hours of sleep, I look at this hotel. When Fred had described it, I had thought, "Yeah, another Howard Johnson's." But now I understand; it is unique. The architect was a hypnotist. Everywhere one's eyes roam, they are trapped by some perspective, some slope. There is the airiness of the lobby with its shops and restaurants, eaves rising in dihedral, falling to the ground in anhedral near opposing entrances. It's what was charming about the F4U Corsair. Tiles, color-contrasted, subdued green-bronze extending out to traces of sugar-loaf temples, of pagoda eaves. I think I am beginning to understand. The man had stood out there on the sidewalk, looked at the adjacent Buddhist temple and blended its timelessness with the latest ideas. The result is a watercolor. As I watch, heat rises from the tiles, the light shifts, and the building becomes something else.

Behind me, the Pan Am crew has suddenly become silent. I sit up and look where they are looking. Standing motionless under the covered walkway connecting the lobby with our building are two couples. Apparently, they have been surveying the pool, watching the horseplay. They are European; one glance tells me that. Elaborate coiffures, patrician faces as lean as collies, they are straight from some pavane. Calmly, the ladies return the child-like stares of the stewardesses, then walk on. Lagging behind, their hands clasped on their rumps, are the men, one a gray wolfhound wearing a blazer and a cravat, the other Palm Beachy. The ladies pause again, one smiles down into the other's cupped hands and beckons the wolfhound. He bends from the waist to examine it. His hands unclasp, he extends a finger to touch it, then calls his friend over. They all peer down.

With two pretty girls, both practically naked, within my line of vision, I lean aside to get a better view of the blonde. She is a princess, I decide. She has the complexion for it. Such presence! Elegance and money. Never worked a day in her life. The stews are enchanted. They've quit breathing. I can't catch the language, but it's not English. Now a third couple, Japanese and young, some transistor tycoon and his movie-star wife, no doubt, hail them and catch up. The men shake hands while the Japanese doll, who has had an eye job, is shown the treasure. Whatever it is, it's not a mere princess ring. Probably a big ruby. The ruby is the national stone, I've heard. There are soft feminine murmurs and smiles as reflected pool light plays under their chins.

"Jawhol!" the wolfhound's voice rises in enthusiasm. He beams. *"Unterturkheim."*

Naturlich. All the way from the airport there are billboards advertising the Asian Trade Fair. Heavy German machinery and Japanese electronics. My God, who won that war? And here *we* are, still fighting.

The blond princess lifts her face, laughing in sweet, rich peals, then shakes her head. *"No?"* the wolfhound asks. She smiles and shakes her head again. I have the feeling I've seen them before, and when her eyes eventually traverse and hit mine, I nearly faint. I am back on the Autobahn, hissing along in the rain at ninety; Jenny reclining asleep beside me, her finger still between the pages of *Buddenbrooks*. In my side mirror, I see headlights flashing. Slowly a Mercedes passes, wipers ticking, a distinguished man at the wheel, a blonde beside him. They are younger than this couple. She smiles at me, the same smile, the same violet eyes I see now. Our "US Forces in Germany" license plate, my haircut, tell her all about us. Now her eyes hold mine, and there is no Porsche to steer. Her smile does not broaden; there is no recognition. I'm just another GI—ubiquitous, uncivilized, cluttering up the scenery. No. How could it be? What are the odds?

Coughing and scratching, the oldest brown lizard wraps the hotel's beach towel around his shoulders, rises from his deck chair and walks over to the royalty. When he removes his sunglasses, the wolfhound lights up and the Japanese bows. The ladies address the old man in charming English. The men behave deferentially toward him, agreeing eagerly with everything he says.

"Well," he concludes, nodding to the ladies, "I'm pleased to have made your acquaintance." A wave, and he pads back to his chair.

"Who was that, honey?" his wife asks.

"Oh, just some boys I met in Stuttgart last year. I forget the Jap's name." He lies back, still holding the beach towel around him like a mantle and sips iced tea. Then, fierce-looking as an old hawk, he crunches ice and ogles the deflated stews. At his side, a tiny radio announces tinnily that F-105s have conducted the biggest air strike of the war. I hear something about Gia Lam, MIGs and petroleum, and I rise to walk nearer, but her country voice rises: "These people just don't know the first thing about making iced tea, do they?"

The old man snaps his fingers in slow motion. "Not Stuttgart, Geneva."

"It's too strong, and they don't even know what mint *is*," she explains indignantly.

The announcer is talking about Dow-Jones averages now. Quickly the old man holds up his hand and leans down to listen. A cynical smile comes to his face. The airline captain is interested, too. He is probably even richer than the lizard.

I gather up my stuff, walk in a fog of distraction across the putting-green lawn; enter the teak sentry box of my room's entrance, and shiver in the dark, air-conditioned hush. There's not a sound. I switch on the radio and search for AFN, but we're between newscasts now. After showering, I lie down. By God, they *did* it, and I wasn't even there. Scooter must have briefed it, he and that new Weather sergeant and the Intelligence lieutenant who says, "Expect heavy thirty-seven, fifty-seven, and eighty-five-millimeter . . ."

Restlessly, I rise, shave again, dress and walk downtown. The streets are wide and clean, the weather like Waikiki's in August. There's the Erawan, where the admiral always stayed in Bangkok. It used to be *the* hotel, and its tropical courtyard and pool are still inviting. I order a beer and a sandwich. It's crowded, and I notice an American looking for an empty table. I wave him into a chair. It turns out he's from Seventh.

"Have you heard?" I ask.

"Yeah. I just came in on the courier. Goddamn madhouse over there at Ton Son Nhut."

"Any word on losses?"

He holds up two fingers while he drinks.

"Which wing? Do you remember?"

He shrugs, ponders, finally shakes his head. He orders a round and eyes the girls swinging past. An hour later, bloated on beer, we switch to martinis.

"Yeah, I know," he says, sighing. "A piss-poor war. It makes no sense. The other wars did, didn't they? Or were we just younger? This one beats me. Sometimes I wonder if we aren't being conned. Y'know? Look at Ky, a high-school dropout. Now how can he communicate with Lodge, for chrissake? *Harvard*, no less. What do they talk about? Land reform? That's the basic trouble, you know. Here, Mexico—shit, California."

My mind keeps floating away. I'm cold sober. I should get back up there. But it's done now. It's over. And it would be stupid to go six months without a day off, then ruin an R&R worrying.

"Land and money," he's saying, "like every war since the Crusades. *That's* the last time anyone fought for ideals—the Crusades."

I wonder where I can find a phone that speaks English, as Joe used to say in France.

"Well," the LC continues grimly, "we've got hold of a tar-baby this time. Goddamned French tried to suck us into this one back in 1954, but old Ike knew those bastards. Over here they were saying, *'Oh, mes amis!'* and in France they were saying 'Yankee, go home.' Ike gave 'em some birds out of the boneyard and told them to go fuck themselves."

I have never admired obscenities in public. Coldly, I excuse myself and head for the lobby. In my mind, as I stroll through the tourists, through a whole busload of Japanese expectantly unslinging their Nikons, I see, in slow motion, a funereal, three-ship echelon on initial approach. They smoke in, growing in size and majesty as they approach and at standard interval, pitch out—all in absolute silence. No rustling of the air overhead, no calls on the speaker. *Who?* I can't stand it. I pick up a phone on the counter.

"I want to call my base," I tell the girl behind the counter. Girl? She is my age, and she gives me the eye, but she's nice about it. While I wait, I ask if she knew the admiral.

"Sure. Here," she says, and takes the phone to put the call through. No more eye, just friendship.

"Who?" I ask the captain on the command post. He's a sharp kid, so I won't have to compromise security.

"Nobody from here, Colonel." Ah, thank God. I'm released, I float.

"Thanks, Norm. You have my address here?"

"Yes, sir. Hey, Colonel, *relax,* okay? Forget this place. Go get laid."

I walk until I'm exhausted, completely beyond town, out past the embassies, then catch a cab to the Oriental Hotel for dinner and the floor show of Thai dancers. Most are just children, twenty-year-old children; tiny, full of joy.

The three days drift by, each a whole week of rest. I sleep late, buy silk at Thompson's for Jenny and my mother, inquire about rubies at Alex and Company. These must be famous stores because they are hard to find, and quite small.

A teenaged Thai girl, slender and deft, pours out an envelope of rubies, weighs a few on tiny scales. "Color is more important than size," she whispers, looking at them. Her jet-black hair, clean and tapered, hangs forward, even with her chin, and shades her face. She is *not* teenaged, I realize.

"All of the national rubies have flaws, you know." When she raises those liquid eyes, I quit listening. My mind has to replay her words, and then I am almost too stunned to absorb them.

"But that's not important?"

She shrugs, smiles briefly, pushes her hair back. "Yes," she murmurs, "but, unless you want to pay a thousand dollars, it's not important."

I walk. I have sworn off cigarettes but have no pipe-cleaners. The clerk holds up a pack. "Two *baht.*"

About ten cents. I nod and he extracts a single cleaner, bows a little. What the hell, I buy a half dozen.

Cocktails before dinner. The pianist is American—British?—tall and dignified in a business suit. Away from the piano, he could be mistaken for one of the guests. He returns effusive greetings with a warm nod, a trace of a smile. It is almost startling to see him enter the dining room like some ambassador, then walk to the grand piano. With good wide chords, he plays Lerner and Loewe, Richard Rodgers, once a little Bach, almost as a joke, for the little German lady who nods dreamily. Poker-faced, he splashes out old favorites full of such joy and rhythm that the couples can't resist dancing. Their food grows cold. Every twenty minutes, he stands, smiles his gentle smile and hurries away. He seems without vanity, a sober professional who would perform in exactly the same manner if there were only one uninterested customer. Does he ever go home to America—or Britain? He *is* English-speaking, isn't he? Suddenly, I'm not sure. I watch him say something to a waitress. She answers, with a paralyzing smile and a toss of her hair, in her own language. He pats her arm, nods, and walks on.

Beyond the bridge players, beyond the Pan Am crew, past the CIA pilot, I notice an unsettling scene. Within fifty yards of our lounges, Thai laborers are building a tunnel to connect a new wing with the kitchen. I rise on one elbow to see them wrapped in filthy cloth against the afternoon sun. There are no backhoes, no hard hats. They have probably been there since dawn, swinging picks ceaselessly. As I watch, one straightens painfully and I see that it's a girl. She is looking right at me.

What must she think of us foreigners paying absurd prices to lie in the sun? Without releasing me from her dark eyes, she adjusts her dusty hood and settles the cardboard shield about her crown to a more comfortable position. I lower my beer to the tiles and almost rise. Someone should lead her up out of that trench, wash her, dress her, educate her, then lead her to this pool. Americans are so naive. We are all Pygmalions. Until it begins to hurt our standard of living. The labels in our clothing now read Taiwan and Korea. Our trucks are Japanese, our stereos and cameras. The Germans still smile at us, but it is a superior smile.

She lifts one sleeve and brushes her lovely cheek with it, still looking at me but without a challenge in her eyes. She isn't that much older than Becky . . . what is she—twelve, fourteen? No, she has breasts. But her face is that innocent. What, I wonder, during this frank exchange of stares, does she think of her life, leaning there on her pick, of the beauty of this hotel, of the privileged, bikinied stewardesses?

The sun settles behind the roof tiles, and the shadow of the western wing advances quickly. We swing our lounges around to catch this last glow and settle back again. I listen for their voices; they are becoming audible. Their picks chunk less rhythmically into the earth, and I open my eyes when I hear a *mama-san* (our absurd Japanese pidgin for the matriarch) chatter at a teenaged boy. *Dig*, she must be saying. He grins and pitches a clod of dirt at her. The other workers laugh. They realize that they have caught our eye, and some of them like the attention. The men seem to gain strength. Lighting cigarettes, they look around, briefly at us, then gesture at their work. It is noticeably cooler now. The women who have been carrying dirt in baskets and dumping it onto ground-cloths pause to shake their clothing and nod good-humoredly, but their gaze never seems to include us.

"Look at that face," a woman lying nearby murmurs to her husband. They are British; I have heard them pronounce "not" as "naught."

"Yes," he breathes, and quickly pulls a camera from their beachbag. "I must have that." He rises, walks to the edge of the pit, and consults his light meter. Their faces turn away.

"I say there," he calls and raises his camera. "Come now, don't be shy." He frets, murmurs encouragingly, finally shouts.

The noise draws the Thai foreman, who bows to the Englishman. "Yes, sahr?"

"That girl. I want her picture." He points her out. It's the girl who had looked at me. Uncertainly, the foreman approaches her. He twists his vertical palm around, says something, smiles. She shakes her head. He frowns and mutters something. Slowly, reluctantly, she turns and lifts those luminous eyes.

"Think you," the Britisher nods, and resnaps his camera case. He waves to the foreman, who bows, and strides back. Sadly, the girl hangs her head. She whips away from the consoling *mama-san*.

In the dusk they leave the pit, walk wearily to the small pond on the hotel grounds and begin unwrapping. It is a natural pond and possibly the home of snakes. Most of the hotel guests have gone indoors. Finally, only the Air America—CIA—pilot and I remain to watch. The laborers bathe, the men in shorts, the women still chastely wearing a wrap of some sort. Smiling, inhaling against the chill of the water, they ease into the pond. Now only their heads show. In the gloom they could be us in our pool.

The Air America pilot sighs, looks at me, and shakes his head. I nod. It's coming. A cold breeze sends us indoors.

It is a withdrawal, a disengagement that begins at the pool, a gathering up of towels and lotion, of a paperback I'll never finish, of the Barling pipe I bought in Prestwick twelve years ago. A last look around at the people, who seem familiar now. Where will they be next week? At another pool somewhere, I suppose. But, wherever they go, they won't likely find another hotel this perfect. I pause to take a last, long look at it.

It's like a quick, God-sent sketch that can never be exactly duplicated. And yet it must have been. Somewhere there has to be a filing cabinet brimming with blueprints, different elevations and perspectives, alternative sketches, financial estimates. The architect would smile at my naiveté; like the pianist, he is a professional artist. It's a living, he would probably say, and shrug.

I catch a taxi to Bangkok International, board the C-130, where a jet engine is lashed down between the rows of bucket seats along the sides, and sit there in the whistling drone for half an hour.

My other world, equally unreal, is waiting. Laden, I climb that yellow, metal ladder again. It seems that I go from solitude to solitude. The crew chief will see it in my eyes. He will stand on the ladder until all my straps are cinched tight, then nod and descend. I am already there, I realize. The actual ladder is lifted away from the canopy rail. I stare at my checklist under my flashlight, but I can't seem to concentrate. My hands are a page ahead. Someday they are going to forget something and blow the tail right off this big mother.

It's all so strange, as eerie as the smoke of the starter cartridge enveloping me. For a time, all I can see are the soft, red instruments, and the amber illuminated words of the caution panel. Some birds, they say, even have a sexy woman's taped voice soothingly mentioning that the aircraft is on fire or out of oil pressure. I wouldn't leave without her. Dreamlike, this smoke. The cockpit becomes a little balcony, footlighted in the fog. My helmet earphones crowd busy voices at me: "Killer, check in." Click, click. "Killer Two . . . Three . . . Four . . . Spare." "Killer Leader. Let's go Channel Two." Below, his earphones and boom mike plugged into my fuselage, the chief is asking me something. He wants me to extend the ram air turbine—the RAT. He wants me to cycle the refueling probe out and in, the speed brakes. I lag in confusion. Most of me is still back there by the pool.

20

THAILAND

I HAVE BEEN here eight months, seen a whole generation of faces pass. Of the original group, only I and the grunts—the other grunts—remain, and we drink too much. It's becoming harder to distinguish the Gentlemen's Flying Club from a bunch of drunks. Last night one of the new jocks called the wrong grunt a grunt and got dumped on his ass. But he was too drunk to visualize round two, so I had to ease him out of there and put him to bed. Mother Copley, Scooter calls me.

"Wasn't I always?" I ask him.

Scooter is a veteran now—strong, usually tired, capable of leading all but the most important strikes, but flying too seldom to seek that brief glory. I have sixty missions, he forty. Not that it matters. Lately we've been fragged for a lot of Laos stuff, so we fill in there when needed. Counters, smounters, Scooter says airily. He seems content, I think; and then one day (after he'd pinned on his major's leaves and, wearing his bush hat jammed down over his ears, rung the ship's bell for having entered the bar covered), he tells me that he'd like to become a squadron Operations officer.

"No way, babe," I tell him.

"You promised, Mother John."

Yeah. Maybe I did. God knows he's earned it after twelve years in fighters. I talk it over with the Old Man—the *new* Old Man—and one day when the Ops slot opens in the 33rd, Scooter cleans out his desk, winks, is gone. Our idiot major looks askance at me with his brown monkey eyes until I tell him to snag a jock out of the next inbound group.

"Okay," he nods, and lights his dead cigar with new authority. "Okay." He runs his short finger down the list. I don't have time to worry about it. Tomorrow I brief the vice chief of staff who is reputedly a nice guy, and a senator who is a sonovabitch. Goddamned cannibal who's always after headlines, the Old Man says.

"Ya see this guy here?" Einstein says, tapping the list and spilling cigar ashes all over it.

"Almost."

"If he was at Chanute, we used to bowl on the same team. Good, too." He gives me his Cheetah smile.

"That's fine," I tell him. "Just what we need."

Ah, God, Roscoe's in the Old Man's plush chair, and the general is coming. Long ago I learned not to try to drag Roscoe out of that chair by his collar. He bites. He's really Ray's dog, but Ray's up North somewhere, buried in the ground or buried in a POW camp. And if you tip the chair forward until gravity overcomes the toenails, Roscoe comes up all teeth, so you've still got a problem.

"Sergeant!" I call to the big black projectionist, but he shakes his head.

"With all due respect, Colonel . . ." he begins.

"Then go out on the porch and meow," I order.

"It ain't gonna work," he insists, but, resignedly, goes out there. "Who'd believe this?" he asks an Intelligence sergeant.

"Meow! Meow!" his deep Southern voice calls.

"Goddamned *lion* out there, Roscoe!" I tell him. He lifts his head in disgust, lowers it again. There's only a minute—I hear them in Intelligence calling Attention—so, violently, I dump him and run for the door, clapping my hands. Helluva way to win a Purple Heart. But he's not chasing me all the way. Instead, he compromises by climbing into the adjacent chair and showing me his teeth. Cautiously, I circle and brush some of the hair out of the plush seat before retreating to the stage and the rostrum.

"Meow! Meow!" the big sergeant calls.

At this moment the general enters, leading two three-stars and several lesser luminaries.

"Tenchut!" I yell. Roscoe answers with a deep growl, and the sloppy, giggling Intelligence sergeant begins coming apart.

On the porch, his heart no longer in it, the black sergeant switches desultorily to bird calls, trilling like a bastard. When the Old Man, near the end of the procession, enters, he gives me his most pained what-the-hell-is-going-on look.

"At ease," the general murmurs and, frantically, I jerk my head at the Intelligence sergeant, who finally leans outside and beckons. In comes the smug projectionist, who has proved his point, but who, seeing all these stars, pales. We exchange tragic glances, and he tiptoes in long strides to his machine.

How can I warn the general? Seeing Roscoe, the Old Man gives me a quick glance and then foolishly steers the dreamy vice chief right to the plush chair within six inches of those teeth.

"This is Roscoe, our mascot, General," The Old Man explains with false heartiness and looks at me exactly as Roscoe had. "He came down from Japan with the Fifty-third last year. A great morale-builder, but he's been known to bite." He suggests a chair farther away, but the general, who has recently testified on the Hill where everyone bites, nods absently, waves away this lesser threat and slumps into the doghairs.

The lights dim and, not hearing any chewing, I distractedly begin, keying my spiel to thirty-five-millimeter slides and a home movie. But it's not the Blue Plate Special we'll give the Washington silk shoppers next month. I mean, they don't care, those crooks from the Hill. They're just coming over to buy Christmas presents. Once they realize that Thailand is off limits to the press, they mostly lie back and sleep off hangovers. But the vice chief is the guy who really runs the Air Force, so I throw in some fairly controversial stuff, stuff I'd want to know if I had his job. I even take a crack at Seventh, well aware that one of those three-stars out there commands Seventh, and I hear the Old Man loudly clearing his throat. By golly, he really has Roscoe's expression now—that drawn grin warning of a lunge—and he keeps crossing and uncrossing his legs. Jesus, I'm beginning to sound like old Hopwell, who must be in a loony bin by now.

During a bright slide, however, I see that the general, slouched a little, long legs crossed, is scratching Roscoe's head, now in his lap.

Back in the hooch that evening as, sipping gin, I recover from having briefed the bristly senator—a little battle damage after that one, I'm afraid, judging from the Old Man's final, dismal expression—I thumb through an old issue of the magazine *Air Force* and see a snapshot. "Can you identify this officer?" the caption reads. A young pilot is sitting in the cockpit of a shark-faced P-40 and holding a black mongrel puppy. I recognize the lean face immediately, the calm eyes, and show it to the Old Man at dinner.

"Yeah." He takes the snapshot and closely examines it. He nods. "Well, we lucked out, didn't we, Copley?"

I get his implication. That wasn't a very professional performance. Yeah, we did. But the general lucked out, too. As a rule, Roscoe bites. Like that vicious old senator.

Two days later I discover that my luck is holding. I take out a bridge, a brand-new thousand-foot-long bridge. I mean, it wasn't the Golden Gate or anything, but it was loaded with big Russian trucks every night, so its loss will hurt them.

I can't believe it. It just shows what a series of canceling errors can do for you when your luck is running. I looked back and watched those bombs walk right down the centerline, collapsing all three spans.

"Shit-hot!" everyone yells. "Mr. Magoo *did* it!"

A nice warm feeling, that. Most days I miss all to hell, rusty as I am. I can't get this old hog to turn straight into the chute, especially when I'm carrying a centerline tank. It's like one of those long, tourist surfboards then. But this time I had the inboards and the seven-fifties, and she just greased right into the old forty-five-degree chute.

Nevertheless, my bombing isn't exactly computerlike. I was steep, but slow today. Sometimes I'm steep but fast, or shallow and slow, and then all I can do is fake it with body English at the last second, jerking or pulling the stick to sling the bombs in the right direction. Usually I know before I depress the pickle button. Maybe I know when I release brakes on takeoff. What hurts is when my impacts aren't even close, when I see geysers of earth or water way out in left field. That's when all the North Vietnamese applaud—all those who weren't in left field. Big toothy grins. "Yeah, yeah," they probably say knowingly and nod, "Wing wienie."

Anyhow, it's a new experience for me to taxi in and see all these jocks with their thumbs up. Aw, hell, here comes Scooter with something gold hung on a chain like those the sommeliers wear. What's he got? Yeah, it's a real wienie painted gold. Better than an Air Medal, I think . . . until it ripens.

The C-130's props haven't been still a second before he is out on the PSP, arms akimbo, looking around. He's sharp, I can tell already; he's wearing a flying suit to save his uniform, and he's also wearing his billed garrison hat with all the farts and darts. I packed mine instead, and now it looks like a sailor hat. He's smart but, nevertheless, so obviously new in that getup—we're in silver-tans and overseas caps—that he's behaving rather stiffly. He's cordial enough when he returns our salutes and shakes hands, but his eyes roam around as though he's expecting the king and queen or somebody. A little guy who has compensated, he's five-eight at the most but with big shoulders and strong hands. He walks like a boxer entering a tough bar.

I don't know much about him, but some of the jocks whistle when I mention his name. "Hey, *shit-hot*," they say to each other. He's especially famous with the guys who flew F-104s at George. Once he flew one that Lockheed had hopped up to a new world's altitude record and then had tumbled, flamed out, back through a hundred thousand feet. He had been their DO at George.

While they unload his baggage, he doesn't look at us much. Occasionally, he removes his hat to wipe his brow, and I see that, despite that young boxer's face, his crew-cut is almost gray. Formalities over, he heads for the staff car with the Old Man while I follow in his jeep, Hopwell's special version with softer seats and a UHF radio.

We pull up beside his trailer, and he comes back to collect his bags. I notice that he rolls his shoulders as he walks, that his head is down and that he has an unlit cigar centered in his mouth. I pick up a bag and carry it into the trailer. That embarrasses him. Then I show him his jeep—a little pointless because DIRECTOR OF OPERATIONS is painted just below the windshield—salute and walk away.

The next morning he beats me to work.

"I wanted to catch some mission briefings," he explains. "You know."

He's shy, I realize, probably the first shy hero I ever met. I'm shy, too, they tell me, so we'll probably never get acquainted. I show him around, introduce him to everyone in Ops and Intelligence. In the Command Post he lingers before the grease-penciled names, glowing in color on the backlighted Plexiglas. I think I know why: he needs a familiar face to introduce him *properly* to us. His eyes drift down the schedule, his jaw muscles flicker. Seeing him now, I doubt that we'll ever become close.

He doesn't ask questions; he just watches. He doesn't want to become beholden to anyone. His desk has a view. Mine is across the office. I'm Deputy Dog theoretically but, actually, I still run TOC, too, so I'm in and out.

I wish I had the guts to fire our bowling champion. He should be down in the motor pool. Well, he *should* be retired. Every time I hear him breaking in our new major, I tell him that I've got more important work for him. I need a message drafted, I say, and I would like him to compose it in privacy and take plenty of time.

"It's secret?" he asks, his eyes shining.

"Yes," I whisper. "I want *your* thoughts on this. *You're* the only other old-timer here, understand?"

"But I don't know anything about tactics." The enormity of it is taking him down.

"There are the manuals. When you've finished, bring it to me."

I reenter our office. Our new DO is spinning his swivel chair to accommodate his shorter height.

"Was your last DO a gorilla?" he asks, trying the new height. He slaps his overseas cap on the desk, props up his feet. "How long you been here, Copley?"

"Eight months, sir."

"What's your background?"

Here we go again, I think. I tell him. He simply nods and starts patting his pockets. I doubt that he's ever heard of CINCPAC. All he knows is fighters. I could have told him I'd been a brain surgeon at Walter Reed, and he'd have just nodded. He can't find his lighter, so he starts opening and closing drawers, the cigar dead center. I pitch him my lighter, the first of a thousand pitches.

"Say," he says, after he's filled the room with smoke. "I got a problem. One of my old guys is going home, and he's got a piss-poor assignment. He wants me to get it changed. How do we go about that?"

They haven't wasted any time. One night at the bar and he's already enmeshed.

"I see. Well, it's been done, Colonel." I consider alternatives, but they're too slow. Still, I don't want the Old Man to start trading favors with him right off the bat.

"Can *I* call anyone?"

"Sure. If you know someone at Clark or PACAF."

He doesn't. I can see that.

"Y'see," he explains, "this guy's just a major, and they're trying to send him to the goddamn Pentagon. You know how it is," he adds, pitching my lighter back. "The guys are all watching to see how I settle in as DO, whether I can handle their problems."

I phone the Wing Exec. We've been pretty close. Two old grunts. He says he'll slip one more name on the Old Man's list of "inappropriate assignments" going back to Randolph. No sweat.

"Thanks, John," the colonel nods, and relaxes, his feet up again, his hands clasped behind his head.

"It may not work, sir."

"Oh, bullshit," he says, grinning.

The weeks pass with neither of us taking a day off. Einstein is on his fourth draft, but I can't find him a job anywhere. Big missions are briefed, a few are flown. November is here, and the monsoon winds have shifted. Here we're having tourist weather; across the mountains in North Vietnam it's clobbered in most of the time. All that Maritime Tropical Air comes in off the Gulf of Tonkin, hits the upslope, and there go the counters until March or April. For the past three days weather has diverted everyone to Laos. The jocks try to talk the Forward Air Controllers into letting them look for holes in the undercast over in the panhandle. A counter is a counter.

274

But the big missions are still fragged and briefed, as always. Who knows when, with little warning, the Red River Delta will open up for a couple of hours? Meanwhile, of course, the truck convoys are running south without interruption. Sometimes they duck out into Laos when the fords in the panhandle get too deep, and then there's a turkey shoot. *I* even got a few trucks with the cannon as they snaked through Mugia Pass the other day. But they've got thousands of them. And, really, it makes no sense to risk losing a two-million bird to nail a few trucks.

I used to say that it would all be over by now if they had let the Navy mine Haiphong last spring, take out those two rail lines coming down from China, and let us bomb every airfield and POL storage area we saw. But now I'm not sure. Those ARVN guys down south can't seem to get it all together, as the South Koreans finally did in the Fifties. And, of course, we've got to have a little public support back home. I realize that we aren't as important as the big bowl games or, say, the Green Bay Packers; but if you're going to put your ass on the line for somebody, it's important that that somebody notices. All I can say now is that if I were President Johnson, I don't know what I'd do. And obviously, he doesn't either.

It's 2200, and there's been a big last-minute change in the targeting. Seventh is on the scrambler speaking pig latin or something. All I can make out is that the new frag is coming on the teletypes.

"For afternoon strikes?" I ask.

"Negative. Same TOTs."

"It's too late," I tell them. "The jocks need some sleep, and I'm not waking them before zero-two-hundred. Slip your Times on Targets, and we'll do it. Otherwise, forget it."

"*Who is this?*" a hard voice asks.

I tell him. I should have said, "Marshal Foch." Aw, Jesus, now I'm off to join Colonel Hopwell in the loony bin.

"Give me the phone," the colonel says from behind me.

"No, sir. Let me tell 'em. I'm expendable."

"Give me the fucking phone, John."

He takes it. "Who is *who?*" he asks belligerently. "*What?* Aw, c'mon, who is this? Jack? Is that you, you fuckin' bomber pilot? Yeah, yeah." He grins. "How ya doing, Jackson? Okay. Yeah. She's fine." (I am omitting the necessary scrambler pauses here.) "Now what's this going against Air Force Regs? . . . Yeah, *violating crew rest* and all that. . . ."

He shuffles around, winks at me. His cigar has gone out, so I hand him my lighter. We're using about a can of lighter fluid a day.

"Yeah, yeah, I know. I *heard* there's a war on," he says when it's his turn, "how'd you pansies find out?" He laughs.

He's tired though. He hangs onto the phone and gesticulates but wearily with his unseen cigar. He's been up since 0200. I know, because so have I, and my legs quit about an hour ago.

He hangs up. "They're gonna slip 'em," he tells me. "They just got carried away. Shit, it's not gonna break up anyhow, is it, Sarge?"

"No way, sir." By now the new sergeant knows the patterns. "Look at that flow." He taps his charts. "And *this* new trough."

The colonel finds his cap with the corroded eagle on it and pats it into place, also dead center and precariously forward. I've always said that the main thing is to get it well forward, not like the Legionnaires wear them. "You on the schedule?" he asks me, then swings around to check the board.

"Spare," I tell him.

"Aw, it's not going. Come on over to the trailer and I'll buy you a drink."

He's right, fortunately, because I'm reeling when I leave. He'd shown me snapshots of his wife—predictably a little blonde with high boobs and a cute rump, standing by their Cadillac convertible. "It's baby-blue," he says with satisfaction. His kids sun-grin at the camera. They're just later printings of their parents. "She's at UCLA," he says, "and I sent *his* ass to the Academy."

He wears no ring. I can't tell.

"Are you an Academy man, sir?"

He bursts out laughing. "Who, *me?* Shit naw, I busted outa reform school."

I tell him about my Coast Artillery training, and we end up hanging onto each other, laughing so hard that our cigars keep falling. "Aw, Christ," he says weakly, "how do they expect *us* sorry bastards to run their fucking war?"

Christmas is coming, and so is Jayne Mansfield, a sign at the club says. "She's my mother's age," a lieutenant shrugs.

"Yeah?" a major answers. "In that case, don't look. Is your mother forty-plus here?"

I no longer have time to catch mission briefings, much less fly. There's always some crisis and if not a crisis, then a VIP to brief. "One of you," the Old Man tells the colonel and me, "will brief all senators and congressmen." He may as well have said that *I* would. Every other day, the DO is airborne, or if not airborne, attending mission briefings and debriefings. He has no time for these boondogglers from Washington, these silk-and-ruby shoppers.

He's too much, this guy. Beats me how he conned everyone into assigning him here. He arrived without ever having flown the F-105. In fact, I can't visualize him sitting still for formal instruction in *any* bird. I imagine he's skimmed the Dash-Ones and read, at the least, the bold-faced type. If you've flown as many fighters as he has, you become like a parking lot attendant sitting in a new car. "This thing *can't* be that different," they must say to themselves.

But it's amusing to watch him listening to transmissions when a bird malfunctions. He stands there by the radio and frowns while he shifts his

276

cigar around. In Mobile or the tower is some old head giving the jock the standard emergency procedures.

"Shut down your ATM, Jaguar Three."

Inhaling, puzzled, the colonel slides his cap to the back of his head and holds his hand out. I hand him my lighter. For Christmas I'm going to give him a sackful of zippos.

"What's the ATM have to do with it?" he asks.

The Command Post captain and I exchange glances. I explain it as briefly as I can, and the colonel frowns considering it, nods and files it away. He's simply not a reader, and his pace allows no time for formal instruction. Well, I did see him reading an article by Arnold Palmer.

After a few missions, his name appears in a Pack VI gaggle, and I try to talk him out of it. Our wing has always tried to keep full bulls out of Six. To date, the enemy hasn't captured one, and God help the one they capture. I remind him of that, but it's like talking to Roscoe.

The target is an important bridge, concrete and steel, just northeast of Hanoi. And our Weather sergeant decides that this one might go. I erase the colonel's name and write my own there, but he comes in later, sees the change, and restores his name. "Keep him outa here," he instructs the captain.

If he's nervous, he doesn't show it. It's an afternoon strike—that's the only time the weather's good at all now—but he makes the 0300 briefing as usual, then goes back to bed for an hour or so. At 0830, a little red-eyed, he calls in all four squadron commanders and raises hell about the condition of the airmen's barracks. They are the Old Man's primary concern now because they are the Alligator's primary concern. The Alligator is the commander of the Thirteenth Air Force, and we come under him for everything except combat operations. With perspicacity, the colonel remarked that the Alligator doesn't like being upstaged by the war. So everyone's rendering to Caesar.

When the squadron commanders have settled back with their coffee, the colonel says, "Okay, gentlemen, you can probably guess the subject . . ."

Foley interrupts him with some droll remark anticipating the subject of the airmen's barracks.

"Right," the colonel nods. "And I—"

Foley interrupts him again and isn't smart enough to notice the colonel's eyes.

"Okay, Foley," he says quietly. "I'll let you call your meeting sometime. This one's mine." Foley is an ex-BMOC, you can tell, and still very much the glib operator who tries to deflect everything with ridicule. The colonel had made the mistake of letting Foley get too close to him that first week.

"Now, then, *listen,* you clowns. The Old Man has been talking barracks to me ever since I got off that courier the first day two months ago. He's on my ass constantly, and I am getting sick of hearing about the goddamn barracks. Now, I want you guys to ground yourselves until your barracks can pass inspection. Every morning at ten hundred, I'm going to begin inspecting barracks, and I want you to accompany me as I go through your area, and—"

"Colonel," Foley begins in his cajoling manner.

"Goddammit, Foley, I *told* you not to interrupt me. *If you say one . . . more . . . word . . .*" His fist is back, and he's half out of his chair.

Gradually he subsides and begins pawing through his desk. I pitch him my lighter.

"Now then," he says calmly, "if you have a piss-poor first sergeant, *fire* the sonovabitch. Don't tell me your troubles. I've heard all I'm gonna hear about those barracks, understand? If you can't handle such a *simple* goddamn problem, I'll get me some squadron commanders who can. Questions?"

Silence.

"Comments? Foley?"

They salute and, in shocked silence, file out.

He sits back, props up his feet. Finally, I look up from the message I have been supposedly drafting and, gradually, his eyes settle on mine. I grin. He grins back, looks at his watch, slams drawers awhile, then rocks to his feet and stretches. "I guess I'm supposed to be drawing lines on a map to somewhere."

Out he goes, striding head down with his muscle-bound boxer's walk, then leans back in to pitch me my lighter. Great eyes when they smile.

Later I see him in debriefing, one foot on a table, his cigar waving around in some formation while he explains what they did wrong. Not much, he concedes, but bad enough to make it rough on old Blue Four back there. He has revived squadron formation attacks. We have a new ECM gadget which makes it possible. It turns their scopes to snow, they say.

"Goddamn Chinese fire drill when we rolled in," he says, "Smitty, you were way out too far to the right with your guys."

He has the cigar dead center again, bobbing it up and down as he talks. His gray eyes are steady, but benevolently so, on Smitty's. His face still bears mask prints, his short hair is wild.

"Murph," he continues, "I thought you'd never get your flight in position. Use your 'burners if you have to, okay?"

Murphy shrugs, slouches in his chair. He's not going to give in. Yes, he is; he has just traded looks with the colonel.

"Okay?"

Murphy nods, "Yes, sir."

Well, they have a leader now, a real DO. They love him already, especially at the end, when he admits, "Shit, I didn't see *anything*—no flak, no MIGs, nothing, I was just hanging on."

Once, much later, after a hassle with his wingman in the local area, he

says, "Where'd you go, for chrissake? I thought you'd crashed or landed or something."

"Right at your six o'clock, Colonel," the wingman laughs.

"Well," the colonel says, winking at me, "I *told* you to turn ninety degrees, you bastard. You turned about thirty, then reversed while I was still turning gently away. Hell, you never really broke formation."

"Colonel!" the lieutenant says.

"Bullshit, I *saw* you."

"Well, I didn't want to get too far away, or you'd never see me again without your glasses."

"Yeah, you wart."

"I'll say one thing though, Colonel: you are smooth. I had absolutely no trouble staying on your tail."

The colonel starts after him, grinning.

"Even updated my Doppler, sir."

The colonel laughs and throws his lit cigar at him.

While we are laughing, the door to TOC opens, and one of our sergeants sticks his head inside. "Red Cross on the phone, Colonel Copley," he tells me.

21

HAWAII

HE IS DEAD; I am next. Self-pity instead of real compassion, the dumb cry of the heart. I stride the shady sidewalks of Hickam. Jets have provided me with this time-machine miracle: from Bangkok to Indiana and halfway back in less than five days.

A December day on Oahu, seventy degrees and clear, with the dry, steady Trades smelling of plumeria. Signer Boulevard, our old street, followed all the way, leads back to the Officers' Club and the Visiting Officers' Quarters. A nostalgic little round robin to remove the stiffness in my muscles, the weariness in my bones, to help reset my internal clock. Yesterday, in Indiana, it was snowing. Here men wearing shorts push mowers over the lawns bounding their low-eaved, pastel quarters. We nod to each other and smile. My mind has not quite caught up. Part of me is still in the Greyhound station in my hometown.

"Well, Johnny," my sister had said when we were finally alone, "we'll look after Mom while you're overseas; but, well—we've always put it on the line with each other—she's your mother, too." Momentarily, she had dared lift her eyes to mine, but couldn't sustain the firmness that her husband had demanded. The words are not hers, but his.

"Sis," I began, "you know I'll help in any way I can, but she can't move around the world with us at her age."

"I couldn't agree more. In fact, she's told me she's not going anywhere."

"Which leaves *me* where?"

"In Indiana," she said. "Right here. At home."

"Doing what?"

"Whatever you like, Johnny. No one wants to run your life."

"Sis, I left here in nineteen forty-two, twenty-four years ago. The Air Force is my home."

"Maybe it's time you got out of the Army, John. I mean, we admire you for having done your patriotic duty overseas and all that, but we've all got problems. Jim isn't well, and neither am I. The plant could close tomorrow. Jim never knows when he goes to work."

There's the parade ground with the memorial tower, actually a disguised water tank, at one end. On either side of the mall the houses are larger. Generals' row faces the quarters of senior NCOs. Old Army. Most of these families have known each other for a quarter century, professionally, at least. At work, the men know who can be trusted with responsibility and who can't. They protect each other. In the commissary or BX, their wives occasionally gush at each other and, in a few cases, the warmth is sincere. Many have done volunteer work side by side, but, socially, the hierarchy—some say oligarchy—is carefully observed. In dress, in general grooming, in ease of manner, the distinctions are apparent. The service did not create these distinctions; they began at birth, or at least before high school. The service simply confirmed them. Their kids grew up together, are perhaps still friends, but the kids are grown and gone now. So there are few paths across the grass of the parade ground.

There's the dispensary with its cool airiness where, almost exactly twenty-five years ago, privately owned automobiles brought the wounded and burned. I imagine that some of those old Army wives could tell me all about it, about the strafing Zeroes just above the monkey pod trees, about the concussions and flames along the ramp, about the bomb that hit the mess hall during breakfast. As a reminder, pockmarked concrete marring PACAF Headquarters has been preserved.

Just beyond the chapel, adjacent to the ball field, is our "tenement." Several of the cars parked in front are familiar. Has it been only eighteen months?

I have just realized that an automobile has been pacing me. Turning, I see a familiar Cadillac and a face I love. She leans across to open the passenger door. "Hey, GI, you want Kamikaze Taxi?"

I slide in and buss her cheek. "GI, you want go RTO catch train?" she asks.

"Okay."

"Ah, so," she hisses, guns the engine and wildly saws the wheel back and forth. "No sweat, GI." Slowing again, she grimaces to show me all her teeth. "I speak werra good Engrish, you see."

"Yes, you do."

"You want *jo-san,* bath, whiskey?"

"Yes."

Betty is wearing white shorts, white boat shoes, and a cotton blouse the green of her eyes. Saltwater tan. Sunglasses perched in her hair, a little gray now. "So what are you doing here, sweet? Is the war over or something?"

"Emergency leave. Dad died four days ago."

"Aw, gee." She bites her lip. "I'm so sorry. Did you get there in time?"

"Almost."

She winces, sighs. "Jenny and the kids okay?"

"I assume so. They were with her parents in Florida. Her folks are thinking of retiring there. House-hunting, I guess. We couldn't contact them."

"What a shame!"

"I'm just as glad they missed it."

In silence we approach the low club with its palms and satellite buildings. Teenagers come out of the snack bar licking ice-cream cones. The air seems golden. Betty turns right and continues past the pool. Immediately beyond the pool is the channel into Pearl Harbor. Occasionally, sunbathers lying beside the pool are startled by the shadow of a flight deck almost overhanging the pool. At that close range, a great carrier gliding by so silently that you can hear voices from her decks is overwhelming. On the opposite side of the channel, attached to a chain-anchor fence along the Navy's housing area, are signs warning of sharks.

Betty turns into their driveway, and expertly swings the big car into its stall behind their impressively large quarters. As I recall, a two-star was once billeted here.

"Where's your footman?"

"Well, let's keep things in perspective: nothing is too good for Eric, right?"

"You are."

She shrugs. "One judges a person by the company she keeps. And, to be fair, he knows how to cope, and that's important, they tell me." She shrugs.

"Where is Eric, by the way?"

"Eric who?" she asks, and opens her massive Cadillac door. "Japan. Somewhere, escorting a herd of fact-finders. Come on in. I'll show you my etchings and so forth." She tugs on the salt-corroded frame of a sliding door leading in from the *lanai.* "Were you here the night we had the *tiki*-torch fight? Eric was appalled. Everybody else had a ball, especially that submariner friend of yours from the Sub Base. He was up in that palm tree screaming something about the Silent Service and waving one of these torches."

"Bubbles?"

"No."

"Princeton Pete?"

"No. Are they all crazy?"

The door finally tilts and slides open. Despite all the art treasures hanging on the wall, it wasn't locked. "When he's home, I lock all the doors religiously. He wants to loan all these to a gallery, purely for safekeeping. But I'd miss them. There's the bar. Build me a drink. Why didn't you phone me, you fink?"

"Just got here at noon."

"Okay, look at Eric's art bargains while I take a shower. I'm covered with salt like what's-her-name in the Bible. You know the Mifflins next door?"

"No, I don't know many generals."

"Well, he's got this dumb yawl that thinks it's a submarine. He stands there at the wheel with just his chest above water yelling commands while everyone else swims around pulling on ropes and smiling. When he's not doing that, he's out jogging. A great intellect."

"Ice in the kitchen?" I call toward the bathroom.

"Wait a minute. Don't go in there or you'll never be seen again. The roaches will eat you." She has only a beach towel wrapped around her and still walks with the easy gait of a teenager. "I'll admit it: I'm sloppy about some things. My *jo-san* comes tomorrow to rake out the place. Hey, nothing with rum, okay? Stuff splits your skull like an axe."

She hands me a full ice tray, pecks my shoulder, and hurries back into the bathroom. She shouts something at me above the shower. I should get out of here, but I don't.

Five minutes later, she emerges, toweling her hair, stoops to the record cabinet, hands me a record, then hurries into the bedroom. Mancini. Four expensive speakers hold me in a sort of cocoon of strings. I find a jar of olives and deliberately mix killer martinis. Voluntary consent of the will, and all that. Out of the bedroom she comes finally, sleek-haired as an otter but in no other respect like one except for fluid movement. She is wearing a lime-green muumuu, so her cat eyes are especially stunning. Having adjusted the volume so that I can barely hear it, she settles back on the couch and draws her bare feet beneath her. She pats the adjacent cushion. As a final gesture, for the record, I point to the flagstone *lanai* with its unlit *tiki* torches. She shakes her head. Wearily, I settle beside her.

"Jet lag?" she asks.

A new term to me. I figure it out, nod.

"How old was he?"

"Seventy. Three score and ten. Cancer."

"Umm. Well, there's really no good time for it, is there? My dad was only thirty-two, I was ten. But, with a male, it's the father's death, isn't it? With us, it's the mother's. I dread it."

"Your mother is still holding up?"

She shrugs. "She walks, she talks, she smokes cigarettes. I guess you get used to being half alive."

"Thirty-two. Lord, that's young." I am beginning to see her differently. "What killed him?"

She shakes her head, shrugs, crushes her cigarette. "Congenital disappointment? God, I don't know." She swings those cat eyes on me, lowers them, reaches over to tug on my overlapped waistband. "Hey, you really did get your ass shot off, didn't you?"

"Scared off. And I'm not through yet. Two more months."

"I thought you were fighting natives with spears. That's the way it looks on TV, burning huts and everything."

"Maybe there are two wars, I don't know. Up north it's different." I try to explain, but it's too far away.

"Sounds like the first team," she says finally. "What say we sell these paintings and bug out to Canada? It's all the rage."

"Well, I would except that I've accrued sixty days of leave."

"With pay, you mean. Right. I'd want to eat right along."

"Eric still talking about getting checked out in fighters?"

"Not since the shooting started. He's trying to get back to Washington. Says that's where the action is." We both laugh. "To make general, he says, you must have a political sponsor. Right? No? Well, it helps, you'll admit that. So Eric wants to become some senator's pet, and he's got his sponsor all picked out. Who's the old guy who serves on all the big committees and thinks he's God? Yeah, agreed, that's half of them. Tommy—next door—says that colonel is the highest grade to which a gentleman may aspire. Had anything to eat today, sweet?"

"An in-flight box lunch on the C-141 this morning."

"Okay, but go easy on that gin. You haven't lost so much weight that I can carry you. How long you gonna be around?"

"Noon tomorrow. I'm booked out on another C-141 nonstop to Clark."

"Well, well," she says, rubbing her hands together. "In that case, come here." She places our drinks on the coffee table. A long, long kiss with our arms tightening around each other. Oh, God, it's been so long. I kiss her ear, the nape of her neck, damp from the shower. Her green cat eyes are flecked with gold. Frowning, they move over my face while, with one long finger, she traces the new lines.

"I changing to Mr. Hyde," I intone. "No more Dr. Jekyrr."

"Ah, so. Well, quit. It's unbecoming." She smells my drink. "This isn't what Fredric March drank. This is real gin, distilled by the queen herself. Well, whatever the reason, give me another kiss before you get any uglier." We kiss again and let our heads roll desperately around each other's. "Hah!" she says. "Now you can't go to the club and play Bingo. I've injected venom. In ten seconds, you will be almost completely paralyzed."

"Almost?"

She smiles. "Meaning not completely."

I sigh and indicate the *lanai*. "Last call."

"My reputation? No sweat, GI. There's no one home on either side of us. Now, time for *jo-san* and bath. Surprise! I not Kamikaze Taxi; I Jo-san Number One!" She leads me into the bedroom and begins unbuttoning my shirt. "Hey, John, relax, okay? Let it happen. See? You're not paralyzed below the waist."

This time I am allowed to make my own decision. There is no child around to save me, and I am sober. She has become serious. Oh, Lord, it has been so long. Her rhythms, so different from Jenny's, are complex. She is catlike in her unpredictability, drifting from moods of arching wildness, while her nails press but never quite tear my skin, to purring docility. Thus, she guides me. Occasionally, she will throw her head back and talk to herself like some jazz pianist. All this excites me so that, even by thinking of the most boring activities that I can summon—quickly, outlining a term paper comes to mind—I doubt that I can last. At some point I simply quit trying. It's that absurd; I'm out of control, gone, pouring my very life into her. It's then that I realize that it's okay; she's there, too. Her body, undulating like that of a wounded snake, stiffens. Her chin, lifting higher and higher, suddenly snaps sideways. We keen together and seem to fall thousands of feet. Intertwined, we sleep.

When we awake, it's almost dark. She curls forward to pull the sheet up to our navels. We tilt our heads to look at each other. If I were more man than clown, I would share Lancelot's shame. Or would that be hypocritical? We are each of us responsible for decisions we have accepted, for becoming soldiers, for loving the wrong person. Well, I love this woman, so I suppose that this coupling was inevitable. Now the consequences. Her eyes search mine. We smile, God help us.

"I'm hungry," she announces.

"We seem to be ruled by animal appetites."

She shrugs. "We're animals. That wasn't our decision."

"In that case, you're a cat."

"What are you?"

"A fink."

"Umm. Well, sure, but who isn't?"

Jenny, I think.

"Persistence pays." Betty nods at the ceiling. "Fourteen years before I got you in bed."

I lay my hand on one of her breasts, let it slide down to her concave stomach. "Or vice versa."

"Whatever. All I know is that we needed that. Now I'm ready to take vows, and so forth. Almost."

I pull her to me. "Not just yet."

"You're bluffing, fella. At our age, we must conserve our energy, right? Later." She laughs. "That's what I tell Eric on those rare occasions when he gets ideas—with me, I mean. I'm sure he sleeps around. There seem to be more protocol duties than there are official visitors, especially at night. I couldn't care less." She strokes my hair and leans on her other elbow so that her right nipple touches me. "Tell me, GI, how do I compare with your other *jo-sans?*"

I shrug, lift a hand and rock it from side to side.

She grins. "Bastard."

"You won't believe this—I wouldn't in your place—but this is my first fall from grace."

"Yeah? Grace who?" She is pleased. "Okay, tell you what: I'll believe you if you believe me. I don't sleep around either. Shake on it."

We shake hands, and a wind chime tinkles. "Oh, oh!" she giggles. "Caught again." She kisses my forehead. "No, I have to love someone before I go to bed with him, and you're it, kid. That's a song title."

"I love you, too, Betty."

"Well, sure. Who wouldn't? I'm irresistible. Except to Eric, thank God."

"Why don't you leave him?"

She scratches an elbow, finally shrugs. "Good question. While I'm still irresistible, huh?" She takes a deep breath. "Well, first, he *is* a good cook. Okay, let go and I'll tell you: he's got all these fabulous paintings, see? Quit pinching, I'll get around to it. Okay, the truth: it would kill my dear old mother. She's—*we're,* I guess, technically—Catholic. Micks are Catholic, right? So there's no such thing as divorce unless you're a very big deal. All marriages are made in heaven, see? Even if the girl is a twenty-year-old college junior blinded by a glamorous Army aviator. I wore his miniature wings on my sweater and made the fraternity pins look silly. The girls in my dorm would faint when he came around. Eric was a little bigger than God there for a while. Mother still ranks him right after the Trinity. So-o, we still play house—but not doctor. When Mom dies, that's it."

"And then?"

"By that time I'll be ninety, so it won't matter." And here she smiles that great smile that first drew me to her. "So-o-o, you've got it made. No sweat. See? I can read your simple mind. You'll still have Jenny and the kids. *And* me, if you like, number one Kamikaze *Jo-san.*"

"You don't know Jenny. She can also read my simple mind."

"And you'd be stupid enough to admit it."

"It won't matter. She'll . . . she knows now."

"Okay, love, but I know women better than you. If she loves you, she won't ask. There's too much at stake. Just don't return beating your breast. In fact, don't mention that you saw me. Tell her that I was still in California with Mother."

My life, it seems, is no longer my own. My soul seems to be darkening. I'll have to confess. But what if she doesn't forgive me? Then the kids will suffer. I can't tell Jenny. Or is that simply rationalization? Suddenly, the idea of returning to combat becomes intolerable; I'll be too vulnerable. Some shield seems to have been removed. Betty's hands burn my flesh. Sensing this, she rolls away and swings her slim legs out of bed, is silhouetted against a dim light like a teenager. She searches for her robe. "Hungry? I'm starving. I really can cook, you know. Unless you'd rather run down to Buzz's or Trader Vic's. Remember that talking myna bird that can mimic the hatcheck girl's sexy voice?"

"Cook."

In the middle of the night, I hear the grim music and cries, face the pulses of light. I yell out, wildly awaken, see that I am naked. Half asleep, Betty pats my thigh, drifts away again. Wise as she is, she cannot imagine what I saw. Determined little soldiers, their pith helmets pushed back, lower their binoculars and yell toward their radar operators. In the vans controlling their SAM, their surface-to-air missiles, a Russian who looks like me paces, checks his consoles, wonders about his dedicated trainees. A sophisticate, he nods and the SAM launchers begin rising. From five points, the points of a star, centered on the vans, missiles part camouflage netting and stand like cobras. From loudspeakers and earphones, men listen for the special calls of their most hated enemy, the Wild Weasels. I see myself flying in that hunter-killer flight and sink back against my pillow as though dying: Major Pierson limp beneath the flags and smoke, Henri Farré's Captain Féquant being lifted from his primitive cockpit.

22

THAILAND

YOU SEE HIM swing down from the cab of a transcontinental diesel, walk into a diner, and settle importantly onto a stool. Everyone knows him. The waitress knows what to bring him and is careful not to slosh his coffee. From all around the diner, other drivers casually gather around him and listen to his assessment of road conditions through the mountains. Perhaps they themselves have just covered the same roads, but they listen respectfully anyway. He has been at it a long time. They watch him stir his coffee, watch his hairy hands trace the curves along the counter, listen to his Southern drawl. Gradually, they modify their accounts of ice and traffic to match his. His eyes insist on it.

But he isn't—in this incarnation, at least—a truck driver. He is a fighter pilot, and we aren't actually in a diner. We're at the bar in the club. Everything else is the same. In flying coveralls, they stand around listening. The waitress is Thai. But the same hairy hands are tracing a route, and occasionally, he looks up from beneath heavy eyebrows at someone.

"Where were you, Watkins?" he asks. "You said you were east of the ridge."

"I was, Moose," Watkins replies. "I went right down the ridge until the ceiling got too low, then we curved around to the east."

"Bullshit."

"Ask Fowler."

"I didn't see you."

"Well, I was there."

"Did you see them launch from Lead Twelve?"

"We didn't see *any* missiles, Moose."

Moose's eyes search Watkins's. He smiles a little.

"Well, I like to give people the benefit of the doubt so, okay, let's say you *were* there. Why didn't you give us a hand when I called you?"

"I couldn't find you."

"You tried your ADF?"

"Sure. I tried it a couple of times," Watkins says, "but that channel was too crowded with voices. The needle was pointing all over the place."

"We could have used some seven-fifties on that site, Watkins."

"Goddammit, Moose, I'm *telling* you we couldn't find you. We looked. Ask Fowler."

Moose's eyes wait for Watkins's to fall before he swings his stool back towards Suzie, who seems to be listening knowledgeably. (For all I know, she's North Vietnamese and has a degree in E.E. from Berkeley.) "*You* coulda found me, couldn't you, Suzie?"

She reaches a slender hand over the bar and touches his left carotid artery, letting her fingers drift up it to his temple, into his hair. "You betcha," she says huskily, her hand curving so sensually.

Moose enjoys his supposed monopoly with Suzie. He looks around at all the swooning faces and, with satisfaction, says, "I'm gonna need another one of these, you little doll. Your old Dad's all dried out from oxygen." He calls after her, "And bring old Eagle Eye here a beer, too. You do drink beer, don't you, Eagle Eye? Or does it have an" (and this in mincing tones) "*adverse effect* on your *perfect* vision?"

It's getting to him. Fifteen to go. Fifteen slow ones. He's begun to wonder if he'll make it. Last week another of our Weasel crews got boxed in and cremated by SAM sites. It's not like the old days. Those SAM guys are getting smarter: they used to launch at anything within range; now they sucker you in. One of them comes up on the air and paints you a few strobes on his scope. When the Weasel bird turns toward him preparatory to launching a signal-homing Shrike, he quits transmitting. Then another site, ahead but on the Weasel's opposite flank, switches on its radar and tracks awhile. A turn, and *he* goes down. Finally, a third, well ahead, comes in good and strong, but he's just out of range for the ground-to-air SAMs.

Only two types of Weasel will rise to that bait—the least experienced and the most experienced. In either case, it takes guts to move deeper into that electronic forest. There are diversionary sounds, and the real beast ahead. As with animals, never show fear, the Weasel drivers say. You're the fucking sheriff. Move in purposefully as though you own the place. Go along with their game for a while. Essing along over the paddies and foothills, you know that at times you are very close to their draped camouflaged nets. Missiles are pivoting to remain within calculated cones. The sector commander, doubtlessly Russian, will tell everyone when to spring the trap. His face, an educated face, glows in the light of the cathode tubes as he moves his pieces to block the queen. The queen is a slim, two-place F-105F, configured with incalculably expensive and rare electronics. Her pawns are three ordinary "Ds," three single-seat '105s. In loose formation these mottled four, delicate as bird tracks in snow, skim now from the shelter of the foothills out over the delta, covered with dirty stratus, bases at three thousand feet.

Unlike chess, there is a short time limit to this game. The two commanders, the Russian and the Weasel flight commander, have to decide quickly.

In his sleep, Moose plays the game, plays it well, though he's probably never played chess. In his mind must exist a grid of some sort, perhaps curvilinear with the arcs labeled radii of action. How far can you go and still have enough fuel to maneuver in 'burner for two minutes and egress in a dignified manner?

"Tails over the dashboard, boys," he tells them now at the bar. "Make 'em afraid to come up next time."

Moose has been all the way across the grid several times, well into his margins. Psychological warfare, the Russian frowning, puzzled, murmuring something into his headphone. A few more degrees of turn and the opposing cones of fire will separate. Then he will nod, the pulses will resume, and the flight will glow phosphorescently like lightning bugs in summer. He lifts a switch cover, nods, shouts, depresses the button. From several apparent clusters of farm buildings, flares ignite and orange dust rises.

High-pulse-rate frequencies are instantly detected by the Electronic Warfare officer in the rear seat of the Weasel bird. "*Launch!* Launch from eight o'clock, Slingshot!"

"Okay, Slingshot," Moose says, "we've got some SAMs out there at eight. Get ready to take it down."

In his dreams, they must never quit coming, curving in like sharks, hidden by haze or clouds until, suddenly upon him, torching brightly against the gloom, they appear, lunging with energy, as real, as alive as MIGs. He has sweaty nightmares. R&Rs do him no good. Forty-five years old with a boy in college. The tips of his country haircut are silver.

"*Up*, Slingshot, in 'burner. Right on up to the bases. Okay, there they go. *Now then,* recheck your rocket switches, and let's go stomp on those boys over there."

Scooter is sitting on his bunk, his back against the wall, his knees drawn up, playing his trumpet. Balanced precariously on the blue blanket is a tall glass half full of gin. I, still in my flying coveralls, am writing a letter to Jenny. Our desk has no lamp, my shadow falls over the stationery.

"You know what we need?" Scooter asks.

"Yeah," I reply.

"I mean for light. We need a bunch of empty bottles with candles."

"Wrong war, Scoot."

"No, seriously. Think of the atmosphere."

"Yong-Dong-Po. Nineteen fifty-two."

"No, no. You forget. Paris!"

"Toul-Rosières, nineteen fifty-five."

He frowns, puzzled.

"When the power failed," I remind him.

"Oh. Yeah!"

Sometimes it seemed an arbitrary decision. With no warning, the French would cut our power, and Christie's sweet voice would falter down into bass register, die. Don, cackling, would crouch in the hall, lunging at everyone, and whirling around while Whit and Dan, our cool handymen, would hold fuses into flashlight beams and agree.

"Hey," Scoot says, replacing his trumpet in its mildewed case. "That reminds me—guess who is flying F-4s over at Danang?"

I keep writing for a few seconds, then oblige him.

"*The Tasmanian Devil,*" he says, and his eyes narrow dreamily.

Don? I'd heard that he'd been sent to Keesler to become an electronics officer. But that was eight years ago. Everyone seems to show up over here sooner or later, as Personnel had promised, as I had consoled Jenny that evening she kept crying and saying that I was going to get my ass shot off. I push my chair back.

"Well, then, Chet-baby," I say, "what say we call him tomorrow and invite him over?"

Wordlessly, he goes into his Ted Lewis routine, easing around and smiling into some spotlight.

Two weeks later, Don appears, and we'd never gotten around to calling him. It isn't ESP or anything. It's simply that Danang is under attack and being evacuated. Mortar shells have already landed near the tower and the fire station. There isn't time to grab more than a toilet kit. Some of the jocks, those airborne at the time, are diverted without even a toothbrush. Of these, Don is one.

Within half an hour of Seventh's call, we hear that characteristically strange shrieking of J-79 engines overhead. Feeding time at the zoo, those wild sounds: screams and roars, blood-chilling throttle bursts through several octaves, all sharps and flats.

Everyone drops what he's doing and runs outside to look up. There they are, yodeling around onto downwind, while others are still pitching out from echelon. One flight is already rolling out on landing, their drag chutes oscillating in their exhaust shimmer.

On the porch of Wing Ops, a lieutenant drops his gaze. "The *MIG-killers,*" he says. "What are we supposed to do, Colonel, salaam or something?"

"Argh," I mutter, waving my hand in fair imitation of Colonel Hopwell. "Who needs 'em? But maybe we'd better show a little hospitality. How about checking on the number of empty bunks in your squadron, and adopting that many of them?"

I find loose jocks from two other squadrons and enlist their assistance. We round up vehicles and drive out with cold beers.

Scooter reaches him first. I see him leaning on the ladder yelling something. Don nods, throws back his straps, removes his helmet, and stands in the cockpit. He waves to me. Scooter raises his own arm, trumpeting in the general noise.

From twenty-five feet away, they appear untouched by time. They communicate with the same sly grins, the same private jazzy pantomime, the same incoherent bursts of speech. Seeing them together again sends my mind tumbling back to a muddy *marguerite* in Alsace where, standing beside a much smaller fighter, I had told them good-bye.

Déjà vu. An endless evening that lasts a second. I am stupefied by alcohol and tobacco, by cumulative fatigue finally released in our mindless hyena laughter. "Do you remember . . . ?" "Is Hank really raising cattle?" "Yes." "Whatever happened to Tim?"

"He's an engineer now," Don says. "In Florida."

"Tim?"

"He was smart, you know. He and Charles."

"*Tim?*"

The mind is the soul. It is unfathomable, its memory banks imperishable. We may forget, but it doesn't. Uninhibited, it can slip backward and forward through whole decades with their bars, perhaps through eons. As we sprawl with the F-4 jocks, I am suddenly back at Hamilton with the F-86 gang from March. The F-4, Scooter tells Don, is sinfully ugly. "Watch it!" Don warns.

Lost in reverie, staring at a miraculously refilled martini glass, I am summoned back to the present by fingers snapping under my nose. Automatically, I hand them my Zippo.

"Where ya been, John?" the colonel, our present DO, asks. He lights his cigar.

"God knows."

Life *is* a dream. The mystics are right: it is a dream encompassing all the lesser experiences. Insatiably, we try to enlarge it, to live as many lives as possible. That is why we read, they say, why we drink, why we play around.

"You checked the weather?" the colonel asks.

"An hour ago, sir."

"The delta is clobbered in. So is the panhandle. Nobody's going anywhere."

"Good thing."

"Look out! Here they come."

It is a scalping party of Map-Clip Bandits. The left legs of their flying coveralls are ripped so that bare legs show. Like shipwreck survivors, too casually, they encircle our table. Most are lieutenants, apparently of junior high school age and leanings. They are whistling and not looking at us. Slowly we get to our feet.

"Oh, Jesus," the colonel laughs, and flails at them as they attack. Over go our chairs and the table. Working in pairs, they rip off our map clips and swirl away to regroup. We lie panting, and cursing and staring at the ceiling. The colonel's cigar looks as though it has exploded. He is delighted.

Aw, hell, here comes the volunteer fire department, another mixed contingent of Boy Scouts. They carry extinguishers of all kinds and, as we lie there, they "revive" us with water, chemicals and foam. Some of it may be toxic, so we call for more water, then lie in the slimy mess, coughing and laughing.

"*This* will be reflected," the colonel promises them. "By God if it won't."

"Aw, c'mon, sir. No hard feelings, okay?" They help us up and offer to flip us for a drink. Pretending to be taken in, we go to the bar with them. Suzie, threatened with a CO_2 douche, grimly waves a bar knife at groin height while she takes our orders. We hold coins balanced on our thumbnails.

"Okay," one lieutenant asks Don, "are you ready to flip, Major?"

Don nods; then, simultaneously, he and Scooter stoop, grab the lieutenant, and flip him over the bar. The colonel and I send another one flying. Suzie screams. We field-graders shake hands.

"Nice form, chaps," Scooter says.

Still struggling for breath, my coveralls flapping like a scarecrow's, I pound the leather cup. Suzie wipes our heads with bar towels. "You pay for glasses you broke," she says grimly. I pause before lifting the inverted cup and look down that long echelon of faces, all expectant, all happily flushed. Where am I? George, Korea, Prestwick? *Time past and time present,* old Eliot wrote.

In the morning we see Don and his flight off. He bends and zips his G-suit up over his tatters. Everyone moves with elaborate care, wincing at the slightest noise.

"Okay," Don says. "Briefing. No 'burners, no calls, no Gs, nothing." His eyes are not quite in focus. "Are there gnats in here? No? God, I could use a cold brew." I reach into the fridge and hand him one. "None for *him*," Don indicates his backseat lieutenant, his GIBS. "He's driving."

We hold their survival vests for them. They pull up antennae, listen for the beepers' whine, snap them down.

"Uh, Major," a sergeant asks Don, "have you checked your revolver?"

"No," Don replies thoughtfully, "no, I haven't, Sergeant." He pulls his .38 from its shoulder holster and nods to the sergeant. "Stand over in the corner, please."

Hamburger is as well known as any jock in the Air Force. He practically grew up at Nellis. He has instructed there in three different fighters, has flown with the Thunderbirds, and can put on an impromptu floor show that once actually upstaged a famous comedian at the Sands.

He has never trusted our new ECM pods and volunteers to avoid them and the wing gaggles.

"I disapprove of electronics, missiles and computers," he says half seriously, ticking them off. "I am a *low-level mutha*. The general likes low level? Shit, we got low level. Would you believe twenty-five feet at six hundred knots? Yessir. The grandmothers shoot each other trying to hit us, and we ain't on *nobody's* scope. All you guys with the big theories are up there dodging SAMs and colliding.

"Listen," he tells us, "yesterday we were coming down these tracks, and I see this canal coming, so I call for 'burner and up we go, jinking through all the flak and crap you guys stirred up, but just for a few seconds. And, as I climb, I'm looking for this important JCS target, which is a Communist outhouse. And all my vector strobes are lit up like Twentieth Century–Fox, but it's too late for those clods.

"I roll in. I'm too steep. I'm in about a 100-degree dive angle, so, if I drop my bombs, they'll fall on *me*. I go right on down, keeping my ordnance, and lead them back into the hills. This dumb Academy kid on my wing still has his bombs, too.

" 'You stay here,' I tell him, and I go back. Dumb, but I deserve it. Back into 'burner and up again, watching my fuel gauges fall. Up and over, and this time it looks good, so I pickle.

"But now I'm almost out of gas, see? And when I look out, there's the kid. I do a double-take. His bombs are gone, too. We cross the Red, then the Black and I see I'm not going to make it. I've gotta stick a tanker, see? So I get on the horn and tell this tanker to head north. The tanker guys have balls *this* big. I love 'em.

"Jesus, when I call for a fuel check—and I know I've gotta subtract five hundred pounds from what these lying bastards read off—the Academy kid is right with me. He must have followed me in that second time.

"A minute later, this idiot calls, 'Hey, Sapphire, trucks!'

" 'Where?' I reply. I see 'em, of course.

" 'Four o'clock,' he tells us, all excited.

"Now, what do they *teach* these kids? I ask you. Eight million dollars' worth of machinery running on fumes, and he wants to shoot up a few trucks.

" 'I see 'em,' I finally say. 'Forget 'em.'

"Oh-h," Hamburger draws back from us, holding up both palms and turns his lifted chin away in disdain. "You think this Air Cadet is going to let me forget that?" He shakes his head tragically, his eyes as sad as a hound's. "I'm chicken, see? Me! Fifteen years of trying to kill myself, and he's thinking *no guts*. That's the trouble with kids. They think about *that far.*" Hamburger's forefinger is almost touching his thumb. "And now I got this cold and I can't fly and the Air Scouts are going up there tomorrow without me."

The Air Scouts are, in fact, flying wing positions in our flight. Tom, who replaced Fred several months ago as a squadron commander, is leading; I am the element leader. The tankers meet the drop-off time to the second so that, simultaneously, the four full strike flights ease down and away, accelerating and converging into a loose diamond of flights. On go the ECM pods and, to the enemy radar, we must look like an approaching snow storm. Hamburger can have his low level and his pop-ups; this is the way to go, this big bomber gaggle. *Unless* the MIGS are up in strength, and they haven't been since Robin Olds and the other F-4 guys from Ubon had their turkey shoot.

Ahead, motionless even to her bow wave, is the last destroyer, alone in the flat gulf. We are abeam the Communist island of Hainan. Somewhere in our vicinity is an EC-121 airborne radar "site." We hate it because it exists not for its avowed purpose of warning us of threats. It is really orbiting to monitor *our* positions, identifiable by flight because of our IFF codes. It exists to protect those areas declared off limits in our frag orders: the buffer zone along the Chinese border and the circles around Hanoi and Haiphong.

Very well. Fair enough. Protect the United States against an embarrassing violation of Chinese airspace. But let him maintain absolute silence at all other times. We don't need his warnings of known threats on Guard Channel blocking out critical calls on all frequencies. Using severe language, I have drafted messages for the colonel's signature. He scans them, nods.

"Send it." He shrugs. "Big Mouth has to go." Moral courage.

Water off a duck's back. Seventh is like my old civilian instructor in Primary, our teletype like his Gosport. All I had was earphones. *He* had the speaking tube. Actually, having served in the long chain of command, I realize that Seventh is simply following orders. The orders originate in Washington. Seventh has become like a placatory politician listening to the mutter of the rabble.

Over the Elephant's Ear, an island of that shape near the Chinese Mainland, we tighten our scrota, retraction having proved impossible, and head inland. The late afternoon sun lies straight ahead, red in thick haze. The green of summer is gone. The land lies dead in winter grays and brown, ominous, seemingly hostile in itself. They are waiting for us, these tough little men dedicated beyond Western reason. I can almost feel their hatred rising. Ahead, the Weasel flight is calmly working the signals.

"How's she look, Merc?" Tom, our mission commander, asks.

"Aw, it's okay," Moose replies. "About three-eighths cloud cover and three miles. Maybe four."

We are going after a railroad marshaling yard northeast of Hanoi. The general, probably striking a pose for pictorial history, has finally received approval from Washington, relayed with cautionary addenda down through CINCPAC and MACV. His preparatory messages are triumphant. For months he has been tasting this particular target, its rails multiplying into a great complex complete with turntables, repair shops and warehouses. Even our weather teletype had begun spattering out NASA-like pep talks: "All systems are go!" one had routinely repeated. Our forecaster had turned away, grinning. Generals think positively when it suits their purposes.

"Where are you now, Mercury?"

"Aw, we're down at Romeo, about twenty southeast of Kep."

"Okay. What are your cloud bases, Merc?"

"Stand by, old buddy. Break, break. Okay, Mercury, we're getting strong activity out at one o'clock. Get ready."

"You have us, Vulture?"

"Affirmative, Mercury," a new but familiar voice says. Vulture is our F-4 escort. "No sweat." Don?

"That you north of X-Ray?"

"Rog."

"Flak, Vulture. Four o'clock."

"Okay."

"Flak at twelve, too."

"I see it."

"They're *shooting*."

"Okay, let's hold it down. I *know* they're shooting." Is that Don's voice?

"All right, Mercury," Moose clears his throat, and I detect the first note of tension. "We've got a launch indication. Let's take it down."

"Bogies at two o'clock, Killer Flight."

"That's Vulture. They're F-4s."

"SAM! SAM, Mercury! One o'clock."

"*Up*, Mercury!" Moose yells. "*Up!* Here they come."

"THIS IS EVERGREEN . . ." says the scopehead on Guard Channel out over the Gulf. "SHOVELNOSE BRAVO FOXTROT FOUR. TIME: ONE ZERO FOUR ZERO ZULU."

"You okay, Merc Four?"

No answer.

294

"Mercury Four, are you okay?"

"I don't know," a voice answers weakly. "I think so. No, my arm . . . it's . . ."

"Take him home, Mercury Three," Moose orders. "Get him outa here."

Droning in, we see no enemy activity. We move in a globe bounded by haze. Below, there are mountains, rivulets of snow. Suddenly, dead ahead in the haze, a flash of flame and a pall of black.

"Vulture Leader! *You're hit! My God! Get out, Vulture Leader! Get out!*"

"Shut up," someone snaps. God, let it not be Don.

"GET OUT!"

"THIS IS EVERGREEN," the deaf scopehead intones. He is fortunate to be two hundred miles away. Any one of us would happily shoot him down.

Now, without warning, we become engulfed in flak. A broken cloud layer had hidden the muzzle flashes, I guess. Some bursts are so close that I can see, almost subliminally, their microseconds of fire. Suddenly, from the corner of my eye I detect wild motion, and turn my head. A tailless F-105 is tumbling out of the formation.

"Hectic Three, *eject! Get out!*"

". . . SHOVELNOSE, BRAVO FOXTROT FOUR. TIME . . ."

"Okay, Mercury Two, let's head out. I've got a Bingo."

Now I know how those poor goddamn B-24 guys felt over Germany. All you can do is keep driving and sweating. God help us if our electronic magic fails, if they've moved in SA-3s, if . . . well, the undercast is skimpy from here on in. We're coming out of the foothills. To our left lies Hanoi. We can *see* it.

"Bogies at nine o'clock low, Killer."

"Watch 'em."

"They're MIGs."

"Okay."

Sunlight glints off metal: the northeast rail line. Our eyes follow it southward. I can't make out the marshaling yards. At eight, low, are specks curving in. *Jesus.*

"Dragnet," Tom's calm voice begins, "the target is at—"

"THIS IS EVERGREEN . . ." the scopehead says.

". . . o'clock. Let's. . . ."

". . . BRAVO FOXTROT FOUR . . ."

Tom's afterburner is alight. He pulls away. Cursing, I engage 'burner and wait for the kick. Now, in a vision gained from dim photographs, I see the railyard. It seems unimportant.

"MIGs!" someone calls. "MIGs *right behind us!*"

"Use your call-sign," Tom says.

"Dragnet! Dragnet! They're firing missiles!"

We are Dragnet, I realize with horror.

Tom's speed-brake petals open and he plummets toward the target.

Automatically, I follow. Down into a vortex we swirl. An aircraft drifts in front of me, slides right. Tom swerves between us. I am buffeting in a stall, hanging onto him like a World War II wingman, hanging on, whatever happens. Suddenly, our swirling transitions into a forty-five-degree dive. I glance ahead at a hillside sparkling with heavy flashes and fuzzy with blowback smoke. I diverge slightly to my right, look at my instrument tapes: *we are too fast,* so a little humping and, *now!* I depress the red button, feel her jump. Tom is suddenly in plain view before my nose. I dump the nose to clear him, then pull hard and roll in back trim. God knows where the others are.

Everything is completely gone. I am blacked out. I'm unconscious? No, the doctors say. Now, only gray. I'm jumping and twitching spastically. I can't focus. My hands are limp on the controls. Gradually, my vision clears. I look around. I'm alone. No, there's someone—Tom—fifty feet above and to my left. I ease up until I can see the numbers. It's Tom, thank God. Where are the others, the Air Scouts? There they are, their fins rising into view, flying exactly where they should be. Gs don't bother Air Scouts.

"Hey, *beautiful,* Dragnet! You done good!"

I look back at the hillside. All the lights are out. Smoke hangs over it, boiling from a perfect, giant ellipse.

Relief floods through me and, in the middle of Package VI, I almost relax. *We have done our job; we have suppressed the flak.* Thousands of antipersonnel bomblets have cauterized the area. No, they have killed or wounded hundreds of gunners, but even now replacements are crawling from bunkers to man the guns. We have simply bought a few minutes of relative safety for the strike flights now diving.

Supersonically, we climb. At this speed we can relax a little. Wherever the MIGs are, they'll have to hump to catch us. The Twenty-ones, I mean. The old Seventeens are out of it.

Tom calls for a check-in. The flights respond. There is a gap in the sequence.

"Panther Four?" Tom asks.

"Direct hit," someone says. "A MIG."

I look back at the target and see only a rising brown cloud in the haze.

"THIS IS EVERGREEN . . ."

In my mind I am already drafting a message for the Old Man's release. It will be flagged EYES ONLY for the general, and it will be more strongly worded than a military message should be. But, if heeded, it may prevent the unnecessary loss of one of our radar early-warning aircraft to the guns of nominally friendly fighters.

Tom is going home. We have arranged an evening barbeque before the hooches. They will present him with the usual plaque bearing the squadron heraldry, but there hasn't been time to have it engraved. Ironically, he has presented almost a score of engraved ones. He makes a touching commander's farewell speech, his long-lashed eyes resting for a moment on each of us. I have a little trouble maintaining eye contact when he looks at me. Then, lifting the plaque to the light and laughing, he pretends to read it:

"It says that I, 'the World's Greatest Fighter Pilot,' on this date, obtained the favors of . . . who? Ann-Margret? Hey, I'll treasure this. *If my wife lets me.*"

They pepper him with spent flashcubes. He yells, "Flak!" and ducks, bats them back with his palm.

"No," he says, standing again. "*I really will* treasure this." His smile becomes shaky, his lips purse. "I . . . Christ . . ." Wheeling, he walks into the darkness.

Eleven months. Mentally, I am already home. I vow to myself that I will fly no more Pack VIs. It would, in fact, be nice to come down with pneumonia and be grounded for this last month. My letters glow with optimistic plans: she will fly to San Francisco to meet me; we'll rent a car, drive around the Bay and down the Peninsula, eat at all those restaurants that we, as lieutenants, couldn't afford. (We still can't afford them.) We'll cross the bridge to Sausalito and see our old basement apartment, drive up to Hamilton. In other words, not too imaginative.

Jesus, I just remembered: I'll have to learn how to drive on the right side of the road again. Why is it that every time a war comes along, the first thing we have to learn is how to drive on the left side? Deductively, then, to abolish war, all mankind needs to do is . . .

I have had too much to drink.

Vinh lies just below the southeast corner of Pack III. Traditionally, it has always been a Navy target, and they are welcome to it. Estuarial, a hive of industry and shipbuilding, it is well protected. In effect, it is a transplanted piece of Pack VI, and everyone who isn't fragged for it automatically avoids it.

During our briefing, our flight leader, an experienced captain, remarks that he plans to stay at least twenty miles away from it. Thumbs up all around the table. He smiles. "No," he says, "I just want to check out this new site down near Ha Tinh. We'll just troll along past it a few times as though we're road-reccying. They won't know we're breaking in a Weasel crew on my wing."

The Weasel pilot is brand-new to Southeast Asia, one of a third generation of faces in my memory of Thailand. Neither he nor his EWO has tackled a real SAM site yet. They haven't been farther north than Three. Moose and his EWO have gone home.

Now we are over Nape Pass in Pack II, flying northward along the ridge of mountains that separates Laos from North Vietnam. To the east, there is a low stratus undercast covering most of the panhandle. Beneath it, trucks must be racing along as though they were on the freeways of Southern California. The roads must be alive with them. I'm flying Number Three again, element leader, and my wingman is a virgin to combat. He is continuously calling out specks that I can't even see. You'd think we were in a dogfight and, for all I know, maybe we are. My eyes are gone. Mister Magoo, the Air Cadets openly call me—openly, because I laugh, too.

But I can see *one* thing and that's this long, forked strobe on my miniature scope. It's the real article. Somewhere to the southeast lies a FANSONG Radar and, probably, SAMs. The Weasel bird mentions it, and our leader acknowledges. Fine. Play dumb and keep driving northward. Now, as we come abeam Vinh, the leader and the Weasel start a gentle right turn. We slide over them, two thousand feet higher, then again in the opposite direction as they roll out heading south. Every controller in Vinh is wide awake, I notice. My scope is a mess of various patterns, all bright green overlays from that old city.

We cruise along the jungled foothills and I am curious as to which way he will turn when we reverse course again. Not eastward (left) surely, for that will take us too close to the new site at Ha Tinh. An experienced Weasel would turn westward and simply maintain that right turn through 270 degrees if he decided to cruise out over the water. Or would he? This flight leader has flown twice as often with Weasels as I. Oh, *Jesus*—a *gentle left turn*—and, equally grim, a gradual descent. My apprehension has become fear. We aren't carrying jamming equipment and, if SAMs climb out of that undercast, we'll need all the visual warning we can get. I cut across the lead element with my wingman and maintain altitude. Longevity is my motive.

Around he goes, maintaining the same rate of turn, the Weasel bird holding classic position. Soon we'll have our tails to Ha Tinh. My heart begins thumping. I debate whether to tell these guys their business, decide that I shouldn't. Instead, I veer farther north and climb another thousand.

"Where ya going, Cadillac Three?" the leader asks me. "We're down here."

Ha Tinh's site remains quiet, our scopes dark except for spurious blips and chirps in our earphones. Hindemith. We're tail-on now and not far from the water, paralleling the coast. For once I have a precise Doppler. Vinh is only twenty-five nautical miles from Ha Tinh, so we'll always be within range of one site or the other. In my estimation, there's not enough time to react intelligently.

"Is that right?" I can practically hear our cocky leader ask. Yeah, I'll admit it: I've become an old lady. After all, the name of the Weasel game is to tempt them to switch on their guidance radar. *They've* got the sophisticated equipment, *they've* been through an intensive training program, this Weasel crew. And this isn't their first mission in Pack II. So I decide to maintain radio silence.

The sun is sinking fast now. A mean, gray day without horizons, without blue. I just realized that I haven't heard a word in several minutes, that all other friendlies must have gone home. We are alone, we four. I can imagine some master controller down there relaying *that* information.

Well, here comes Vinh. Through a break I can see the Song Ca River curving below the city. Let's turn quickly, I think, head for the water. No, he continues northward. I'm beginning to get long Stravinsky strobes from a site west of Vinh. Turn *right,* I think, turn right while there's still time.

"Hey, Cadillac," I finally say aloud. "How about this guy at eleven?"

"We know, Three. Keep it down, please."

I take the element still higher. Jesus, we had better do something quick. I'm tempted to tell my wingman to break right and follow him. But I don't: I don't know why. Stupidity, that's why. Air discipline, it's called.

"Cadillac," the Weasel pilot calls, "we have strong indications of prelaunch activity from both ten and two o'clock." *Sweet Christ, two* of them. Now, belatedly, the Weasel turns to leave the leader.

Suddenly, flak is bursting all around, rocking us, and the green strobes jump to the rim of my scope. In my headphones is the rattlesnake clicking. God, why am I laughing? How ironic to end a wienie's tour in absolute panic!

"*Launches,* Cadillac, from both sites!"

What I can't understand is why anyone is surprised. Our leader pulls his nose up and fires a Shrike toward ten o'clock, the Weasel launches another toward one. Then we all claw in afterburner for altitude and watch the cloud deck below. Ahead, diverging, the Shrikes are arching in trajectory, leaving white smoke trails.

Now, in the clouds below, strange, moving, orange lights forming a sort of fiery ring ascending appear and suddenly break free. There are *six* SAMs converging on us from two directions. I do all that I know to do: I roll over and plummet back through the layer of cordite. As they rise, my wingman and I fall. The other two planes are now diving, too. But *this* controller, I realize, is experienced. He has probably seen this a dozen times up in Pack VI. Instantly, his missiles deflect downward, but their control surfaces are so small. Once they seem committed in this new direction, I call, "*UP,* Cadillac Four."

Graphed, our flight path must look like the sine wave for a damped spring, like the hood ornament of an old car after it hits a railway crossing. All that saves us is that old Ivan down there can't get his guidance guys in phase. It is a relatively primitive control situation. But terrible in their swiftness, as mottled as we are with camouflage, the SAMs race beneath and explode. Now more orange lights appear in the undercast; a second salvo is on the way. SAMs rise while our tiny Shrikes descend, homing in on Ivan's radar. Unless his control van is sand-bagged, Ivan is in as much danger as we. Surely he knows this. He's a pro, watching a sweep-second hand, gauging times of flight. There may just be time before he must switch off his power. Once we commit ourselves to a climb or a dive, he can direct the SAMs with one final correction, cut his radar and fake the rest of it. A little imagination and a command detonation button.

I think he's right. Inviolable rules have been violated. The launch lights in the Weasel must now serve as a hard reminder to her crew. Abruptly, our leader twists downward. Instantly, the orange lights reduce their climb angle, and simultaneously break into the clear. Undeniable, blurring at Mach 3.0, they converge on him. There is a bright yellow explosion. A wing flutters and spirals like a maple samara. The fuselage whips crazily like a thrown torch. Against the gloom it is all so brilliant. He can't get out. His arms must be flailing like a rag doll's, his brain gorged with blood and disoriented.

The Weasel pilot is screaming the usual things at him. Aw, *he's dead, man,* I tell him; but I am not depressing my mike button, of course. Then, miraculously, I hear a beeper and see a parachute. The torch falls into the undercast, burning a hole in the clouds. Colorfully— international orange, white and mottled green—the parachute follows. Ah, God, which is worse—to be killed instantly or gradually? Below, in Vinh, exhausted, angry men are waiting. He will be beaten to death like a snake.

Assuming my now-proper authority as flight leader, I call the Weasel up to join us. "Let's go to Guard Channel, Cadillac," I tell them. They switch and check in.

"Crown, this is Cadillac Three on Guard."

"Cadillac Three, this is Crown." Crown is an airborne Rescue C-130 command post.

"Roger, Crown. We are about twelve miles southeast of Vinh. Our leader ejected at the following coordinates . . ." I read them off twice and wait for them to sink in. To the Rescue guys, these must be fairly famous numbers.

"Rog, I'll repeat them." And he does, without any dismay. Aw, these Rescue guys are too much. "Have you established UHF contact, Cadillac?"

"Negative. And I don't expect to."

"Understand, but I've scrambled the whole gang, so we may as well make sure. How's your fuel?"

"We can orbit ten, maybe fifteen minutes," I reply, "unless there's still a tanker airborne."

"Negative tankers, Caddie. They're on the ground. Okay, leave when you hit Bingo." (I guess he knows that we're already at Bingo.) "Break, break. Sandy Leader, Crown, I read you loud and clear. Do you have the coordinates?"

Before I can stop myself I push my mike button and shout, "Crown, forget it. I'm sorry I called you. He's *downtown,* man—don't you understand? *They're gonna get their butts shot off."* Ah, Jesus, what's wrong with me? I'm crying like an eight-year-old. Whatever it is, it should be written up as a discrepancy because, as a mere spear-carrier, I'm not entitled to emotion.

"Ah, roger, Cadillac . . . break, break . . . disregard, Sandy Leader. Cadillac Three, attempt voice contact with the downed pilot, please."

I nod and laugh, wipe my eyes, acknowledge foolishly. Then, in a voice I'd use to call Lazarus, I transmit. Nothing. He's either dead or on his way to the Hilton. I try again—and think I hear an answer. My blood boils. But it's just another Rescue bird. Duckbutt Alfa? A Duckbutt is an SA-16 amphibian, as anachronistic as an Amish farmer's carriage, but useful if a guy ejects over the gulf.

"Cadillac Three, this is Duckbutt Alfa, over." I can hear his propeller background noise. What does *he* think he can accomplish? I'm not going to answer him, this spade-bearded holy man clucking at his horse. I can see him better now—clean-shaven, traces of headquarters pallor, me maybe. *He* decides where he dares fly and that is wherever he is needed. I see his eyes, sense his ancient dedication, am humbled, cry again, raising my visor and nodding at my black complicity. Yes, they recruit these guys from asylums but, yes, *they are what we should be,* all of us.

We are almost at the southern end of our racetrack pattern. One more lap, I decide. It is almost too dark. My panel lights are dimmed, but my little scope still writhes with busy, green ghosts, telling me of all the ways we can get shot down. That bastard over near Ha Tinh certainly is military. His strobes begin forking again.

It hits me. "Duckbutt Alfa, Cadillac Three," I call quickly, "there is an active SAM site at Ha Tinh. *Keep your feet wet. Acknowledge.*"

I can visualize this sedentary fool, a classmate perhaps, bifocals lifted to scan his acetate-covered map. He is stationary at 130 knots and without warning gear. His face is that of a saint.

"Ah, rog, Cadillac. Ha Tinh, you say?"

He is coming in out of habit, this idiot, out of some innate need to help. Whatever happens, he *has to be here.* I have never understood these guys. They look normal enough at the bar but, they must recruit them from asylums. I remember the lunatic who landed in the mouth of the Yalu, MIGs taking off right over his head, to pick up Rocky. His voice sounds the same. They are a type, like firemen.

Ah, Christ, I'm crying again. I can't see. I'm full-scale loony, my eyes full of tears, my hands weak on the controls. I grab my scarf and mop my eyes again. When I can see again, my eyes, unbidden, are focused on the dedicated Shrike attached to my right wingtip. Angrily, I deny its existence, but there is no way to stop the mind.

"Caddie Three still has a Shrike." I look over at the Weasel pilot.

"So?"

"So."

He pushes the mike button so I can hear his sigh. "Oh, well, why not?"

How unprofessional can you get? I am becoming angry. How ludicrous! Professionals do not feel emotions. Black and white is for Birchers and liberals. Still, *it's there;* I'm like old Moose, bent on revenge. I head straight for him, while the Weasel, my Sancho, calls off range. We are idiots and fools.

"Twelve, eleven, ten." There is no longer any escape, honorable or otherwise. Well within the SAM's envelope, we enter the Shrike's. "Eleven . . . high PRF!"

Okay. I recheck my switches and ease the lovely nose of the bird upward twenty degrees. Now! I depress the tiny red button. *Whoosh!* Streaking too fast for the eye to follow, the Shrike is already a mile ahead, a white, burning arrow. Burnout. The trajectory arches, steepens, disappears into wisps.

"Launch, Cadillac! Launch!"

"Roger," I reply. The undercast shimmers with orange orbs drifting and growing. Here they come. Strangely, I almost feel contempt for them. Their very momentum defeats their control surfaces. Bullets can't turn, and neither can these clumsy things. MIGs would present more of a problem. Gently we angle down, and they follow. The controller has no choice; we hold the initiative. He is beginning to appreciate this, I think. No computer can predict what a loony like me will do next. The missiles are diving now, steepening, committing themselves. Over my shoulder, I watch them.

"Engage 'burners now, Cadillac," I call. "Okay, up and hard right!"

My last view of them is of hogs on ice. Their small vanes are fully deflected, but Newton's laws remain valid. They are like coast artillery projectiles.

"Hey," the Weasel EWO calls, "you got him!"

I look at my scope. The forked strobes have disappeared. All we have now are the usual thistle patterns and chirps. We disengage our afterburners and half-roll to watch the SAMs. They have gone ballistic. It is like a resolved dream. Now we can sleep.

By coincidence, we are headed southwest toward home. In peace, in relative silence, sleeping, really, we climb. I check out with Crown. My voice is not mine. It is too professional.

"You *got* him, huh?" Crown asks in wonder.

"Apparently, but *please* tell that Duckbutt to go home."

"Good show, Caddie. Okay, you are released. Did you ever establish contact with Cadillac Leader?"

"Negative."

I release the mike button and almost slide into unconsciousness. I shake my head, check my oxygen blinker. What the hell is wrong with me? Why am I trembling? It's not hypoxia; crying isn't one of my symptoms. I haven't cried since I saw Spencer Tracy in *Captains Courageous.*

"You okay, Cadillac Three?" my lieutenant wingman asks.

"I don't know," I reply.

"Want me to take the lead?" he asks quickly.

The Weasel pilot is senior, but this kid is so eager. "Affirmative, Two. Take the lead."

Confidently, he surges ahead, flicks his navigation lights to "Dim-Steady." Almost laughing, I slide back through space and time. We are following the last of the light.

"Fuel check, Cadillac," he calls importantly. For him, it all lies ahead. We read off our gauges to him, and he takes us over to GCI frequency. He's okay, he's going to be good. Like an old idiot, I laugh and nod. Then I dope off.

We are letting down. Jesus, where are we? That looks like Sussex down there, so soft and violet-green with its dark villages. Ahead is an airfield, spectacular with its colored lights and white beacon. Burring in the dusk, we curve in a half circle and slide into echelon for initial approach.

My loony mind shifts in whole decades. I am no longer sure where I am, or how I got here; but I have the distinct impression that I have completed a much larger circle.

EPILOGUE

THE LONG GOLDEN cabin is hushed with soundproofing. Voices don't carry far, soft music is everywhere. Stationed along the aisle are the stews, all characters, I would judge from their repartee.

"I'd like to hang this suit-bag in a closet," I tell one.

"Well, *that's just tough*," she says, her eyes blazing. Then a big smile as she takes it.

Another, black and cute, sighs when two black sergeants pause to flirt. "Get to the back of the bus," she commands. They howl. She pouts and smiles.

I'm surprised to see a few dependents. MAAG and embassy people, I guess. All down the aisle, men remove their blouses, fold them precisely inside out, and lay them on the overhead racks. I take an aisle seat by this Airborne lieutenant colonel and his wife. It is a mistake, I realize almost immediately, because she is a compulsive talker. He just nods constantly like a giant drinking bird and looks around, sighing.

My hands keep groping for something—shoulder harness, I realize— but here all you have is this narrow lap belt. I click the ends together. Big deal. I doubt that the seat is even fastened to the floor. No chute, no dinghy, no ejection seat. Insane. The airlines treat everyone as though they are trusting, not-too-bright children.

"Wave, Henry," the Airborne wife commands and, obediently, like some tame Mongol chieftain, he bends his bullet head to the window.

His pale, Husky eyes relax a little, his lips curl in a bouncer's smile. His hand waves from the wrist, as a child's might. Abruptly, she pulls a tissue from her shoulder-slung purse, which is the size of a full field-pack, and blows her nose. A few tears, more waving and lots of fussing with her poor corsage, but her emotion never interrupts her monologue.

Wearily, Bullet-head swings his martyr's expression toward me and introduces himself. With little hope for its survival, I extend my hand. He shakes it gently and asks where I've been stationed. The name registers. His growl becomes respectful. He tries to cross his big legs, but gives up.

I feel a slight tremor and realize that one or more of our engines is running. It is all so civilized. Within a minute, the door has been closed and dogged tight. Sunbeams shift; we are moving, swinging, gliding like a limousine. An incongruously sexy voice explains emergency procedures while the other stews point and mime coquettishly.

We line up, and a smooth surge of power eases us back into our seats. Instinctively, I look for the runway markers. Seven, six, five, four, three thousand. We must be doing at least one seventy. *Now*, I think, and, yes, the cabin tilts upward, the jiggling ceases. We are climbing. Faintly, I hear the hydraulic pumps whining and feel the wheels bump into their wells. Gradually, the complex wing becomes a blade. In a gentle, climbing turn, I see Thailand for the last time.

The LC's wife squeals and taps on the glass. *Engine fire?* No, he leans across her with the faintest smile. His smashed nose permits him to get really close to the glass. Finally, they settle back, and she fluffs up her flowers and lace. Then, brightly, she leans across him to ask me how I enjoyed my stay in Thailand.

"Not much," I reply.

He whispers something into her ear, and she backs away, her eyebrows rising. Considering it, she pouts and looks away in puzzlement.

Around Cambodia we curve and follow the airways eastward. The sun is already overhead and moving rapidly. Our wing is motionless against the horizon.

By now the morning mission should be down. I can see the fuel trucks crawling past the bays forming the herringbone. At Fort Apache the milk trucks are coming in. Roscoe is out to meet them and hitch a ride to the club for lunch. Laden and jingling, they shift their loads to rough up his ears. Who is missing? Was Scooter flying?

On the screen, Jack Lemmon is hopping around in his underwear while this frantic girl stacks clothes in his arms and pushes him out the door. Bullet-head elbows me and laughs. He has his tiny earphone on the ear nearer her.

The lieutenants explain to the stews, who are now giggling like coeds, how they may limp when they get home. "Oh, *that* one?" one of them looks down to where his ribbons will rest, "The pale blue one with the white stars? That's the Medal of Honor, honey."

"No," another lieutenant says. "Amnesia!" He vibrates his head, reaches up to touch a stew's cheek. "Don't I know you from somewhere?"

Bullet-head jerks once with laughter.

"Goddamn lieutenants," he says.

"Yeah."

"How'd you like to be that young again?"

I consider it.

"And be as smart as you are now, I mean," he adds.

"No,"

"Me either. *Everything* is boring the second time around."

The second time around. In my attaché case are orders to the Pentagon. CIA agents have poison capsules they can pop down when torture seems inevitable. All we've got is gin. Ops this time, however—down in the Bargain Basement. The Return of the Wienie, as Scooter said.

Well, I am fortunate. I should thank God I'm alive and not a POW. I couldn't take that, I know. And I'm so lucky to have Jenny and the kids, and—Fang? Anyhow, here we go again. I guess we'll need a new car; Jenny writes that our old wagon sounds like a Coast Guard ice-breaker moving through heavy floes. How would she know? Nothing exciting though. Only orthodontists and lieutenants can afford Jags and Porsches.

I lie back and close my eyes; then rouse myself to reset my watch to California time. With that simple act, I leave Southeast Asia.

"*Air Force Times,* Colonel?" One of the lieutenants hands it across the aisle. Without interest, I scan it, see my name in the Transfers column: DCS/O, Headquarters, USAF. Big deal. Three or four years of pulling on some oar with other slaves. Three, if I can arrange it. By then it will be 1970 and, if I luck out and make full bull, one more tour. Thirty, as newsmen say. I'd like that last one to be quiet—say, ROTC in New England. Elms. A chiming clock tower. Peace.

"Gentlemen," I'll say, removing my horn-rims and staring out the window. Too bad the Sam Browne and riding boots are gone. Without the creaking leather, I'll have to use rhetoric to stupefy them. "*Professionalism,* gentlemen. Dedication! There are no substitutes."

When the athletes begin yawning, I'll mention the F-15, still experimental. It can accelerate while climbing vertically, they say.

Separately, there is a list of general officers' assignments. Two names fly out at me, both brigadier selectees, both returning to Headquarters, USAF: one, our dedicated squadron commander at Hamilton (I thought he had retired years ago), and the other—I may, for the first time in my life, become airsick—Eric Camston? I think of Betty and wonder how that will end.

In his last Christmas card, Smitty wrote that our beloved Fat Stuff is also back in the Pentagon. Who else is there? Charles up in Plans. A fast burner: consecutive promotions below the zone.

All in all, not a bad cast for a morality play.

I turn the page to the obits. Taps. There are separate columns, Active and Retired. The names are listed alphabetically without regard for grade. I'm almost afraid to scan them now. So many are already gone, and I've missed more issues of the *Times* than I've read. If it wasn't an aircraft accident, it was a heart attack or the Big C—two Big Cs actually: Cancer or Cirrhosis. Among the Retireds I've already seen listed are: Cat Man, Possum Slocum, Colonel Nasser Bronton, Pete (forty-two, a real shock) and, a long time ago, our old Irish colonel at Hamilton, the one who flew with Chennault in 1933.

Most sadly, in that same Christmas card, Smitty added that "our old doll, Minnie"—Mrs. Minerva Caldwell, the professional's professional— "died in November." I find that I am having trouble in absorbing this particular loss.

Not that the others are easy. In those minutes before sleep, in mild necromancy, I say a little prayer for them, both the dead and the captured. Two litanies, really, both becoming quite long. Don, it seems now, may be alive. No one saw a chute, but two F-4 jocks swear that they heard him on Guard. So I'll hang onto that for a while.

Neither the dead nor the missing are really gone for eternity; all of us know that. It's in our bones, in our genes. Ever since we were fish— sharks, some say—we've been heading for the light. It's simply a matter of maintaining a reasonable rate of climb, trusting in one's instruments and not deviating toward those sucker holes which seem to lead immediately to blue skies.